Merle H. Horwitz is a retired attorney and litigator to Hollywood stars.

To Mary,
Jac, and Charles.

Merle H. Horwitz

AUGERS AFFAIR

AUSTIN MACAULEY PUBLISHERS™

LONDON · CAMBRIDGE · NEW YORK · SHARJAH

Ordering Information:
Quantity sales: special discounts are available on quantity purchases by corporations, associations, and others. For details, contact the publisher at the address below.

Publisher's Cataloging-in-Publication data
Horwitz, Merle H.
Augers Affair

ISBN 9781643782782 (Paperback)
ISBN 9781643782799 (Hardback)
ISBN 9781645367369 (ePub e-book)

Library of Congress Control Number: 2020909812

www.austinmacauley.com/us

First Published (2020)
Austin Macauley Publishers LLC
40 Wall Street, 28th Floor
New York, NY 10005
USA

mail-usa@austinmacauley.com
+1 (646) 5125767

Special recognition to the staff at Austin Macauley.

Foreword

Sarah is not too tall and definitely not too wide. She has sort of a self-assured bearing that you see in a princess about to become queen which makes her taller as though walking on her toes. Her hair is not too long or too dark, her skin is not too pale. She has a look in her unflinching gaze that hides all sorts of secrets. As she luxuriates under the Pacific summer suns on the white sands in front of my condo at Venice Beach, her body changes to a glowing polished redwood, and for reasons that are inexplicable, make her need an immediate warm shower and me. Hurray for sunshine.

Except for that impenetrable shadow in her azure eyes, which I'm sure comes from the DNA of a slightly disturbed father, Sarah is just about right in all departments. She fits precisely into my six two frame as if having been carved according to my own renderings. However, that bothersome look in those unsettled eyes unsettles me. They want something else…something beyond reach. Or, is it merely my insecurity about not being the right guy? Actually, I know I'm not – but so what? She is just right for me. Taken as a whole, she radiates an inner florescence causing people to turn and check her out to see just exactly who that was who just passed by. Nothing about her is fixed – which may explain what eventually became of us.

Unfortunately, we are terribly different, and yet, in love. Genuine, honest-to-God, actual love. At least I am, which is and was an entirely new sensation for me. I am a gambler. A life-long, addicted, no sleep, card playing, devoted horse playing, gambler. Casinos too often through the night and thoroughbred racing during the day, checking the point spread of various games in the morning LA Times. And I'm good at all of it. A two-hundred and thirty thousand winner at a Las Vegas poker tournament last year. One of those sharp-eyed little ladies beat me out of the bigger prize.

Indeed, I am all Sarah is not. It creates heartburn. She is a nine to five person who needs a nest and all the collections and things that go along with that disposition. Good China, pastel towels, proper silver, chatskas, and something seriously more – still hidden, perhaps still unknown.

We are sitting in the patio of my Venice Beach condo, drinking laced lemonade; she in that sinful black bikini, and me in my bathing suit boxers, when she says, "We have to talk." This is not good. Definitely not good. Every male human knows this is not good. She prefaces the "talk" by reaching out and touching my arm and then sliding up to my bare shoulder, her fingers digging a little on the way. She sits up very straight as she clears her throat and shakes her head, one of those I wish I were elsewhere shakes, and all at once, as if struck by a live wire, changes her mind, gets up and goes into the condo and sits at my Baldwin upright, which I have serviced twice a year because of dampness at the seaside.

She lifts the walnut cover with delicious care, lips curled into joy, and stares at the keys as if the piano was a well-behaved child who would do what she wanted exactly how she wanted, and is like a person she would miss. I am ready for the worst. I know she doesn't need music to play because I know a good deal about her life. Years of lessons, a year at the Colburn/USC school of music under some of the very best concert artists, and then local concerts for which she would get great reviews and terrible pay.

Her hands rise – the fingers extend, they come down like steel pins and she begins one of those short Rachmaninoff pieces that start at the top of the keyboard. She begins and thunders her soul-searching way down the scale in reverberating chords as if the composer was arguing with God about the end of the world and she was saying "right on!" At the bottom, the music detonates into something not of this world, perhaps because Rachmaninoff knew something about the end of it. The explosion echoes from hardwood floors through the room and then slides into an achingly beautiful melody that the composer is noted for. Who can adequately describe such emotional music? And our emotions of the moment?

This girl astonishes me and I know she is about to bewilder me even more. I am holding my breath.

All at once, she turns, closes the keyboard cover, her eyes reflecting a bunch of unhappy tomorrows, her hands come to her face and she begins to cry, furiously, almost without control. Her hands climb into her hair, crawling through its thick layers. I hand her my handkerchief. I don't dare say anything or touch her.

I know it is Sarah who I want and need. I was whom she wanted but maybe I was not what she wanted. Like I said, it was unfortunate. Actually, more than unfortunate.

Chapter One

How can a guy have a close friend assassinated, lose his girlfriend, piss off a double of his sixth-grade teacher, and win three hundred thousand dollars all in the same day? I ask you.

Don't ask.

Okay…ask.

***

It was just after 7 a.m., on a gray Saturday morning. A January drizzle stretched over a sullen Pacific Ocean and clawed its way into the dry interior. The beach from the wall-sized window of my condo was desolate. Pretty sure no one enjoys beach volleyball in the rain.

Not possible to determine where the edge of the sea and sky tangled with one another. A hundred yards to the north, the Santa Monica pier was a dark skeleton. Black waves lashed against the timbers of the pier and next to it rose up and broke down in angry thumps like a recurring headache.

Shirtless and cold, I picked up the Times from my front steps, pulled off the cellophane covering, and opened it. Below the fold, a twenty-four-point headline screamed the news of the midnight assassination of John Augers and the kidnapping of his ten-year-old son, Frankie, all occurring at the *Backside* of Santa Anita.

It took a breathless few seconds before the reality of it hit me. My friend, John Augers, had always been a pain in the ass, a successful one to be sure, but this? Assassinating him in the dead of a moonless night? On the wet streets of the thoroughbred stables of Santa Anita Park, the Great Racing Place? And grab his kid – an autistic ten-year-old?

I took a deep breath, sat in my little den, and read the entire article. And then again. I understood why someone, or several someones, might want to grab the boy. He was a Wheeler grandson. One of those *a couple billion here and a couple billion there and it eventually adds up* type of moneyed families. That alone was meaningful. But Johnnie? He was aggravating, I know, but not *that* aggravating.

I threw the paper down, stared at it, then picked up the frayed pages, carefully folded them back together, and laid it to rest on the small table next to me, the one Sarah bought. I couldn't turn the clock back and undo yesterday. At the same time, the headline was not going to be the end of the story. Assassinating friends, kidnapping kids? No, not for me it wasn't. Not by a very long shot. I sat there for a while trying to make logical connections. Except for the wealth of the Wheeler family, I could not.

Then habits took over. Thank God for habits. Plugged in the coffee. Turned the hot water on full blast and stood in the hot needles shower like a shock-waved mental patient. Thank God for habits. Shaved, spent five confused minutes choosing the right necktie and the right socks (they were all black) – but this time, on the way out, I reached into the back of a kitchen drawer, pulled out my big forty-five, checked the clip, and shoved it into a shoulder holster, took a last gulp of hot coffee, and clicked the garage door button. It sounded like I felt as it slowly suffered its way open. Three cement stairs down and into my almost new juiced up '04 Jag that was in the shop half the time. I could actually feel the emptiness in my heart since Sarah walked out. I jockeyed my way through narrow streets of Venice and headed to the I-10 freeway. Although the news was already old, considering the deadly and emotional events, the big forty-five was probably a good idea. I don't like guns – but now and then…

***

Smart people know that gamblers are trouble, which is what I am – and generally in the middle of trouble, which – I can assure you – I do my best to avoid – in spite of what they say. So, now and then, my big forty-five couldn't hurt.

Not only was I anxious to know everything possible about last night's assassination of my friend – the who, why, what, and dammit, who the hell would kill that roly-poly, feisty, hair in his ears, pain-in-the-ass, first rate horse trainer, and kidnap his autistic kid at the same time?

I knew, deep down, like a scratch on my soul, that there are always dark reasons for such terrible events. My mind was clear; I would find the kid and kill the bad guys. Maybe kill them twice. And I would dig out the secrets. There are always secrets; persistent emotions and stories hidden away. There was no way 'they' were going to get away with this monstrous crime. I would get them and their secrets.

Traffic was already building on Interstate 10. I f
wipers to clear away the anemic drizzle and weavec
traffic, got illegally in the fast lane, sped past downt
crowds which were navigating the freeways like litt
ladies, but take the damn bus next time. No one in L.A.
wet weather. I headed over the canyons of the railyar(
Garfield Boulevard and north to Huntington Drive,
edged by great green lawns of the manicured Asian
County and finally down into the vast wet south belly of Santa Anita, the
Great Race Place, my home away from home.

In the midst of my anger and upset about what the headlines screamed, I
was still trying to get a handle on what had happened with Sarah, who I had
believed was my final and lasting lady love. Why the hell was it so damn
important to her that I become what I wasn't? What I didn't want to be?
That's exactly what it was when I split all those years ago. Get a job. A
regular job! I didn't want a job then and I don't now! Get a fucking job! Into
my fifties with a twenty-two-year-old daughter and the same fucking
thing…be someone else!

I zipped down into the huge parking area of the complex from the lush
greenery of Huntington Drive and parked at the Backside gate, not sure what
misery was hurting more – losing Sarah or losing John. I flipped up my
jacket collar thinking I should have worn jeans instead of getting duded up.
Long time security guard, Estavo Hernandez, guarding his gate, waved and
grinned his lopsided grin, showing his unfortunate rack of teeth, missing a
left incisor. He rolled the gate back just enough for me to get through and
asked, *"La eleccion hoy?"* He could speak English perfectly, having
graduated from Roosevelt High right in the middle of Los Angeles without
ever having been in a "continuation" class. But his native precise Spanish
was a point of honor. He was taller than most of his indigenous brethren.
Indigenous Mexicans and Central Americans were small which is why
jockeys were almost always Central and South American.

Estavo ran a hand over his bald head and kept smiling. I took out my
Racing Form and pointed at the fourth Race, *"Numero Tres."* I could count to
ten in Spanish. More than most gringos who grew up in Southern California.
As I turned away to enter the backside area, Estavo grabbed my sleeve.
"Senor John?"

All I could do was nod.

Chill coastal mists had followed me and grasped stubbornly at the angled
rooftops of the stables dancing shadowy little minuets trying to hide from the
sun, from the reality of death. The morning had climbed into nuanced clouds

and pink pastels, and the ebullient yellows of the mid-street
the *Backside*. My life of late, however, had been a persistent gray.
known since I was a kid that gambling was not a sensible way to make a
ng. But, once you begin…well, why would you want to get rid of those
sensational jolts of adrenaline? All those exquisite highs and even those lows.
It became the incongruous foundation of my life and I became good at it. One
bet led to another, like the first stone in an avalanche: the addiction of
winning, and the addiction of losing would not let go. There was always that
sense that something wonderful and special would happen – gamblers believe
that *La eleccion hoy,* that one bet would grow into the Emerald City, every
loss, disappointment, every pain that ever existed in my soul, in anyone's
soul, would vanish. You know what they say – it's not the winds that decide
your direction, it's the way you set your sails. I set them and no one liked it.
Ever. And it was always the same. Be something else. This is not a way to
live. Live what they want? Screw it. Screw all of them. Exactly when do I
stop being me? Tomorrow before the sixth race? Tonight before I take my
last pill, the little white statin? Or after poker at the Hustler Casino? Or after I
find John's killers and kill them? Which is what I intended to do.

I've seen Seabiscuit win the Handicap here, and I've seen him beat War
Knight in an evening match race against that eastern champ (although it was
in a fuzzy kinescope replay). I've seen Citation, the Triple Crown winner,
and Swaps, who was probably the best of all but mistreated and mismanaged
by the owners and trainers; I've seen Citation prance around the track in a
special final appearance before shipped off to the stud farm – and I saw that
awful race where the English champion NOOR came out of nowhere and
beat him by a nose in the Santa Anita Handicap. I've seen Determine, Silky
Sullivan, Armed, Assault, Cougar. All the greats – and in recent times, the
California mare Zenyatta, who was the best of the best. I saw her last race
when the jockey mistimed her closing rush and lost by a whisker to ruin a
lengthy and perfect record. The crowds in days of long ago would swell like
a pregnancy ready to pop, eighty thousand excited people rushing to get into
the pari-mutual lines and plunk down two-dollar bets that would get them
next week's meals and an extra six pack. Dollar and a half to get in, corned
beef sandwiches piled high, sixty-five cents. Beer, frothing and spilling over,
a dime. Fifteen-dollar afternoons of hope were the best ways to lose the rent
ever invented.

Already into my early 50s, gambling is what I do in the persistent,
undoubtedly neurotic belief, that in the end it would all work out, that
something special would happen, that something would come my way and
make it all worthwhile – and not so neurotic. However, at the moment,

stopping to catch my breath, watching early strikes of light chase blue shadows from the unfamiliar drizzly morning, I was struck with the notion – maybe not.

That's what Sarah said this morning. One of the things she said – maybe not, Harvey. When does it all stop? Five years? Ten years? I didn't answer. I remembered a line from Dickens – tell the Missy, Barkus is willing – there was only one response: Tell Sarah. Ace is willing, but unwilling. Sarah was smart and solid as well as luscious. She was a nestor. Wanting her nest and her things, a vase here, and a photo there, chatkas filling up the corners, I suppose that is the final goal of all women (but what do I know?). Especially this handsome Jewish girl from a mother who resembled a recreation of a Nefretiti, the ancient Egyptian Queen. I gathered over time that Sarah's mother. in spite of her looks, was a lady who eventually gave her life to cleaning, cooking, soap operas, and checking her countenance in the mirror every couple of hours. She eventually began forgetting things and applying lipstick every hour and forgetting she had already done it several times before. Sarah's father Sol, also known as Sollie, six-two and an amateur boxer as a kid, was an advertising exec who gave his life to womanhood, girlhood, all those in between and finally, sillyhood. So, I could understand where Sarah was coming from, that she needed stability, order in her life, a clean kitchen, her nest, as much as she needed to eat and to sleep, I still couldn't swallow what had happened to us.

Add that to the assassination of a good friend and the kidnapping of his kid at the same time, and the added sensation that John's death was not the end of it, and you get the sense that I really needed to fix things and make everything alright.

The coincidence of events left me with one hope – one final exciting, eternal hope. My filly – Winning Silks. She was that something that would change my life. We called her *The Silk*. She was bigger than most, fast and well bred. She was out of a very good stallion, Lucky End. Thirty-five thousand stud fee and a three hundred-thousand-dollar Grade I winning mare and *voila!* A big, fast filly. My filly would overcome all these recent events, all my character disabilities, all my regrets, and make my dreams come true. Neurotic dreams, but so what? They were great dreams…and hopes. At the moment, she was all I had. John's assassination, Sarah walking out on me, left me with a horse. A horse! Can you beat that? My best hope – my last hope? Maybe my only hope. *The Silk* would change my life. I believed it. She had to.

OK, I had some weird friends. That's true. But they were hardly comforting. Maybe just the opposite. Horse Blanket Billy, Jimmy the

Mummy, Nails Nirenstein, LowDown Larry Litowsky. They were all strange. But the filly was not. As soon as she was mine, (a pair of black Queens did it.) I had a jockey's shirt made with white satin, over-sized sleeves and a big Ace of Hearts on the back. That's who I am. An Ace. Harvey Ace. More like a solitary Ace of Spades at the moment.

I picked my way through the damp saddling areas of hard packed dirt streets of the *Backside*, the sweet smell of horses, mixed with itchy hay, straw floors, companion goats, and lazy cats. Whispers of steam wafted up from the nostrils of horses in the shadows of the morning mists after early morning workouts, or just leaving to get their morning workouts of four or six furlongs.

Carefully tended lawns and brittle bright flowers were planted down the middle of the slippery streets of the Backside, colorful iridescent spreading petals in the now assertive morning. Undecided breezes tossed bits of hay and dust in lackadaisical swirls at my feet. Blue morning dew hung from feathery strands of new spider webs hanging from the stable eaves. Cats, uncurled in their carefully cultivated beds, gazed somberly at me, tails swishing at the ever-present flies. I would stop now and then and pet one of them but they didn't care. They didn't even purr.

Grooms and hot walkers and exercise jocks were all moving at once. All of them waved as I walked by, as if I was one of their innumerable illegal cousins. As a kid when my father brought me here for "some business", I thought something is not right with all these horses that ran like crazy, and little men who beat them and huge crowds that screamed bloody murder and wanted the little men to beat the horses even more. Didn't figure it out until I made my first bet with my own two dollars.

The sun suddenly intruded into the moment and reflected in the round traffic mirrors at the end of each row of barns, called shed rows. The reflections created bright, elongated ovals along the dirt streets. It was all wonderful. It was my life, but John was dead. Dead! His kid gone!

Why? What the hell did he do? Who did he offend?

The San Gabriel Mountains were still shrouded in the gray distance but their snowy tops rose above and shone in the morning sun like a kid's ice cream cone. I know, I know, all time is borrowed – nothing is ever the same. I'm resigned to that – but those purple mountains and their vanilla tops were for always. I dodged the sweaty and snorting horses parading about and their solemn looking jocks, helmet straps loose, carrying their whips, each of them about hundred and ten pounds of muscle. I waved at all with two fingers.

I thought, *Perhaps I'm waving at a killer.* Somewhere among all these people might be the person who pulled the trigger on John. Was I part of the final scheme? Someone was there who knew the answer. I was certain.

The Backside was a small city that housed the entire support community of racing thoroughbreds. Apartments and trailer homes for the families of the grooms, exercise riders, hot walkers, caretakers. Baths and showers and first aid stations, a meticulously equipped hospital for horses. The trailers were parked in neat lines with yesterday's wash still hanging next to them; grassy areas and flowers and ever-present goats. And flies. The pervasive buzz of flies. Most of the Backside workers suspected that the Feds didn't raid them because they hated the flies. Raid the Backside, as the Feds repeatedly threatened, and the racing cosmos would cease to exist. Hispanics can hide from the world at a racetrack. They had found a spot in the world they loved. The flies and the cats protected them. They knew horses, worked hard, gathered their change, and now and then made two-dollar bets with inside knowledge. Twenty Federal agents sweeping down on the track at any hour might find a total of five illegals and ten dozen that could demonstrate that they were longtime citizens, with driver's licenses and social security cards. They knew how to get credit cards and driver's licenses, social security cards. Some were over sixty-five and collecting social security. Most had begun their paths to the promise of America from everywhere south and north of the border. They had come because the USA gave them hope. Can't beat hope.

***

There she was, Gertrude Wiseman, standing at her barn, tight black jeans and an unbuttoned checkered Pendleton hanging over a white tee hugging a serious bosom, tall and tough, tapping a black high-heeled booted toe against a bale of hay, staring unhappily at me as I approached. She was a little gray and a little sun and sea weathered with intense gray eyes deep into sleepless blue sockets at nearly the same level as my own, and I'm six one. An imposing woman and a first-rate thoroughbred trainer; a testament to John's taste and his small man's appeal, whatever it was. She had a history with John and a history of life. It was there in her eyes and in her manner. There was simply no fear in her. It was, however, like greeting my sixth-grade teacher. She had that look. Even so, I always wondered...

She took over John's stable including my filly. But she needed my final say so. She didn't want to waste her time with mere gamblers who are never to be trusted. She kept tapping a toe against that bale of hay. We shook hands and she moved into the shade. I wanted to hug her but I had that fucking gun

17

in my armpit. The big red ribbon around a peppered ponytail and a bandanna around her forehead and a sling of rings under her eyes made her seem like one of the stable hands. Except they were all Hispanic and small. Although she didn't actively dislike me, she was dubious about my character even though I had spent months as an investigator for her years and years ago, looking for her lost baby sister. Even though I had a California Detectives license, I was a gambler and that was close to the bottom of the barrel so far as she was concerned, not believing for a minute that the horse training business was also a gambling enterprise. She was good to her stock, treated them like kindergarten children, and good to her staff. Good food, exercise, and discipline for all. One of only four or five local significantly winning trainers.

"You're late, again…what the hell is that bulge? fer chissake, are you carrying a fucking gun?"

"In case."

She contemplated. Her creases creased. "Carrying a gun around horses? You couldn't use it even if you had to. The only ones that use guns around here are the killers. And they ain't around just now! And why late again?" She shook her head and gave me a sad eye.

"Take it easy, Gert. I had a little problem earlier." I did not intend to say anything about Sarah and what had happened between us.

"Traffic or women?"

"Forget me for a while. Listen, whoever they are, they knew what John did and when he did it, when he got here, where he slept, the works. And I'm guessing they know what I do and when I do it." I waited for a response. She was still. Had that grammar school look on her face. I went on. "They didn't assassinate Johnny and take the kid without a plan…whoever they are, they know I look for people. And find them…so…"

She sighed. "You can't live down all those headlines, can you? Finally catching up to you, eh? Knowing your rep. Listen, there are cops crawling all over the place, and they don't need you and that gun of yours. Tell your friend, that Paul Sampson cop. He seems to be in charge. Anyway, dammit, don't start complaining about your miserable life, Harvey Ace. You chose it. No excuses. Your finding skills didn't do me a lot of good back then." She shook her head, remembering that past loss. "Don't see what that Sarah girl sees in you, anyway. You may be a half-assed almost good-looking hunk…sort of, but that's a so-what item. And this is the last time you will be late."

"Never again, Gert. Promise." And among my promises was the promise that I would prove to Sarah that I was more than a gambler. That I was a first-rate detective. That I was the owner of a champion filly, that I had helped a lot of people, found a lot of missing people that the police and others couldn't find. And I would find John's kid. And the assassins. I put a hand on her shoulder which she shrugged off. "You doing OK?"

Her shoulders sagged. "Didn't find out until early this morning. Johnny's assistant, that Raul Besakie fellow who used to work for me, told me to take over. Hired him on the spot." She took a deep breath and turned away and then back, tried a smile, and adjusted that loose strand of hair again. My buddy, John Augers, probably didn't deserve this formidable human being but go figure relationships. Same with Sarah who wanted what I was unable to give. But I still wanted her. I needed her. Such things are not explicable. I am a fact person but Sarah was in my heart maybe like a fantasy, which I couldn't explain and she wasn't leaving.

"Can't tell you how it feels, Ace. Can't. It's a bitch, Johnny being dealt with like that. Right here at the track. Trying to get away on one of his horses. I'm sure he was probably trying to put distance between him and them and his son. Trying to save Frankie. Why he was a target, I don't get. And why did they take his kid. Why the kid?"

The reasons seemed obvious to me, grandson of a rich and famous old man. The Wheeler family fortune. A ransom note would come soon enough, but "obvious" was almost always wrong. Can't predict an assassin's conduct.

"I found out when I got here," she went on. "The cops have been busy." She pointed at the yellow tape around the barn of John Augers. "Couldn't tell them anything. Don't know anything. Just that John always had fistful of money at all times and managed things for old man, managed some of his real estate stuff. But that's all I know. And he managed and trained Wheeler's FKW stable. Of course, it didn't do him any harm to marry that crazy daughter of his way back when. Who the hell knows what else? Johnny had secrets; you know. Even from me." She took a deep breath, turned away, bottling emotions that refuse to stay forgotten. She clawed the bandana from her head and put her fingers through her hair. It wasn't too long ago that she had been close to John. Body heat close. Until the Arise debacle in the Santa Anita Debutante. It was a Grade I race for baby girls. John took the race from her. Her share of $350,000 down the drain. John kept every penny of the winner's money except for his staff. She reached out and held my hand and we stood there for a minute. "We weren't – you know…close anymore. But I can't shake it. Our past sticks in my belly right now. He would have a pile of cash in his pocket and I would ask him, where'd you get that and he would shake his head and shrug and sometimes…sometimes he would point at old man, Wheeler, and just grin. You know, Harvey, he was full of secrets."

19

It looked like John Augers' past had settled on her shoulders along with her share of their secrets. "They have to find the kid. Somebody does," she said. "He's just a little kid. With plenty of his own problems. He's autistic, you know."

"I know. I'll find him. I promise."

"And you have to watch yourself, Harvey. Lots of past to deal with. God knows what. Wouldn't doubt that you might eventually need all that iron you're carrying."

"I'll watch out. Promise."

"That's three promises so far."

"I keep my promises. You know that. What odds you give me?"

"You're bad, Harvey. Just a fuckin' gambler but I'll give you hundred to one. And you have to keep every damn one of those promises."

I peeled off a twenty and laid it on a bale of hay.

"You're on."

She grinned and reached into her pocket. I was sure it was the first time she was able to smile in a very long morning. She looked down the shed row to John's barn where the yellow tape was still surrounding the area where Herman Barnes, the night security guard, was found with two slugs in his back. All at once, she started to cry – very softly, as if it was something new to her. She turned away, but I could hear her sobs. Somehow, it surprised me. School teachers didn't cry. I pulled her into my arms. "Harvey, I know you. I know you want to get them…but maybe, just maybe this time let the cops handle it. Forget the promises. Whoever they are, they could get you, too." She pulled away, put her arms on my shoulders, tears down those weathered cheeks. "Really. I mean it. Just take care of the legal business John left and let it go. Forget the promises. No bet. None of it makes sense." I gathered her hands and held them.

"I'll get them, Gert. I will."

"Famous last words. I can understand taking the kid for ransom. Killing Johnny doesn't make any sense. What's first on your agenda?"

"John's lawyer, Harry Moss first. Called him already. I'm John's Executor. He was mine. I'll see Harry and then his accountant and then old man, Wheeler. Those fellows have to be where the secrets are. Then I'll nose around a little. If they wanted money, why kill John?"

She shook her head, took a handkerchief from my breast pocket, and dabbed at her eyes. "He was the golden goose. Maybe that's what they thought. He was always involved in something, wasn't he? All his secrets."

Then she did something unexpected. She put her arms around me and whispered, "You're an idiot, Harvey, you're a definite idiot, you know that? But you were maybe his only real friend. Maybe mine, too."

I wanted to do the same. Hold her. Just the two of us holding on. Tell her that I had lost Sarah. Tell her how I really felt. But you don't do that with your sixth-grade teacher. You don't reveal your insides to teachers. If you are in the second grade and you wet your pants, then OK, you say something.

I dropped my hands. She dropped hers as if they were hot. Neither of us was the hugging sort anyway. It could be that was our problem. People in our business put away emotions as best they can. Can you imagine betting a pile of money on a six to one shot because you feel like it's a good bet? No. You do the math, then you use knowledge and experience and that's it. Gamblers need to be without emotions or commitment to any one gamble. You can feel a win streak when you are throwing dice, but the dice control, you don't. As she turned away, it was like that vision of Sarah as she walked out the door that morning. That was a picture I won't forget. And I would never forget Gert Wiseman at that moment.

"Everybody has secrets, Gert."

She looked up into my eyes, "You didn't find her. You didn't find my baby sister. You told me you would. You don't always win, Harvey."

"Oh, God, give it up, Gert. That was not…she was not findable. That was fifteen years ago. And I didn't want to find a broken body, like the cops did. I didn't want to come to you with…fuck it. You hold onto the anger. Keep it. Makes you feel good? It was a lifetime ago. And you know I gave it a good shot."

I tried hard to find her little sister who had vanished as an infant. But, I never did. It was a terrible failure that I couldn't kick. I was good at finding people. My license was always up to date. This time, I would succeed. I would find the killer or killers and find John's 10-year-old. It would be a trick. Midnight killers planned their events very thoughtfully. However, as a gambler, a player of the odds, I had a bag full of tricks which I carried at all times along with a little .22 and a big .45. More tricks than fifteen years ago. The solution to finding the boy and the killers would be in numbers. Dollars.

"Cops said they would talk to me later. I should stick around," she said, "those two down there and those guys with the cameras are still poking around. And, wouldn't you know it? I saw that Mondozo creep friend of yours nosing around too. The one you got your filly from. Don't like him even a little bit. Latin gamblers? Way too slick for me. Take a look. Still there – up near the top of the grandstand section. Even see his grin and that creep with him. Don't like his looks at all. Pinstriped suits, Gucci shoes, and hard faces. I know he wants your filly. Might kill to get her back." She hesitated. "Shit, is that a pistol he's pointing at us?"

Sure enough, the gonzo with Aurielano Mondozo was holding his jacket over a pistol he was pointing at me. They both grinned and waved.

I smiled and waved back. Mondozo was the person from whom I won my filly in a card game, my ticket to a different life. He was not a good loser. Nor was his family.

"Westrum's kid said they would pay a pretty penny for your filly. Maybe four hundred. And maybe it's a good idea. Get those creeps off your back. Either they are financing Westrum already, or they will outbid him."

"We never sell, Gert. Never. Won her fair and square. She's my ticket. I told you."

She gave me a dismissive glance. "Yeah, yeah…and when that Mondozo kid shoots you in the eye, then what?"

Chapter Two

One day, I would tell Gert Wiseman the story about Aureliano Mondozo and his famous south of the border family. I would tell her how a pair of Black Queens could give birth to a gorgeous eleven-hundred-pound composite of muscle and heart – Winning Silks. It was a dicey few minutes alone in an expansive dark red "ranch room" at his hacienda, a hundred Mexican miles from anything or anyone who might rescue me. Aureliano Mondozo was supposed to be a good friend. I had saved his drunken nineteen-year-old ass several years earlier from the wrath of some really bad guys at the Fronton Palace in Tijuana, his own extended backyard. He was the son of Mexico City wealth and power and that made him invulnerable and unstable at the same time. He grew up learning to use a cultivated sneer and his cruel coffee eyes by the time he was a teen and took to using muscle men to intimidate whoever stepped into his path; which always worked – but not among the low-minded soldiers of the north, our own highly moral gamblers and their bent nosed protectors in the USA. Muscles were rarely useful. But money talks. I thought to a time back then, when dark eyes and sneers were standard accoutrements for Latin gamblers, and procurers of women and children and perhaps clerks at the IRS. In California, we could always call on Mr. Universe, good ol' Gov Arnold, in or out of office. Or, we could hire all of the Muscle Beach crowd, all oiled and ready to go. Hey, my guys are bigger than your guys. Meanwhile, all I told Gert was that Aureliano was still young and didn't have the chutzpah to do anything but sneer and call Papa if things got too tough. Papa didn't need muscles. He had money and guns.

She said, hand on hips, "Okay, Mr. Smart Ace, I don't care how you got *The Silk* but like I said, people want her and this is a dog eat little dog business. That kid Westrum Junior would probably give you a terrific price, maybe more than three, maybe four. Mondozo doesn't seem to like you. He will bid Westrum up. That kid simply wants to beat you. And buy the filly. Not sure what he'll do to get her."

"Just add him to my screw-you list."

It pisses you off when people tell you the truth. Who wants to hear the truth? I was a really disappointed that she was even asking. "Really, Gert, you want to be rid of me and the filly so easily? You want to sell?"

A sly smile came onto the tip of her lips; eyes widened – they were green and then dark and then flinty green again like light passing through an emerald. Her sixth-grade teacher's face softened…just a little. For a minute, I thought she would ask to see my homework. She didn't know it but she had a certain unavailable sex appeal. You don't think sex thoughts about your sixth-grade teacher, do you? In my chauvinistic way, I was sure most ladies are unavailable only on their deathbed.

"Never cross anything out. Let's see what happens. And, you know, hope springs eternal." John gave her a few easy outings.

"Anyhow, dammit," she fussed, "we haven't got the time around here for late, Harvey. No more late." She brushed strings of gray hair from her eyes, tucked it around her ear, and grabbed me by the elbow. She smelled a little bit like fresh leather. Warm scent. "She seems ready to give us a go. We had her out for a little gallop yesterday and she was bouncing and ready. However," she waggled a finger, "we take it easy for now. Too much shoving these two-year-olds into tough situations. But we'll give it a little bit of a go this morning."

"You're the boss. But, we're going to talk after? Things I need to know…"

Her forehead furrowed. Traces of vulnerability rose in those alternating green eyes. For a moment, she was a lady in the middle of mourning a lost love. "Not about Johnny. Not now. Not about him. You want to talk about him, call your friend Paul Sampson in the LAPD. Ask one of the cops still hanging around back here. Or, just let it go. You don't need to save anyone. Get over it."

Gertrude might not talk at all; afraid the past would grab her and we would both be in that deep emotional stuff we couldn't handle. We're people who make quick decisions and have trouble in the muddy soil of relationships. "You remember Juan? No more talk. He has your favorite girl over here. She's grown a little. C'mon. Say hello."

As the day warmed, the scent of hay, hot dung, and fresh sweat created a new medley of magic potions, and along with the flies made a person love it or…like most, hate it. I loved it. It took me away from the tidy, clean world of my tidy condo, my clean beach sand, my books, my walks on the morning Pacific breezes. It took me away from everything, from the moment, the headaches, the heartaches, the nights, the days, the everything. I was not me at the racetrack.

I was *"Hey, Ace, you killin' 'em? Whatscha got in this one?"* and *"See ya tonight with the rest of those card sharks you call your buddies."* My name was hey, Ace... Sarah once said to me, "Ever think you really didn't want to be you?" It was like a dagger...you know where.

Gert and I sauntered to the saddling enclosures next to the paddock circle, behind the enormous green Santa Anita grand Stands and the Pari-mutual windows at ground level. My heart was already skipping a couple of beats in anticipation of watching my girl in a hard gallop in her first genuine workout with Gertrude calling the shots. I kept my eye on the grandstands high up near the top. Aureliano was still there.

Juan Gallegos waited. A narrow pink slice of a scar cut through Latin skin next to his left eye. He wore a white kerchief around his forehead, pushed the kerchief up, and nodded. I said, somewhat reluctantly, as I knew of his past with John, "You're OK with Gert now?" Juan Gallegos was half again bigger than jockey size, in his 50s, and had a no-nonsense manner. He had gray temples and short, black, curly hair that was never out of place, jutting chin, black eyes with thick lids. His eyelids went to half-mast and he looked unsure and glanced at Gertrude for reassurance, then back at me. "Very good place here. I have a title, too. Assistant Trainer." He flashed a big smile, then remembered. "Sorry, patron. *Siento mucho.* You want to know about *Senor* John?" He shook his head slowly, remembering. His voice was low. "He was good to me. Not every hombre. But to me, good. But I tell you..." he swiped his nose, "that fella was like a hombre riding three bicycles at the same time." His Hispanic accent was soft and fluid. Spanish was the language of communication among the grooms and stable hands at the racetrack. At all race tracks. There was a kind of pride in using it among the gringos. A touch of his American high school education affected Juan's lilt. "*Senor* John was a good man. Crazy, but good." He nudged his shoulder against me, whispered, "Good with the ladies," and shook his head. "Three bicycles...now, you seriously going to get the bad guys? And the little boy back? And maybe you kill the bad ones? Or just talk?"

"No talk, Juan, I will get them."

He said, again very softly, "And kill them sonofabitches?"

"Yes," I said. "Twice."

"Miss Gert says maybe they kill you. Those people, maybe they don't like you, too. You his best friend so maybe they think..." He shrugged and finished with, "Miss Gert – she says you don't think straight."

"Yeah, that's what all the girls say."

He had a sort of sideways look that was almost menacing and which seemed to say I know how things are, I know about all that bad stuff – so you watch out.

A breeze came up. His blue denim shirttails flapped in the wind. He came to America by the way of an Argentinian horse brought by the stable of Westrum Simpson, who died two years ago and left his stable to his 22-year-old son they called Junior and left Juan Gallegos to John Augers. It was as if Juan belonged to the elder Simpson and was his for the giving. Which was probably true. Simpson got Gallegos his green card allowing him to travel with the horse. That was eight years ago this coming April. Juan never asked how Simpson got the card; he simply knew that Simpson was rich and politically connected and that this combination could do anything in any country. It was normal commerce and merely a matter of price. Try Spain, try Brazil, try Argentina, all the same. Juan never understood why paying for favors was frowned upon in this country. Especially when he learned that we bought and sold people in high places with a lot less money, or merely a free game of golf and a good looking night companion.

Gert was lucky to have Juan. He had an instinct for horses: they had moods, personalities; some were mean, some gentle, difficult, competitive, and some insanely competitive. Seabisquit, Whirlaway, Assault, Affirmed, Secretariat, and Citation were the prime examples of the absolute need of some of these glorious animals to be first at the wire, any time, any wire. I remember Silky Sullivan, overgrown, klutzy young horse, almost walking out of the starting gate taking up space thirty lengths in the rear, apparently supremely unconcerned about the race in front of him, finally deciding what the hell, I can't let all those people down and I don't want to look at those horse asses in front of me – so I'll go get them. And he started to run and was all at once flying, into the far turn, and like a runaway locomotive he roared around the turn, eating up space and devouring his opposition, into the stretch, racing past the herd of horses – all of which seemed to stop, stare, and contemplate this mad golden locomotive that looked like a horse. But his trainers were not too bright and were fat and lazy and they let him get fat and lazy. He failed when he went east. Miserably. Brought his local breeders and trainers down to the bottom of the barrel. He became a loser.

Horses had characters as varied as humans. But more predictable than *Homo sapiens*. Juan preferred horses. With a few exceptions, he was right. And he was probably safer in dealing with them that I would be looking for the Wheeler kid.

Juan nodded. "I know about you. Big famous guy." He looked up from his five-foot-seven height and pointed at me. "I know you will get them.

Everybody says you have a nose." He touched his nose mysteriously then managed a bit of a smile. One side of his lips curled slightly as though unfamiliar with the business of laughter. His dark eyes were alive. "You'll find him. Yes?"

"I'll find him and the killers if you will help me." I asked him where he was the night of the deed.

He frowned, "He always had troubles, that Mr. Augers. Troubles. I cannot help, *Senor* Ace." He turned away and led *The Silk* out in to the sun. But he sagged. He would not look at me.

My Filly's registered name was *Winning Silks*; we called her *The Silk*. The exquisite icy blue of the sky struck *The Silk's* golden coat. The gold of her coat cast its sheen in a halo around her. A Monet moment.

"Juan, I need to know. Tell me."

"*Nada. Senor* Ace. *Nada*." He waved, dismissing me. He turned and patted the horse's neck softly and murmured, "Maybe this the one."

"We talk about it later. OK? Maybe you were here."

He insisted. "Nothing. *Nada*. I know nothing about it."

The lie was in his black eyes. He took a step back. He knew I knew. I would get to him later and find out what was lurking inside. I said, "You like *The Silk*?"

He stopped and brightened; big white teeth gleaming glad to get into more familiar territory. "She's very smart. Big and smart. Fast? Don't know. Just a baby. Maybe. But she looks..." He clucked and shook his head back and forth, "...looks like maybe a good one. Maybe a champ. Still growing. Did six in 58 and change and one thirteen and change for six ...alone...easy...very fast for a baby." He put a forefinger to his lips. "But no one is supposed to know."

Gert gave him a gentle punch on the shoulder. "You talk too much, Juanito."

Six furlongs, three quarters of a mile, in one minute 13 seconds was a very, very good workout for a two-year-old not working with any competing factors. Gert waived Juan aside. She said, "Juan, you just get things straightened and cleaned up around here. And you, Harvey, just don't be late anymore. We'll see about your little lady here. I mean, big lady. Can't push them too fast."

"One thirteen? Impressive. There are exceptions," I said.

"And that's what they are. Exceptions. Maybe your girl. Just look at her. How many babies this big? Sometimes too big. Remember. Determine was a small guy. And Seabisquit. But John loved this one." Then she stopped. "He loved her a lot." She turned away. She removed the bandanna from her

27

forehead and wiped her face and squinted. The sun chased shadows into oblivion. I took a breath and took a slow stroll around the filly being careful not to get too close to her hind legs. Most lady horses are temperamental. Boy horses are temperamental. I thought to myself, *All ladies are always – whatever.*

The Silk was, indeed, a big girl, even before she was weaned when I first saw her and fell in love. She had that big person's kind of muscle that didn't need developing, just regular using, educating. It was all there. She had sturdy hindquarters, something akin to a quarter horse, but not quite. It meant to me that she could dig in and go after any animal and sale on by...if she wanted to. She had an eighth of a mile spurt of speed at any point she was asked. A Pulpit filly, and a very good Dam, and that genealogy had a good history.

I patted her and scratched her under her chin, reached up and put an arm around her and whispered, "Whad'ya say, Silk baby? Look, I got it right here. Maybe that mean ol' mama will let you have a little cube." Her big, moist eyes turned towards me, lips daintily covered the sugar cube and then she pushed against me and turned her head and I scratched the other side of her neck. She knew her friends.

"You get all the good-lookin' ladies, Ace."

"They never stick."

"Well, Sarah seems to be a good one. I like her. Although you gamblers all die broke and toothless. Or maybe end up like..." She couldn't finish.

She had hit close to home. In my heart of hearts, I knew Sarah deserved a better destiny than mine. She didn't deserve my addictive life. And I knew in that same heart of hearts that someday in our relationship, I would lose her. Who would stay with me to the end? She once asked me, "Exactly what are your values?"

I said, "I'll take my chances on anything as long as the odds are right." It was, of course the wrong thing to say.

"Anyway, stick around," Gert said. "Cops said to go about our business, so we're giving her a little workout. A little more serious maybe. We've got Miss Donna Camina, youthful women's advocate, to go a half with her. I'm gonna get her to go the half, four furlongs instead of the three today. She seems to like the last part of the work better than the first. Later, maybe in a few days will go another and then five, and then in a week or so, six... And then..." She was talking about furlongs. Eight of them made a mile.

Gert added, "Ocean View Farms, where I went to pick her up, said she was doing regular threes at 37." It was racing spiel for 3 furlongs in 37 seconds. "That's a little too fast for their slower training track. Fortunately, they never let anyone near her. No clockers except their own. Jack Aquilar wanted a piece of her in exchange for boarding. Told him to forget it. Harvey, he told me, you know, you might have a good one. Just maybe. I've just galloped her a few times to stretch her legs, but the times were…interesting."

"This time will do a little more. Nothing really quick." She turned to the young lady holding her red helmet, who I had met briefly a couple of days ago.

"Got it now, Donna? Do the first two medium, no pushing, but don't let her loaf," Gertrude instructed, in a no-nonsense voice. She wiped her forehead again. "Then when you get to about the middle of the far turn, let her go a little and let's see how she likes it. Push her in the stretch but leave the whip here. No whip. Not yet. Then ride her out for a full five."

"Full five" meant five furlongs.

The lithe young lady listened attentively, patting Silk on the rump during the instruction. She put on her helmet and strapped it carefully. Donna Camina squeezed my arm, leaned close, and said, "Thanks for puttin' in a good word the other day. They don't much like girl jocks," as I cupped my hands, lifting her gently into the saddle – like tossing a dandelion into the air. She couldn't have been more than 100 lbs. soaking and naked, which drummed up a nice picture because she was a very handsome young lady, big blues and sandy blond short hair in all directions all over her head. She checked her chinstrap and grinned a confident Colgate grin. Gave me a small salute.

Gert laughed. "Like I said, you guys are all the same. Cute tush and you go bananas."

"Wouldn't have it any other way," I replied.

"Problem is these jocks don't think or act like kids. They're old at thirty-five and heavy at forty and washed up at forty-five. Very few exceptions."

The Silk didn't need a lead pony. She was quiet but on her toes. She was led out by Juan through the tunnel-like area under the stands to the main part of the track. Gertrude explained that the Filly seemed to be enjoying herself. Going through the tunnel was part of her training. *The Silk* understood her job. Thoroughbreds, good ones, love to do what they do. It's like conjuring up any workday morning and going to work, doing what you like to do. Donna waved her whip and tossed it to me. "No whips for this monster. Old lady will kill me."

"How good is Donna?" I asked, when *The Silk* was out of voice range.

"Plenty. Strong as an ox. Shoulders like Pincay. Lifts weights an hour a day. And good hands. She'll never weigh more'n 106, maybe 108 tops. Her father was a jock. Joey Camina. You might remember him. Had a heart attack at end of a workout. Dropped straight to the ground. You remember? Joey was good but Donna is going to be better. Wants to be the best. That's the key. Keep telling all of them, "if you're proud of yourself, the rest generally works out pretty well." I just have to keep the guys around here from doing their macho stuff. One day she might clobber one of them with anything she can get her hands on. She really doesn't like it."

"I can understand why they try."

She slapped her knee. "Just like I said, you guys are all the same. Give it up, old man."

"I wasn't suggesting," I protested.

"Yeah, I know, you're all the same. All you guys. The same." Her laugh was all at once lost and hollow. Her forehead creased. Pains diminish in time but memories grow – we were, for that few seconds, joined in the middle of our own junction of memories. I did not like memories. They included regrets. Hated regrets. Tomorrow was always best for me along with Saturday's racing card.

Suddenly, I heard an unmistakable shout. "I told you, Harvey. You gotta get them!"

I turned to Gert, "That's Jimmy, the Mummy."

"What's he saying?"

"He's a little crazy. Getting old. Really old. Forgetful."

"You gotta get 'em, Harvey!" Jimmy hollered and waved, strands of capriciously red dyed hair sticking out from under his hat.

We watched as a security man in uniform guided him gently out of sight. He waved again. "You gotta get 'em!" Jimmy had a history. Everyone at the track knew him as Jimmy the Mummy. It was always hard to squeak history out of Jimmy; a little bit here and little bit there. A bad guy's history. Cuba in the wild years. South Florida, guns, gambling, and mobsters. Now old and down and out. The usual status for no longer young involved mob hanger-ons. I waved back, turned away, and rested my binoculars on my nose.

"Where do you get these guys? The Mummy and that Larry, the Low-Down nut case. He keeps trying to tout me. And Nails Nienstein. And Billy."

"My friends, Gert. All of them. High minded and card-carrying citizens. Where did you get your guys? Arnie and John? Arnie, your first husband, ended up somewhere in gambler's hell, and now, John and his secrets."

She stopped in her tracks. "That was low, Harvey. Low."

It was. I walked away. Separated. We would never get together fully or understand one another. She was in business and I was a bum. I liked my friends. Larry the Lowdown, Billy Fitzer, Nails Nirenstein, and old Jimmy the Mummy. They were what friends were supposed to be. Loyal and interesting. Of, course they also cost money as not one of them was a good gambler and not one except Billy had any source of income that I could see.

There were only four other horses on the track. Most trainers did their work earlier. A few trucked their crews to other local tracks, trying different surfaces, trying to outwit the workout results of various private handicappers and clockers. The *Dailey Racing Form*, the horse racing Bible, always had a couple of clockers watching the workouts. These results were made available to everyone. The private tout sheets had their own clockers and analysts. If a trainer managed to get his all her horse worked out without a posted result, the odds on the animal would not reflect the fitness or preparedness of the horse. The State of California and the California Racing Association would not like this, so trainers used a variety of legal subterfuges; such as tossing several horses from one barn on the track at the busiest time, work their animals in the fog, or just before dawn, or switch to much heavier workout jockeys. Do their workouts on the outside of orange markers placed on the track, changing the time of each workout. It's not the trainer's responsibility to assist the clockers. They are adversaries in a friendly but very serious game. Workouts are one of a gambler's most valuable bits of information. Was the finish labored or easy? Was the regular rider up? Was the workout just one to freshen up the animal or a real test? Was this trainer one who works the animals fast or easy? How did the horse finish the last quarter?

Gertrude pointed at the "clockers" hut in the lowest stands at the head of the stretch. They had their glasses on "Winning Silks" because she was new and was indeed a big golden beauty.

***

Silk was way out at the clubhouse turn, to our right, cantering lightly with Donna nearly standing. The sun was now just over the horizon, deep set in a south seas colored sky. Mists had burned away. The San Gabriel Mountains had climbed into a half dozen shades of green, canyons mauve, and still shadowed. There were people living in those low-lying canyons and hills. To get a bottle of milk, each had to traverse a couple miles of twisted road and traffic. Had to plan your days more carefully. The television towers at the top of the western end of the range seemed about as close as a Little League second base. To the east were the higher peaks still capped with snow.

It was hard to pick my filly out from the other horses until she got away from that glaring eastern sun almost into the distant straightaway. They were a little more than six furlongs away from the finish. Donna was high on her back. As she came around the turn, she began to crouch. And the filly began to move, not abruptly, but like a locomotive beginning a downhill run. She could reach 40 mph. From 0 to 40 in less than 60 yards. If she wanted to. A Porsche Carrera might be able to stay with her that first 60 but not much else.

There was another horse out there with her, ebony hide reflecting the morning, gliding along in tandem.

Gertrude held her watch high. I set my binoculars to the top of my nose. Just as they came out of the Clubhouse turn into the straightaway, the other horse began to crowd *The Silk*. The jockey apparently had instructions to test his colt. Gert said, "That's Calculator, Jorge Silva's colt. He's already won Special Weight Allowance. Silva is high on him. Don't want Donna to deal with him yet. Not yet."

Before they hit the half-mile mark, Donna's shoulders went down, her head high, higher than most as she was all legs. Her white helmet went down into Silks flowing mane. The dark colt went with her. Silk and Donna were no longer two beings out there – just one. Part of one another. The Colt and his jockey nudged to the front. I heard Gertrude mutter, "Damn."

They hit the far turn and longer strides took over. Both horses had shifted into another gear. Shifted their lead foot to the right foot around the left-handed turn. It was as if the ground beneath them disappeared. They were going smoothly with the colt remaining in a lead. Silk's legs came up high. Now they were nose and nose and it had become a contest. Just what Gert didn't want. My pulse was about 120. "She's got a high step, Gert."

"That's good. More dirt and cushioned races than grass in California." She took her glasses down and muttered "damn" again under her breath. "Don't like the way that colt is pushing her. We don't want any stupid race here. Not ready. Looks like Donna's got her relaxed pretty well. Let's see if *The Silk* changes leads again natural like." A horse changed leads when it shifted from one foreleg as the first step to the other foreleg as a first step, refreshing its strength around the turns and into the middle of the stretch. Donna hit the button and they started to accelerate. You couldn't tell their speed from merely looking at them. But the clock affirmed it. And their ears were a dead giveaway. A horse that was having fun running had its ears perked straight up, enjoying the feeling of speed and strength, losing itself in the pure joy of running. Everything was still. Except the spindly legs and the flowing golden mane of my teenaged golden horse and her menacing ebony experienced challenger. In my mind's eye, I created a phantom race. "24 and two." Gertrude said, referring to the two-furlong quarter-mile time. "Just about right. She rated nice too. But they've quickened. That damn Silva jock is turning it on. Donna better not take the bait."

Under my breath I said, "You don't want her to come second to anyone…" But Gert didn't hear. In the glasses, I could reach out and touch the faces of the two young people beginning to thunder in the middle of the far turn. They were calm, knowing faces. Donna's lips were clucking. The colt began to pass her on the inside. The jock was smiling. He was playing with her. He knew what he had under him, and knew my filly was new to the game.

Problem for the colt was that he didn't know who he was playing with. *The Silk* slipped into another gear. In the middle of the turn, her left front leg took over, providing that final speed gear and stability. "They're not going at the 24.2 clip anymore," I murmured.

"What the hell is she doing?" Gertrude suddenly bellowed. "Dammit! Bring that filly down; take it down! This is not a race!"

We were watching them at the head of the stretch. The two horses melted together as they straightened out. Nose to nose. Donna low on her back. Silk wanted to run. You could see it, feel it.

Gert stared at her watch and shook her head "Three in 36 3/5." We knew that was way too fast for a baby workout. Now Donna slapped at Silk's side with an open hand. She waved her hand out where *The Silk* could see it. The filly moved again. So did the colt. It was a race like it or not.

Gertrude was swearing under her breath.

"C'mon babe," I said to myself. "You're my girl. You can take that guy. Into the straightaway of the stretch."

Gert said, "48.2. Dammit. Way too fast. She's not ready. That colt is. Let's see if she changes leads again."

The colt was touched with the whip and he moved a half-length ahead. Donna hand slapped *The Silk* and they were neck and neck again. You could see that both horses knew they were in a race. Neither was giving an inch. Heads bobbing in unison. Bit by bit, *The Silk* inched ahead and was leading by a head bob just into the stretch. The jocks had turned it into a personal contest. Gert kept muttering, Goddammit, Goddammit under her breath. Neither horse gave an inch. The colt's jock was not going to let the girls beat him. He hit his horse once. Camina didn't. They were glued together. First the ebony colt by a head, and then Silk by a head. Gertrude didn't stop muttering. I started rooting aloud. "Go, Silk Baby! GO!" The horses remained locked together. Nose to nose. In spite of my apprehensions about the filly's first real workout, I knew it wasn't too early for that big girl to run her contemporaries into the ground. If you're good, OK. If you're better, then no harm strutting your stuff. At mid-stretch, I could see the reins loosen a little, knees tighten against the horses. I could almost feel the pounding of the

33

hooves against the ground. And then at the sixteenth pole, the girl jock's body shoved at *The Silk*, knees squeezing and both arms pumping, moving *The Silk* forward with her strength and her will to win. They pulled a half-length in front. She had him. "Get him! Get him!" The girl had the boy. The colt came at her again. He moved up almost eye to eye. *The Silk* would not let anything pass her. The colt got another hit. Made no difference. *The Silk's* stride lengthened, and she began to move away, a half-length, then a length. "Atta Girl!" The colt's jock stopped trying. The lead lengthened. They hit the finish with Silk a couple of lengths up, pulling away, and going like she wanted more. All the Clockers saw it. I could see some of their heads shaking, showing their time-pieces to one another.

Donna touched the reins and her horse realized that the fun was over. She rode out to the turn and began to wave one arm and then the other above her head, like Rocky Balboa, imagining the cheers. I love that adrenaline high. I had lost my "highs" much too long ago. But maybe this girl of mine would make it all happen again. I needed to beat the statistics, to win my own races. I wanted it all back. For every reason I could think of, I needed it. Deep down, I knew it was a product of my own abysmal psyche. I had watched my father win, get to the top, and then lose, hit the bottom. It wasn't that I loved him, or even liked him, but it was watching it all happen and how it damaged him and all the lives around him. A big-shot ending at the bottom of the barrel. It left me with a sense that winning was the only salvation, my only salvation. I could hear him when he was at the top, saying, "Dammit, kid, don't you ever get it right? Second best doesn't exist!" This from a father who was physically beaten so badly by the hired hands of those who came second in his corporate world to his first that he was sick and miserable the rest of his life. Second best was obviously not what I wanted. Just win. I would win. *The Silk* could get it all for me. *The Silk* would create a new life, I would own Doug O'Neill's stable and get Sarah back and, well, maybe, I would re-carpet my condo. And I would find Frankie Augers and kill the bad guys…twice.

To a breathless and peeved Gertrude Wiseman, who was also feeling the high, I said, "No matter what, winning is still the best." It was true. Owning a winning horse was like nothing else in the world. Better than 7s and 11s. It changed your life.

"You're full of crap, Ace. Just like a gambler. Just like a fuckin' gambler. I remind you that wasn't a race." No smiles on that sharp face, except for the smile in her eyes. "We got a 24.2 and a 23 flat second quarter. Way too fast. That Donna girl has got to follow instructions." Her forefinger punched the air. "We have to be careful. You understand that?" Her tired face was not tired anymore. "Maybe that baby horse of yours is that good. If so, a half million is what we're looking at. I wanted maybe a 49 on the four and maybe a little more than 1:00 flat for the 5/8ths of a mile."

"But she was coasting, Gert, and loving it."

"She wasn't coasting. She just didn't want that colt to get by her. Don't get excited, Harvey. Horses kill. How many times I told you that? How many?" She pointed at my nose. "They eat your hearts out. You should know. Gamblers lose because they make all these assumptions that the world is peachy keen. They would always win. And they end up like Arnie Wiseman, that big oaf of a husband I had, and now like John. It's total shit."

I looked at her as if she were my sixth-grade teacher again trying to get long division through my head. Tears started dripping from her eyes, now faded and gray. "Horses kill, Ace. They lose and then if they're lucky, they win a little. But they all end up losing. And sometimes, you have to stand over these beauties and watch a doctor kill them because someone abused them early in life, or because they break a foreleg, or because they were doing what they want to do, run their hearts out. It's like watching a doctor shooting poison into your pet dog that you've lived with longer than most marriages. It's terrible. And you have to be with them and hold them when someone kills them." She shivered. "They stare at you pleading with you to stop the pain, make them young or make them whole again. Breaks your heart…time after time…and hearts can be broken only so often, Ace. Then it dries up and crumbles…and gamblers are just the same. Everyone who puts two dollars down loses in the end."

I said, "I know… I've heard it all." I'll send for my things – I'll send for my things.

She gave me a dismissive stare, untied the kerchief about her forehead, and wiped her face. Her eyes had that vulnerable look back in them, set in ebony holes. She was working at staying in the moment, dismissing memories. "Who knows what will be with this baby? She's got breeding, but who knows? I never know. You just hope. Maybe she's the one. We all want THE ONE. But, maybe she won't like the crowd or the gate. Or she won't like the competition. Maybe Mondozo will want retribution and kill you or the horse… Or both. He would do that, you know. That's his local rep. You got her on a bet, Harvey. No secrets at a racetrack. You damn well better make sure he doesn't try to renege on your deal. And you have to deal with Franklin… Franklin Wheeler. The old man had his beefs with John."

"Don't know where you heard your stories but Aureliano Mondozo knows better. My deal was all on the up and up. He's a spoiled kid. Besides, I know his family. They wouldn't do anything to me."

"They're the ones who own like half of South American TV or something like that. Right? And in the Government Pemex oil program. Right again? And a few ponies here and at Saratoga. Uses Westrup Simpson's kid as his trainer here. Yeah, sure. Don't know this Mondozo kid, but he wears that suit like it's an anti-depressant. Has that damn half smile. He just looks like he might send your own ear to you in the U.S. mail."

"He's just a blowhard kid from a very rich Mexican family."

"Yeah, but I'll bet they get whatever they want. Whenever they want. You suckered that filly away from the sonofabitch, didn't you?"

"No way. It was legit, Gert. Legit all the way."

She looked at me sideways, not believing a word. "Nothing happy ends with people like you." She waved a finger in my nose. "People like us are dust to them." Her eyes fluttered. She looked faint. I grabbed her arm. "Hold on…" I held her for a moment. "What's going on, Gert?"

He breathed heavily. "Fuck it. The world. My life. Maybe memories. They get to me sometimes." I straightened her and she brushed nothing from her bosom.

"Tell you the truth, Ace, I'm tired." She hung onto me. Loose limbed and miserable. "John. The kid…all that. Hard to deal with." Memories had finally flooded back and had taken over. Juan Gallegos came to her side and she leaned on him.

We would avoid talking about everything in our hearts. Feelings were dangerous. They all say trust your feelings. Bullshit. Nothing about people is unique except from the neck up. Brains are all that counts. I told myself that over and over.

"You're just a gambler, Harvey. An addict," she whispered, trying to straighten up. Juan murmured to her, but she pulled away. "I'm just getting older. So, don't pretend or give odds on how dangerous that Mondozo kid can be."

I had no answers.

"OK," she conjured up a quick smile, "so, we maybe have ourselves a winner. Something special." Juan discreetly backed away. But stayed close.

"Your words to God's ears."

The three of us started walking back to the barn area. "You see those guys at the top of the grandstand?"

"Wasn't looking."

"Bull. In the shadows. Binoculars on the workouts and then shifting to the two of us. Take a look, accidental like."

"Doesn't have to be accidental." I turned. They were still there. Almost at the top row. I waved. The one next to Aureliano waved back and pointed his finger at me and squeezed the trigger letting me know he meant business. No one else around. I did the same and faked a laugh they could see.

"That's a serious family you're messing with."

"Got her fair and square. Told you half a dozen times. I'll keep telling you. I'm close to that family. The old man and I are close. Mexico's finest. He's not letting his kids make trouble."

She tossed a dismissive "sure" at me. There was a twinge in me that knew that family was always first in Mexico.

The sun was just hitting eight o'clock. The haze had cleared. 1080 pixels in HD. Two lazy seagulls squawked just above us assessing the world below. Where did those airborne sailors come from? We were 30 miles from any gathering of water. Some of God's creatures could go anywhere they wanted and would make do. Nice.

"Don't worry about this filly," I said, "Jack Aquilar at Ocean View said she went into the gate real nice on a regular basis. John said so, too. She's big and put together. Nothing is going to happen to us or to her."

Ocean View was the breeding and training farm down the coast near San Diego where my girl was born and raised and cared for like a princess, and where she went through her early training. "This filly is not afraid of anything, Gert."

"And you?"

"Absolutely everything."

We rested our rears on a bench near the entrance to the Backside. Stared at one another, smiling. Juan had followed us every step. "Miss Gert." His soft voice was comforting. He cared about Gertrude Wiseman. He would be there whenever she needed him. "She was flying, Miss Gert." His face grew serious. The scar deepened. "We need to think about running soon, real soon. Have to prove her – find the right race to enter. She's ready. Wait too long and she loses the edge."

"We got lots of time, Juan. We'll see. Another month or so. She's got some growing still to do. Just keep your mouth shut. The clockers aren't really sure of what we have or exactly what to think. I told Donna what to do. If you want to make money, keep the face quiet."

He straightened. Somber. Reincarnated from a regal tribal heritage. "Problem is the hombres, they see. Everyone around the Backside. They see this workout. All the tout sheet handicappers see it. And, we all know, everyone has cousins."

Silk came back wet but not lathered. Donna Camina, dusty face, had a quiet grin spread across her face, her helmet tilted back. "She could've done a 57 flat easy, Miss Gert. Even better. Coasting all the way. Just waved my hand at her. Just remember," she added, pointed a finger at my nose, "don't let anyone take her away from me, Ace. I'm good at this and I don't wanna be second string all my life."

"I know how you feel," I said.

Gertrude ran a practiced hand over each leg then grabbed the reins. "Take her on back, Juan. Cool her down. Check every inch of her."

He glanced at her impatiently. He didn't need anyone to tell them how to treat a horse. Especially this one. But Gertrude persisted. "Wait a while before you wrap her. I'll be back in a little bit." Then she motioned to Donna and pulled her aside. They huddled serious expressions on both faces. When they broke, I asked Gert what was said. "She has to do things my way. Or she's out. I just made it clear."

Trainers had their routines. Early mornings, they unwrap and check every leg and then wrap them again if there is no schedule, although most want their stock to get out for a little exercise. They wrap the dainty legs of their charges a half hour or so after every workout. Grooms wash them down and talk to them and check every inch. Like checking the serial numbers on a thousand-dollar bill. They check the feed tub and fill it. If the feed tub is empty, it tells them that their prize is feeling pretty good. If not, something is wrong and they checked the horse's temperature immediately and feel each leg carefully for warm spots that aren't visible. They look in the mouth and check the teeth, remembering that Secretariat lost to Onion when he had an abscess in his mouth and could barely hold the bit, and couldn't tell anyone. His feed tub was half full. The groom knew something was wrong but no one asked him. No one checked the horse's mouth that day.

A half-hour later, Gert and I sat in a local Denny's. "I'll take her on," Gertrude said. She smiled. Wrinkles disappeared.

I put the menu down. Not interested in what Gert wanted at the moment. "Who could have done this, Gert? The boy is bait for money but killing John? I don't get it."

Her gray streaked auburn hair curled down to her shoulders which shrugged helplessly. No smiles. No words. Coffee was poured. I ordered scrambled eggs and Gertrude waved off the waitress. We sipped coffee for a quiet few moments. Then Gertrude pushed her coffee away, "I really don't like this stuff. But my doctor says two cups a day is good for you."

"I'll remember that."

She sat back and sighed. "Tell you what I'll do, Harvey. Seeing it's you. Seventeen hundred a month plus feed expenses and vets specials and the usual rental plus 15% of net winnings. About four to five thousand a month. A bargain at twice the price especially here at Santa Anita. We can talk about some of the other places. And you always get a fair count. Not from a lot of the others." Her price was a pretty standard one. 15% was a little bit of a surprise. I thought a moment, pretending a serious and thoughtful decision.

Maybe this animal of mine wouldn't break our hearts. Maybe we would all live happily ever after. Maybe *The Silk* would be IT. Maybe we would make a million. But, maybe not.

"Twelve fifty a month, plus some feed and vets, and special expenses and 12% of net."

"Fifteen hundred and you gotta deal." Her hand came out and so did mine and we gave one another a good squeeze, a real shake. It was better than a written contract.

"I'm going back to the track but first I have to know, tell me what I don't know about John. No more avoiding. There has to be a reason for what happened. You have to have guesses."

Her eyes closed. Shadows fell over her face. Her high cheekbones made her sun-dried face seem hollow. "Sometime, maybe. Right now, you're going to see Harry Moss and then see the accountant. Ron Cable. He knows more'n I do. After that…well, you have to think about old man Wheeler. Johnny had money, always had money, whether up or down. He always talked…a blue streak…but never said anything. All he told me was there were trusts and he was in charge. And I heard Wheeler and Johnny arguing more than once."

"About?"

"Never could tell. Never let me get close enough. But that old guy's eyes gave him looks that could kill. Damn those big-shots."

"Eyes don't kill, Gert."

She looked up and gave me a quick false laugh. "But how about –" She shrugged and didn't finish.

"And now you're handling some of his stock."

She pushed the saltshaker back and forth. Her arms locked against her sides as if squeezing out the pain. "I'll do fine. Don't worry about me."

"When do we get serious about John? There's more, isn't there?"

"Gimme time, Harvey."

***

I was looking for Juan. The sky was already dark. The world of racing had shut down for the night. A few neighs and whinnys. The damp streets were as empty as my life at the racetrack. I contemplated heading for the Hustler Casino. Poker would be about right at this hour. Sitting at a two and four poker table was sort of like a necessary dose of dope. I walked down to the end of the darkened street. Jorge Santomeyer, a very good jock I knew, in his jeans and a heavy jacket, came out of the new mist and darkness, hunched over. He looked up, unhappy, dark face, brows lowered. I waved. He shook his head and walked quickly by. Everyone has troubles.

A slight drizzle began, then a heavier one. The rain soaked me. Low-cut Florsheims were not made for rain-soaked muddy streets. Feet wet, rain in my eyes, heading to Gert's barn, figuring Juan would be nearby. But he wasn't and what the hell was I doing there at this time of night? Getting soaked, hoping against hope that Juan would know all the answers and rescue the night for me? I almost expected to see John stride up and wonder what the hell I was doing there and tell me to stop nosing around. Sally is dead – the old man is crazy. Sally was John's deceased wife.

But the only human being that appeared then was Donna Camina, small and shivering, huddled in a corner against the barn next to Winning Silks. We were mutually shocked at seeing one another. She got up quickly. "Just had to... I couldn't..." She shook her head and started crying, softly. "Sorry." Hard to understand but most of these jockeys were just kids, in early twenties, sometimes in their teens like this one. She whirled away quickly, and said, "Sorry. Just alone. Leaving."

But she didn't. She stood stiffly in place, wiped her nose with a bare arm. She was wearing a white t-shirt that stuck to her and something like running shorts. Shivering. I approached and wrapped my arms around her. No resistance. I pulled her in and massaged her back but she kept shivering. Her bottom lip was red along with her eyes. "I'm OK. Really. I'm OK."

"You're not."

"They needed their space."

"Who is they?"

"Sister and that damn husband of hers." She shivered again and I pulled her in and then let go quickly.

"They just tossed you out?"

She told me she lived with an older sister and brother-in-law in a house trailer along the south end of the living space at the track, along with another dozen trailers. "Just over there. Can't really afford anything else. They work here, too. She's in the bookkeeping – payroll and such. And he does PR for them. He's a son of a bitch. Can't live there much longer. I just hope this big filly of yours will do for me what I can't do myself."

"Join the party, Donna. Join the party."

"Told me they were leaving early. She has two days coming and they're going to Vegas. Probably gone by now. I can go back."

"Maybe I'll just go back and make sure."

"Yeah, that's OK. Maybe you can beat ol' Kenny boy to death."

Took a couple minutes and were at the steps into a trailer that was about ten or twelve feet wide and maybe twenty-five feet long. Not much bigger than my kitchen. It was nestled in a row with at least another ten similar trailers.

She knocked. Twice. Then twisted the handle and took the three stairs up. She motioned me in.

To my right was a bed, covers messed, shelves in the corner with what looked like more bed clothes, and a bed covering the rest of the space. Right in front of me was a commode and shower, door half open. To the left was a small stove, two burners, a cast iron frying pan and two plates on top of one another. Cabinets overhead that carried two glasses and nothing more and a sink full of dishes. Too many rags strewn about the kitchen to count. "Sorry about the mess. She tries. But Kenny-boy just pulls at her and they forget about cleaning up and he just takes her hand and off they go into the sack. Fuck away and leave everything. I sit outside. I clean up most of the time."

She shook and then quickly turned and took off her wet T-shirt. No bra for that girl. I started to leave. She came to me in one big step and put her arms around my neck and hung there, her lips on mine, pressing. There was no place to back into. I pulled away. But she held on. I said, "Wait, Donna. Hold on. I mean, not to me. You're not old enough for any of this."

"Plenty old enough, Ace." He voice was full of sex. I have to say, she had me confused. "How old?"

"Twenty." She reached under my wet sweatshirt. Hands cold. "Couple months."

"I'm a hundred and sixty-seven. Honestly, you're just not feeling good right now. I would love to oblige. But we can't do this." I pulled her hands down, away. She grabbed my jacket, started crying.

"Don't you have any other relatives, kid? Mom and Dad? Or anyone else?"

"No one. Died four years ago. Both. Grew up with this sister. She never knew I was around."

I held her. Seemed the easiest way to avoid things. She did a fast dip away and slipped out of her pants.

What do the writers say? The bad writers? Naked as a Jay Bird.

Her hands went to my belt and had it undone before I moved. Then they went down. Cold hands, shocked genitals. "Oh, no. This is not happening." I pushed her away.

She pulled me back. "Just this once," she whispered. "One time. Just once."

41

I pushed her away again. Hers arms were muscled, but her shoulders blades protruded. Waist tiny, thighs strong. "Listen, kid. We both need something now. But, I'm telling you, you don't need me. And you don't need this. I need you to ride *The Silk*. Not one another. You should talk to Gertrude. Get close to her. She actually needs you. She always wanted to find that kid of hers – the one I couldn't find. The one I failed to find. Go see her. Just not me. Wrong person. Wrong time, wrong place." I held her closely for a moment, then untangled and hurried to the door. "I'm sorry, kid. Honestly."

The last thing I saw was this little girl, naked and sobbing and miserable and very needy. And there I was, naked soul and needy heart. I jumped out and began running along the next street and along the flower beds, all drooping in the rain, just as I was. Inside and out. I thought, *I have to call Sarah. This can't go on. I could change. Maybe enough to make it work. I would go to the track on Thursdays only – or maybe just on Thursdays and Saturdays – maybe when there was a big cap, and home by 6 p.m. Or maybe I adopt a three-year-old and take him or her to Chucky-Cheezes on Sundays. That ought to do it.*

***

I'm getting into my car in the vast empty parking lot when Jimmy the Mummy, elbow on the top of my Jag, soaking wet, holding a soaked VONS bag in one hand, hollered, "Wait!"

His shout jerked me back to the world. "What the hell are you doing? What're you yelling at? Look at you. You're soaking! Trying to get double pneumonia? Dammit, get your ass in the car." He happily jumped in and slumped, head on his chest, dripping from everywhere. Old and gray. Leather seats would have to be wiped – but he was a good friend, except when he wasn't. He dropped forward almost slipping onto the floor. He had big hands and good shoulders, large forearms and biceps. Made him more than eighty. Born in the middle of WWI. He was out of someone unknown by someone unknown. Fabulous breeding. He looked like a onetime muscle man. Jimmy was always on the wrong side of events like all horse players, like all gamblers eventually are. He was persistently broke. He wore the same pin stripped jacket that once had been part of a thousand-dollar suit. And his shoes were polished, as old as the hills but were of first rate leather.

Jimmy, however, was at the tail end of his adventures, and rumors were that there had been plenty. An early life in Cuba and then working for some casino in Florida. He once told me his whole story, slightly buzzed and needing to talk after I gave him a couple hundred dollars to "tide him over."

42

Said he was born Johann Garfein in 1915 (but wasn't sure) in some tiny shtetl between Hungary and Bulgaria or somewhere around the ever-changing European borders. He and his family managed to find their way to what was then Palestine during WWI when the pogroms got serious. It was a place where no one wanted them to be, especially the Turks, later the British, and then all the indigenous tribes. There were established forces that led them to an agricultural Kibbutz, called Habhan after the founder, where the family grew melons and eventually became spies for the British against the Ottoman Empire that was coming unglued. Jimmy became a messenger carrying messages on camelback and horseback to a ranking Brit about locations of Ottoman Battalions and usually received a couple of pence for his trouble, along with frowns and comments that made him realize that he was only a pawn in the fight against the Turks and that they really didn't want him or his family when the fight was over. After the war, the only place the family could get to when trying to immigrate to the United State, was Cuba. The family survived, barely, and Jimmy grew into his thirties in a strange land, coping with language, once commenting that he did "a lot of bad things" about that time.

He sat quietly for a few minutes and as I was about to ask about the bag, he finally shoved it onto my lap, flipped it over and dumped bundles of cash, rubber band around a dozen bundles that fell into my lap and onto the floor of the car.

"Thirty-six hundred bucks," he said. His eyes flashed proudly. Then he shivered. I could've sworn he didn't have a dime to his name as I was always buying him meals and shoving bits of cash at him.

"Whoa, there, Jimmy. Lot of money. Start talking."

"Been saving. Not to worry." Then he stopped, looked at me intently with grim unrevealed eyes. "Gotta tell ya'." Then he insisted that I – for god's sake – figure out what happened to John and his son and to avenge them because the people that were stalking John and killed him were the same ones stalking him. He said he was connected to the tragedy. "But I can't figure out how. But I am, Harvey. I forget things. But I'm telling ya. I'm somewhere in the middle of this. And you gotta be, too. I'm not crazy." He shook his head slowly with low painful moans. "I'm telling ya. It's true. They been following me. Harvey, ya gotta believe me."

I gave him an OK and figured he was in a stage of paranoid dementia. I assured him I understood. Over and over. And then drove him home, a small apartment, midtown, near Western and ninth. "Find the boy!" he said. "He's the key. Gotta find them. The whole fuckin' bunch."

I took his key and steadied him in the door and onto his bed, pulled off his shoes and tuned on the heat. "Get some sleep." I put the piles of money on the dresser in his nickel-sized bedroom with a bed and dresser, no mirrors, tiny closet. The living room was just as bleak. A very worn checkered brown upholstered chair, a small couch and table, and a 13-inch TV and that's it. I didn't look but I suspected that the frig was empty which I couldn't fix just then. A let down of significant degrees for someone who was once a somebody. Reminded myself to call social services and send them out.

From the bedroom, he hollered, "Get the sonofabitches, Harvey, before they get us!" Paranoia had to settling in deeper and deeper. So I thought.

I was sure the Augers Affair required people who had a great deal more involved than just money. However, money is everything, which seemed to lead inextricably to FK Wheeler.

I was on my way.

Chapter Three

It was only a couple of days ago on that same drizzly Sunday morning when this whole episode began.

Sarah lived with me at my beachside condo at Venice Beach, California. It had taken three months and a dinner at Spagos to convince her to move in sans ring. Who knew that girls had so much stuff, that there were so many details in moving in and moving out; gas bill, phone bill, DMV, voting, locating a pharmacy, pots and pans, of which I had few, as well as enough forks to last more than one meal at home. On that unhappy Sunday morning, we had been together for seven months (three days and eleven hours, but, who's counting?). We met at a Frontier Airlines Ticket Counter on a warm Friday night in Phoenix, Arizona, a year ago, each needing to make connections. Since we could not make connections, we ended up in Super Eight Motel, the only room within miles of the airport.

We, without the details – think Clarke Gable and Claudette Colbert decided that night that we weren't going to waste more time looking for anyone else. I liked this girl. She had dark eyes that told stories. They shifted from a clouded hazel to dark walnut depending on mood and she definitely had moods. Big time.

Some specially constructed noses are perfect, and Sarah's would have been, too, except it had a little tilt up at the end, just a little which meant that it was not specially constructed.

She was pretty much an "as is" product and pretty much perfect in the tape measure dimensions; maybe five feet five. I could cup my hands over…well, pretty much everywhere. She was in flight two, sometimes three, days a week as an attendant on Frontier Airlines, bouncing between Denver, LA, Phoenix. I tried to convince her to quit her job – over and over. But, hey, I was often at a local casino playing poker or at the Santa Anita or Hollywood Park, and in later summer at Del Mar just north of San Diego, doing what I do. So, it was hard to insist and our schedules didn't give much persuasion time.

Little by little over the years, I had accumulated a comfortable bundle. I invested in GE and Telephone and Disney and a little in Apple. Telephone did lousy, but the rest did reasonably well and I kept adding to Apple. Sold telephone and GE, but what this investing business did was convince Sarah that I was not crazy, a ne'er-do-well, and that all I needed was a steady job, something just to keep me busy during the day and home by dark. Something regular with a paycheck. Her mother had a regular paycheck, even her idiot father had a regular paycheck. She worked hard at convincing me to "get a job, Harvey, a regular 9 to 5 job."

Where would we be if you had bad luck? If I quit gambling, she would quit. Told her my bundle would carry us for a very long time maybe until we died and were buried, and showed her my Merrill-Lynch last report. She didn't understand money. Unless you live with the contemplation of money, with how it works, about compounding, and the risks and rewards of investing and how to measure each, and understand that money has to work for itself, that a hundred dollar bill is a working piece of paper, and that you don't always win, then there's no explaining it. There just isn't.

Gimme a break. Nine to five? My answer was always, and do what? Her persistent reply was, "I don't care…just get a real job. I won't quit until you do." She figured, along with the vast conglomeration of the rest of the known world, that people had to have a "job." Not complicated. Get up in the morning and go somewhere, and be there by nine. And leave by five, now and then by six and get a check in the mail on Tuesdays every other week. However, I liked "complicated." I tried to explain. Gamblers aren't like real people, they are more like several people in one, trying to fit themselves into one package, figuring the risks, jumping whole hog on sure things, being where you needed to be. It was not a JOB; it was a profession. I borrowed these thoughts from some writer. I added the "Coup d' Grace."

"And aggravation keeps you thin!"

We were at an impasse. The last couple of months, the air had grown heavy between us, turning back to back at night, not knowing what to say, except good night, did you take your pills? I didn't want to lose her, I needed her in my own way, actually needed her in a way not fully explicable then. A person needs care and attention at the beginning of life and care and attention at the end of life – a person needs to know someone in the world actually cared. But the blush was definitely off.

We were going through a month of dead Sundays. I knew, intellectually, how others felt, but that's about it. I vaguely recalled how I felt at the end of my first short marriage, which was like 100 years ago; I hated going home in the evening, but my car kept driving me there – I would look up and sure enough, I would be home. That car had a sick magnet in it.

Nothing, however, was the same as this. All new. Problem was I was in love. Which makes everything different.

What was it that created this wanting? Hard to figure. For me, it was new and something akin to fear. Persistent fear of saying something wrong, doing something wrong, being at the wrong place in the condo at the wrong time. Wanting to do what made her happy but not able to do it. Upset half the time and not knowing exactly why – yet, at the same time, she was it. Sarah infected my fucking spleen. I would tell myself nothing else mattered. For whatever reasons humans were stuck with, I had to have this girl.

I vowed over and over to make it work and still win, pick the right numbers, draw aces every time.

I thought I could change. I wanted to. Winning Silks would make it all possible.

Then on that damnable Sunday morning, just as the sun rose, I turned in bed and her spot was empty. I pulled on a pair of gray sweats and hurried down the stairs and there she was walking to the front door, dressed in that pale blue sleeveless blouse that barely covered her, just throwing a black sweater over her shoulders, brown slacks, almost indecently gorgeous, rolling her Hartmann and carrying her one and only Gucci bag which we bought in Chinatown together for twenty-five bucks. She looked at me a long time like checking me out one last time before I died, said nothing, and opened the door. The ocean drizzle swirled in greedily and she stopped, checked the inner sanctum of what had been our home, dropped everything and strode briskly into the small library area and returned a James Lee Burke paperback to the shelf, returned and retrieved everything in a smooth practiced movement, her eyes absolutely blazing. I was waiting to hear something from her, anything – at a complete loss about what to say or do. I put my hand up and finally stammered out with, "I think…"

She put up her hand. "Don't say it. Don't say anything. We've done all the talking. I'll send for my things, whatever is left."

She stepped outside into the mist and was gone. I heard the Honda door slam and then she pulled away.

I believed she was the IT girl. I was sure she was…open and tough and smart. So what was it? What exactly did I do?

Or didn't?

I knew – but I didn't. And not a word except, "I'll send for my things."

Took me about five minutes to absorb the moment before I ran madly out to the beach, to the great Pacific Ocean and screamed like a banshee. What is sacred about nine to five?

I didn't understand any of it. Not the relationship. Not Sarah. Not anything. The mists held onto the sand. The gulls were caterwauling above me, and I screamed back at them. Runners along the cement frontage gazed at me like I was mad. Which I was. I dumped my ass on the damp sand and watched the earth and interminable sea and one lonely fisherman on the pier, about seventy-five yards to the north, yellow hat, with his pole bent – hoping. Hooray for him. Fuck hope. I stared at him for a long while as if he caught a fish. If he did, it would end my misery. Finally, I told myself it was okay to have my coffee and read the paper and screw the world. I had my life.

I had a life, dammit! My gambling life and my nutty and misfit friends. If no one liked it, fuck 'em. I hollered at the runners who had stopped and stared. "What the hell are you looking at? Never saw a crazy man screaming at the ocean?"

The population where I lived consisted of teenagers who shared living quarters and seemed not to understand the concept of school or gambling or work, or anything. They played volleyball all day long. There were also the homeless and the local shopkeepers all along the boardwalk to the north. I bought my condo, one of six in the complex, all in a row, before it was finished in 1991 after a big win at Hollywood Park, long before prices went beyond good sense.

The thick LA Sunday Times always plopped in the same place on the top step of the small porch of my condo which fronted on a narrow street behind the beach. Except this time, it was at the bottom of the steps half into the street. I tossed an inch-thick sheaf of adverts onto the floor which I promised I would take to the large trash bin on my way out. I make a lot of promises. The automatic timer on the coffee maker which I had set up the night before buzzed and I poured a cup and settled into my Eames Chair looking through my picture window at the beach, at the licks of malicious little whitecaps the ocean breezes made, then picked up the front section of the Times. Sunday morning rituals. The top right of the fold was the usual national news stuff, "Republicans against…" About the persistent bickering of Democrats and Republicans on every subject, all of which had been droning on and on ad nauseam since this President was elected. The opposition is supposed to aggravate and oppose but also create; however, this adversarial group was making sure nothing worked.

I flipped to the bottom of the fold. The interesting stuff is usually there. It didn't sink in when I first glanced at the brief article, two columns at the bottom left. So, I squeezed my eyes and read it through and then again. "FAMOUS THOROUGHBRED TRAINER MURDERED LAST NIGHT AT RACE TRACK!"

"John Augers, respected trainer of thoroughbred race horses remembered for his role in bringing a filly named ARISE to fame and fortune, winner of the GOOD FORTUNE Stakes at Hollywood Park late summer last year..."

The same article also revealed that the night security guard, Herman Barnes, was killed and that John's autistic son had been kidnapped.

Like Herman's death and the kidnapping of a 10-year-old was an afterthought. My first thought was that the kid's life would worth a fortune to old man Wheeler, his grandfather. There would be a blackmailing ransom note corning soon.

I dropped the Times like it was diseased. John was a friend. A pain-in-the-ass friend but a very good horseman and, in spite of his boot long list of shortcomings, he was someone I knew for a very long time, someone I worked with and cared about. I cared for the son of a gun. He had his secrets and I have mine. But, however difficult he was, he was a good guy. There really aren't that many. Percentagewise, I mean. I poured the coffee and recalled John Augers apprehensions.

It was no more than two weeks ago when he told me he was not long for this world.

"Sometime soon," he said, was what the voice claimed at the 2 a.m. phone call. He told me it was the third of such calls. His round, red face sagged. He had passed a hand over his baldpate and thought a minute and shrugged, stared at the table and mumbled. He had big ears and an architectural molded significant nose and a growing belly. As he spoke, he seemed weirdly resigned as if he was ready for whatever came, a condition that was grossly incongruent with his usually agitated, glass half-full personality. The only thing he revealed was that he was sick and tired of his father-in-law Franklin Wheeler's ravings about his daughter Sally, about John's training methods, about the Wheeler Foundation's CEO and everything and anything else that crossed his mind. Sally was John's wife. I should say, she was his wife until her death in a mental institution several years ago. John was tired of the imagined conspiracies between himself and Sally to steal old Wheeler's fortune and kill him in the process. It had become the old man's mantra. "She's out there. I'm telling you. Sally's out there. Gonna kill me! Johnny, it's me or her."

The late-night calls John complained about were not merely prankster's calls. He was sure. It was real. A finger went to his temple, his eyes squinted.

Right or wrong, he was sure. I knew Franklin Wheeler to be an impatient old geezer. If it weren't for the fact that John's wife was dead, and suspicions remained, I would have taken his description of Wheeler as over the top. Way over. But John insisted. Wheeler was crazy. And the calls he kept getting were serious. John may have been over the top himself, but he wasn't a liar.

Chapter Four

I told myself again I would get the killers and kill them. Twice! And find the little boy I was good at finding people.

I even had a license-Harvey Ace, Private Investigator, California# 62381 a-2.

A pair of Black Queens made Winning Silks mine about six months ago. We were at his spread-out ranch home, rather the home of his parents, just south of Tijuana on the inside of the coastal road that took one straight down the Coast to Ensenada and on further all the way to Cabo San Lucas. Thought Aureliano would lace me with bullets in that dark, rose colored den with the fake book in neat shelves and perfect green felt poker table when I turned up my queens.

But, he was a friend. He owed me. And blood in his father's den was something he would not risk. He stared at me with hate in those ominous ebony eyes, pistol within reach, however, I walked away intact and with her papers.

I had high hope for the golden filly. She had great breeding.

She was my ticket. Maybe my final hope.

Which in the last couple of years had become something larger than the Queen Mary and empire State Building combined. It's not that I was always looking for that final hope. I couldn't carry on like I had been for a lot longer. That was my belief.

Beliefs are always wrong – in spite of hope and beliefs, we carry on and carry on more and then more, until the inevitable end. Beliefs from childhood and hope are the primary genes inside all of us, especially gamblers.

John was an insistent, little man carrying luggage under his eyes, who didn't break five foot six. A former exercise jock who got big in the belly. Even so, I could put my arms around two of him. He wore that silly old straw hat of his at all times and spoke in half sentences…over there, go…and, that done yet? Check that Mare's teeth! He would wave a finger and expect everyone in sight to know what, where and how. He quoted biblical phrases, his favorite being the Song of Moses, Listen, Heavens, while I speak…which, of course, meant listen to me because it is vital and I'm not

51

about to repeat myself. He had a history: paying off auctioneers at thoroughbred auctions preserving the best yearlings for himself, a history of giving bundles to charity, a history with rich women who seemed to "just adore" him and a history as a winning trainer. And a history with Arise, his Breeders Cup winner. A clown? Maybe. Sometimes a bully. However, if you were his friend, he was the man to call in a pinch…

John and I had dinner at least once a week. He always paid, kept that idiotic hat on his glistening pate. We talked about racehorses and racing, other trainers, the weather, my love life, but avoided anything resembling serious emotions. He married the "Wheeler girl," the very pretty, social, and sought after Sally Wheeler, twelve years ago when she was just nineteen. The "Wheeler girl" was Franklin Wheeler's daughter. *The* Franklin Wheeler. Big time tycoon type.

Owned a third of the western world. FKW Stables. Construction, land, Malls, Movie theaters, Savings and Loans, fingers in everything – whatever made money. And John was a beneficiary in ways I didn't ask about.

I always found it hard to understand what possessed Augers to marry the "Wheeler girl" and stick with her all those years before her sudden and inexplicable death. She was in and out of mental institutions. A persistent problem, as was her father in dealing with her. And dealing with John.

Old man Wheeler, however, according to John was getting long in the tooth and not so fearsome anymore. It was claimed he had become a paranoid, a nagging old man. Just a couple weeks ago, the last time that John and I spoke on the subject of Sally, he said, "I just finished a bull session with the old man. He's fixated that she is out there. A ghost. Thinks she and I are in cahoots somehow. Thinks she will strike at the stables.

"Crazy stuff.

"Sophie didn't help. She is like nails. I know all those things they say, But I know all the fucking rumors, too." He took a sip of water, his lips dried visibly as he spoke.

He was telling lies or plain scared. "People keep saying she is not gone. Don't mean people. Wheeler. That's who. She has risen, he says. She hated her old man so much he is sure she has come back to get him. Especially around the stables which was her favorite of all places. I tell him to stay away from the barns, the employees. But he just rants.

"I'm telling you, Harvey, Sally died. She was miserable in her skin. She died, goddammit! That's all there is to it. She died! And I really don't know why! Or how except, what those idiot doctors said.

"I wasn't there. But she's dead. And that old crazy man thinks she is following him around." His forefinger pounded the table, "And Carole is dead. Her death really hurt. I didn't want them dead. I admit, Sally was a real problem. But she is dead. Gone! Someone has to get that into that old man's head!"

Carole was the wife he took on a year and a half after Sally's death. She seemed to be the right one. Until her violent end at the hands of a derelict. Or so it seemed. The story of John's wives was out of a bad movie. He looked down, fingered his coffee cup, stuffed his loose blue tie into his pants, pushed the saltshaker around. "And now I get these phones calls. Middle of the night. One of them said, That Ace man can't help you. Why you are in middle, I don't know. But someone doesn't like you. The voice was different each time. Why your name is in this?"

"I'm famous the world over."

"C'mon, Harv…no jokes. If anything, you're infamous."

We speculated as to why I was part of the equation. No answers. Finally, I said, "Maybe Franklin is just an old guy with regrets and trying to scare you into giving back all the rights in those trusts. I don't know your deal with him. Don't want to know. But maybe he doesn't like the situation anymore. Maybe he regrets the whole damn thing. I have a long list of my regrets. Long as my arm. Maybe he feels the same."

"Maybe so, you will dig out what is going on. Everyone knows we are close…and for a long time." He laughed and then looked quickly away. Round face suddenly drawn; cheeks hollowed out just enough to make shadows out of every inch of that face. He suddenly glimpsed something in his past. "Shit," he murmured, to himself.

I was never privy to the police inquiry about Sally's death, or the rusty debris of memories from those years. But, what do I know about relationships? I was always under the impression that a good relationship was a matter of always saying thank you and you're welcome, getting home by seven and doing the dishes, except for Saturday nights. And of course when she showed you a leg all the way up to her hip and said tonight is the night, you had to be ready. Could be I had a relationship quotient of zero minus three…maybe four.

John occasionally spoke about the care of their autistic son but, other than those rare moments, we did not get close to gut feelings, which was fine with me. Gamblers work at steering clear of emotions. Of course, I had heard all the rumors and persistent scuttlebutt about the Wheeler Trusts of which John was the beneficiary of at least one, and the rumors about old man Wheeler's unhappiness with the way his trusts had been handled. I heard all those stupid rumors that Sally was actually alive and seeking satisfaction for some unknown misery thrust upon her by her father.

But they were all merely rumors that seemed to grow with telling.

Rumors abound at racetracks and are worth about the same as a stock tip by a broker. I studiously ignored them.

During the Del Mar racing season in late July six months ago, John and I were at a Fidel's, a celebrity hangout serving first-rate Mexican cuisine. It was a mile or so from the track, after a day of significant winning, when nothing could go wrong. There were such days when you were ten feet tall, when gambling triumphs were substitutes for food, sex, life itself. You become, for a few moments, the Chief of the Clan, head of the Mishbucha, King of the Tribe. Trouble was it was all so damnably fleeting that you keep trying to do it again and again! The final hope, the final triumph. You're supposed to have a thousand dollars on a pick five, win the whole thing, and then drop dead relishing your final high.

What I wanted to do was tell him about my plans with Sarah.

They were monumental plans to me.

Mariachies played in the background assisted by the melodious tinkling margarita glasses – salty rims on margaritas by the tub and soft romantic words in the background.

The fiddle played, Jerome Kern. John and I didn't need the mood of the famous Del Mar taco, rice, and beans hangout.

Nevertheless, I felt like I wanted to buy the whole house a drink. I wanted to celebrate winning and what I hoped was a new beginning for me. Normal came to mind. I was ready to ask Sarah to move in with me and maybe even to suggest that M word. Told him, slowly. "This is it."

His eyes narrowed. He shoved that idiotic hat back on his head. He gazed at me for an extra-long moment like checking to see if it was really me. I thought he was going to congratulate me.

Forget that. If you win a big race for a big number, he would say something as endearing as "Fuck you, Ace" or "why didn't you say something, you misery?" Instead, on this occasion, he said, "Sarah? Sarah Finkel. Miss Gorgeous? Are you kidding? Harvey, look at me – are you kidding?" He put his finger on my folded hands. "There's something I don't think you ever understood." He shook his balding head sadly as if ready to cry...or laugh. "You gotta be kidding. A person your age has no business being dumb about love and that stuff." He leaned back and took that hat off and placed it gingerly on the table in front of us. Then he took a sip of what was left of his coffee.

"Listen, Harvey," he spoke slowly like lecturing a ten-year-old. "There are six parts of a relationship. Six. Count 'em. Pay attention."

He ticked them off, snapping fingers as he spoke. He was Socrates, Aristotle, Jung, Freud, all together.

"One, there's lust, two, there's like, three, love four, boredom, five, dislike and six, out in the Alimony cold.

"The evidence is in; you're not made for the domestic life. You're still trying to fix the last one. And a Jewish girl? They want picket fences, regular paychecks, big ones. And babies. I can see you holding a little Harvey. He would look up and say, "Gimme two across the board on number four." Jeez, Harvey, give it up!"

I should have known. My life had been a series of mistakes interrupted by misbegotten triumphs. Sarah had been one of the significant triumphs.

Mr. Wiseguy, Augers the horseman, the horse training genius, was always telling me who I am. So, I told him who he was. "You're an idiot, you know that?" I said. Not a question. "And you're wrong about her. Just plain wrong. I don't know why you think I'm not fit for normal. I am. I'm normal. I want that life!"

I wanted to punch the aggravating little man. "I'm very normal. I'm going to get even more normal. So get over the damn judgments.

"She's perfect for me." As I said it, my stomach turned. The question was not Sarah – the question was me. Knowledge hurts.

He sighed, grinned broadly, knowingly. "And you for her? Don't you know who you are?" His small, green eyes all at once grew flat and somber. I knew he was going to start telling the truth. About me – again. Which. Of course, I hate.

"People like us are not normal, Harv," he said somberly. "You recall what happened after I married Sally? Glamorous and beautiful Sally? How I struggled with the Wheelers, both of them, and how Sally was in and out of the nut house? How I gambled like a madman? How Gertrude and I…" He didn't finish that thought. "How I had to figure out how to even begin to manage those trusts? Now the old man claims Sally is haunting him from the grave. Ready to kill. And he thinks maybe I am a threat to him. I'm conspiring against him somehow as a trustee. They're all crazy, Harvey. Nut cases. Even when I'm crazy, I'm not like those people. Marriage is not for people like us. We have to move on…to the next race, the next deal, and then move on again." He whispered the last, "Then again…fuck it." He shook his head slowly. "And you remember you can't even contact your daughter after all these years? Somehow you fucked that up, too."

John was convincing. Maybe I should wait. Waiting. That never got me anything. I rose. I wanted to punch the little man because that was one thing in my personal life I didn't fuck up.

55

It just ended up that way. He waved. "Sit down, Harvey. Just sit the fuck down. Sorry. Low blow. But, fer chissake, don't you know you're just at the lust and like stage? I give you six months."

Then he described the telephone calls threatening both of us, though I can understand threats to him, he was in the horse flesh business. But I was a loner. Except for Jimmy and a couple other off the charts nut cases. Why me?

***

A little over six months later, missing the exact day by three, Sarah dumped me. It was not a classic dump. It was quick and uncontestable. Sarah Finkel, beautiful Sarah. Dark hair and fair skin and dark eyes with those touches of gold in there that seemed to say I know more than you do; and she always stood straight and looked you in the eye. One of those girls you can't ignore even in a crowded room. Losing her changed my life – not for the better. The only thing I would sleep with now was a horse and a bank account.

I never had the chance to tell him Sarah had walked out. Never told him he was right and what was wrong with me? Six months almost to the day. *"I'll send for my things."* No angry words. Nothing.

Merely, I'll send for my things.

And she was gone. Along with hope. What do they say? I remembered…hope is a bitch. Was she really gone – never to return?

Not a good morning. What I needed was to know more about John's death and the kid, and I needed a big winner. Then maybe I could quit. *The Silk* would make it happen.

***

Naturally, Gert was right. Mondozo was stalking me. He knew everything I did and when I did it.

I don't know how many people he had on my tail but they were invisible. I'm the guy who is supposed to know these things. I know them when it comes to someone else.

Pretty clear, I don't know shit when it comes to me.

Chapter Five

One couldn't simply stop an addiction. Whether booze, pills or gambling, or cracking your knuckles. Addictions wrestled their way into your bloodstream. They were with you when the sun went down, when the sun went up, and when it did neither but hid out somewhere behind lightning, thunder and black clouds – every damn minute of every day and night.

I would awaken at eleven in a restless evening, stare at the ceiling, tell myself not to do anything, take a piss, drink cold water, hit the pillow – then I would dress and head for Larry Flynt's Hustler's Casino, right off Interstate 5 in east LA twenty minutes that time of night. It was like "O'God, I don't even know how to change, even if I really wanted to…which I did. Really."

I would sit with old ladies and similar stricken quiet people in those lonely red draped upholstered rooms, each one a first-rate card player. There were consequences. I knew that, or *The Silk* would win and win and win and I would become legitimate…an owner. I would sit at my table in the turf club and talk to trainers about what filly or colt to buy at the yearling sales…or to claim in the claiming box, and deal with an entirely new set of consequences.

Maybe I would call Sarah and maybe she would feel differently. She was one of those people who had mapped out their futures carefully. Structure. That was it. An inflexible way of being; breakfast at seven, lunch at noon, count the paper clips at your desk and then have a coffee. Unfortunately for her, she met me. All cylinders clicked. But, I was not a person with a structure. Well, maybe it was that I was more structured than she, at this track in December, that one in July, another in the fall, and perhaps Saratoga now and then in August. More than anything my future was tomorrow's Racing Form.

We met at a car rental at the Phoenix airport.

A day later, in bed, she looked over at me in a quiet moment and said, "What on earth is gambling going to do for you in ten years?"

I never answered that question by Sarah. There I was sitting at "my" table at Santa Anita, trying to figure out how to win betting on flesh and blood.

How the hell could I answer her question except with promises she wouldn't believe? That I wouldn't believe?

However, I said to myself, as Teyva might have argued, Sarah is a good one and you love her. Stick with it.

But, I was simply a middle-aged fellow who gambled, played the horses and everything else, and seemed content in the process. I won more than I lost, at the Casino, at the Track. People paid me large bucks to find missing people, isn't all that enough?

In quiet gambling rooms, hearing the clickidy clack, clickidy clack, of betting chips, counting mine with fingers, not looking, casual like, turning them and counting again. I got lost in the words I would have liked to say to her – like, I love you, down deep where it counts; how even a numbers guy could be hurt. And I wanted to tell her how it hurt to lose John and how strongly I felt about finding his unfortunate son... My thinking processes didn't get as far the future. They didn't have to. I had my State license. I had a home and a bank account and a reputation, albeit different to different people. So what if Sarah didn't understand. So what? I didn't want to know more than a couple of tomorrows anyway. Three and a half years with the Los Angeles police department, a car cop, before I quit. Not a heavy resume. Then learning the gambler's trade and making headlines when I found someone who was seriously lost. I always thought of Heronimus Bosche's wife, the gambler. His make-believe wife, very real to me. She would sitting alone at a black jack table and there she would be to end of her days, interested in the rest of the world but not enough to turn away from the dealer's next card. I had to admit it, we were serious addicts.

Then came that card game with the Mondozo kid and *The Silk* was mine. A baby girl horse had taken hold of my future. It would be different.

A skinny, delicate lady sat two tables down toward the Clubhouse turn smoking incessantly. The smoke naturally drifted my way and disturbed me. I kept waving it away. Hated cigarette smoke ever since I stopped December 25th Christmas day at about 10 a.m., almost ten years ago. I had the flu and I couldn't smoke without choking to death. And there were no smokes in the condo, and way too ill to go out, simply hoping someone would put me out of my misery and then give me a smoke. Shit, if I can quit the fucking cigarettes... I can...

Jimmy the Mummy, collared me at my table. He sat down heavily and grabbed my arm. Jimmy was maybe two hundred years old going on more than eighty. Strands of red hair fell to his forehead. He had a thousand crevasses in his checks and sallow skinned, slipping down from under a batter black fedora. His before the dye hair was actually snowy white but I was the only one who knew. Almost twenty years ago, he had been shot in an alley by a doctor who thought Jimmy was engaged in unmentionable adventures with his wife. The irate Doctor chased Jimmy down an alley in Beverly Hills. Can you feature that? A white coat chasing a has-been gambler?

The doctor got close enough to shoot. When Jimmy went down, the doctor ran. It confirmed my opinion of doctors. Cops got the Doctor and Paramedics hauled Jimmy to the hospital. He was white as a ghost when I visited him. In fact, he was so white the hospital staff started calling him The Mummy.

"Wanna see the Mummy? Room 324. The nurses directed everyone to Jimmy the Mummy. The name took hold and that was that.

However, if a stranger called him that he would turn and say firmly between clenched teeth, "My name is James Gaines. I do not know any Mummy. You understand? James Gaines."

Billy often called him James. Billy Fitzer, known as Horse Blanket Billy. All these people close to me had these character names, but never responded to them. And Billy had a temper, so everyone watched it.

Jimmy pulled at me.

"I gotta talk to you, Harvey. Now. Gotta. They're after us. They think we did something."

Jimmy was a smart old man, getting sort of paranoid with age. Been told it comes with age. He was a walking, talking genome of opposites.

Strong, dependent, secretive but never stopped talking. A history about which I learned but about which he never spoke. I discounted his personal fears. Those pale, red-rimmed, eyes were genuinely blazing and fearful this time. He shuffled back and forth waving a folded newspaper and said, "You hafta believe me, Harv. They're after me. I'm not crazy." He dumped a Von's paper bag on the table.

"Go slow, Jimmy. Just take a deep one. OK? You're hyperventilating. Here's some water." I handed him my glass. He stared like I was crazy, then finished it.

"Harvey. It's all connected." He wiped his mouth with his sleeve. "I'm tellin' ya. It's all connected. Maybe you're part of it. Unnerstan'? Got John in the middle of the night. Can't kill someone in the middle of the night without knowing exactly where he is, when he is gonna be there, and then take his kid. Gotta be connected. Harvey! It's coming clear to me." He waggled his head. His voice lowered. His eyes faded. "They're after me, too." Then he went silent and shook his head back and forth mournfully. He whispered, "I know what everyone says – I forget things. But I know." His chin fell to his

59

chest. I thought he would cry. Then from his VONS grocery bag, he dumped thirty-six hundred dollars cash in three thick newspaper wrapped bundles. He pointed a finger and squeezed the trigger, "Find the kid, find Frankie, or he's deader than dead. And you, too. Your buddies at the police department ain't gonna do it. Everything is connected. I know somethin'. I know somethin' – I don't know what, though…damn them. Damn them all."

His head dropped to the table.

"Breathe, Jimmy. Breathe? I don't know who you are talking about." I grabbed the money and shoved it back into the bag. Then gripped his hand his and held it. "It's going to be OK." I waved at one of the busboys, who was about Jimmy's age and short as a jock and told him to bring coffee. I put the bag on the floor between my feet.

"Cool down. Tell me what's going on."

Jimmy still had that graveyard look, sallow complexion, thin frame, deep set eyes, big ears, with a history no one knew much about. He had these big strong hands which I always thought could take his weight plus twenty pounds and come out a winner…if he wasn't as old as the hills. He was always saying something like "Don't fuck a duck, Harvey. You gotta duck a fuck." I had no idea what he meant and never tried to learn.

"The money. For you. They are definitely following me. I'm not crazy. They are. Take a look over by the kitchen entrance. Take a look."

I did. Someone was there. In a suit and tie.

Looking very Latin and suave. "Who is that supposed to be?"

"I keep seeing him."

"So?"

"I don't know. But he is after me. I'm tellin' ya."

I rose and went to the spot. The fellow was nearly my height, bulkier, almost fat, black eyes. "My friend thinks you are after him. Following him. Tell me what's the story."

He looked at me like I was crazy. His eyebrows raised an inch and he took a step back. "Don't know what you are talking about."

"But you do."

"See that man – table just below on the that level? See him?"

I looked. Someone perhaps in his sixties, neatly dressed, tie and suit, sat alone with the racing Form open in front of him but unopened.

"OK. What about it?"

"Know him?"

"No. I've seen him there before. Always alone."

"That's all you need to know. Now get yourself back to that crazy old man." I gave the fellow a long look and went back, patted Jimmy on the back and told him, "No one is after you, Jimmy."

"You think I'm crazy like Billy." The rest of them definitely. But I thought you were sane." Live it up, Jimmy. Guy has someone else on his mind."

"Take the money, Harvey. Find that kid. It's all connected."

"You said I had something to do with it."

"You do. They know who you are. Big investigator."

I sat back. I couldn't be bothered anymore.

Jimmy got his coffee in a nice chrome decanter and the waiter smiled and poured.

"Take a swig, Jimmy."

"I ordered a chicken salad sandwich. You'll feel better when you eat something. Meanwhile, I got a race to think about."

But Jimmy had turned my mind to my own mishugas. No one was following me…or Jimmy. No one.

I would know. Suspicions and fear has a way of insinuating themselves into your psyche, but they hadn't gotten to me yet.

My mishugas were Horse Blanket Billy Fitzer, Larry the lowdown Lowenstaff, and, of course, Nails Nirenstein. Nails let his nails grow on one hand only so that they curled around into a five-inch circle which he had to carry around with the other hand like a frail child. Nails had been very well-known in some unsavory circles as the best safe cracker ever. Billy Fitzer had his own problems; obsessions, avoiding cracks on sidewalks and never without one of his multicolored sports jackets, yellow orange, blue, red, in strips or checks, looking a little like a wrapped Indian Doll. Larry, long and lanky, was an incurable liar. He was Beverly Hills blue blood stock; home on Roxbury, north of Sunset Boulevard, where the bottom price on any home within a half mile was upwards of six r million. He had been thrown out of his family home when his father figured out why the family Kristof silverware was disappearing. Larry had been pawning it to pay Willard Spearman, his bookie, who, it just so happened, lived in a French Norman baronial affair two doors down from the Lowenstaff mansion.

Lawrence was twenty-eight years old at the time with a Masters in Business from UCLA with a specialty called "Statistical Leveraging." I figured it; it was a specialty that taught you how to cheat Wall Street bankers, hard not to approve.

He was emotional and stubborn, loose limbed, notoriously clumsy. And, better yet, he was not good at statistics. He had written a couple of

61

Hollywood gossip books under the alias of Lou Archway, which was his way of cheating on Ross McDonald, and which that made him into a second string Hollywood celebrity especially when the McDonald estate sued him. Larry could always get a table at Spagos. He made his living selling bad information…a small-time tout who knew everyone who was anyone in the news business and sold gossip picked up at the track or, often enough, whatever he concocted, like some politicians.

Jimmy got his sandwich, ate it hungrily. And when done, kept shaking his head slowly murmuring something private to himself.

The man in the good suit was gone.

All in all, my friends were a defective group. I watched out for them and they watched out for me.

However, I paid most of the bills. They say I am one of them – birds of a feather – a gambler who shoves his tickets into differing pockets based on a winning or losing streak, someone that cannot resist opening doors that say "Do Not Open." Someone who needs to win. But someone who believes he can and will win with a new hole in his heart and a new horse in his life.

My reputation came with the headlines about the case involving Willa Katt, the celebrity shrink and the nut case who believed she was Satan. She didn't look like Satan. More like a svelte Jane Fonda exercise devotee with good boobs and long brunette curls. There was no truth to the headlines. I was merely a hired hand, a licensed detective.

I might add, I didn't kill her. It was that kid who I found in a bar in Jackson Hole, Wyoming, and who had two other kills to his name, all lady Satans. Unfortunately, he managed to shoot me after I collared him and had him down. I survived but he didn't.

Big headlines. The notoriety got me business, most of which I didn't want as it got in the way of the Hollywood Park and the Santa Anita seasons. I hated it if someone tried to hire me during the August Del Mar season, the jewel of the California racing scene, situated just north of San Diego and a half mile from the ocean often had the biggest crowds. During that late summer season, my habit was to play golf (12 handicap) at the La Costa Resort in the morning, then head off to Del Mar, sit on a little porch in the Turf Club overlooking the paddock, and then go to the Jai Alai games in nearby Tijuana, Mexico, just over the border. With a little luck, I could win quite a bundle from the wise guy golfers at La Costa and not lose too much at the Jai Alai games at which Aureliano Mondozo always seemed to win.

I always believed I would come out OK in the end. A persistent delusion Billy regularly repeated, "You're delusional. When you quitting this game? Set up a real investigation shop."

I never answered. However, it was not how I felt now with Sarah gone and John done in. Problem was that for the last several months, it didn't matter whether I won or lost. My adrenalin highs were about done. My situation with Sarah (the word seemed right) had gotten to me. But the past couple of months, I had been losing more than winning. There were few highs and my lows had settled into a serious abyss. Perhaps I would climb beyond my father, who had climbed far beyond his own deficiencies. He would always say, "Gotta take care of things," and never did.

Maybe, fighting to get beyond these new lows, I could even forget Sarah. Or get her back. I'll send for my things. What a way to end things! I felt like a kid at the top of a slide afraid to go down. Once I started sliding, it would never stop, down and down, ending in a heap…at the feet of some nervous horse. But the Silk would save me.

***

John Augers' history was over the top in tragic consequences. Mine was full of undeserved romantic gossip.

Absolutely undeserved. All of the other gossip and rumors.

I did not have that affair with June Silberman, the diamond heiress, and we were not wrapped around one another at the beach in Acapulco…we were discussing the weather. And I never cold-cocked that fellow she called her "honey-boy" – he tripped. Swear!

I had been hired to find her runaway child and I did. But I never saw June again. She swooped that child the world had abused and I had to call a certain large sized bent-nosed friend in order to extract my fee from her equally large bent nosed and crossed-eyed "Business Manager."

In spite of my desire not to get involved in anything that disturbed my gambling career, I would have to peel away the layers of John's life and probably those around him. And figure out how to take care of Jimmy the Mummy. It wasn't very long before I simply forgot that violence has terrible and twisted consequences.

Jimmy finished his sandwich and I handed him the bag of money. "Not mine, Harvey. It's yours," he said, "Find the kid. And the killers and watch out. They know I know something. So they want me." He shook his head and I thought he would cry. "Just can't remember. Can't remember anything." He got up slowly looking like every bone in his ached and started to walkaway unsteadily. "See?" I called after him, "No one's after you."

"Bullshit." He took a savage bite of his whole wheat BLT.

He disappeared. I gave up and went to the mutual window. The horses were approaching the gate.

I smiled at Helen. Helen smiled back. She was my favorite betting clerk. She wore a lavender blouse and a small lavender paper flower in her hair. A tooth on the upper right side of her mouth stuck out half a mile.

I had offered to pay for the dentist to fix it, but she seemed to be afraid of my intentions, which, I assured her, were honorable.

"What's with the bag, Harvey?"

"Squash and tomatoes."

She laughed. "No onions?"

"No onions."

"You gonna win today?"

"Stick with me, girl. A hundred to win on three, box a fifty exact three and one and parley three in this race to number five and the next, make it for fifty… And a ten spot on number three again for Jimmy."

The computer betting tickets came spitting out.

Still holding the Vons bag close to my side, I had trouble reaching for and grabbing the tickets out of the machine. Helen pulled them out and handed them to me which I shoved into my jacket breast pocket. I always started with my breast pocket.

If I lost, I would stick all new tickets in my jacket side pocket and if I lost again in my pants and so on, until I won. Then all over again.

I'm not superstitious. Horses are flesh and blood and bone. Mathematically I should win every time but I don't. No one does.

"You know how to cook squash?" she asked. Big smile, protruding tooth.
"Of course. In the oven."

I took the time to rush to the valet at the Turf Club entrance, gave him a ten, took the keys and dumped the bag into the trunk, parked the car myself and was back at my Turf Club table staring at the Racing Form all within eight minutes. I was in the middle of pretending to be absorbed in the Form when Billy Fitzer sat down as though the world was too much for him. His hands covered his eyes. His trademark jacket was decorated in squares of rainbow colors. His hands came down and finished Jimmy's water. His cap was stuck to the back of his head. He had a pink fat face and a pug nose just like his little pug dog, Geraldine, which he often carried around with him.
"What about Jimmy?"

"Haven't the foggiest. Just being Jimmy."

"You going after the boy?"

"Try. I don't know anything. I'll call Paul, see if I can find out something."

Paul Sampson, a childhood friend, was a Lieutenant in the LAPD. Sampson was a good cop, except he always, but always, followed the "rules."

It made life easier for all employees of large institutions. Follow the "rules," stay out of trouble.

Except that one time when he was close by when I was shot. He didn't take time to call his crime lab, his superiors, anyone; with Billy helping, he just carried me into his black and white and, sirens screaming, got me to Saint John's Emergency. He saved my life and got himself into trouble not following the rules which required him to call the parameds first and to report a shooting. His trouble was a reprimand – except it was placed on his "sheet," like a rap sheet for criminals.

"Paul isn't gonna help you."

"He will. He knows I was close to John."

"He's a cop. Ain't in their rule book."

"That's a tired old saw."

"Whatever." He shrugged and again brought his hands over his eyes, then dropped them and stared out over the crowd. "He would get like that. Solemn.

"Listen to them," he said, "the crowd in the grandstands."

"Maybe eight thousand today," he said. "It's all so fucking haphazard."

"What if that boy was not a Wheeler...No one in the whole world would care. How do normal people live?"

"Not like we do."

"You're with Jimmy?" He shook his head. "What does he want now?"

"Wants me to find Frankie."

"And?"

"That guy Jimmy spoke to, he's an IRS guy. Checks on where the IRS money is going. At the track and Indian Casinos all the time. Now and then, he finds someone spending their money. You knew that, didn't you?"

***

Billy owned and operated a used car business, a very used-used car business, on South Figuerora. His nephew filled in when he was at the track. Kid couldn't escape high school He had joined me at my table when Jimmy ambled off.

Billy looked at me, up and down slowly like checking animal flesh he wanted to buy, and said, "You sick or something?"

"I'm fine."

"You look shitty."

"Can't tell if those eyes are green or brown or what. Except you look angry."

"I told you, I'm fine."

"Not bothered by anything except, John, the kid, the next race and, I suppose, Jimmy."

"Crazy as usual."

"Stupid talk. Crazy."

The track announcer began. "Horses are loaded up."

"Gotta stop taking care of Jimmy," Billy said.

I shrugged.

The bell rang. The world stopped. The gates clanged open. The horses were away. Horse players screamed; old ladies screamed. The hearts of two-dollar bettors pounded as if their world hung in the balance. I heard almost nothing until the horses were at the far turn.

Transfixed as always.

The horses were coming into the straightway. Crowd thunder rose. It filled the emptiness in me. I felt better without caring what the horses were doing. As they came into the stretch, my choice burst into a two-length lead. I smiled inside. I was right again. For whatever reason that existed in past, or in my genes, I needed to win and to win, and to win. And I did. I was right. But the feeling wasn't there. I was becoming a gambler without highs.

When it was over, I unfolded the Times and read the article on John over again.

I was the Executor of his estate and John had been of mine. Dinner couple of times a week. But we didn't really talk.

However, actually becoming his Executor, officially, wasn't on my agenda. Death wasn't new to me and was no longer an emotionally difficult event.

So death, when it came my way, was out there somewhere on a far horizon. I couldn't afford to spend emotions on something as ordinary as death. Except every time and this time. When I first read about John and his boy just two mornings ago, I felt strangely guilty. And then, I felt very, very angry. Tight in my belly angry. The rhythms of my life were upset. I was angry with everyone.

Including Sarah and maybe with me.

Billy said, "Jimmy said you would kill the bastards, send them to the jungle. So, you gamble and win and the world is OK again. Shows an enormous lack of character."

He ran a hand over his face. "However, I'll admit, winning is better than losing." He shrugged. Kept talking. I wasn't listening.

A few minutes later at the pari-Mutuel windows, I heard him say, "This whole John killing is something like peeling an onion. More you peel, the more there is. Somehow, it seem to involve you, doesn't it?"

"If there's a connection, I'll find it."

"Famous last words."

"I hope not."

Chapter Six

Unable to sort things out almost a week later, the racetrack authorities made an official Track statement about the events of that Saturday night. They wanted it known that the Santa Anita community; owners, trainers and all personnel, were very sorry about what happened to John Augers as he was a "respected trainer well-known in his profession" and that the race track and its family are all safe and cooperating with local police to bring "justice to all." They went on to state that management knew nothing further about the tragedy. The statement claimed that management had provided adequate security on the backside every day and night of the year and one of the security guards, Herman Barnes, a valued employee, was obviously doing his job having made the ultimate sacrifice in so doing.

Ward Wilson, The Times writer, in an "in depth" article, in the California section of the newspaper, provided interviews with some of the track employees and quickly concluded that the death of John seem to have been the result of an "apparent planned assassination unrelated to track business," that the police did not have any present theories as to motive although there were rumors about money laundering, white slavery, importation of elephants, Rhesus monkeys taking over and you name it. Wilson described Augers as the primary trainer for F.K. Wheeler, owner of the FKW stables who was an important and respected member of the Thoroughbred Racing Fraternity. The writer also gave an almost blow by blow of his conclusion that Augers had tried to elude his attackers drawing them away from his son sleeping in a nearby improvised bedroom made in John's Tack room, by climbing on a horse named *Misdirection* trying to outdistance the attackers and draw them away from his boy. His attempt at outrunning the bullets didn't work, maybe he thought he was Superman, but the bullets won. Augers and the horse ended up bolting through the automatic door into the pristine lobby of the Hyatt Hotel about a mile from the track, collapsing and bleeding to death on the marble floor. Ward went on and on…and even more on about the Wheeler estate which included various trusts, charitable and otherwise, valued at maybe 4 or 5 billion and about John's relationship with Wheeler who was, he insisted, the elder Trump of the West, and not crazy.

Wilson gave the reader a rundown on Franklin Wheeler who was generally known as an irascible character, on his second wife, having lost the first to insanity and an early death as well as the mysterious demise of his daughter, Sally. A person could not make up the stuff of John's tragedies even with a capital T.

Little more than a year after Sally's death, he married Carole Turnny.

Seemed like a good match.

She doted on Frankie. Within six months, she fell or was pushed or jumped off the ten story high bluffs that rim the edge of the ocean at what is known as the Palisades in Santa Monica.

That narrow mile long strip of parkland, with its Malaluga trees winding through the gardens like interminable pythons, housed its share of the homeless, the joggers day and night, and mere strollers enjoying a special green place above the Pacific.

It happened on a quiet Sunday afternoon while John, Carole, and Frankie were walking along enjoying a chocolate ice cream cone along one of the paths at the Palisades.

John was in front of Carole and Frankie, who were walking together when, according to John. Someone looking like a bear leaped out of which seemed like a hole under one of the earth hugging Malaluga trees that caressed the gardens, and shoved and/or carried Carole over the edge, and then he or it ran and disappeared before anyone could gather their senses and react.

Ward, apparently happy with his big by-line on the first page, revealed that FK Wheeler had bestowed several large trusts upon John as a trustee when he married his daughter and then when his grandson, Frankie, was born. Ward reported that the old man had also made John a trustee of the FKW Charitable Foundation. Apparently to take up dead space. Wilson reaffirmed the basic facts of John's demise – and added that John was watching over a valuable Wheeler two-year-old colt named Sky Colors that had come down with a hacking cough. It had been a chance for father and son to spend time together and to involve Frankie in John's life's work and hopefully improve Frankie's disabilities. Maybe it would have helped. But Frankie was gone.

Stable hands, hot walkers, the entire Hispanic backside community, as well as his fellow trainers, had all met Frankie and had given him a warm welcome. Warm welcomes in the horse racing business was a seldom event. If you've ever seen a shark smile, you know what it's like to do business with thoroughbred horse trainers. They all have great smiles. However, all of the sharks, including all of the backside citizens gave Frankie a genuinely big welcome and their attention because they knew of John's rather strange and sad history and because they knew that Frankie was "not quite right."

The more rational scuttlebutt about John's death was that he was a target because of his control of these trusts and corresponding prodigious amounts of wealth, and to his activities as a trainer for the large FKW Thoroughbred Stables, and that Frankie had become a hostage. Everyone knew that old man Wheeler would pay a pretty penny for the return of his namesake. The thought was that Wheeler had dumped the end of the rainbow onto John's shoulders with malice afterthought, expecting his benevolence to somehow get his disturbed daughter off his shoulders, or to get rid of her in some way – which made her death even more suspicious. John was supposed to be the patsy. But anybody's guess would do at this stage. All roads seemed to lead to Wheeler. He was either stupid or very guilty…at least that was the talk.

My guess was that talk was cheap and that I would find answers when I finally got to Wheeler himself.

***

It was about seven in an evening that was warmer than the usual October Southern California weather. But it was growing darker each day, and as the sun set in the midst of gray clouds along the beach communities, sometimes with thick shapeless clouds bathed in all colors of red, pink, orange blue/white bursts of light within. With the display of the sinking sun came the sense that smart people ought to be home with the doors locked. Clouds hid the sky and it became very dark. I knew I had to go to that Pacific Palisades scene and see for myself how Carole's death could have happened. Touch it and feel it on my own without anyone's description. I was just tossing an apple core in the garbage disposal and tossing away the paper plates of my cinnamon roll when a call came on my landline. I decided to let it ring figuring no one would be calling me except some robot call selling solar power or Viagra (*they somehow get your name the minute you turn fifty*) but I looked at the printout on the phone and I grabbed at that sucker trying to control my breath.

"Harvey?"

"Sarah?" Like I didn't know.

"Yeah, it's me. I'm ready to fly out in a few minutes. You know the same old grind. I just wanted to say…" She hesitated and her voice became quieter and vulnerable, like music. A Chopin Nocturne or perhaps the end of a Mahler symphony, fading reluctantly into the excruciatingly painful and diminishing end of the world as in the last few moments of his Ninth

Symphony. All I remembered just then was, *"I'll send for my things,"* and an empty doorway.

"I got a call. A strange call about John Augers…said you have to give them what they want or else. Meaning you. Then they hung up, or he hung up, rather. A muffled voice. 'A man or woman?'"

Whoever it was, was getting to the heart of the matter. My heart. "Oh, just a crank call. I'm sure. I get those. Wouldn't pay attention."

"But how does this person know I have any connection to you? Or my number?"

"Sarah, there were very few people who didn't know…our connection."

"…and what was it they wanted?'

"It's a prank call, Sarah. Pay no attention."

Long silence. A whisper. "I suppose." Long silence. "I, I miss you."

"Likewise." I thought I would take a chance. "Can I meet you somewhere? Before you fly out? Where are you staying? You live in town? You set up in town? You have time now?" All of it came out in a tumble.

"Hold it. Hold on, Harvey. Slow down. I took a one bedroom in Denver with Josie. Josie Turner. Remember her? A little blond, a little softic? Think you've met her once or twice. Our schedules out of Denver are usually different so it works out pretty well."

"Just wanted to call anyway." Maybe it was merely what my heart wanted, but there was that end of world sadness in her voice. It was the kind that comes over you when you want something badly, and you hope, and know you can't have it.

"Know what you mean. I've been wanting to call. But the question is (me, the punctilious nut case), can I drive over to LAX to see you? Is there time?"

"No. Not really. I read about John. And this call. Thought I needed to tell you about it. And tell you how sorry I am about what happened to him – I knew you worked closely with him, and well," she coughed. A small nervous cough. A good sign. She always coughed one of those little deep in your throat coughs when she was most vulnerable. "Maybe. You know. Maybe sometime…you think the call was just one of those robot calls? Or something like that?"

"I'm sure of it, Sarah. I have nothing anyone wants."

"Well, maybe…"

I stopped. Full stop. I didn't want to fall back in and then get punched again because I knew in my heart of hearts I wasn't going to change. … I wasn't sure I could change…but I wanted to. "Yeah. John was a crazy guy. But you're right I did care for him. I really did. The call had to be a prank."

71

Confessions are not good for anyone, even prosecutors who get confessions with promises and smiles who then rely on the confessions and become lazy and don't carry on with their due diligence. If confessions in relationships were good, people would be confessing their way to heaven every minute of most every day expecting confession to cure bad behavior and cut a path to forgiveness. Makes you feel better for a half hour then same old, same old. Maybe it's OK when you're shouting at friends, but girls remember every word you say for years and years and take every damn word very seriously and personally.

"You still winning?"

"Every day. Except with you."

Another one of those silences.

Dead air that you could feel. "Well, just wanted to tell you I was sorry about John and that call. Any more news about what happened?"

"None. But I'll find the boy. I promised."

She laughed a soft laugh. "I expected to hear you say that. Oh boy, here comes Harvey on his white horse to the rescue." We both laughed. "Anyway, it was good to hear your voice again. I do miss you. But…gotta go. Gotta be at the gate in ten minutes and getting through the lines even for a service person like me is a bitch."

"Hold on…Sarah. Wait. Please. When can I see you? Where?"

She clicked off.

I swore up and down and backwards and leaned out the sliding glass door of my Condo and let the night and the birds, the joggers and strollers and the Pacific Ocean have it with screams of pure misery.

***

Midnight after the Sarah call, there was no sleeping. Couldn't even close my eyes staring out at the dark Pacific and the last lights of the neon Ferris Wheel that lit up the end of the Santa Monica pier where the world was young and everything was neon and light and gay and full of fun, when Jimmy called.

I let it ring and ring until the automatic picked up and heard him tell me that he had seen Sally Wheeler and, "I'm absolutely fucking sure, Harvey!" And he went on to tell me where the sighting had occurred. "I know she was a nut case! I heard the stories. But she was there, I'm telling you. Alive! Looking at me from across the street!"

The last time Sally was committed was when she came at old man Wheeler with a very large carving knife one evening at the Wheeler home.

She was sent to the home in Mara Bay, her usual institutional residence, up the California Coast not far from Pismo Beach. Jimmy assured me that she was no ghost. Bad people come back as ghosts, he repeated – maybe you believe that crap but this was no ghost. Half-naked in pink. Boobs hanging out. Ran to the phone to call you and turned around and looked out the window and she was gone."

I picked up. "Jimmy, had to be like a mirage, one of those mirages, with the night lamp light and the sky. Had to be. Take it easy."

"Bullshit. I know what I saw."

I recalled what the assigned detective, a fellow named Cochran, told me at the brief memorial John had for Sally, "She was cremated before we had a chance to take the body to the Coroner. The mortuary license was lifted for a month for that bit of nonsense."

"Who ordered it?"

"Think it was the old man's wife."

And I recalled that Frankie was also at the same institution at Mara Bay, particularly after the death of Carole, to which he was a witness. After that event, the kid broke down completely, and they took him to the children's section of the Institution while they tried to diagnose his ailments and behavior. Doctors have knowledge. Knowledge is deceiving. One presumes a high degree knowledge alone can solve problems. It misses half the time. It takes more than mere accumulated facts to understand anything fully, and in this case, to fully appreciate what had happened to this unfortunate child. It takes all of that and more. Knowledge alone can be stifling. A lot of really smart people make things happen because they don't have the specific knowledge that it can't.

I would do now what I should have done then. Talk to those mortuary people when I got to Mara Bay and get to Wheeler.

Chapter Seven

My appointment with Ron Cable was at 10 a.m. My last accountant was fussy about time but crooked as a used car salesman, so I arrived at Cable's office at 9:45. The 1900 Avenue of the Stars Building in Century City is a twenty-nine story thin black structure overlooking the two Aluminum trimmed Alcoa Structures across the avenue which were the first of an entirely new complex built in the early sixties.

2011 Century Fox had fallen on bad times. They owned about 1500 acres behind its façade on West Pico Boulevard where it shot portions of Dolly and Cleopatra; the costs of Burton and Taylor as Antony and Cleopatra, the star crossed lovers in fiction and life, a massive naval battle, and a couple of pyramids, was not a star crossed enterprise and brought the studio to near total disaster.

Century City was created when 20th Century Studios found their savior in Bill Zenkendorff, a highflying real estate gambler from New York. He saw the potential of the location, right in the middle of West Los Angeles, and took an option on half of the acreage for six months for five million. Gamblers always see limitless futures. Gamblers see the future rather clearly. Someone has to take those starry-eyed chances. Gamblers and dreamers. However, it always takes big time money which they usually don't have. Within a year, Zenkendorff tried to sell his option for more than fifty million and got the bidding up to forty-three million which became the negotiating floor for the property. He called off the sale at that forty-three million mark. No one knew why. It was his gambler's instinct or it was the fact that he had a friend who was the Real Estate VP of ALCOA, the Aluminum Company of America. It had accumulated a bundle of cash just sitting there asking for a home. Pays to know the right people – I learned early that it is an immutable lesson in success. ALCOA came up with thirty-eight million and returned Zeckendorff's five mil and they made a deal and the land was theirs, good old Zecky baby kept a small piece of the whole.

You have to have balls of cast iron and relatives who will not die from anxiety in working through and managing such things. Zekendorff ended up on top and became a key player in the development of Century City. ALCOA put up the first two buildings and the developers were off and running.

Century City became the home of a Macy's, a Bloomies, a couple dozen upscale shops, two major hotels, high-rise condos, and office buildings, open air restaurants, along with very expensive ones. The new city housed enough people during the day to fully populate Toledo. It had its own twin towers, cavernous parking garages going down more than a ninety feet into the earth displacing enough expensive dirt to bury the entire city of Beverly Hills a foot deep. The studio still maintained a large complex fronting on Pico Boulevard where remnants of the "Dolly" set could be seen from the street.

Cable, Sherman, and Kirtchner took up the north side of the tenth floor of the North Twin tower in Century City.

Ron Cable was taller than I was, very thin and tanned and he sashayed a little, flailing fingers never seemed to stop. He wore a conservative gray pinstriped suit, black tie and orange Adidas that had to be in the size 13 or more category. You had to walk a half mile to get anywhere in the Century City complex so tennis shoes were "in" – all colors. He had these narrow eyes that seemed persistently worried, angular features, and a chin that might have come out of a Toulouse drawing. You had to notice his feet with those orange Adidas. They could have carried three of him.

White teeth flashed with his opening hand shake – a little too much pink gum displayed. His office looked like a professional decorator had been given a free hand, money no object. Every decorator designed office looked the same. Dark furniture, desk about the size of my dining room, small, twisted chrome lamp on top. Delicate vases casually set here and there, very frail multi-colored crystal bowls with candies in each; a twelve-inch replica of a Remington Sculpture, cowboys rip roaring to their destiny, along with Modern American artists on the walls; Lichtenstein Cathedrals and two Rauschenberg's Apollo series lithos, or copies thereof, and one four by five foot Ellsworth Kelly's apartment expanses of blue and white, all of which lined the forest green papered walls. It was all dimly lit except for a spotlight on the Lichtenstein and Rauschenberg and a light beaming onto his desk like an unwelcome but necessary intruder.

"Must've played basketball at some time."

I remarked as casually as I could.

"I lasted two weeks at Cal...Berkeley...but I got in and got room and board for a year and an education. And the right friends."

"And you kept the shoes."

75

He didn't even smile at my quip. Lawyers and accountants must look cheerful and seem serious at all times, as they were dealing with your most precious possession…money.

I offered a card for his records but he said, "Yes, yes, I already know you." He pointed at his head. "Memorized your address and phone number."

Having earlier searched internet, I learned that he graduated Cum Laude from Berkeley. Got his Masters in something called Statistics of Global Economics similar to Larry the Lowdown's degree.

I said, "If you tried to impress me, Mr. Cable, you have. The Lithographs on your walls must be worth quite a bit."

"Not as much as one would think. The Remington is worth a nice penny. It's an original. Not a copy. I chased it down all the way to Wyoming, to buy it from a Jackson Hole dealer. Naturally, I had it authenticated."

"I have a couple originals from that era of American Art."

He looked at me sideways. I ignored the doubt. "You know why I'm here. I am –"

"I know, Mr. Ace. I know. You are trying to find the boy. Detective Sampson told me you would be coming. He was here early this morning." My friend, Paul Sampson of the LAPD had beaten me to the punch.

"I didn't tell him I was coming."

"He seemed to know." He gave me his superior grin with flashing teeth and pink gums. "I presume he told you not to cooperate, that I was merely a private citizen butting in."

"Actually, no. He –"

I waved a hand. "I know we're doing the same thing in trying to determine exactly what happened to John and his boy and why…and who.

"So, it might seem like duplication. Fact is, I am the Executor of John's estate. Whatever it may be. And a close friend. So, I have what lawyers would call prima facie rights."

"Sampson said you were good at what you did. Licensed and all that. And as long as you didn't get in the way of the police department, he said I could cooperate…if I wanted to."

"And I'll bet he said I was a pain in the ass."

Smiled again. "Something like that. Just tell me what you want, please. I still have a long day coming. Ask your questions."

He sat back in a big black leather chair about two sizes too big.

"OK. You are on the board of the Wheeler Foundation?"

"Yes."

"Their accountant and financial advisor?"

"Yes."

"Your lawyers told you to just to answer yes or no?"

"Yes."

"You kept notes of your meetings?"

"Yes." He couldn't conceal a faint smile.

"Where are they?"

"At the Foundation."

"You keep copies?"

"Yes." He picked a pencil from a load of pencils and pens in a cup near his right hand, leaned back again, waved it, and pressed the eraser against his tanned cheek.

"I want copies. Past two years would be enough."

"Not sure I should do that. Confidentiality, you know."

"You told me Sampson said to cooperate."

"And do something improper? I don't think so." He sat back and stuck that pencil between his teeth, waiting a long moment while he contemplated more. I could see his wheels turning, as his mouth turned down at one side and turned away. He knew what he was going to do but had to make sure I knew he was doing me a favor. "OK. It's a job and a half to dig it out but OK, I'll see that copies are delivered to you within the next, oh, let's say, 48 hours."

The look I gave him made him add, "Maybe 24. I know your address."

"You didn't get the address from Sampson."

He smiled. I waited a full minute. "Don't give me that doubting look, Mr. Ace. You're in the fucking phone book...Harvey Ace, Venice Beach, Missing Persons, etc."

"Of course."

What I wanted to say was, I am going to bend your neat little nose one day, Mr. smug, His real name was Cabrera. He wasn't the only one with access to the internet. From Boyle Heights. Eastside Los Angeles. Roosevelt High school and a Berkeley graduate Cum Laude. Family was in the electrical contracting business and had sub-contracted with Wheeler Construction on several projects.

"You must know old Franklin Wheeler pretty well," I said.

"Met him a couple of times at the site of one of my dad's deals. Maybe fifteen years ago. And at the meetings of the Foundation. We hardly ever spoke." He leaned forward. "Far as I can see, Mr. Ace, to get to the point, all I need to do for the estate is to verify bank accounts and deposits, stock, bonds, and that sort of thing for Harry Moss's report to the Probate Court on the estate... I guess I do it for you as Executor. But..." His fingers pyramided in front of his nose. "The trusts are not in the probate which is the purpose of a trust. It's not your business or my business to get into it...unless invited. I don't do the day-to-day accounting for the Foundation. Done over there at their office. They give the information to us and create the proper forms to send to me and I merely translate into a proper IRS filing. You must know that the trusts have oodles of money in them. I help Wheeler now and then with some of the investments as well as John, or did, but he made and paid most the bills in the Sally trust, Frankie's trust and his own. I did help him now and then with that, and of course. He gave me the data and I did the trust tax returns. Numbers are extent of my knowledge. But, as I said, the trusts are not in the estate, not part of any probate. He is...was an exclusive Trustee in each of these trusts. John, that is. And I'm sorry to inform you that the probate estate is just a house. The house in Hancock Park he lived in. Trusts are private contracts that carry on after death requiring the Trustee or Trustees to deal in specific ways. So, all there for you to deal with is a house, a nice one, but just a house in Hancock Park, June Street I think, and its contents. So I can't help you very much. I'll send over the legal description and the tax returns and a description of whatever other odds and ends in the estate but that's about all I can do...along with the notes of the Foundation...but only because Mr. Sampson said it was okay. Right? You need to inventory the contents."

"How long has it been since you've seen John?" I was sure John was not a friend of his, merely a client.

"About four months since last year when we talked about the quarterlies and his tax returns."

"Any changes, surprises in the Will to your knowledge? Discussions with him about his personal life. Just off hand talk? About difficulties. Anything?"

"Nothing."

"Mr. Cable, John was a talker. He could go on for hours?"

"True. That's true."

"He had to say something about his life. What he was doing. Small talk. What did he say? Anything? I'm trying to find that boy. You can't hold back. He's in deep shit, right now. I need help."

"You're suggesting that I'm holding back?"

"Not suggesting anything. But I was pretty close to John. He talked."

"I recall nothing." He smiled.

I leaned over the massive desk, pointed a finger at his nose, "Cable, you are full of it. Listen, you can "no" me all day. And smile your way to hell and back, but I'm not leaving until I empty everything in your head on this. You want to see a kidnapped kid murdered? It's OK with you that John was assassinated? I can do things the police can't. I can do things and get away with it. They can't. Maybe you are involved somehow. You had your fingers on all the important stuff. Numbers. I'll ask Sampson to subpoena your records, every damn one, subpoena you and half your staff and take as much time away from your $250 an hour billing as possible or you can just tell me what you know."

I was ready to pound the table.

He straightened abruptly, flattened his hands on the desk. "Are you nuts or something? Why would I be involved? Why would I have anything to do with that family? I take care of reporting numbers to the IRS! That's it. I put numbers together. I don't like being accused." He sat back again realizing that the hotter he got, the more involved he seemed.

Decided that pounding a table, shouting like some losing lawyer wasn't going to get me anywhere. Figured anyone who dealt with the IRS on a regular basis didn't scare easily. "I simply want to know what you know about John. I'm trying to save that kid."

"Leave it to the police. That Sampson fellow seems competent."

"Yes, he is. But I can go places and do things he can't. I told you. Just tell me about anything in the Will or Trusts you know which might lead to answers. Or anything. Suspicious phone calls. Something in the trust data, or in his cash dealings."

He didn't flinch. "No, no, and no. I don't really know anything. Numbers. That's it."

"Numbers tell stories."

"Go see Moss." He lifted the phone and told the other end not to disturb him for any reason. He leaned back pulled the yellow pad to his lap and doodled on it for a minute while I was still leaning over him. "Sit down, Ace. Threats are useless. Really. It's been tried by the best. Feds, bad guys, and weeping widows. Told you, I represent numbers…the numbers created by good people, bad people, and pain-in-the-ass people. My hundred and sixty pounds can't make you sit down but please, I'm not holding out on you. I presume you will see Wheeler and Sophie. Feel sorry for her."

My eyebrows went up. Sophie?

His voice was reasonable and deliberate. "Just in that whole situation. Her son sure didn't like it. Left town a while back. Whole family is nuts, including that boy."

"Didn't realize the old man had a step-son."

"Get Harry to give you what he can. Tell you what he knows. I really don't know more. I have ethical obligations. So I'm stuck there. But…" He smiled, this time only with the tip of one side of his mouth, just lips. "The advice I would give anyone is…don't make notes of anything, no emails, no texts, if you are up on new internet things. Telephone. Use it. Nothing in writing. It's a lawyer's lesson. That police Lieutenant, he had his finger in my face just like you and it got him nothing. All the police need is a fall guy. I'm not that guy. Maybe Harry Moss. Harry is the smart lawyer. So...he set up everything."

He smiled that cunning smile again, "So, cool it. What I can suggest is that you check on the death of Carole Augers...John's second wife. She went off the palisades cliffs like some bag of old rags...which you must already know about."

I nodded. "Carole was suddenly shoved by an apparently homeless maniac over the edge to her death nearly a hundred feet below. It naturally caused a big hullabaloo and additional trauma to both of them. I mean Frankie and John. Everyone had suspicions but the creature was a homeless maniac."

His hands went over his eyes. He sighed. Spoke slowly. "I'll tell you something, I never believed it was a homeless nut case who attacked her. I heard all the stories...explanations. Never believed it. I didn't trust the Santa Monica police report or any of the stories. Stuff like this just doesn't happen. They shoved the whole business down the toilet. Bad PR for Santa Monica, letting the homeless camp out at the Palisades. Letting the public know about the homeless along the Palisades is not good business. Scares tourists which is about a third of their income."

I believed him. "Appreciate your candor, Cable. So...tell me what you think...why would anyone bust up that marriage with such a weird way of doing it. And in front of the kid. Tell me...anything that will help me get to the boy. Something that helps me understand the plain why of it."

His finger pounded the desk. "I need some coffee. You?"

"Black. And let me change chairs."

He pressed a button.

I moved from the hard oak chair to the left and sat in another hard oak chair with another. He came around and sat next to me. A silver tray of coffee appeared at my side, with sugar, and cream and tiny silver spoons and fragile china with gold trim. I poured a cup, held it carefully, and sipped it quietly for a contemplative moment, and waited for the exit of the secretary or whoever it was.

"I don't need to be behind that desk. Not giving advice, solving problems, saving money."

"OK, Cable, appreciate it. Start."

"I have nothing to go on...I admit that, Ace. But the whole thing all the way along is too improbable for my taste. After all, John was settled. The new wife seemed just fine. They are getting along. But she, I mean Carole, calls me and complains that John is not getting a fair shake from the old man. She complains that Wheeler is on his neck about something – she is not sure of but thinks it's about Sally and her trust. Or the kid's trust. And it's driving John crazy. She is trying to protect him. At least it seemed to me from that one call. This had been going on for a while. Then bang, she gets it. Tossed overboard and no way to find out why or anything about the bozo that ran her down like that. Murdered as far as I am concerned."

"Doesn't make sense."

"Can't be just a coincidence. Santa Monica police mark it up to a crazy nutcase who they can't identify. Makes it easy. You know what they say about coincidences?"

"They don't exist. That brings us to Wheeler," I said. "But why would he or people at his command take the boy, hide the boy. Kill the wife? That also doesn't make sense. He can certainly control the estate of his eleven-year-old grandchild."

"Yeah. With John gone." He shrugged again, his eyebrows raising and lowering. "Maybe not. Maybe it's just not him and somebody outside of the probable."

"Keep talking."

"Well, how about this, John was at the last Board Meeting of the Foundation. Unusual, actually. He was the Chief Operating Executive, not the policy wonk. The Foundation had an operations man for every day functioning. Don't know if Harry Moss was the one who was behind the creations of all the Trusts, or he did it solely because Franklin told him to do it. I advised them when Harry wanted to do it. Saved a bundle of taxes, of course. But there has to be more."

"Wheeler did all those trusts just to protect his daughter, to keep his daughter happy by making John the power behind the power? Or out of love? Or hate? Meeting with Harry Moss should be interesting."

"Sampson has probably been there. Harry will tell what you have to do. The details. John could push a lot of buttons, you know. What about you? You involved in this in any way? You were close to him."

Of course, *Jimmy the Mummy,* came to mind, but explaining anything about him was not in the cards. Explaining any of my friends was not in the cards. "Wish I knew. We'll see. You have any idea who is going to take his place or who is the alternate trustee on that Board of Directors?"

"*Nada.* There's a Board meeting soon. They should let me know."

"Why you?"

He straightened. "Well, they just usually do. You have to see Harry about that. Anyway, that property along the 101 near Mara Bay might be the answer. 28 acres, or more. Big parcel…just near Mara Bay and only a half hour to Santa Barbara. The Foundation has a twenty-two percent of that property, John's trust had…has twenty percent and the kid's trust another fifteen percent."

"You have the Trusts. Show me. Or tell me. Show and tell time."

He put his hands to his face. Each palm over his eyes. "C'mon, Cable. No damn reason why you can't tell me."

One hand came down. "I want you to get the kid. The rest get from Moss."

"And the remaining percentage?"

"Sally's trust had ten, which John administered along with Frankie's. Then Wheeler himself at thirty-eight.

"Far as I can tell, if they build that property all the way out like they planned, John would have been manager. The Foundation has its own Board of Directors. That's a glaring conflict between Wheeler and John and the Foundation. I can guess that Wheeler wants control. Moss somehow talked him into this. And now, I imagine he regrets it.

"He has his own management people to run it.

"The Foundation may come up with nothing by the time Wheeler and his personal FKW Trust gets through with it.

"Conflicts abound. Sort of like politicians in business. Everyone knows that Franklin extracts a ton of expense money through a variety of small corporations or LLP's and LLC's, controlled by him in this project as well as everything else he has.

"These satellite groups build, pave, obtain permits, etcetera, and etcetera."

"A lot of conflicts to digest. He's a perfect suspect."

"He's a clever guy. At least he was. Anyway…" He leaned back somberly, cupped his hands over his eyes for a moment. "My eyes are shitty. I rest them every now and then.

"A lot of fucking conflicts. Not my concern. I add, subtract, double-check, and send to the IRS. Guess no one in this scheme gets the upper hand. Except Wheeler is one of those who has to be a winner. Life is a game to him. Win and win and that's all there is. Except Sally was an exception. Doted on her, then, of course, worried about what she had become. Maybe even a little afraid of her. She was some piece of work."

"Know what you mean. Every discussion on every subject is a game of who wins."

"That's him. Anyway, this Carole girl, a pretty girl, was against Johnny taking over all those trusts. She was not a silent partner. She was a noisy wife. And smart. Sally was just a sad case at the end. She never got over being a pre-teener. Had this *thing* about her father. Then suddenly, she was gone."

"But the Foundation was a charitable enterprise that Franklin created. Why let it be divided?" I was hoping he would say amore about the *thing*. But it was a though he realized he was talking more than he should. "Ace, get real. Unless you live in the Charitable world you don't know – there are too often accounting finagles. Enormous deductions. Shifting of companies to and from relatives. How to do double duty and win is the scenario. Get deduction for contributing, and provide expenses and deductions for nearly everything. No tax...as long as you have me or someone like me to do it right. I keep it legit. That's Harry's job, too. Been fifteen years. Frankie wasn't even born. Then when he came along, they did a whole new trust in dividing the property and carving up a piece for him. It's value has escalated like mad. That land along the 101? It's about priceless in today's world. Instead of talking millions, maybe talking a billions: Population moving in that direction and huge malls are the winners of the day. It's the hey-day of malls. You sell them for triple the cost the day you break ground. Or keep them and the bucks roll in till the depreciation wears down and then sell.

"By the way, check this out with Harry, the kid's trust owns some of the land in the middle of the right-of-way to the highway. Can't get anywhere without him."

I had the feeling that this Cable fellow was feeling as though the whole business was like some sickness. But, when he took his hands away from his eyes, they gleamed as though he was counting a sudden pile of money.

I poured a little more of the coffee and waited. Cable extracted a small white pill from a plastic box in front of him, tossed it into his mouth, and downed a half glass of amber liquid. "Apple juice and pressure pills. Hate coffee or booze. Pressure gets too high. The pits, growing old."

"How old...if you don't mind my asking."

"Nah. Fifty-two. Fifty-two! Shit..." He sighed and wiped imaginary sweat from his brow. "You know how John and Franklin argued? Quietly. Not vehemently or anything like that. Politely. But I know those two. They were bulls in heat holding on until the right time."

"John talked a mile a minute," I commented. "Not sure he ever said anything pertinent to any argument, but he was a fast talker. You must know that.

"He didn't like this and did like that, hated this trainer or that one, loved to buy this horse or that…but really, said nothing. And Wheeler, as you might guess, is used to getting his own way. No way anyone is going to stop him from building his Mall and may a resort of some kind there. Plenty of land."

"But can't be sure of anything. John controlled everything. Or did."

"Anyone else witness these arguments?"

"Sophie. She was everywhere. Nice lady. Smart. She's a member of the Board of the Foundation. Has a smart nutty kid somewhere. Told you. She pops up now and then and is just another vote for the old man. Sort of cunning."

He poked a forefinger on his desk. "The way she talks to Franklin before the meetings. And after. She whispers, he nods. And John? Think on it, Ace. One minute his first wife is in a mental institution, and the next minute she dies and gets cremated all within about eight hours. A little more than a year or so later, second wife is mysteriously attacked and tossed off a cliff. That, Mr. Harvey Ace, does not sound like mere happenstance.

"What about Moss? Don't know what he thinks about Sally or her claimed resurrection, or Carole or anything else. Looks like he is counting shekels whenever you meet him. That lawyer's head is going a mile a minute. At the Foundation, if there is a vote he votes with Franklin. But he creates the language of the vote. Most of the members vote with Wheeler, which is to be expected. But the language…you have to read some of the notes and minutes."

"The books at the Foundation? Are they here?"

"The Foundation keeps their records. They compile the numbers and send them over for the quarterlies and the returns. The other Trusts are private. Since the Foundation is Charitable, they are subject to public inspection.

"So, you can go there and insist on the books and records. Ask Harry and he won't agree, then you see another lawyer and he'll get them for you. Eventually."

He stopped for a moment, eyes fixed on the ceiling, then back at me. "Don't envy your spot."

"That police lieutenant said he wanted every piece of paper in the Foundation and here. Said he would subpoena.

Let him subpoena away.

"I'll call Moss. He's the lawyer and he will tell me what to do."

"You won't have a choice. In they will come right past you and start emptying drawers."

Whatever there was to hide would be hidden ten minutes after I left. "There is something more, Cable. I can see it there in that obvious face of yours. I hope you don't play poker with the boys."

"No chance. Tried it as a kid and learned my lesson. I might be good at what I do, but I have a face like a child's book…even a four-year-old can read it. But there's nothing more. Honestly." His hand went up. "Swear to God."

"OK. OK I believe you, but what's going to happen with all these trusts and all the assets in them?"

"No idea. And don't care. I'm not the lawyer. Now that his mother and father are dead, guess somebody will have to go to court for Frankie, if he is found alive. Maybe Wheeler ends up with it all. Someone will get a guardian or conservator or something for Frankie. John's share I am sure goes to Frankie. I think that's the way it is set up. Go ask Moss."

I poured another cup of coffee.

"Cold?"

"Cold."

He buzzed. Same girl there within ten seconds. She held a hot flask of coffee, steaming. She was steaming also. Dressed in close fitting sheath of light brown, red shirt almost down to her belly button.

Blue eyes.

Hard to resist.

"Careful, Ace. Watch it." He waved a finger.

"I am."

"One more thing that might help. He might be, I mean old man Franklin Wheeler, might be genuinely paranoid. You've probably heard it already. He believes his daughter has risen. That she is out to kill him and get control. Don't know much more. Remember, Ace. I merely count pennies. That's it." He shook his head, put his hands over his eyes again and then pressed his buzzer one more time. Smiled. Big public relations client smile, with the pink gums. "You figure it out. I can't. Good luck."

As I moved through Ron Cable's hallowed halls, a young fellow about the size of my filly, with exaggerated comic book shoulders and arms, smiled a winning smile and handed me a file jacket about an inch thick, said, "These are copies." He opened the door out and watched me leave.

***

On my way home, I'm thinking I have got to talk to Wheeler and check out the stories myself.

Then maybe I talk to Paul Sampson. The kid has to be alive and reasonably well, otherwise there wouldn't be a point to grabbing him. He has to be close. I knew it. Well, I didn't know it. I don't really know much so far. But the kid was close.

Billy called. I picked up my half-pound cell, pushed the speaker button, tossed the cell on the passenger seat.

Billy's voice came in loud and nervous. "What's up?"

"Where you goin'?"

Told him I was on the way to get a steam bath and a massage.

"Don't give me that nonsense. You've never ever had a steam bath and massage in your life. You're chasing something. I know you are doing something really stupid."

"I'm not getting more involved with this case. I told you."

"It's the only thing you do. Jimmy is acting crazy. Don't see Wheeler around. Coming to the track tomorrow?"

"Same time, same station. One more interview and that's it. Maybe two." I could hear Billy thinking over the dead ether.

"Harvey, it's pretty clear, the people who killed John had to take his kid. They had to. No point to John's death otherwise. Not going to leave a witness and the kid is the path to all those trusts that you talked about, that Johnny bitched about. Has to be. I don't even know much about them, but it has to be. These are serious pros, Harv. The way they set up the kill. If it's the Mexicans then OK, you have the filly legit but you and Gert have something to worry about. If it's somebody else, and not the Mondozo family then God knows what, and even God isn't sure. So why not play it cool? Just let the cops handle it. Let it play out on its own."

"You mean I should do nothing? Sit back and do nothing? C'mon, Billy, I know what you're saying. But the boy is autistic. He's an innocent. Another of the calamities in John's life."

"If the kid saw anything or anyone, he won't be able to say anything. He can't. The kidnappers probably didn't know and maybe still don't know he is autistic. Seems to me if they wanted ransom – they just take the boy. No need to kill anyone. And bottom line, John was the golden goose. And stalking like that? At the track at midnight? Pretty clear they were instructed to get rid of John and my guess is they were surprised by his son being right there with him. The kid was not in their plan. Now they're stuck with him and will probably have no choice but to send a ransom note and get rid of him. Or just get rid of him, anyway they can. He's cover for their real purpose."

"Which is?"

"I sure as hell don't know," I said. "Kid was in the room asleep. Until the shots were fired.

"Then John ran. I disagree. Kid had to be part of the plan. Everything in life is power, which is money. That's generally the ultimate purpose. Wheeler seems like he is in the line of fire. But it's awful damn neat, isn't it?"

Billy took off his cap and with a small handkerchief wiped the sweat on his bald head with the fringe on top.

"You know the Arcadia police Department is involved with this, too. "Even the State might be involved, with all the training licenses at stake."

"I figure the old man needs ultimate control," Billy said. "John was the target because of his control of the future and his share of the power. The detectives have to be all over that Old man's life and business affairs. But logic is seldom the answer. It's always something in left field."

"You are usually right," I told him. "Going over to see Moss. And I have to see those shrinks at that place they put Sally in Mara Bay. You know, Jimmy swears he saw her. Ghost stories are fun," I added,

"And Wheeler is too obvious," Billy said like it was the definitive answer. "Alright, wise guy, tell me what you think."

"I think John was wanted by the KGB, by Putin himself, because he dissed Stalin in 1956 while picnicking in Red Square. Called Stalin a pedophile and an old fart to boot. And said Hilary was more man than Putin. Said that Putin was a KGB second string assassin and not very good at it. Putin never forgot and sent a hit squad to get him and take Frankie back to Moscow to make him into the youngest Communist spy."

"Yeah, and then he is supposed to steal the top-secret love notes from Kennedy to Marilyn Monroe. It's all a Hollywood screen play. Anyway, I appreciate all your help and serious insights."

"Gotta go. Nephew told me he is trying to sell an old Dodge. You gonna be at Matteo's tonight with Sarah?"

"No Sarah."

"She just out of town?"

"Yeah, out of town. Denver…someplace."

"Have you called Kim lately?"

"Every fucking week."

***

You're supposed to know what you want by the time you're twenty or twenty-five. I didn't, except for the next bet.

Now, I wanted yesterday – all my yesterdays – and wanted to promise Sarah I would be different. And I wanted to win. I wanted the highs. I wanted the kid back. In short, I wanted everything to be perfect.

Winning was my drug of choice. But I would be different. I really would. I would tell her. I would get a job. Nine to five.

Fuck it. I don't to the Casino until most midnights.

She would know was a lie. It would be the same old Harvey. I knew that, too. She would get tired of the charade once again. Even I was getting tired of the charade. Maybe I would change. This John thing and the dizzying series of connections would get me back fully into my "profession." Being a finder, a good detective, wanting to fix things, find things, people. Maybe, I would get a job selling shoes. High heels fitting a size eight, or a size six on a fat lady. I can just see me trying to shove a fat foot into a size six.

"By the way, you know that Gert and John hated each other. She has her own story with him."

"I know the story. But who cares anymore? My filly doesn't give a damn. Gertrude is good at what she does. I've made up my mind."

"You'll be sorry.

"They had a history. You keep playing with fire. Don't get too close to her."

"She's okay."

***

Later that night, when I got home, the front door of my condo was jimmied open. An inch open. Dark inside. I pulled out the little .22 from my ankle holster which I always carried and nudged the door with my toe. The top hinge had come partly loose. Not a professional job. I was silhouetted as I entered and bent down. Perfect target. It would have been better to wait. Wait it out. But I pressed myself against the wall and slid inside. I knew whoever was there had nowhere to hide. Neither did I. The distance from the entrance to the large wall sized sliding windows was thirty feet of open territory. To the left was the small dining area and library against two walls. The kitchen behind a wall. I reached up and flipped the light switch. Standing there, black cashmere sweater and butt hugging pants, cool as ice, pointing a very big forty-five at my gut, was Aureliano Mondozo. My good friend...

He wore a slight confident grin barely touching his lips as if anticipating blood. His eyes were black and dangerous. He whispered, "I've got the biggest gun, Harvey. I always had the biggest gun."

"You have to be crazy, Aure. You gonna shoot? What the hell do you want?"

"I want the Filly's papers. I said I would pay. But maybe I won't anymore."

"We're putting the guns down. Then you are leaving."

"That BB gun of yours won't do anyone any serious damage."

"You'll have to take your chances."

"I like mine. I don't like yours."

The library area just behind Mondozo was a mess. Books and shelf decorations, some valuable, were dumped everywhere. I hate disorder. Made me want to shoot first. However, like all good gamblers I assessed my chances and figured talking was the way to his heart. Hah!

"This is stupid. Where is your brain, Aure? You think I keep such things where anyone can find them? "Dammit, it'll take forever to get the books back in alphabetical order on the shelves. I hate that. I could shoot this pea shooter and hit your eye and no consequences except blood on my carpets. You shoot and you spend the rest of your life in San Quentin or get a needle in your arm. Aure, this is what we are going to do...I'm going to tell you exactly..."

He laughed a short snickering laugh, the laugh of someone accustomed to getting his way.

"You would never shoot, Harvey. But I would. I will. I want what I want."

I spoke very softly and slowly slid myself into one of the dining chairs, still holding the pistol. "We put our guns on the table...and we both sit down. You first. Slowly. I keep my pistol until you sit. Then I put mine down. Then I pour us a drink. Lemonade. I have that Paul Newman lemonade. Very good. And then we talk. *Comprende*?"

He laughed again, nervously. Dark eyes, slick black hair. A modern Valentino, with a big pistol. A rich, coddled young man trying to be something more. "Harvey, you got balls. Always did. I'll say that for you. Always told my father that, even when I was a kid. It isn't gonna help. You do the sitting. Just remember Mondozos don't go to jail. Never have. And you would not be the first person..." he sighed. "Just cut out this crap, Harvey. Maybe I shoot just your knees. Just to let you know that I'm not that kid anymore. And your pea shooter doesn't do the trick. You know my family. We make people do what we say. It's the way it is in our world. They never not do what we say. And you are not shooting anyone. We both know that, too."

"Double negative, asshole. Your NYU professors would disown you."

"You can buy professors, Harvey. At least some of them. Now, shut the fuck up. Just tell me where."

"Looks like one of us is going to get hurt. Listen, Aure, you take that kid to get to me?"

"That Wheeler kid the other day?"

"That one."

"You gotta be crazy. Who needs a kid to deal with? Now where is it? I'm not waiting." Perspiration rose on his upper lip with its very thin moustache. He pointed the gray nose of his big pistol to a spot just over my shoulder. "I want that filly."

"You aren't getting her. You lost. In your own home. With your own cards."

"Fuck you." He fired. But not at me. He missed a Joseph Albers black and white lined abstract. Not a print. It had taken me two years to find it in San Francisco and make arrangements for its purchase. It looked unprepossessing. But wasn't. Thin white lines outlining black and gray squares – among the earlier abstracts of its kind and father to many later abstract artists.

Aureliano's shot created a big ugly hole in my dining room wall, a powerful reminder of the punch of a forty-five-caliber bullet.

"The neighbors will call the police. You forgot a silencer. You're just not smart, Aure. You lost your bet with me. That's it. A bet is a bet. Get it straight. You lost."

The smile was gone. "Next time I hit the picture and then a couple others. They gotta be valuable. I know your history. You gonna kill me for that? No way. Not you, Harvey. You can't kill. I want the papers, that's all. I want them endorsed to me. Find the filly's papers and sign this transfer, too. No one gets hurt." He pulled out a folded document and placed it onto the dining room table. His pistol kept its aim at my belly. "Where are the State and breeder's papers?"

"Poor Aure. You were never the Mondozo family's smart kid. Your father will kill you if I don't. He loves me."

"Put your cap pistol down." He came close and shoved his pistol hard into my right knee. "I'm counting."

"OK. I'm putting it down." I raised my hand high over the table. I pushed aside several books that had been tossed there with the other hand. He was pointing his gun at the wall, at one picture and then another, a small Rauschenberg, a Liechtenstein Cathedral in blue, squinting as if trying to hit a special place on each. Arm and hand were extended with his pistol creating a small but neat target. Big Mistake. An amateur's mistake. Can't extend your hands. Makes them vulnerable and slower. He kept going back and forth between pictures. He was laughing. Having fun. Aiming at one picture and then another. "Which one, Harvey?"

As my hand lowered the pistol on the table, finger still on the trigger, I twisted, pulled the trigger and clipped Mondozo's arm midway up the forearm. His pistol dropped to the floor like a hot frying pan. He screamed and jumped and squirmed and held his arm. "You shot me! You shot me! You son of a bitch!"

"I tried to tell you," I said calmly, but shaking inside. Playing with guns is way too dangerous for children to play.

"I grabbed a kitchen towel while he was bellowing and wrapped his arm. You're getting blood all over, for God's sake. You have to stop bleeding."

"Are you crazy? How do I do that?" He started groaning. "You bastard. Why you shoot me? Why you shoot. I ain't gonna do nothing."

"Tell it to the cops."

"You turning me in? No fucking way! Not you!"

The wound, fortunately for both of us, struck across the thickest part of the forearm, flesh and muscle only and lodged in the binding of one of the books on the shelf. The wound would make him into a lefty for a while. But that was the extent of it. A small pistol has its advantages. Hardly ever going to kill anyone. I pulled him into the kitchen and stuck his arm under the faucet. He started screaming. "Stop it, Aure. Stop. You'll wake the neighbors."

I got a handful of ice and wrapped the towel over it. "You can bleed in here. In the kitchen. But nowhere else. Nowhere!

I don't want to have to clean all the carpets."

He looked at me like I was bananas. He was in his early thirties and still a kid. Believed the world owed him."

"When that stops bleeding you're going to have to leave, Aure. Don't even think about coming back. No more chances. I won Winning Silks fair and square."

I sat him onto a chair and held the ice hard against the wound. I pulled up a chair and held the ice towel against him and we stared at one another. Finally, I said, "Idiot," and grabbed him by the collar of his sweater. "I see you here again, you're dead meat. I'm taking you to the hospital."

"No hospital." His slight build and weight surprised me. He couldn't have been more than one forty soaking. His eyes fluttered. "Whad'ya doing?"

"Dumping you. Hold your arm high…won't bleed so much. Feel faint?"

I carried him through the front door, down two steps to the walkway, and sat him down. "You got anyone here?"

He pointed. "My gun."

"Forget your gun. Where's the car?"

"You sum-bitch. I'll get you."

"You kill John Augers, too?"

"I ain't killed no one."

"John. John Augers."

He turned his head. "No one. Sumbitch."

A black limo started up and came down the alleyway. The door opened. I waved my pistol at the driver.

"Aure, next time you come here you are dead. Not saying that again, Mr. Aureliano Mondozo. You want to forget the past? OK. I forget it, too. But you come back, I kill the car and your driver and everything…dead."

"Fuck you, Harvey. Shit, I think I'm gonna faint."

"Not on me. I pushed his head down to get the blood into it again." He wavered. "Next time I bring my army, Ace. My father's army."

"Bring 'em on, little man. Bring 'em on. But you know better."

He managed to nod his head. The Mondozo's couldn't be ignored. Aure's father was a gazillionaire in Mexico City. With his own entourage in the TV business.

And every other Mexican business. All with guns. But the father loved me. I had saved his son, had dinner with the family, stayed at his hacienda. Walked with him through grape vineyards, talking about the stock market and businesses I knew nothing about. The old man and I had history. He knew that this second son was a little short in the clever department. I was not worried.

I watched his great big black Lincoln Town Car drive away. It lurched a couple of times and then turned back and came by. An automatic rifle stuck out from its driver's window. I flattened and rolled into the dip that substituted for a gutter. The blast tore about ten splintered chunks out of my Condo's stucco and doorway. It skidded away and disappeared. Worry? Me? Worry?

Chapter Eight

I called the local Venice police station. As they answered, I hung up. What were they going to do? Arrest Mondozo? Assault, breaking and entering? Making holes in my walls? With a hole in his arm?

Aure would be out in a couple hours and then call his brothers and his father and I would have an entire army after me. Never act with emotion. Calculate the payoff and the odds. If emotion was the core of my life, where the hell would I be? In an accounting office, wearing a green eyeshade? Standing behind a pari-mutual window dishing out tickets?

Married and fat. Screw it. Aureliano could go patch his arm and wish he was a better gambler. But I would not make it worse for myself.

Called a repair company, poured carpet cleaner on the carpet, and scrubbed until the rug looked reasonably clean. I left one spot of blood for forensics to get a DNA sample if I changed my mind. Then I took a hair dryer Sarah had left in the bathroom. And spent another few minutes using the dryer on the carpet, then gave up and had an epiphany, what woman forgets her hair dryer? No. Not going to let emotion get me again. Didn't want her. Didn't want her.

Didn't want her. Where the fuck is she and why isn't she here? I can fix things. That's what I do. Just let her call.

Finally went to my large window door, slid it open, and watched the evening light fade from blue to gray to streaks of apples and oranges and then watch the sun, the size of a glowing dot, disappear into the black Pacific horizon. Strangely enough, I was not feeling unhappy. Not worried about Aureliano Mondozo or his brothers and I know he wasn't worried about me. I doubted if they were careful or calculating enough to be behind the entire mess while still holding Frankie Augers. Didn't calculate.

I needed to clean myself.

That same miserable feeling that too often came over me. I needed to get clean. Scrub everything like wiping away the past, memories, the mess I made of my relationships, whatever dirt had stuck to me during my fifty-five years. Sarah told me that I was scrubbing my sins away, like doing penance. I

93

resisted, then, what the hell, what difference would it make to anyone if I cleaned something? I scrubbed my hands in the kitchen sink. Until they were red, then took a shower and scrubbed everything even more.

Decided to call in the event. Punched out the Venice police station numbers once again, gave them a brief review of what happened and a patrol car came with ten minutes. One of officers, the one who didn't seem to be big enough for a high school wrestling team, sporting a black moustache and the word "Angela" tattooed in black on the back of his left hand and "Mother" in red and blue on the other, asked, "No one hurt? We didn't get a call for an ambulance."

"My feelings and my property." I didn't tell them who it was but described the person in vague terms, while they assessed the damage to the front of the condo, and after they made their notes and left, I called Paul Sampson and he had the same reply, "No one hurt?" I told him to figure out a better opening and told him that it was the Mondozo boy who was the bad guy.

I could hear Sampson thinking, "Maybe we let this one go."

Paul Sampson was a childhood friend. Thin and tall and curly black hair. One of the very few people who could actually beat me up. Grew up going to the same schools in LA through high school. Watched out for one another. He spent a good deal of his time in outhouse…the food was better and there was plenty of it. His dad was a cop. He went off to Santa Monica City College, one of the better community colleges, and ended up like his dad and now was a detective in Homicide at the new Downtown Headquarters. I ended up at the Wharton business school at University of Pennsylvania. I had decent grades, actually liked school, and my dad, the asshole, had money.

"Harvey, just let this one go. Mondozo in jail doesn't help us. Venice can handle it. I'm assigned to the Augers murder along with the Arcadia Police. We'll find the kidnapped kid. And the bad guys. Don't worry."

"You'll find the kid alive?"

He was silent for a good long moment. "Why don't you go there and sit down? Maybe I should send those patrol offers back there and arrest you. Dammit, Harvey, stay out of this. Something more is going on. Not something you can handle."

"I'm an upstanding member of the public and damaged and you're going to arrest me? "That's good police work. Just like the LAPD."

"You actually want me to go pick up the Mondozo boy? You think that's the thing to do? He's out in an hour, back in Mexico and even more pissed at you? Forget it. The officers filed their report. Whatever happens after that is not up to us."

"Give me forty-eight hours. I'll find the Augers kid and bring you Mondozo and save you a lot of trouble."

I could hear the wheels turning. "Stop and think, idiot. He's wounded and pissed off."

"Okay. Okay. I'll deal with him, Paul. My way."

He sighed. Shook his head. "Listen, you ought to know this...Franklin Wheeler has been calling my office, calling McCullough, my Captain. A half dozen times. Claims his daughter is alive and out to kill him."

"Already heard it."

"OK, Mr. Hero, now you can go and calm him down. Then we'll pick you up for obstruction and put you in a line up."

***

Threw a frozen hamburger on a frying pan and watched it sizzle and then shut the burner, not hungry in the slightest and walked out, to the cement "boardwalk" then to the Venice Pier which was north a hundred yards.

I took deep breaths of the comforting cool sea air and strolled out to end of the pier. It was a symbolic end, as nothing seemed to end for me. Maybe the same with Sarah. The Ferris wheel loomed over me. I looked back at my window. I had left a light on and I could see into a portion of the living area. Got to get that window shaded with one of those green window coatings that let you look out kept people from looking in. I would have to shut myself in and the world out.

Looking for Aureliano Mondozo was harder than just waiting for him to try again. Which he would.

Soon.

He was a hot head. Not like his father who was deliberate and calculating, smiling all the while in round faced grins.

I wanted John's killers.

I didn't believe that Aure was connected to John's killing. Told myself it was too obvious. If he wants the filly, he kills me. But not John and not the kid. I would get the bad guys. I would get them – in my own way, in my own time. And then kill them again. And I would keep Gertrude. And Jimmy would get his money back. And I would get Frankie back. Alive. And I would break Aureliano Mondozo's other arm just for good measure.

***

95

The next morning, I ran. Ran and ran in those new shoes Sarah brought home a week ago. Old shorts. Old thoughts. Breathing like an old horse. Looking over my shoulder for Mondozo or his goons.

Running always gave me time to think with nothing else interfering. Sarah and my daughter, Kim. How would it be when they finally met?

If they met?

Didn't understand any of it. Or either of them.

I called my daughter regularly and she refused my calls. Let the machine take the messages.

I ran until I had to stop, at the end of endurance, and found myself almost four miles south of the Marina, halfway to Redondo Beach, dripping sweat like an old wash rag. The worst part of running in any direction is you had to get back. Can't keep looking over my shoulder.

I walked and jogged slowly back toward my condo, pulled my cell from my shorts, snapped it open, and called Harry Moss's office. Sat on a beach side cement bench. His officious receptionist, Ms. Beaton; had a voice like nails on glass. "Need to see him as soon as possible," she said, "I couldn't do that, that it would be at least three days before you could see Mr. Moss."

"I'm a paying client. And he knows me."

She wasn't fazed, told me to "stop being silly."

I told her I would be there at 3:30 that afternoon whether anyone liked it or not, that I knew Moss would be there, and that was that. "Does he know about John Augers?" I asked.

"Of course. Naturally."

Her voice had the sound of a one-cylinder scooter and contemptuous at the same time. The world was full of one-cylinder voices. Officious and always just a little bit nasty. "Who else would they call? Mr. Moss was the first to know."

"Except the killers, the police, the Coroner, the newspapers and Wheeler."

She clacked her teeth. "Won't do you any good to come at 3:30, Mr. Ace."

"Mr. Moss is in court. Maybe at five this evening, that's the best I can do. Don't you start telling me what to do."

"I'll be there at 3:30. So will he."

The sun pushed its way through the dappled gray skies on one of those late February days in sunny SoCal. I was hungry. Sweat dried on my lips. Still in my shorts and sweatshirt, I came to the end of Washington Boulevard, just where it touches the luminous dazzle of the white beach.

Sea gulls snapped at remnants of breadcrumbs tossed out by tourists.

The *Egg and Omelet* a popular breakfast outdoor restaurant next to the wide beach sand at the end of Washington Boulevard occupies the prime space. f. I went straight to its men's room and scrubbed. After scrubbing my hands to a bright red, I entered the open-air patio and settled into a quiet corner against a huge Unicorn and a veiled naked nymph perched on top printed on the wall-with a bloody dagger in her hand, raised high, about to strike. I asked everyone what it meant and got answers from – 'don't trust women' to 'don't trust women on horses'; never leave a woman if she has a knife. Why didn't the guy paint her genitals? Is she on one of your losing horses'? Send her to my house, without the horse; send the horse' Go figure.

There would be plenty of time to get home and shower and get there. From there, it was no more than a fifteen-minute ride to Mr. High class lawyer Harry Moss's office. I had no money. No wallet. It's who you know that counts. I knew the entire staff of the restaurant as I had been a good customer for at least ten years.

Valerie, thick glasses, A bulk of curly hair built-like-a-football-player, my friend and waitress, always grabbed my table. She peered down at me, great breasts as close to my nose as the management would allow, and said, "How you gonna pay for this, wise guy?"

"You confuse me with your delicious body. I don't remember how. Maybe you just carry a tab. "

"Stop staring 'cause these babies ain't going away real soon."

"How about an IOU and a hug?"

"Big talker. "I always cover you. So we get together and then you cover me."

"C'mon, Val." I could never handle you. Anyway, no time for fun."

She came down to me again, "Yeah. Yeah. Some day."

"Some day."

She stood up and sighed like she had lost a big bet. "I don't meet good guys in this job, Ace. Just wise guys and kids. So you come along and you keep saying *no*. Not healthy for a girl like me." She touched my shoulder. "You don't know what you're missing." She had a nice smile, an inner smile that you knew was genuine. Nothing hidden there... Or anywhere. Nothing. She shoved a lock of hair behind her ear.

"What I don't know won't hurt me. I'm high school sophomore at heart."

"Say, did you read about John? John Augers? You must've known him."

"Yes, I knew him a little."

"He used to come here. Like a chubby, old, little man – zombie like. I mean he had something going on all the time. He was always in a funk. I know those moods. Every guy I ever knew had those moods. I'm telling you he had some female problem going on somewhere. Those moods…" She shook her head and did a tsk, tsk.

Valerie once told me she didn't remember any of her boyfriends, not one face, not one body, and there were plenty. We both knew that was a lie.

She swore she could conjure up either one anytime she was in the "right situation."

"Hellava talent, sweetie. So what else do you know? Go on."

She pushed her black hair back again, pulled out her homed rimmed glasses from the top of her shirt, and shoved them onto her nose. "I'm just a waitress, Acey Ducey. I go to night school to be a beautician, not a detective. I can make more money fixing hair than any detective. I'm telling you, I know female trouble when I see it. That chubby wise guy had a real problem."

"God knows, every guy is entitled, Val."

"God doesn't know, Harvey. Some guy believing in God is like hiring someone to go to work, do the dishes, clean the house, pay the bills, make nice on the spouse. Someone else is taking over the details. Big relief. "No wonder people believe in God." She laughed. Had a slow rumble of a laugh. "Saves them a lot of work and worry. They kneel and say God is everything, then they're not responsible any more. God will take of it. Don't you know that?

I shook my head.

"Every guy is not entitled, Harvey," she went on. "No way. None of us.

"You gotta know that."

She gave me a disapproving stare. "It was more than that, Harvey. Believe me. It was like that Augers guy did something wrong."

"I never much thought about it before. Until the news reports the other morning. He was carrying a picture of someone. Couldn't see it too well."

"It's not our business, Bullshit. It's always your business."

"You know what they say."

"Alright, oh, wise one…what do they say?"

"Once a chaser, always a chaser…of anything. Everything. I could spend a week with you, but that's it." Wide grin. "What, a week! But you find these people and bring 'em in. Like Sheriff what's-his-name… I'm just telling you. But you're the guy who ought to know all this."

"I'm a gambler, Val. Just a sort of mathematician,"

I pulled her arm gently toward me…"and I don't know much – especially about women. I know a little about odds and less about horses and much less about people. And I try to stay out of things."

She leaned down and showed those breasts again, and wiggled a little and whispered, "One night, Harvey – and you'll never leave. I'm telling you. when you pull me close like this. I can smell you." She straightened abruptly, shoved her black rimmed glasses up her nose again. "And I see those eyes, like sort of gray…they want to kill, don't they? It's sitting there right above your nose. Wanting to kill. They go flat all at once. Dead giveaways. There's a girl in there, too. I know men. Yep, there's a girl in there. And you're still sweating about her. Why is that?"

"Let up, Val."

She stared at me for a long moment, shoved a wisp of hair behind her ear again and murmured, "I've known you, how long now, Harv? Maybe eight years? I know you're perpetually horny and always sticking your nose into stuff you shouldn't. I read the papers. That's the part I know. Except, this time you look tired and shitty and you need a shower. And you're really upset. Maybe horny, too… I could oblige. Say the word. And those eyes."

Waitresses know everything.

"Thanks, but no thanks. It's a great offer but…" I waved a finger and tried to smile. "I don't want to start anything I can't finish. You said so yourself. You know we would make a mess of it."

Here was a nice human being, pretty, hardworking, not educated but plenty smart, and I was stuck in some past fantasy about the person who would be best for me for the next hundred years, not seeing what is and was real and ready and good enough for anyone in front of my nose – except what was it my mother used to say, when she could and when my dad wasn't around?…"If we were all the same we would all have to be committed."

Valerie leaned close again and whispered, "You need me."

We shrugged at the same time and grinned. Wonderful girl – bad idea…for her. I ordered a three-egg mushroom omelet with jack cheese and with an onion bagel, about half of which I would not eat.

The coffee would make me reach for the TUMS. She brought the order a few minutes later without a word, dropped it in front of me without looking at me, eyes down, and hurried to another table. After a few bites, I pushed it all away and waved at Valerie and gave her a credit card and then a large tip to assuage my guilt, a guilt that was not because of her but was just there as a persistent part of my past and all future misadventures. I went to the men's room and scrubbed my hands again. It was like scrubbing my soul.

I had to.

The Daily News vending machine was open. No quarters needed. The product of down in their luck locals. I took a copy. Promised myself to leave a dollar next time I was there. I read its account of the murders. Nothing was reported differently, but the *News* made more of the mystery of Carole Augers death and Frankie's resulting psychological trauma.

Harry Moss would have answers.

Old legal warrior on his way down. They have retirement homes for broken down racehorses. None for used up trial lawyers or depleted gamblers. But Harry had to have answers.

First, I had to make some money a. I had to deal with odds and animals and insane people making a living from the courage of racing animals. In short, I needed to win. A big time need. Most people don't know what a gambling addiction is like. Same as a drug addiction.

***

I drove north. As I got close to Pasadena, the San Gabriel Mountains rose like mute sentinels in front of me. They were cold and clear. The lower reaches of these silent overlords were punctuated by forest green and mauve patches. Here and there, a red shingled roof peeking through. Higher up the trees thinned to piney watchtowers, touches of snow drifting off limbs like dying moustaches.

As I turned off Huntington Drive down into the vast acreage of the Santa Anita Parking lot to the valet attendant, I could reach out and touch the ice cream topping of Mt. Baldy. Further to the east, Mt. San Gorgorio arched white veiled and majestically up to more than eleven thousand feet, guarding the great foreboding and wintery Mojave Desert on its north side. To the east and the south of the San Gabriels, like a luscious Kentucky farm, was the balmy date palm greenery of Palm Springs fed by underground aquifers of the Colorado River. As a teen-aged kid, I hiked up and through those mountains, resting now and then to survey the world below, the world I wanted to own.

Santa Anita was nestled just below the alluvial sweep of the mountains. Its stately, polite pale green art-deco grandstand accommodated an easy forty thousand. It was embellished with ivory painted iron works decorating its four stories. It was polished and stayed above a green and tan couple of one-mile ovals, inside of which were lawns and betting booths and umbrellas and chairs and benches and food, and kids and swings and slides and three-dollar cokes. It was where the two-dollar bettor could lean over a fence and be not much more than ten yards from the horses in the stretch or at the finish line. The interior of the Turf Club, on the other hand, had four massive crystal chandeliers overseeing a mahogany and marble curved lounge and bar; sedate people sitting around brass rails and that mahogany bar – brass palm trees, cherry wood carved tables – all trying to remain sedate when the announcer got hysterical. There were small alcoves for special patrons who could sit quietly trying leaning over tout sheets and racing forms trying to figure out how to bet on animals…all of it with painted portraits of farmlands and famous horses, televisions hanging everywhere. It had the smell of a kind of decadence that got better with age. Decadence was fun. The lounge was the daytime dalliance of people who owned coal mines and utility companies and put on a coat and tie for breakfast.

I always expected to see Tallulah Bankhead sashaying into the room sporting a long filmy satin gown and saying in her upper crust southern rasp, "Darhh-ling, that fucking nag cost me a fortune!"

Every time I sat down at my table in the Turf Club, at this track the years bounced around in my mind like child's marbles sans gravity – the characters, the crowds, the horses; animals of pure courage, like the elegant Citation, arched neck, prancing to the gate, running down the stretch, winning sixteen in a row. And I remember the English invader, Noor, carrying twenty-two pounds less in the renown Santa Anita Handicap, against Citation, and pounding down at the over raced and tired Citation like a truck downhill and on steroids, winning the race by not much more than a nose. And the marvelous maverick Seabisquit, ridden poorly and losing the big Santa Anita Handicap – twice, before winning.

And Ruffian, the greatest of all lady racehorses of her era, breaking speed records in each of her Handicap races, finally breaking down and grinding her forelegs to a pulp and still racing for another hundred yards before she collapsed in her match race against Derby winner Foolish Pleasure.

I remembered Armed, Assault, and Artillery and Cee-T-Cee, the last two twenty lengths head of their field and racing to a dead heat; Round Table and Cigar and Whirlaway, with his tail caressing the wind as he and Eddie Arcaro blew away his foes; and, of course, Silky Sullivan, breaking through the air like a sudden golden hurricane from a quarter mile behind the pack and sweeping past them and their jockeys all of whom seemed to stop and stare as he thundered on by – they all danced in my mind as if alive, pounding down to the finish line, crowds roaring.

On the other hand, Hollywood Park, at the south end of Los Angeles where I spent my summers, was like an early Monet, lakes and fountains, spewing rainbows and swans and "goose Girls" in their row boats on the lakes; very Hollywood – casual blouses barely covering gorgeous mammary glands, suntanned stars and starlets drinking champagne sitting across from their graying "dates."

Sedately planted flowers wherever you turned. It was the same as a movie set in the 50s. Then there was me, needing the adrenaline. How could you not love it?

Santa Anita was the coat and tie granddaddy, Hollywood Park was the puerile exciting Bikini clad Beverly Hills teenybopper. I loved them both.

I heard the crown roar.

Life went deliriously on. I made my day. Twelve hundred forty dollars.

I saw Jimmy in the midst of a crowd as I left. He saw me and motioned for me to come to him and then was lost in the crowd. He always had news.

Chapter Nine

Ms. Beaton was a skinny, bleached, sharp-edged badger. If she were actually a badger, none of the other badgers would bother to hump her. Not even Billy's perpetually humping male Pug, Geraldine. Don't ask why he named him Geraldine, he just liked the name. The Pug didn't know the difference.

Dear lady Beaton had thin sharp lips, sharp eyes, sharp chin and temperament, an incongruously large set of breasts, and brown dyed hair slicked back into a bun.

Ideal for a legal secretary. Nothing seemed quite to fit and was at a persistent edge of anger. Anger grows with age. I was sure of t. She wore a light gray blouse and a gray long skirt, with a gray pallor. She didn't bother to look up. Told you. Mr. Moss is not here. He won't be."

"Buzz his secretary. Ask her to come out…please?"

"He's not here, so it won't help."

I Looked up, trying to give meaning to my mood and narrowed my eyes. "Listen, Miss Beaton," I dragged out the 'Ms.' "He's in court at 8:30; at about 11:30, he runs over to lunch at Glenn's on Sixth Street including at least one vodka martini, and he usually shows up here at 2:00 p.m. sharp. You have exactly five seconds to go back there and get his secretary for me…that's if you want your check this week."

I knew that would hurt. Jerry had a growing reputation for being in persistent financial trouble; big mortgages, huge loans from Sotheby's on his art and book collection, too much booze, and an authentic love of the ladies. All of which dear Miss Beaton knew.

"You gamblers are all just alike, just alike…thinking there's gold in some stupid pot somewhere." She gave me a superior smirk and flounced into the recesses of the suite. Her butt was puny. A minute later, Anne Whitson appeared and smiled a soul-striking smile. I remembered why I liked her. She was built for liking. Her hair was curled and not quite red – ladies have names for such colors. It surrounded her enormous jade colored eyes which had a come-hither look. There was a long eyelash over the side of one eye and she wiped it. This was a Miss America with an edge. Colgate advertisements didn't hold a candle to her smile. Naturally, she had all the appropriate curves in maddening abundance. And she wore something low cut. Made a person forget the past and future…only the moment survived.

Seemed unfair to the rest of womankind.

Especially to Miss Beaton.

I wondered why she wasn't a Malibu wife, or a Beverly Hills north of Sunset Boulevard mistress. Then again, maybe she was. "What happened to Mister Wonderful?" I asked.

Whitson laughed gently. Her nose crinkled when she laughed. "He had to see a dog about a man. A big dog, and an annoying man. But…"

"You're sort of new around here."

"What part? You have to define your terms."

Harry Moss was suddenly on top of us and interrupted as I was about to try a one-upper. He grabbed my hand and began pumping. His nose was red, a slight film over his heavy dark eyes, a day old peppered beard. A definite red two-martini lunch streaking across his eyes. A couple inches below my forehead, a shiny Southern California tan topped his bald head, with a tiny fringe around the edges like Oscar Hammerstein's Surrey. He had soft hands and manicured nails. His face was scarred with small fissures of meddlesome age, a crevasse on each side of his nose, although recent vodka had smoothed his crevasses. Not the same as I remembered him from newspaper items about his significant triumphs and low points of the past not the guy with the ten-million-dollar verdict against one of the local hospitals, a sixty-five million judgment representing AFTRA against Millennium Films for cheating their actors and directors. He was closer to the low point of a near indictment ten years ago for alleged siphoning off a couple million dollars from the Peppercorn Junction, a fast food company that went public and broke in nearly same month. He was, in short, a tired lawyer with memories but not a lot of left-over dollars.

"Whad'ya say, Harv? Sorry we get together just because of this tragic John thing. Goddamn terrible mess. Just terrible." He kept shaking my hand as his face screwed up just as though he were in front of jury. He thought of it as a mess. Which it wasn't. It was a murdered friend and a missing kid. And a tangle of tragedies.

It looked like any minute he would squeeze out a tear or two to demonstrate his sorrow. Hell, I'd vote for him. President of the *Has beens*. He ushered me to his office, to a small table in the corner and sat down heavily and motioned. "Miss Whitson, will you please get the Augers file and those other two files I asked for while you're at it. We're late."

The walls of the office were in forest green and red plaid – a rectangular leather shade on a tiger sculpted ivory desk lamp cast just enough light to notice it. A four-volume leather bound, gilt edged, set of Shakespeare Tragedies sat on a small mahogany table in the other corner. Files were piled on one side of his the extended desk about foot high and a row of sharpened pencils in a drinking glass sat next to them. There was a three by four paned window on one wall with the branches of a large wintry elm hanging just outside. A long narrow window was set into the highest part of another wall through which sunlight beamed. He turned, immersed in his Hollywood sorrow.

He stared at me, worried eyes, wrinkled brow. I understood that he didn't know how to begin the conversation. He knew FKW, but he didn't really *know* John.

I recommended Harry when John wanted his Will done but that was the extent of their connection.

I also knew that Moss had drawn the various Wheeler Trusts, for his Foundation, Wheeler's own trust and that of his deceased daughter and John. He had the best education and at one time had been among the brightest and most renown west coast lawyers.

"Terrible," he said again.

"This John thing."

"Yes," I murmured. "Terrible."

"But life goes on." He tried a smile and a light tone.

"It does."

"I hope you understand how hard all of this has been on me. It just has affected me. Yes, it has. I can't do the same things I did years ago. Not the same. Breaks my heart."

"What part of that heart thing of yours is busted? You're a little older, Harry."

"You had to remind me." He put his hand over his eyes and leaned back. "These events drain me. Yes, they do. They drain me." At that moment, he was the reincarnation of King Lear in real pain. My vote was that his pain was in his pocket book.

Whitson slipped in quietly and handed him a six-inch stack of files. "We have to finish these Declarations with the Motions on Shigati case this afternoon for tomorrow morning, Mr. Moss. They're right on top."

"I know. I know. I won't be long." He grimaced. He turned and smiled a wan smile. "I don't know why I got into this business. It was my mother, you know. She was always on my neck. 'You gotta be a lawyer! Gotta be somebody'!" He laughed softly to himself. "She was always in a hurry and I always seem to be late. Fat woman who moved like a bolt of lightning. You know, Ace, I can't keep pouring the work out like I was forty again. This racket ain't what it used to be. Twice as many forms. The powers that be think that the more forms you have the more efficient the system. Just the opposite. Stupid, too. But they ain't too swift. None of these Judge guys have ever been in business. Well, hardly any. They spent all their time trying to become Judges. Bar Committees and things like that. But it leaves the way open for restless dogs like me to make a living. I charge for every piece of paper they dream up."

I waited, thinking…when you're young and ascending the scale of life everything seems to work out. This guy is the epitome of when you run out of steam, and have to figure how to prolong the highs and use whatever other assets you have – guile, flim-flam, and plain old deceit just to get by. Even experience and brain power. Had no idea, yet, what Moss was using.

I had saved up this line just for this moment. "Restless dogs rely on discipline and maybe a good urinary tract, Harry. How about you?"

He humped a cynical taunt.

"Worry about your own damn urinary tract. I'm as healthy as I ever was. Listen, this old body is holding up. You want a drink or something? We got whatever you want. A Snickers Bar, a coffee, a shot of vodka."

"No, Harry. Nothing. Just tell me where I fit in all of this. This Will business and the funeral and being an executor."

"Yeah, yeah. You fit in, alright. But more than you think. FK's all shook up. He said we have to have all the trimmings. Memorial and Funeral over at the Sacred Rest Cemetery, up the coast a ways. Know it? Just past Point Dume? Maybe day after tomorrow, Sophie Wheeler's handling it. She handles everything. Got the Mortuary. Did it all."

"I know the place. You take that cut off along that narrow road along the ocean for about four or five miles. Then turn in. The place hangs just above the ocean."

"Right. That's what John wanted, according to Sophie. Whatever Sophie says, goes. She must have surveyed the whole county herself. It's out of the way. She's pretty much calls the shots now. FK seems to like it that way. He's tired. You get old you wear down pretty easy.

"That's probably why she picked it. They can avoid the media hype that comes with this mess. Road is too narrow to accommodate the media types."

He nodded and then started shaking his head back and forth in a kind of rhythm. "Terrible, wasn't it?" He looked up, red-streaked wide eyes. "Thieves, murderers, that's what-the world is full of; junkies and killers and fools! Who the hell else could have done it?"

"Not a bunch of fools, Harry. But they were pros. Hired assassins. Out to get John. Everything carefully planned. Pretty clear. Now they have the boy. And no ransom note. Yet. I'll bet the boy being there wasn't in their plans."

"You think Frankie is alive?"

"Of course. The boy is insurance as well as money.

"One dead kid, no live witnesses."

"But worth a lot of money alive. The answer might be deep in all the legal work you did for Wheeler and his daughter. Frankie became a bargaining chip. It's money, Harry. Always money. And power, too. It's apparent these people stalked John and followed him as he tried to get away on one of Wheeler's horses. And now, the kid is the key…and a liability, but won't be for long if they don't get what they want.

"So, tell me where do I fit in? Fill me in."

He did that soft hand over the eyes thing again, then leaned forward. "I'll tell you everything I told the police."

"Tell me about the trusts? What about –"

He didn't let me finish. "You are now trustee, my dear Harvey. You are the 'it' boy. John made you the first alternate after Carole. You are also the executor but there's not much to the estate. There is no alternate trustee after Carole. John must have told you that he added you as an alternate in his trust.

"So here we are, no John, no Sally, no Frankie. Just you."

I sat back and caught my breath. "Whoa there, Harry. John never said a word. Didn't know a thing about it. Don't I have to consent to all of this? I know about being Executor, but don't I have to sign something to consent to this trust business? John can't just say you're it in secret and it's a done deal."

I thought Moss was smiling when he said, "It's a done deal. You're it. You can resign if you want but everyone who has any knowledge of the trusts beyond this office, like the banks and Franklin and Sophie and whoever they confided with, knows you are the 'it' boy. You can resign, sure, if you insist, but it pays good. State of California sets the fees, but if you resign, we have to go to court and petition to pick a new trustee, like some bank asshole who picks your heart out… But you're the guy. After all, you know all the people most everything that counts… Maybe not about the house."

"Like a man riding three bicycles at the same time?"

"Apt. Very apt. Anyway, whatever might be the good and bad of it, you will be in the middle."

"You know what this means, don't you?" I tried to make it sound menacing.

He wiped his face again, closed his eyes. A streak of sun light came across his face. "Whoever is behind this mess will…well, you get the picture. You're the it guy."

"You've thought this all out?"

"I have."

"You agree. It was not merely a haphazard killing and kidnapping."

"Someone suspects something about all these trusts. These billions or potential billions. The plans for that entire new section off the 101. Like I said, if you resign, the court will appoint one of the banking type pros that do this. But I figure you'll still be the 'it' guy anyway. Up to you."

"I'm not the 'IT' guy."

"Suit yourself. I'll get a resignation prepared. Come back tomorrow."

We pondered one another for a moment. I was flummoxed. I was pleased that John had enough trust in me to make me an alternate and dismayed that he didn't trust me enough to tell me. Or he knew what my answer would be and wouldn't take a chance on my refusal.

"You know, he wasn't killed because he was a bad guy or good guy or anything like that. He was done in by people who have their sights on control of the trusts and oodles of money. Did I say oodles? I mean oodles and oodles. I like the sound of oodles and oodles. So, kid, if you resign, I make more money going through the hassles of replacing you. Don't you want a drink?"

"Not during the day."

"Day, night. Whatever. OK. No drinks.

"So, I'll get things ready for your resignation and it actually takes work and office time and a little court time.

"I can bill FK at a very good rate which he will scream about. But I won't bill the estate in court, so I don't want you to resign. He'll scream either way. That's my take. Also I don't really want the hassle or the work. And I don't like banks or these pros that fill in when appointed by the courts." He closed his eyes just thinking of the extra work and arguing with Wheeler.

Lawyering must make a person very tired.

"Have you asked Wheeler what he thinks?"

"No. But, so what? He won't like it… either way he isn't going to like anything we say."

"If he said no, seems to me that such a position would make him a prime suspect."

"Nonsense. It isn't Franklin."

Explain," I said.

He sighed and locked his hands behind his head and stretched his shoulders. Shadows of leaves undulated in a small breeze through the long window at one side of the room leaving intricate slits of dancing sunlight. They contorted his face like a Braque painting. "Controlling the various trusts means controlling what they do, what they buy, where they invest, the income of the highway project, who they hire…and fire, the contractors, all that. I don't think Franklin would like anyone telling him what to do on any score. For you, of course, there's the salary… Two twenty-five –"

"Thousand? You're kidding."

"That's what I think the court will go for."

"Sounds like bribery. Dammit, Moss, you had an obligation to tell me this long ago. When we did the Will and we named each other Executor. You knew then all about these trusts."

"Couldn't say anything. Sorry, Ace, just couldn't say anything."

"You were acting for Wheeler in this whole damn thing – not John. That's plain. You are and were paid by Wheeler. You were Wheeler's boy. Not John's."

"I represented John."

"Bullshit."

He waved those hands dismissing my upset. "Listen, Ace, it doesn't make a fucking bit of difference. This is was what they wanted. I represented John. So, don't go into your detective's mode."

"This is what John wanted and Wheeler paid?"

"Yes. FK was basically concerned and thinking about the care of his daughter, and…" I interrupted. "And she's dead."

"Right. Listen, John wouldn't have anyone other than you in the middle of his life and death. You were his friend. Maybe his only friend. Very simple."

There was a trace smile on one side of his tanned wrinkle scarred face. Made a person want to punch him. He was never John's lawyer. He was stuck with Wheeler because that's where the money was. "I'm fucking dealing with everyone's life but my own. Different if I chose this. The only thing I chose is to get the killers and find Frankie. I didn't think this business of getting in the legal middle was part of it."

He asked, "Was there any trouble between them? John and Wheeler?"

"How should I know? You know Wheeler better than I."

"'Cause you were John's best friend and he didn't have many of them. He had straw hats and horses and doomed wives."

"I never got into his skin. That was one thing about whatever John touched. It was at arms' length. Never got too close to anyone excerpt his horses. Tell me what you know about those last days. What was his attitude? His demeanor? No women talk? Finances?"

"You're right. He was polite, and loud and funny but distant. What about you?"

"I saw him must've been last Saturday, early morning…almost a week ago. There was nothing going on. We talked about my filly. About Wheeler's Sky Colors who had a little fever and we talked about the Santa Anita Derby. He got busy with a jock at the clearing barn, asked me to follow him to the paddock – which I did. Passing talk. About horses. He acted like he wanted to tell me something. Kept starting to say something, his forefinger would start to wave – I thought it would be about FK – but he never quite got to it. Was he just being John?"

"I don't know. That's it. Just talk, about nothing. He didn't like FK but that was strictly whispers and mutters under his breath at different times. I don't know if he actually had a falling out with him or not."

"He said nothing about Wheeler that particular morning?"

"Just what I said. And later about the Derby. He was distracted. Talked about his sick filly and my new one. That's the most I can say. He was definitely distracted, though. I saw him several times during the weeks before. You saw him, too."

"But, I was not his confidant, like you, Ace. Didn't really know him. He wanted a Will – you referred me because I assume you told him I did yours. That was it."

"Seems to me Wheeler gave away a lot of power to John and you were the one who made the whole thing possible." I tried to sound casual. "It was a tax situation I figure."

"Yeah, yeah, that's what it was."

"Maybe Wheeler is sorry now about the whole thing…transferring power to John."

"Enough to kill him? Don't believe it."

"No. Not old FK. Too much to lose."

"Too much to gain."

He looked at me as though I had a Billy Club in my hand. Harry was an unhappy guy. "No. Ace. Besides, don't start reading stuff into just business. I'm sure it will all come out in the wash and that the police are all over Wheeler already. They probably know most of what they need to know by now."

I wondered how much Harry Moss had to gain personally with John's demise. "Everyone had a lot to gain. Everyone," he said. Still casual. Low voice. But the anxiety was there…maybe if I kept him talking long enough. "So, go on."

"There is a "no" to everyone, Ace. This estate planning business a mystery to you? If you don't understand something, does it have to mean something bad? Get over it. Franklin was creating these trusts out of necessity…or he would end up with a huge chunk of his life going to the IRS. Maybe the whole Real Estate venture he is the middle of. Maybe enough for a new submarine or a couple extra airplanes for the military which they would just dump into the desert after a few years. Feds buy metal things and then just dump them. Bragging rights, I guess. You take the Revenue Code, and you make it work for you. Wheeler wanted a series of trusts. He wasn't going to buy a submarine for the navy and he wasn't going to give Sally control. That was it. You know their history. She hated him. Crazy girl. He was afraid of her."

"Just stories."

"Franklin felt he owed John, because of Sally," he went on. "That much I know. And he saved a bundle by diverting income and protecting heirs at the same time. I didn't make the old man do anything," He poked a finger in the air like a wounded warrior waving for help. "I just didn't. You understand? And I didn't do anything wrong. For god's sake, lawyers always get the short end of the stick. John was the recipient, at least the manager, the trustee, of maybe a couple of billion. That's a couple of billion. Maybe more. The staff at Wheeler's charitable foundation did the basic bookkeeping for itself, and John for the trusts. The Foundation had their own billions to worry about. There's nothing for you to be suspicious about." He took a breath, rose and did a quick parade around the room, sat down again, and did that eye thing with his right hand.

"Ace," he went on, wearily, "Wheeler told me what he wanted. He wanted John to handle things. He trusted John. He was afraid of his daughter. He had so much trouble with her over the years. They ended up at one another's throats.

"The emotions between them were sickening. John was a savior between them. I got the fucking forms and created a bunch of really good and well done trusts. I adapted to fit what the old man wanted. I listened carefully and did it. I'm sure I kept my early notes. A trust to Sally, one to John, one to Frankie, then a larger chunk to the Foundation, and, of course, his own, FKW trust which had created several years earlier.

"Wheeler was Wheeler. He didn't pay attention to what I suggested. He did what he wanted. I did what I was told. I'm telling you – you have to know this, all that Wheeler gang is fucking crazy. You have to believe that. I figure John got infected by their craziness. Like a shot in the arm. Wheeler did everything compulsive like. All the Wheelers are..." He made quick circles around one ear. "But she has a smart son somewhere doing sensible things. That's what Sophie tells me. And I'm telling you. "Hate to say that. I shouldn't have said it. But who cares right now? Who cares? Franklin's first wife, Marian, was a nut case. Ended up institutionalized. Sally was the product of her and Franklin. Same thing with Sally when she grew up. Can't believe one fucking word any of them says. Nut cases."

He sat back and closed his eyes.

That old man even talked about running for President...of the United States! Can you beat that? Egomaniacal son of a bitch!"

He closed his eyes and let his chin drop to his chest. It signaled enough was enough. "Did I ask you if you wanted a drink?"

I nodded.

Moss was in the middle of unwanted recollections. "Okay. I got the picture," I said, "Wheeler asked and you delivered."

"I told the police, that Paul Sampson friend of yours. But I'll tell you one thing. Probably means nothing. I'm remembering. Wheeler did say something strange. A little strange, anyway. I'll remember it in a minute. It's up here, in the head. Takes a minute. Anyway, John kept going into the trust office and straightening out what Sally messed up trying to deal with her own trust, actually just spending more money. They both did that. John and Wheeler. John would straighten out Sally's mess. He wanted Wheeler to stay out of it.

"He corrected things and then Wheeler corrected him. Power corrupts, Ace. An old saw, I know, but it's true. Sally with power and then John with more. And Franklin was and is getting old. People get paranoid with age, you know that, don't you?

"Maybe he and Sophie were just afraid."

"Afraid of John or Sally? Or were just crazy."

He thought about it a minute and shook his head as if tossing the thought away. He was taking too much time to think. He was creating answers.

"You know, Harvey, forget all this killing and these mysteries for the moment. Let's get this legal business behind us. You're merely an Executor under the Will. You just inventory the house and furnishings, which could be worth a bundle, and whatever John had in the bank and at Morgan Stanley, which also could be substantial.

"He owned a couple of minor interests in some of his racing stock. The rest of his life, like ninety percent, is in his Trust, along with Sally's and the kid's. I'll get the books and records of the Trusts and call you and get you to sign a receipt and then you are the boss. Until you find Frankie…alive. Then we go back to court."

"I'll find him. Don't worry about that, Harry. Tell me more about operating the trusts."

He closed his eyes.

"Is it nice out there? I can see the sun now through that Maple."

He spent the next twenty minutes giving me a quick review on the various Trust holdings, explaining that John handled Sally's trust since her presumed death. And John managed his son's trust. Finally, he said, "I think we're done here. You have the legal authority to act on behalf of the trusts now. That's what it says in the trusts as well as the Will. There's nothing to do there. But the estate outside of the trusts has to be inventoried and tended to. Mostly, the house. Probably just sell it. The rest is mostly passive. I'll write the banks and brokerages about you. Get it out today. I'll file a declaration in the court under a new case number. You're good to go. You ought to go see the Administrator of the Foundation. When you can."

He closed his eyes again…a way to dismiss me.

"I'm not actually in charge of anything, am I? I don't actually do anything. Just inventory everything in that house."

"That's the estate. Not the trusts. I get an assignment from you to FK and the Foundation and get it recorded, so you don't have to manage anything if you don't want. Franklin will take over. But, until then, we need something to be able to sign checks, pay bills, stuff like that until I get it done. Come by the office tomorrow, I'll have it all ready. If you are not resigning."

"I'll let you know."

"Then you are now the official 'it' guy. You read it in the Will. You take his place in several things."

He straightened himself and brushed off although there was nothing to brush. The law business is an interesting one. You tell people what to do, how to deal with fortunes, deal with their belongings, tell your staff to prepare this or that, and then sit back and let everyone wrestle with your pronouncements. You make trouble and alleviate trouble at the same time. And you better get everything right. You have to be right all the time – all the time."

"I assume lawyers get used to it."

"I wouldn't trade places with almost anyone," he finished. "I can tell you this, as you've seen, you will need help. Ann can help. Just call. She knows what to do."

"Just get me signature cards and anything else I'll need. Then we'll see. You said Wheeler said something strange? Or was it John."

113

"It was Wheeler. Did I say John? Maybe both. I don't know. It was weird. Weird. They're weird." Harry gazed at me intently for an extra moment.

Finally, I said, "Come out with it."

"Just seems silly. How are you supposed to know, with such crazy people? Take it for what it's worth. The old man said he thought Sally was haunting him. Looking in windows.

"That's what he said.

"Said it more than once.

"Like she was a real living thing in his life.

"Real and close by."

"But still a ghost. John said things like that, too. Seemed like foolish talk. She's dead.

"Cremated. Nothing's deader than that."

He sighed, stroking his face once again.

"Enough. I'll have everything you need tomorrow. But I would suggest you not get in the middle of the Wheeler family itself.

"Just face the fact that John's powers went to Sally, if she were alive…and if not, goes to the child or its guardian.

"You check things. So, we're done here. Just watch yourself."

"Why?"

He gave me a hard stare like I was the local idiot. "You are in charge. Don't you get it?"

"But when she died, I mean John's wife, something had to be done to change her power to John. You're in charge. The buck stops with you. Like having a target on your back. Changing of the guard is automatic. Built in. None of that is a problem So, Harvey, it's not my responsibility any more. I'm not their keeper. You have to understand that. Try to keep it in mind. It's their responsibility to make the decisions. I'm a Dog-soldier, in this Augers affair. I never handled their day-to-day affairs. Their family michugas. It's theirs."

He gave me a helpless gesture.

I didn't respond. He continued. "Harvey, all of these damn trusts settle onto you, the eleven-year-old trust and the Charitable trusts and even Wheeler's trust. John was s trustee for the whole lot of them. Imagine. Kid will come into his legal positions. You now know the whole ball of wax. I tried to tell Wheeler at the beginning."

He closed his eyes.

"I tried."

"I'm sure you did."

114

"I called them. Told them. They ask me to do something, it's done."

"I'm supposed to hold their hands? I never foresaw the transfer of power like it happened." His forefinger hit the top of his desk once again. His favorite gesture. "Big, fat, self-righteous people who are thieves at heart. They knew the terms. John and Wheeler had copies of everything. They created it. I was a scribe at best. Have fun."

Ron Cable didn't think so. But Moss had opened up. I let him go on without comment. "It was Wheeler's baby. I can tell you this – that old Sophie girl was watching everything. Keeping track. Kept saying the old man was too old to 'fuck a duck' – that was the way she said it. That lovely old lady," he grinned, cynical twist to his lips. "Crude as they come. But you won't see it. And I can't be the old man's damn alter ego. Or any of them. It's not my responsibility. You see that, don't you?" He laid his palms flat on his desk. "You do, don't you?"

He stared off into the distance, struggling to dampen his defensive manner.

I watched him turn away and bring on a smile and then turn back. It was like he was admiring how hard he tried to do the right thing. Excusing himself. "It was Franklin Wheeler's show, Harvey. I'm a lawyer, not a life planner."

He was through physically. He slouched back in his chair. The end of his endurance for that day. Suddenly, too old for the game and the sorry series of events. The gaze went blank.

Shoulders sagged.

Shadows consumed the space. "John did alright, didn't he? Yes, he did," he murmured to himself. You haven't figured it out yet? Well, hell, you don't know the whole story, do you? For all I know, maybe Sally forced Wheeler to do all of it her way. She was spooky. And mean. Or John was involved and all of it was his idea and Wheeler bought it. Who gives a fuck now? Wasn't me." He pointed at his head. "Don't know why the hell he went into that marriage... Yeah, well, money. That's easy to understand." His hands went into the air as if tracing the truth of life on an invisible slate. He wasn't done. It came more easily now. "Somehow I had the idea that you knew it all because of your friendship with John. I guess I shouldn't be surprised."

His eyebrows went up. A crease formed where his hair used to be.

I thought he would suddenly begin quoting from his exquisite leather-bound set of Shakespeare tragedies in the corner of his desk. He wanted to pull one out, sit down, open a page to anywhere, and shut out the world. Harry's wife died a dozen years ago. Since then, he had wallowed in the tragedies of Shakespeare, booze, leftover glories, and a good client list. He shivered for a moment as if Yorick was in the new shadows falling like gray intruders in the late afternoon.

A sudden thought escaped him. He tried to pull it back and gave up. He continued. "The story is this, Ace," his voice was just above a whisper. "Franklin K. Wheeler was married to Marian Heinzel when they were kids. Nineteen, twenty years old. Their first child was born deformed and retarded and died within a couple of weeks. FK went crazy…kept trying to prove that the deformed child's death was Marian's fault. Except what did they do? He got her pregnant again a few months later and in nine months had another child, Sally. She seemed healthy and beautiful and FK lavished a lot of attention on her. Too much. They were close. Anything she wanted. He was doing very well even then but began to make the bulk of his fortune after Sally's birth, like he needed to prove himself to this infant. As you know, he was as tough as cowhide. Turned everything into money. Very big insurance agency, you know, the buy and sell for corporations and partnerships, and then got into everything else. His history says he was a money-is-a money is everything kind of guy. In the early years, it was Sally and money and talk about money and deals, and oil and units and more deals…and Sally. She grew up very pretty. He had to keep making more. He had to get rid of Marian, so the marriage didn't last.

"Marian started drinking is the story, stealing from him to support her booze habits. Forged checks. Empty bottles in the linen drawers, that sort of thing."

"They made a movie about such things. Ray Milland. Remember?

"Then what?"

"Then a divorce. Marriage of six or seven years. Franklin got custody of Sally and Marian ended up in some institute in Mara Bay. He was glad to get rid of her. I referred the divorce lawyer to Franklin.

"At the end, Marian was awarded a small bungalow, a thousand dollars a month for ten years, $23,000 in cash, her clothes, jewelry, and some furniture and that's it. I don't know how he did it but screwing women in a rich marriage is not very unusual. He had her watched every minute of every day and she continued to drink. Just exactly what every divorce lawyer loves. He had money. She didn't. She moved up the coast a ways to that Mara Bay, went into that institute up there and then she died after four or five years."

"A quick death?"

"Very. But Sophie took care of everything. Smart lady. Everything about the family, every new article, every gossip column, went into the Court files. I traced it all and found out as much as a person can know. Sally was a princess. She would trot out a new hobbyhorse, or a new maid, or a new

116

dollhouse as big as your apartment. She was kept in silk and satin. Had boyfriends galore as a teenager. And she had her father. Went 'Hollywood' in a big way."

"And the unhappiness grew."

"She had no mother. Money instead of care. Sort of like a psychiatric case book."

"Did this Marian keep in touch with her daughter after the divorce?"

"Perhaps she did, but not that I know of – several news articles about it, particularly in the Santa Barbara Newspaper. Nothing in the Court files that shed any light as to the reasons of the divorce except incompatibility which is a catch-all in California. But it was obvious Marian was a sick human being. And something was the matter with Sally too." He went on, "In spite of doting on her, Sally lashed out at him. After Wheeler married Sophie, the two of them, I mean Sophie and Sally, became close to one another – closer than to anyone else, sort of a unit in cahoots against the old man.

"Sally was a nut. True. Spoiled rotten but not dumb, as I read the files." He coughed and reached for a cigarette from a blue wrapper, one of those French brands. He was not a pack a day smoker. I could tell how he held the cigarette, high in the first two fingers. Later, I would meet a doomed real smoker.

A sliver of light from the garden window struck him in a momentary pose, cigarette in his fingers, Betty Davis style, smoke wafting upwards, and then curling down back at him as if ready to strangle.

He was an old dog trying to be relevant again. "The world is crazy, right? I've seen it all. I suppose John told you all of this."

"No. He didn't. Go on."

"I ought to let you find out everything yourself."

"Finish the damn story, Moss."

He smiled.

"I think I'm gonna quit this game. But, you know," he grinned a sly grin, "several things are coming due."

"I don't care if three virgins are waiting in heaven for you, finish."

He shook his head in that same exaggerated way. "I guess this story is a lesson to all of us.

"Like Henny Youngman always said, 'Take my wife…please.' But do me a favor, take my son…please. My boy is twenty-six years old and I don't have the slightest idea who he is…lives in a bedroom apartment in the garage. Goddamn terrible. I don't deserve it. Sophie has the same problem. But her kid is successful. I think, though I don't know much about him."

"Maybe you drink too much."

"Fuck you. I don't drink enough." He laughed a wheezy laugh. "Old, old, joke."

"And a bad one.

"It's pretty clear. Franklin dumped her mother. That could cause resentment in Sally and even hate. But there was something there. Hidden."

Moss leaned his head back. Stretched.

He was itching for a drink only two-steps away. But a mile.

Just a small drink. "Who the fuck knows?" he concluded, "they're all crazy.

"Of that I am positive." He punctured the air with his forefinger and began laughing and coughing. The cough took over. The jag lasted a good two minutes. Face nearly purple.

At the same time, he looked defeated. It was an inner acknowledgement that there wasn't much left, that he was supremely alone. He needed something to make his life relevant again. He caught his breath and put his head down on the desk, cradled by his arms. He breathed heavily.

Sunshine streaming in the high window faded with a passing cloud like someone had pulled a shade over the world.

In a minute, he raised his head. "You must think I am crazy, too, don't you? Old and diminished."

I didn't reply.

"I'm not. You can be sure. "I can handle whatever they throw at me."

"What could that be?"

He waved. "Screw it."

"Finish," I said. "Finish the damn story."

"Right. Right.

"You know, whenever that young Sally got, let's say 'manic' and couldn't handle things, and had to be," he made quote marks in the air, "put away, John would work like crazy to get the trusts and all the madness in the management of her own affairs back in shape.

Give new orders. Get the books back to understandable condition."

"Ace," he pointed a finger, "I'm telling you, you should stay out of this thing. Resign. John is dead, fer chissake. Nothing you can do. Except maybe get yourself killed. There is a very dark side to the whole fucking thing. I'm telling you, everything keeps pointing backwards." He closed his eyes. "It all goes backwards."

"Just finish the damn story."

A plan was formulating, seeping slowly to the top of my head, around in circles, then compacting into something resembling a genuine scheme of events.

"Early on, Franklin forced Sally to go to every doctor known to mankind. He was obsessive about it. Guilt is part of one's birthright. Don't know why but guilt is familiar and thus in some strange way is comforting. Wheeler possessed guilt to a fateful degree. Then along came John Augers. And..." He waved that finger again, shrugged his shoulders again, like his entire being was part of that unrelated past. "You know that story." There was a look, though, in the back of those eyes that contemplated an ending, something you could actually grasp. Could be the reason he was successful with juries. "Naturally, they fell in love. If you believe in that sort of thing. You know, Ace, don't you, that love is just a sometime thing?"

I thought of my parents and was almost ready to blurt out a family secrets.

He continued, "Who could fall for that kind of person? Nothing made her happy. Nothing."

"Maybe John made her happy."

"Baloney. Never did. He had his own agenda. Listen, you give kids your life, your guts and whad'ya get? "They get money and then are cut loose on the world without a damn idea how to deal with it. You could give them a million dollars, two million." His arms went up like he was washing the sky. "And it wouldn't make a difference, they're not ready for the world and some of them don't want to be. That's the sad part. They don't want to be ready. Same everywhere. Anyway, I'm just going on and on – nothing made her happy. Sally, I mean. Not her mother, Marian. Not anyone else. Got that? But that little girl had fair skin and bright eyes. Disarming smile that was as phony as a six-dollar bill. I met Wheeler briefly years and years ago in a real estate deal. He was huge pain. But I also met the little girl." And Marian. Moss's mind's eye was busy conjuring it all up. For him, the past was his present. He had no future. He knew that. And his present was substantially less than what he had spent his life hoping for. "So she got married to John. Franklin created that enormous trust for her. For John. Tried to make her love him. She became powerful. And she was social. She had access to the glitz in the racing business. To west coast culture. Whatever that is."

"Breakfast at the Palm Room in the Beverly Hills Hotel. And, of course, Franklin promised to give her a world that couldn't be taken away, and I drew an irrevocable trust to John when they were married; a separate one for Sally, and then for Frankie when he was born with John in control. You won't like this but that sucker sold himself for the bucks. I'm convinced."

I wasn't sure I wanted to hear more.

He leaned on his elbows, palms up. "What the hell, we all sell ourselves, don't we? One way or another. You know, Ace, you're a fucking, prudish

119

son of a gun." That lawyer's controlled face, like an actor not quite sure of his material, suddenly dropped the frontal pretense his face had gotten used to… "Guy like you taken in like that. My God, you think John was a good guy? Ace, you live a parallel and different universe. You recognize the value of cards and horses and ball games and whatever goes with it. But people? I know your history. I can go to California Who's Who and find you. Your marriage, your daughter, Wharton Business School, waspy upbringing. Too smart for your own good; too soft, maybe, is the right description. I read about how you got shot helping the police – in Santa Barbara, was it? Now you are the IT guy. You ought to get out of this mess, Ace. I can handle all the legal falderol. The rest is up to the police."

"So far as the world is concerned, I'm in it. The Foundation must know everything you've told me. Wheeler has to know."

"I still think…"

I held up my hand like a crosswalk cop. "Harry. I'm not resigning." I wanted him to keep talking.

"Okay. I get it. Anyway, the upshot of it was that the two of them, Sally and her father, kept the tragedy going, like fuse burning inside of them. Daughter and father. Had to explode. Frankie had every childhood problem you could imagine. Which didn't make it easier. "And Sally got nuttier and nuttier until they finally put her away. It's not a prison. So, she's in and out of that Bright Paths place. Sometimes they took her to place in Tucson that catered to such but not as expensive…or comfortable. They kept putting her away. Finally, John had enough and he filed for divorce. Gave her everything he could think of except his racing business and that big house off Beverly Boulevard."

"All the modern conveniences," I interrupted.

"Yeah, I grant you that. She was in and out of that Mara Bay institution pretty often after that. Maybe the whole fucking craziness and al he trusts were all his idea from the start. Who the hell knows?"

"Like I said, it doesn't sound like the man I knew."

"You didn't really know him, Ace. Certainly not the rest of them."

"That's why I'm asking."

He shook his head again in that slow wagging way. "Once she tried to cut old FK into pieces. I handled the mess. Big kitchen knife." He threw his palms straight ahead as if against a force pressing him down. "Anyway, I made the trust irrevocable – at the old man's request – and it lasted for John's lifetime. Franklin couldn't touch either of them.

"So, they struggled with that vast wealth divided up into all those disparate parts. He and John argued like that was their business – arguing about cutting up the pie, Sure as we're here the old man was pissed at himself."

"What was the upshot with Sally? You left that out."

"Sally, yeah, I'm getting to it. John managed the rest and kept fixing her messes. Except for that house."

"The house in Hancock Park.

"The house was not in any trust. You know the area?"

I did. Hancock Park. Broad quiet streets, magnolia trees and Jacaranda lined streets in the center of Los Angeles – homes the size of ancient baronial castles, five mil minimum, the home of all the late Mayors of the city, Richard Riordan and Tom Bradley, the Hollywood set. Anyway, Sally got out and went off to live in Vegas, and then Tucson, and then Mara Bay. Mara Bay was familiar territory so she seemed to gravitate there. I guess it was the place that seemed most like home. Last I heard, she ended up in a small bungalow at about the middle of the rise up from the ocean. It was part of the properties owned by the Wheeler Trust. It's where Marian had lived. You may know the place, right on the coast, north of Santa Barbara. She kept threatening to take Frankie back from John and FK and Sophie, and to try and bust the trust. Bunch of bad lawyers tried. More bad lawyers than good ones. She had no chance. I'm good at what I do. Easier to defend than attack in the law business."

I said, "So, she ended up living in an bungalow in an old sea village which was a trust property managed by an estranged husband. She had dollars. Franklin saw to that."

"And you were part of all of it. planning and scheming."

"I accept the compliment, but there are special places reserved in you know where for lawyers."

"And for gamblers?"

He laughed out loud.

That was a touché, so I shut my mouth.

I knew Mara Bay. I knew it too well. It was a picturesque village at the side of the Pacific for upscale retirees and a few downscale ones with just the right amount of derelicts and ramshackle clapboards to make it almost "interesting" for a tourist's drive through. It was also a village just big enough to hide in. It was a good coffee stop and a good meal at the widely known and respected Sidney's restaurant. Looked broken down but food was top notch. I knew the proprietor very well.

"Bottom line was that Sally died a few years later at one of the small hospitals up there. There was some question about how she died. Seems all the Wheeler women die before a decent allotted time. You know all the rest, about Carole Augers and Frankie, and what happened."

"It was 1991 that Carole and John were married."

"September 23. And at first, it seemed like it was made in heaven. Carole was perfect for Frankie. He responded to her."

"But?"

"I don't really know, except the craziness that had infested John's life seemed to take hold again.

"Just telling the story is painful. How kids suffer sometimes is beyond belief…and yet come out of it. Carole couldn't handle the problems of the family, or its history. Frankie, Trusts, ghosts, in-laws. She up and ran out. The old man and Sophie didn't like her anyway. So she was on the outs everywhere."

A sliver of sunlight hit the gold embossing on the set of Shakespeare's plays like the last light in Lear's eyes.

"I know the rest," I said, putting words to the scenario to make certain we understood the same facts. "Carole and John go walking with Frankie one warm, early evening, after buying an ice cream. They were trying to patch things up. A last try is the way I figure it. Walking out at Palisades Park in Santa Monica right next to the bluffs, high above the highway. Straight down eighty feet.

"Apparently, an evening stroll was an old habit of theirs. Witnesses said they were right along where the low fence protects the winding path, among the Mellaluca trees that spread out like dead snakes at your feet. Suddenly, from the bushes, in the middle of the park area, Carole is attacked. Two people rush at her. Two big blobs of attackers. Not identified. My guess is some of the homeless that live along there. The information I have," Moss said, "was that they were attacked as if there was malice aforethought. John was holding onto Frankie for dear life. These two…grunts, whatever they were, kept shoving her closer to the edge. She is separated from John and Frankie's grasp. In the prolonged struggle no one came to their aid. She was finally pushed over the bluff and falls screaming all the way down to the highway below. Frankie starts screaming too, and it went on for maybe a couple of hours and finally he stops speaking altogether.

"According to John, the child so to speak went off the deep end with Carole. Kid didn't even cough for a couple of months. Utterly autistic or catatonic or whatever they call it."

Moss stopped.

Murmured resignedly, "Kid never had any luck. "Lost his real mother like she just disappeared. He didn't know why. Found another and learned that his grandparents hated her, or something, who the hell knows what he knew, and then saw the replacement mother get tossed over a cliff – all crazy and scary stuff. Meanwhile, his grandfather is a major pain in the ass to everyone."

"Seems like a string of events that could only happen in your Shakespeare stories."

"Can't blame the kid for shutting down. Wouldn't you retreat? Shut everyone out?"

"That's my M-0," I said.

"Seems to me that John would have said something about his recent life. Especially to you. He said nothing I'm surprised"

"Nothing."

"No women, no complaints?"

"Nothing."

After a long few moments, he said, "Well, I'll admit he would complain that now and then. Handling all the trusts didn't leave enough time to do his real job. Would call me. Wanted help. Told me once he thought there was some funny business at the Foundation. Don't know what made him wonder. And then, he would blame it on Sally. Like "has to be that bitch." Then he would complain he didn't have time to be a father. I tried to get him to tell me specifics, but nothing. Talked about everything except what was important. Never talked about how Sally died.

But that Frankie –" Moss touched his forehead mysteriously. He has to know things. He saw it all. Lived it all. He is not dumb. Autism doesn't mean you're dumb."

He sat back and gazed at the ceiling, satisfied that he had relieved himself of responsibilities. He was a man working at shedding responsibilities, like letting an overcoat drop to the floor. Ann Whitson leaned in. Even that quick sight caused a little jump in my lower intestine. "You have to call Franklin Wheeler, Mr. Moss. He's called twice. You promised him."

"You call him."

A tinge of a smile came to her lips. "I'm not you."

There was no anger in her, a little resignation perhaps.

Smart employees know when to tolerate and when to confront. They both knew that when the money dried up so would she. Her thick auburn hair slightly tinged to a lighter color, looked something like a clouded bit of sunshine. It fell across her shoulders. Fair skin. And the rest was beauty queen stuff. At that moment, I decided to get closer to her. As close as possible. She could make a person forget the past. Maybe.

"Mr. Moss, grab the phone now, he's waiting on the line."

123

She pointed at the receiver at his elbow. Moss reached and with a red eyed wave at me and said, "We're done. Ann will get what you need."

Out I went. I stared at Miss Whitson while I stood by his door and tried to hear his conversation without luck. Turned away. "Nicely done," I said.

"Not so nice. "Just necessary. If he makes money, my life is much easier. His mood is much sweeter. Wheeler is probably calling about you. Face it, there's really no way to actually like the law business."

"So you have to make up for it by making a lot of bucks. Does the law business leave time for dinner?"

"Now and then."

"With me?"

"Possibly." Smiling.

"Are you making it hard for me?"

"Is it...hard?"

"Very funny. When?"

"Sometime this century.

"Call me."

"Coffee later?"

"Five thirty." Without invitation, I went back in as Moss was hanging up. "Okay," I said, "Last thing, how did Sally die?"

He went to the table in the corner, tilted two fingers of the contents of one of the bottles, motioned to me. "John left a letter to you. Remind me to give it to you."

You're just remembering?"

"No. Just wanted to see who I might be dealing with up close."

The bottle was a nice single malt brand but I shook my head.

He downed it in one gulp and sighed and perked up. His face reddened.

"So, how'd she die?"

He gave me one of his cunning smiles like a cobra ready to strike. "Okay. Sit down. Let's see. After several run-ins with her father Sally moved to Mara Bay. But I told you that. She made trouble in town and for the local police. With Franklin's assistance, probably John, too, they got her into that institution. She had some kind of caretaker. Big woman. Nut case, too. Doctor Stan Simon arranged it all. Then she died suddenly. No autopsy or anything like that. By that time, I was out of Franklin's life. Sophie made all the arrangements for Sally's funeral. She took care of all of it. Apparently a very efficient woman. Did it all in a matter of hours. Got her cremated before the stove warmed up, so to speak. So, that's it, now you know."

Something was missing. "Harry, you gotta be in the middle of all of this somewhere. You created everything. Smart old top gun like you? Letting

124

himself be shut out by a client's wife? Letting the entire house of cards tumble and there's nothing in it for you?"

He got up quickly. "Enough, Ace. You're barking up the wrong tree. Enough. You can leave now."

I got up. "You don't want to finish the story?"

"Get out. Told you everything. Dammit! "You should be on my side! Not questioning me!"

He came around the desk.

I backed up.

He needed another drink.

"Go. Get out. Just remember, as soon as I file the Death Certificate of Sally and of John and you give me an inventory for the Probate, you sign whatever I shove under your nose like all good clients. He gave the house in Hancock Park to someone who no one knows. Just the house. No relation that I can tell. But somebody he must have known pretty well. Name's Carly Klein. Never met her but I suppose she's a nice-looking secret. Ann will give you all the documents you need. Addresses. Whatever. And I'm giving you this envelope. Now you can get out." He pulled it out from the top drawer of his desk and handed me an eight by eleven mailing envelope. "Maybe you can find answers in his letter. "Gave it to me six, seven months ago." He looked up and grinned. "We're done. That's it. I'll do the closing and that will be that, as far as your job as Executor of the Augers affair is concerned."

"Am I missing something?"

"What?" His eyebrows went up.

"Just now filing the Death Certificate of Sally? Why wasn't it done when she died?"

"That was her doctor's job. Not mine."

"Then why now you suddenly decide to file it?"

He went again to his small breakfront in the corner. A crack of sunlight moved directly over his face and split it in two. This time he pulled out a bottle of Gray Goose with a small tumbler and waved it at me. "Just something different."

"None of that stuff is "different" to you. Why, Harry, why wasn't it filed?"

He waved the bottle.

I shook my head again.

He downed a shot, put the bottle away as if he had had his allotment for the day and, face growing redder, said, "Not interested in your detective bullshit, Mister Ace. John got in someone's way. That seems to be the long and short of it." He squeezed his fingers together. "Money. Makes the world go round. Now, go home. Leave me the fuck out of this. Go see the Wheelers. He called and wants to see you. Check it out. At least get out of here."

"Why? I don't get it. You should have filed Sally's Death Certificate, Harry. You know that. That isn't merely a doctor's job. You were handling the estates and trusts." He faced me and withered. "So sue me."

***

Chapter Ten

I got to Nate and Al's a little early and I went straight to the bathroom at the rear of the restaurant and scrubbed my hands. I stared at the fellow in the mirror with the thinning hair and wondered why would someone like Ann Whitson want a once rejected, slightly – slightly, mind you, aging fellow like me? – A person with an addiction and a clean hands compulsion? And one with a hidden agenda and a lost love? Then came the old saw my mother used to haul out... *Go figure.*

I flexed my arms and puffed up like smiling Guv Arnie and someone walked in and stared at me precisely as though I was just out of the local psychiatric hospital. I muttered, "Exercise. Doctor's orders."

Nate and Al's in Beverly Hills was the Deli where all the old-time comedy writers hung out, those who were still alive, along with Larry King and, not too long ago, Lew Wasserman, lordly agent and creator, and his grandson. No one knew who was funnier, the waitresses or the writers or the tourists. You could tell who the Midwestern tourists were. Black socks, short pants, white legs, flats, about forty pounds over their limit, belts below their belly buttons, carrying maps. Ladies all did their walking tours in jeans and high heels of one kind or another which they removed once they got out of Beverly Hills. In zip code 90210 everyone is gorgeous and everyone wears black and no one wears short pants except high school girls. And their pants, happily, are really really short. I always want to tell these yokels from mid-America and the southern states that black socks and flats or brown shoes are out. The west coast look down on middle America. They looked different.

Darlene, an incredible seventy-nine-year-old waitress who in spite of her age, and at no more than four eleven and with fuzzy red hair, dumped bowls of pickles on our table, and said, "Okay, now what?," She called all men "sonny boy." Her reservoir of patience had been used up by the time she hit seventy. Now and then, she would try to dig deep down into what might be left of that reservoir and extract a little more. She clearly did not believe in professional hairdressers, as she had a mop which was brown here and faded red gray over there, and sort of orange on top and very thin and turbulent.

She stared at Ann then at me, flipping her pencil between her fingers. Finally, she said, "Listen, sonny boy, you ordering something or renting space? "If you're renting, you need to get a bed and a condom."

She shoved a shoulder in Ann's direction and gave her a broad wink.

Ann's cheeks reddened. "So what is it? Bed or Breakfast?"

"Just want some coffee," I replied as if I heard nothing.

"There's an hourly rate, you know…for the bed. The rest is up to you." Darlene laughed a cigarette laugh. Her thin hair bounced when she talked. This was her fun few moments. Made the job worthwhile.

"Only coffee."

"I get a big tip no matter what you order. Understand, sonny boy?"

She didn't have far to go when she leaned down into my nose.

"I give a dime no matter what I order."

She grinned and muttered, "Wise guy and big shot at the same time. Everybody's a big shot in Beverly Hills. Just ask."

We got our coffee and when Darlene left, we were discretely silent. Eyes on the table. We were both feeling a little guilty like playing hooky from our real work. And I thought, *Listen, Ace, Sarah walked out, you didn't.* There are a half dozen excuses I kept in reserve and could have used, being the great lover boy I was, except I couldn't think of one.

Should my collapsed love-life get in the way of getting something going with this lady? When the silence became a pall over our little world, Ann placed her coffee cup down and looked up, put her hand on mine and said, "No, Ace, I don't go to bed with a guy on my first date. Or second. Or maybe ever. And I'm not sure this is a date."

"Who asked?" I pleaded innocence. "Perish the thought. I am really not trying any monkey business, Miss Whitson. Just a friendly chat. Who even dreamed such thoughts?" Her auburn hair with "highlights" as they say, and contrasting deep set blue eyes, made a needy liar out of me. And she knew it.

"Ho, ho, Mr. Acey-Ducey. I can see it there. You want me. Right there, in your left eyeball. You are at the edge."

She pulled her hand away. "Cold eyes, actually."

"I'll remove the eyeball."

"Leave it." She sounded soft. "Yes, just leave it. At least I know…underneath it all, you are a cold, single-minded son of a bitch. And not sure of anything. Especially women."

I let out a large sigh. "How come everyone knows me? Or claims to? You are very wrong. A single-minded son of a bitch? And this isn't a date, Miss Whitson. It's a friendly chat…two normal people just talking. I have no ulterior motive or desires of any kind whatsoever. None. I hope you hear that. None. I am not interested in that body. No, I am not."

"Alright, already. I got it. You made your point. You want to chat. No bodies coming together. Coffee and creams and no dreams."

"Good line. Besides, I have a steady date. Darlene and I are going dancing. We have a date at the Wilshire Crest Retirement Home once a month. It's dancing night…"

She pointed at my eyes, "But it's there. Then, this is – what exactly?"

There was something sharp inside this lady, I thought. Something to worry about. "A friendly chat," I insisted, "I told you…a chat over a Maxwell House."

"Whatever it is, I'm telling you what I won't do. The only thing that gets my clothes off is time and brains. Maybe a little culture, too. When that happens everything comes off, one piece at a time. Slowly."

"Your mother would be happy to know."

She smiled a great wide white smile, and shove stray hair behind her ear. "I doubt it."

"I'm telling you that I'm not asking…or thinking."

"That's a lie. Just remember the rules." Ann Whitson's baby blues gazed at me without blinking.

"Dinner," she said. "That's all I can promise, but I'll have to check it out first. You said Saturday night?"

"I said nothing about Saturday night," I protested.

Sarah was a twinge at that moment. A big twinge. Ann ignored my protest. "I have to make arrangements for Saturdays."

"I didn't ask."

"You were just going to."

"OK. OK. I was going to. You want cream?" I handed the little cold silver container to her and she declined.

She said, "I've got a kid in high school so I can't leave him on his own for more than ten seconds. Maybe five. He's under the impression that I can still beat him up. Nevertheless, he's seventeen and big. My sister has been in town and she has been keeping him busy. She'll be leaving early tomorrow to go on back to Nashville. All of which makes me old enough…even for you.

"But let's get to the point here, Ace, if you don't want this fabulous body, then what?"

"Okay, dinner. Nothing else. Nothing." My finger went into the air like a politician promising to lower taxes and lying through his teeth. "Just dinner."

"Famous last words." she smiled. "I remember you. When you came in a while back – Harry did your will. You gave it all to a retired thoroughbred horse home or farm or something – some place where famous old racehorses retire. Then you brought in that poor Augers fellow. Too bad about him. Harry was upset. Don't you have anyone to give your ill-gotten fortune to? Other than a horse?"

"Horses are people, too. And more reliable. But no, I don't have anyone. Parents dead."

"No brothers, sister, not even a cousin?"

"Just me. Just a gambler. And, to be frank, I have a slight ulterior motive. I want to know more about Harry and Wheeler." Might as well be direct. Seemed as if she would appreciate it more than indirect probing.

"I checked you out. A loner. You're in one of Harry's books and in that huge scrap book he keeps to show clients all his newspaper clippings and winnings. You're in it a couple of times. Made headlines with some of those cases – you found the kid or the criminals. Put your name in books and there it is. Reputation as a ladies man with that psychiatrist lady, Willa Katt. Big headlines.

"And that case where the bad guy's car went over the edge on the highway right into Lake Arrowhead. And that heiress lady and her jewels. I looked it all up. You want to get secrets from me. I know that. But you're not going to get much. This is a good job. When you came to Harry that first time, you were sort of – what would be the right description?" She puckered up and her nose wrinkled. It wasn't that it made her cute. It made her distressingly sexy. "Sort of quietly cool and cocky. Flat belly, and maybe just a little bit bigger than most. Right around the chest and arms."

"Must be some other guy."

She stuck a finger at my nose and laughed. Then she dipped a forefinger in her coffee and licked the residue. "You." She laughed a soft laugh but there was that sharpness again. "Listen, I'm crazy about Thai restaurants. Are you going to take me to one or not?"

"Oh, my gosh, how did you know?

"They are the only places I ever go."

"Very funny. Laugh, smile…something."

She did. A brief grin. "How's that?"

"Not great."

"Right. I like all those things they put on that new internet thing on my Mac to attract a man…walking on the beach…flowers on every date."

I waited. She was working at conjuring up what other people do and say. "Every lovelorn advertisement says that, but I actually do. And I don't reveal secrets."

"You're in luck," I said. "I live at the beach. Or I'm in luck. Which?"

"I jog at least three times a week. You?"

"I stare at joggers at least three times a week."

She grinned. This time, it was one of those genuine unprotected smiles. She was melting. The old ace charm. I knew I could do it. She ran two fingers through her hair. "You have to know, I really don't talk about my bosses. That's what you're really interested in. You really don't give a damn about me. Dinner is a cheap price for obtaining information. No information from me, except, I'll tell you, he is unusual."

"In spite of booze?"

"Much better lawyer and closer to the vest than he lets on. Or you can figure from looking at what's left. And he doesn't share much unless he has to."

"And lazier."

She nodded.

"Hey, he's seventy-six years old. A tired old dog. Forty-five years or more of litigation can do that."

"So tell me which Saturday is good for you?"

"I'll let you know. Meanwhile, I'll transcribe the instructions on the tapes and give you a copy."

"Tapes?"

"He has a taping system. You didn't know?"

"I'm always the last to know."

"It's no secret. He generally tells everyone. He has a voice activated taping system.

"Like Nixon."

"He doesn't trust his clients any further than he can throw them. Even the big name ones. Especially the big ones."

"He doesn't get the big ones anymore, Ann. That's not news."

She stared at me, lifted the coffee cup and took a sip, and said, "We do okay."

"That's an interesting 'we'."

"A figure of speech."

"Where do you want to go Saturday night?"

"Spoil me."

***

131

I didn't really like Franklin K, with his bushy eyebrows and imperious manner but I didn't have a genuine reason not to.

I think Winston Churchill said it correctly, "He had all the virtues I dislike and none of the vices I admire." Without special reason, I was in Churchill's camp.

Franklin's second wife, Sophie, had approved of John's marriage to Sally. But she had grown up in Culver City, managed to get through Hamilton High school on south Robertson in West LA and got some notoriety in their well-known Theater Arts classes. She starred in what was reported in the Times as a first-rate high school production of Carousel.

She met Franklin at a charity event fifteen years ago at the Bel Aire Hotel where he was a featured guest. She was a well-endowed and a smart charity volunteer.

"Care for a cupcake baked by the children?" She was very good at perfect make-up and bending low when she served cupcakes, those that were chocolate and baked as well as the flesh variety. I never could figure out how those marriages happen, except it usually fit the need of an "important" guy to maintain control of his personal existence as well as everything else around him and act like it. Seems to me important people are driven by a sense that unless they become 'important' they are inadequate. Sophie knew and observed the "Sally Problem" which Franklin described as a "chemical problem."

"A chemical disturbance." The description covered such heartaches as spoiled children and acquired dope addictions, customarily enabled by careless parents."

"Seems to me who your parents are is the heart of every life." But I was the wrong kettle to make judgments about the pot.

"My parents were not at the heart of anything," she said. "Not sure they had one. Old FKW was convinced that when John married Sally, it would bring stability to the family. Sophie wanted to believe it but didn't. When Sally bonded so closely with his daughter, those first few years Wheeler was convinced that he had saved the remnants of his relationship with his daughter. She used to point a finger if she was with him and say, "You did it, you SOB."

When it came to my own daughter, I never knew what I did that was so terrible that she wouldn't even call back. Why was she so callous? OK, I didn't understand anything female. I knew her mother harped on her relentlessly about how useless I was and mean and dangerous, etc. ...ad nauseam. Basically, all I knew was that three to one paid eight bucks. And, I was good at figuring how to get those payoffs. But I never understood my relationship with Kim or with Sarah. There was nothing permanent about my life except my Turf Club tables at various Race Tracks and gambling dens. Perhaps that was the whole story. I was an unavailable human being.

I had been unavailable since my first winner at 15 years of age. Everyone loves a winner and that's what I needed. But not what Sarah needed.

A win a day keeps depression away. Everyday. I figured no winning, no love. No nothing.

I was wrong.

My father told me at one of his fleeting serious moments, "Winning is everything. No one loves you when you lose, kid. Win, just win. Remember what I say. Lose and no one loves you."

I didn't like or admire him, yet he had given me a sense of the world, an education, and an even greater impatience with fools. I was in serious discourse with myself about it when Sarah walked out of that door. What sticks in my throat like a persistent hair is "I'll send for my things."

I was the caretaker of others, but not of myself or what was most important to me. Sarah was young enough to want to settle down, to want a home and a life. But I had created a life for myself and it wasn't a bad one. I didn't hurt anyone. Except the ones I cared about – my daughter, my former wife, and Sarah. Yet Sarah cared. Till that very last morning. I know she did. Maybe even now.

This personal assessment business is not a happy chore – I had no job, no legitimate profession. I was not a marketable commodity in any trade in this year of 1995 or any year. Scrubbing my hands might wash the aloneness and numbness away. Maybe I should keep trying. That was the secret – keep trying.

Could be John actually loved Wheeler's daughter. You think you know your friends and then you find out you don't. Maybe John married Sally for the money, Sex makes a marriage. For the first three months. But I didn't think John would succumb to money. He was in love with his hat and himself – not with money. So I thought.

And then, Sally died. The meeting with Harry Moss helped. There was string tying the old man to Sophie, John, Sally, and Harry Moss except the obvious. I needed to find the knot and cut it. Or follow that one loose end. Frankie was not the final terrible end of that string – there was more. Might get it from the old man.

***

"Hi, it's me."

133

"Told you not to bother."

"But I am." I pressed the phone close to my ear as if that would bring her closer. "I want to see you. You left your hair dryer at my place."

"You called for that?"

I didn't answer.

"Don't worry. I've got a key. I'll drop by and get the rest of whatever is there."

"Why did you leave it?"

"Don't start, Harvey."

"Maybe we can work –"

"And your life is going to be different?"

"I didn't ask *you* to change. I like you the way you are."

"You didn't say love."

"OK, I love you the way you are."

"Harvey," she replied with a soft breath, "it won't take you more than a couple weeks to find someone else. Three weeks tops. Give you eight to one. You're not good without someone and you're not good at changing."

"Sarah, listen to me… I would give it a good try, if you cared to…really cared to –"

"You're kidding yourself. We would play house for a while and then you would have to go down to Del Mar or up to Golden Gate, or to Vegas. And then, we would be down and scrounging for nickels and then you would be God knows where. In some grandstand, somewhere betting show bets. And Billy Fitzer and the motley crew would be in our faces. That's the real end of your life. But not mine."

"We never scrounged. We had money. I have money. You aren't easy either, Sarah. You know that?" I knew at once that was the wrong thing to say.

Long pause. "In case it helps, I know."

"In case you're asking, neither am I."

"Good for us. We both know we're both difficult. Gotta go. Denver this time." There was breathy silence again, then, "Good bye, Harvey. Take care of yourself, I mean it. Honestly. No adventures…"

Right. Fat chance. Goodbye and goodbye. I was angry. The kind of anger, well, maybe upset is better; the kind of upset that left you in limbo. Nowhere to go.

The phone began to buzz.

I didn't answer. I kept thinking she's wrong. She'd done me wrong. Then I remembered some smart guy who said there is nothing so blinding as a self-righteous frame of mind.

***

I stared at the dark Pacific from my living room. The Ferris wheel at the end of pier came alive, beon lights in every color flashing and winding their way around the wheel, then into the center and back. Two person carriages swinging in the breeze. I slipped open the sliding door just a little and the calliope music of the merry-go-round drifted over the night mists and made me wonder how anyone could be happy at anything in the whole world right then. The world was having a fucking good time. How could that be? Kids dying in strange sounding lands. Guns and bombs. I couldn't explain it to myself. I started crying. Actual crying. Really stupid of me. I wanted to wring Aureliano Monodozo's throat. I wanted to win. I wanted Sarah. I wanted the world to be different, maybe just accept me…as is…if not, then, to hell with them, whoever *them* may be.

What helped a lot was just forgetting how I fit in. Who needed to fit?

I started imagining the slow business of undressing Ann Whitson. 1st…, then…A vision of Sarah kept interrupting in the middle and at the most inconvenient moments. She was with me. She had been my big bet. She was my bottom line. But there that bra just fell off, and then thumbs in those lace panties…

Then Billy called.

"Whad'ya want? Dammit! I'm dreaming! It's midnight!"

"George Smith saw you at Nate and Al's with a red head. Also gorgeous."

"I was interviewing a possible witness."

"Witness to what?"

"Stuff. Go back to sleep."

"Harvey, you have to let this one go. It's been in my head. This case is not going be something you can fix. I got this feeling that you end up dead. Swear to God."

"That's what you said last time. Go to sleep. Dream about women."

"I had to call. OK, if you get killed, don't call me."

***

Dinner that Saturday night was quiet.

135

We were at Matteo's on Westwood Boulevard, among the closest to my recollection of deep cushioned fine restaurants of the past. Leather booths and dark lights. It was a yesteryear hangout of the "Rat Pack," Sinatra and Company. His entourage took up most the tables and he picked up all the tabs. Ann remarked on the model trains that choo-chooed along the corners of the ceiling in the bar area, round and round the room. Over a butter lettuce salad, she said she liked TV game shows and red underwear. I could have sworn and bet several hundred that they were black lace. Why was she giving me the red underwear routine? What does she really want? I confessed I liked local versions of Broadway shows at local small theaters, and the fights and horses. And any kind of female underwear. But not on me.

Ann said she liked breakfast in bed and said I liked most things in bed. She asked why I liked horses. I explained that horses had essentially the same responses to stimuli as humans. They nurture their young, form groups for safety and company, are tribal in nature, and are suspicious by nature, they often are content to follow a strong leader. They are willing to accept these leaders and some absolutely need to be leaders in front of the pack. The tough ones, the good ones. The lineage of horses count. Humans? Mamas and papas and grandparents count in breeding horses. Not in humans. But you could have a dud with champion parents and a winner with dud parents.

However, its upbringing that counts for nearly everything. A yearling, male or female, deprived of its mother too long, for whatever reason, grows up jumpy and worrisome and hard to deal with. But, like humans, will respond to affirmation and tenderness – giving them a chance to grow. It takes a while to make these mammals, human and animal, into ladies and gentlemen if they were taken from their mother or were mistreated early in life. Everything needs affirmation. In the long run, horses are more reliable than humans. They weren't devious. You could follow their behavior pretty closely.

She asked how I felt about long-term care and tenderness, and I answered that I had no idea but I had tried giving it to someone just recently and it didn't take. She did a long hum, battered her eyelashes and then another long hum and said, "I get it – you're a gambler. That's what you are. Take it or leave it. Everything including relationships has a mathematical construct. No one gets close. Suspicious for the long term, don't you think?"

Couldn't answer that one. Don't know."

"But you must not have really given, or tried," she added quietly.

I started to reply but again couldn't think of an answer. I did try. Instead, I said I liked scary movies and she said, "Gross." I told her I liked Brown, and she said, "Who?" And I said I liked Mahler now and then and she said, "I knew his brother at Beverly High." We both laughed and she reached for my hand again and said, "Do you know heavy metal? My son likes it."

Actually, I hardly knew a damn thing about Mahler and less about metal, heavy or otherwise, and was sure she didn't either.

There had to be a meeting ground somewhere, like old Spencer Tracy movies. Maybe Katherine Hepburn.

Finally, she said, "Listen, are you buying dinner or what?"

"How about short ribs?"

"Just a salad.

"Then I gotta get home early. Check on Sumner.

"He's getting ready to graduate and he needs me to stick him regularly about his grades and to be there – and, well, stick him."

"Sumner?"

"Yes, Sumner."

"What do they call him?"

"He's six-three, two twenty."

"I guess they call him Sumner."

She looked up now and then as if discretely checking me out. I did the same. I guess that's what people do when they are trying to get closer to someone. Every now and then, a hard streak would jump into her eyes and disappear, like flashes of lightning. It was hard to ignore. The first one caused me to respond with a small startled look. She asked what was wrong. I told her "I get twitches."

"Everywhere?"

"Right." I tried to catch up with those hard flashes, catch the real Ann.

"You know," she said, "You really don't know what you want, do you? Twitches prove it. You are a this – and then a that – you stretch and flex and try to make yourself into something…acceptable…if that makes any sense. Why don't you just settle on exactly what person you are, who you are? Who are you trying to please? Just be done with it? You will never be what you want to be."

"That's upsetting…but…." Couldn't finish. I thought how come other people see what I am and I have such a problem figuring me out? This Ann girl already determined that I was working on trying to be someone else without apology.

"And you?"

"Don't worry about me. I know who I am. Maybe not always so nice," she lit up like a soft lit bulb when she grinned, "But most of the time very feel a little sexy. Filly, I know. I've gotten to this spot in my life the hard way. And, not much ambition to be more, or to travel, here there, and wherever the schedule sends me. And if I don't like it, I'll get a job as an airline stewardess and fly for Delta or Alaska."

"Whoa," I interrupted, "no fly jobs."

She looked at me and guessed. "OK, none of those. Ever. I think sometimes, though that maybe I had to give away too much…just to get here…maybe."

"Compiling regrets?"

Just a hum and nod.

We finished, quietly enough, splitting a shameful profiterole, still wondering about some common ground, other than the guilty feeling between our legs. Sarah and I liked the same music, the same books, the same movies. Everything except my life, my business and profession.

This Ann person at least understood my life. Must be all over my face. I escorted her to her car, gave her a light kiss on the cheek. Total gentleman. She smiled and murmured something that I couldn't hear and returned the kiss on my cheek.

As I turned around, she smacked my rear end.

* * *

I went home and fell into bed lamenting my failure as an interesting Saturday night dinner date, someone who had "twitches," nevertheless feeling a little unsettled about her description of me and feeling the smack on my butt all over again. Ann was not what she seemed. Probably a lot smarter.

I live just a hundred yards down from the Venice pier, right along the cement walkway fronting the beach. The Ferris wheel was lit up every night like on July four, rainbowed neons blazing like fireworks gone mad. I could hear the Calliope from the merry-go-round. I went on merry-go-rounds as a kid but never caught the prize ring.

The egg and omelet and several other restaurants and coffee dives were not far from my condo along with a good Ralph's Grocery just a little walk down Washington Boulevard.

A plethora of pretty girls jogged and skated or biked along the bike path that snaked through the sand.

The sound of the ocean and salt in clean air and misty sunsets were my partners. In short, I had a location and a life.

And I had my routines. Hand washing frequently for one. Not sure why.

I arise at 6:30 each morning, punch the button on my coffee maker, shower, shave, and coffee cup in hand, turn on the TV stock reports and pick up the *LA Times* from my doorstep.

Then I would sit in my Eames chair in the living room, even though I have a nice pale tan quilted outdoor chaise lounge on the porch facing the western ever-changing Pacific Ocean, usually during morning gray skies. I sip my coffee and read below the fold on the first page which is where the news is that I haven't already heard. Then, the International Section and learn that the country is going to hell in a hand basket – all according to the hard right, which they reiterate ad nauseam since Warren Harding's time. Nothing is ever any good. After the paper, I wash my hands again to get rid of the newsprint and face the early murky expanse of the brightening "Blue Pacific" which is not blue and which is always in the process of changing colors and mood.

Within an hour, the sky blossomed and glittered like a painters spread in constructing the first part of a new painting – a few joggers appear heading south from Washington Boulevard where they usually start their 3k's heading toward the canal to the harbor and breakwater and back. Then I pick up my Racing Form and map my bets for the day. A pick three and a four. Nothing higher. Pick fives are suckers bets. Even when they hit there's a dozen successful hits to share with and in the end it's a loser. Add it up.

I head for the track early to watch the workouts, lately more often to see my wonderful filly, talk to my trainer, the clockers, the older retired jocks and everyone with an opinion – which is everyone. Even though John is now gone, the training routine remains the same with Gertrude. Maybe the hole in my heart left by John's loss would not get filled very quickly. Not by Ann and apparently not by Sarah. But I would work through it. I would dig deep and find the bad guys and do my best to hurt them and I would find the boy. And, in the process, maybe find salvation – whatever that is. And who knows what else?

All these routines were as absolute as is possible to make them. I needed routines. It kept me focused on the next hour, the next afternoon, night, the next day. When there is no racing at the local tracks, I will either hurry there very early anyway to check workouts or take a day off and take a walk out on the Venice pier, listen to urgent squawks of sea gulls, watch them glide and dive and merely sail like it was great fun; and listen to the silken Latin sounds of the fishermen leaning over the pier railings, humming old Latin melodies softly and talking to the ocean asking for God to catch them a fish, and could hear the occasional gleeful shout that came with a caught fish. I could smell the delicious sea air and poke my nose into the bait buckets of those Latino fishermen. Are they catching anything or just having fun? Why the hell can't I do that?

And I would check the sky and the sea and wonder how on earth this universe ever happened. And wonder who what makes winners and losers and what and where are my missing people?

Chapter Eleven

Los Angeles is laid out as a large grid, interrupted now and then by small cities and enclaves within – like Beverly Hills, Culver City, Cheviot Hills, BelAire, Westwood, Glendale. North-South streets end at the mountains and hills on the north end and at Long Beach and San Pedro on the South. East-West streets end up somewhere past Boyle Heights on the east and the Pacific Ocean on the west. Street numbers and names often change as one enters a new city. Each new city incorporated was insistent on being independent thus creating chaos out of an otherwise sensible structure.

Just off Wilshire Boulevard, about mid-town Los Angeles, there's a small private street named Fremont Place, ending at a closed vine covered couple of stone sentinels and a gate between at Olympic Boulevard.

It was planned around 1910 as an entirely enclosed park. It was then as it is now, a carefully decorated street of Sycamore and Magnolias trees alternately assembled in a straight line a half mile long, north to south, just west of the major north/south thoroughfare of Crenshaw Boulevard.

The first mansion was completed in 1914 and survives. The interior was designed by Tiffany, every corner, every part of a definitive Tiffany time and place. The plainness of past generations was deliberately changed to ornate corners, swirls of woodwork, every inch decorated with color and fanciful purpose setting the course of architecture and design that became the Art-Deco period. It was built just after what is known as the Victorian Age. The remaining homes came quickly after the first. The wide magnolia lined streets of the enclosed neighborhood sported famous cast iron pillars guarding the north entrance and exit and ivy and weedy stone pillars at the south side exit.

Residences were subject to special design limitations in the deeds along with racial and religious limitations. Replicas of Italian Renaissance was the most loved flavor. However, French Chateau and Colonial Spanish arches were represented. The south end of the street facing Olympic Boulevard was closed altogether in the fifties as if Olympic Boulevard, the east-west thoroughfare harbored infectious diseases or ill-bred intruders that should be shut out. The twenty plus homes on Fremont Place are of the six bedroom, six bathroom variety, pink tile, white roses – a flourishing of rainbow petunias and pansies decorating walkways. Marbled swimming pools still flourished, but were hardly used anymore as there were few children living on the enclosed streets. An almost uniform combination of art-deco white and tan facades were plopped onto the various European designs as though it was a required uniform. It was quintessential baronial, Gatsby-lite.

The era was preserved by such as the old marbled Marion Davies' estate on the beach in Santa Monica, now a fashionable beach club, and the bungalows on Sunset and Laurel Canyon where F. Scott Fitzgerald, Robert Benchley and other drinkers and writers and Hollywood wannabes hung out in the late 20s and 30s. Today, Fremont Place exudes a sense that it is holding on to a world that is and was somewhere else in time and space. However reputable, disreputable English nobles were or are, only they were entitled to reside in the glow of Tiffany windows, lamps and Greene, and Greene carved staircases.

The Wheeler mansion was just across the street from one of the first constructions on the street, a white washed fifty-five hundred square foot mansion refurbished in modern times once owned by Mohammed Ali. Next to it was the old Beaux Arts home of Mary Pickford before she and Douglas Fairbanks moved to their famous PicFair estate in Beverly Hills.

The front door was larger than most, mahogany and carefully carved, and the doorbell a very old-fashioned round button. But the sound was out of Windsor Castle. Sophie Wheeler greeted me. She was not quite plump, her hair not quite silver, short languid curls laced with black threads, and was not quite tall but taller than I expected and in the age neighborhood of social security checks. She had a firm chin, sharply fashioned nose, high cheekbones, green eyes that didn't settle onto you, too much make up, and a quick smile. I could see what a beauty she must have been – and at her age, still is.

She had small gleaming earrings that dangled a half inch and a small wart just under her left ear that did not diminish her finely cared for features. Her lipstick was pale red and her dress light blue silk, perhaps a smidgeon too tight and down to just above her knees, with just a little décolletage. She had been a bit of an actress on the local stages. Had the feeling that she still harbored the belief that someday…

"You're right on time, Mr. Ace. Franklin will be pleased. Always good to hit your mark on time."

It was a show biz phrase.

"Mr. Moss told me it seemed urgent."

"Please come in. I'll call Franklin."

"I want to tell you how sorry I am about John."

As if on cue, her lower lip trembled – or she was about to sneeze. "Yes, yes, we were fond of him. Very fond. There just doesn't seem to be any plan in life does there?" I was still standing on the doorstep.

"I'm sure you're right. It was very surprising."

"Oh, please come in."

With something like a bullfighter enticing a bull, she waved me into the anteroom. Sigh.

I wasn't sure what she meant by a plan.

"I'm thankful when a day goes by without terrible surprises." She flashed a smile, and then said, "I suppose that's the most we can expect."

She could turn emotions on and off like a computer in heat, her eyes blue to purple. Still, first impressions seldom pan out.

She showed me into the Wheeler "China room" straight off the entrance alcove with its enormous grand crystal chandelier specially ordered by Sophie who was reliably advised that it was "An absolute copy of the chandelier of the Sunset Boulevard 'Pink Palace' of Jayne Mansfield and Mickey Hargitay." As she pointed it out to me, she flushed with pride. "Enormous, isn't it? I tried to buy the original but the house seems to be gone."

The "China Room" housed a fifty-year collection of porcelain, silver, pewter, gold, china, plates of all colors and sizes all of which adorned various tables, in two narrow cabinets housing the Jade pieces, and the rest hung carefully on the walls of the large room. There were two Persian blue satin couches shaped like porpoises, and four deep red velvet winged backed Queen Anne chairs in the middle of the space. "Franklin is devoted to this collection," she said. "Loaned it out twice to the Santa Barbara Museum.

"He came from a rough background, you know. This is his way, I suppose, of assuring himself about his accomplishments. He just loves them. I tell him it's silly. But you know Franklin.

"I enjoy the collection, of course. Yes. I do.

"It's quite nice."

She pointed out various Chinese something or others – dynasty plates and trays and a few early nineteen hundred woven Apache baskets in the corner. "How about a nice cup of tea?" she asked.

Just then, Franklin K. Wheeler strode in, creating a turbulent breeze in spite of his slow gait.

He was tall and his body had been hung on a hefty frame. His six-two, wide-shouldered stature filled the room. But, he was, in some unmeasured way, diminished.

Sort of a bull moose in a minor key. Sophie Wheeler faded into the wall.

He stuck out a calloused hand that. The handshake was firm but betrayed the beginnings of Parkinson's. He held onto mine for a moment. He wore a large diamond ring on the pinky on his right shake hand. His eyes were wet black and intense with the lids falling slightly into the pupil space beneath black slightly bushy eyebrows. His beard was shadowy, hair thin and receding leaving two abutting edges. Narrow lips tried to grin, showing just a smidgeon of perfect white teeth. Everything about him was cut into angles, shoulders sharp, and a little bony, square firm chin. He wore a striped yellow tie, big Windsor knot, and a tan sport jacket; light gray, gabardine slacks.

The total was as if he had been put together by Gentlemen's Quarterly for a thirties movie. "Thank you for corning by, Mr. Ace."

His voice boomed and commanded. "Yes, yes, we've met before I think. I told Sophie we've met before."

"We have, at Hollywood Park, but only casually. Through John."

I remained standing as he did.

"And nice to see you looking well, especially after what happened. To your trainer and a good friend. Very sorry," I said.

"Goddamned terrible thing. I know your relationship to John. "Crushing blow. Crushing." His voice lowered as he spoke about John. Was he theater trained, too? "We were close. Yes, we were. I relied on him quite a bit. It's beyond belief, isn't it?" He turned away and then suddenly back at me as if not being sure what he saw on me or in me. "Here, here. Have a seat." He pointed at one of the blue fish couches, shook his head and closed his eyes reassuring me of his deep feelings. He sat down on the edge of the twin blue dolphin couch, crossed his hands, "Well, I'm going to come right to the point." His voice rose. "As you must have guessed, we have to find that boy, Mr. Ace. My grandson. I've talked to the police. I was thinking of hiring my own investigators. I expect everyone to do his part. We have to this hard and fast. Damn those lowlifes who did this." He shook his head sadly. "You know, back when I was growing up – those days we would have said hang 'em all by the you know whats."

His hollow black eyes peered at me all at once looking around for Sophie, a little uncertain as if what he had said was not refined enough for his position in life. Then he sent out a little smile with pink gums showing. Cheeks slightly hollowed out.

"I'll buy that."

"Right. Absolutely. Of course. I know you must have been wanting to see me. As the police did. You were his friend. He spoke of you often."

"We were close." Close was a relative term. "I wanted to know his…"

"Yes. Yes. I can tell you but right now I need your help." I was going to say the same but waited. He was in the mood to talk. He sat easily uncomfortably, shifting now and then as if to relieve his weight on his lower back. Sophie stared at him as though grading his performance. He glanced at her and quickly.

He smoothed his tie, shifted his weight again, hesitated. I assumed he was waiting for some sign of approval from Sophie. He cleared his throat, "I told Sophie exactly what I'm going to tell you. The police are a bunch of dumbbells. Not a smart bunch. They just aren't – lucky to have graduated High School."

"They seem smart enough."

"Are they?"

The LAPD didn't need my vocal support, but I said, "Mr. Wheeler, they do well with what they have. Half of them graduated college. Small number for very large city." I didn't know if I was right. But the Department needed a god word just then.

He murmured something indecipherable and shook his head. "Listen," he said, finally, "I heard about your filly. They call her '*The Silk*,' don't they? The grapevine, you know. Can't keep secrets at the track. And I was always interested in what John was doing for others. Tried to keep him just for myself, but he insisted on helping too many others. Argued with him about that…no sir."

"Well, he seemed—"

Wheeler waved his hand and interrupted. "He spread himself too thin. Told me the connection with you and that you only had this one filly, so I didn't argue about that. Just so you know. "If you ever want a buyer for that *Silk* filly, let me know. John said she was a winner." He reached around to the table next to him. "Care for some candy? We get this great candy. Right, Sophie?" He shoved an open box at me.

"What kind is it, Soph?" He called out like she was not sitting right next to him. "What is this stuff?"

"It's just *Sees*, dear. *Sees* candy. Nougat centers. Remember?"

"Yes, yes, of course. Sees. Want some?

"Tried to buy the whole business must've been thirty or more years ago. But no luck. Family was in control. I'm crazy about the nutty ones. Keep six or seven boxes around. We do, don't we, Sophie?"

She nodded patiently.

I demurred. The air was empty.

After he had adjusted himself on the couch again, he launched into what seemed like a prepared speech about how much he cared for John and how much his grandson meant to him and how shocked and sick he was "about the whole terrible, terrible mess."

When he talked about his grandson, he had a miniscule waver in his voice. He cleared his throat to hide perhaps his only soft spot. His eyebrows had a way of moving up and down with each phrase. It was like a "tell" in a poker game.

I hadn't figured what the "tell" told me yet. But he was certain about everything he said.

He mentioned his dead daughter but stopped as if about to enter sacred territory, and finally, with a hushed voice that didn't fit, he said, "I'd like to change his name to Wheeler. I mean the boy. Seems fitting, doesn't it? – He's a Wheeler and all that's left of the family is Frankie, Mr. Ace. He's a Wheeler. And we have to find him. And that is an absolute and you know what then."

We sat there staring at one another. "Maybe the name ought to be up to the boy. He is John Augers' kid," I said.

Unexpectedly, Wheeler's stood. "That's not the way it's going to be! You ought to know that. John is gone. The boy is a Wheeler. He's my boy now. And he's certainly too young to decide anything for himself." Tears came to his eyes. They may have belonged to a crocodile.

"Now dear," Sophie Wheeler said from her corner, "Don't get so upset. Frankie will come out of it – we will find him. Just give it time. He will decide, I'm sure. If someone wants money for him, we'll give it to them."

She sat with her hands on her lap, prim and proper – the picture of someone who had been forced to sign a pre-nuptial agreement and wasn't sure that caring about anything was useful.

"Oh, stop it, Sophie!" He rose and took a lap around the couch. "All that Pollyana stuff is silly. Your San Diego blue-collar heritage is showing. Those people want everything I've got. Whoever they are. You know that. We will get a note for millions soon enough." He sat down then rose and then sat again. "I planned it all, everything, to go to Frankie, eventually. The whole damn thing, with provisions for you, Sophie, of course. You know that."

Sophie gave him a hard look and a hump. Her back straightened like it was infused with s shot of steel. Then turned away.

"Planned it all. To Frankie. John to handle things and then Frankie. John knew how to handle things. Not anyone else."

"You forgot…"

"I didn't forget anything." He avoided Sally's name or memory. He looked at his wife and nodded vigorously as though assuring himself he was right. "Now that he's gone, it's all upside down. It's just a mess. All my choices seem to be nil and none! You, Mr. Ace, seem to be in the middle. Lots of votes out there. The whole thing is Harry's folly."

"Oh, Franklin, calm down.

"How can you say that?

"You know what you insisted on with Harry."

"He twisted it!"

She didn't respond.

"He made it seem right at the time."

"No one wants anything from you...dear. You did what you wanted to do. Mr. Ace has to know the reality if he can be expected to help." Her eyes flashed sharply. There was resentment in them.

He must have seen what I saw. "You are well taken care of. And that boy of yours."

"A pittance, Franklin. You know that."

"Sophie, this is not the time or place. Enough of this. We have to find Frankie. That will take care of the problems."

He softened.

His temper had caused him to reveal more than he intended. He knew that he should let others do the talking. "Alright, alright."

He got up and turned away and breathed angrily. The sky color of the couch reflected on his face. What was left of his hair was pasted to his head by new sweat, reflecting the vague satin blue.

I interposed, "Can we get to the heart of the matter, Mr. Wheeler? I need to know everything you know."

"Yeah. Good. Thank you. To the point. Right? I'm not thinking straight." He stuffed a chocolate nut in his mouth and chewed, swallowed and said, softly, "Say, Sophie dear, can't we get a cup of that tea here?"

"Of course, Franklin.

"My goodness, I've forgotten my manners."

She disappeared.

"Look here, I'm going to be Guardian of Frankie. There isn't anyone in that boy's life except me and Sophie. I created the trusts and the Foundation and dumped most of my life in them – well, dammit, basically all of it – so I ought to be the one who runs it now that John's gone. Actually, I have to be. "You gonna run it? All of it? Or that idiot at the Foundation? Harry set it up that way."

His right fist smacked into his left palm. "I'm going to do whatever needs to be done. You understand that, Mister Ace? You understand?"

"Hey, Mr. Wheeler, it's your life. Do whatever suits you. Haven't you already start taking over? I need to know whatever you know about what happened. Details." I couldn't help the edge in my voice. He was a hard guy to like.

He waved his hand, the one with the diamonds ring as big as a thoroughbred's ear. "That is the past. What's done is done. Something strange has come up. Not just the horrible crime, but –" he leaned forward, "but something is really funny." His forehead crinkled. He had a way of tucking in his chin when he spoke creating a dark whiskered double chin. He waved a finger. "They want someone else to be legal guardian of Frankie's person. Someone else! I didn't even know there was such a thing; a guardian of Frankie's estate and a different guardian of the person.

"And they want that guardian of the person to become a Trustee and a member of the Foundation. That's Harry for you. I don't mind telling you that I don't like the idea at all! Something fishy going on! I'm the kids' grandfather. Only living blood relative. That ought to be enough! More than enough!"

"Who do you mean – they?"

"Ann Whitson, that's who! Harry Moss and Ann Whitson! His secretary. The way I get it from Harry is that Frankie's shrink, or whatever the hell he is, up in Mara Bay, claims he wants someone who can relate to the kid better than I can. Relate! Can you believe that? I'm his grandfather and Harry has the gall to call me and tell me what's best for my grandkid!

"It's fishy, I tell you. Fishy! Who the hell can relate better than me?" He continued. "I'm his blood. And they say I'm too old. Seventy-nine is too old? Well, Mr. Ace, I don't use these phrases anymore, but bullshit! They're fuckin' crazy!

"That's what. Crazy! Sorry, Sophie for the language." He turned to her with a stone face making both of us know he wasn't sorry one bit. "I know how you hate coarse language. Can you imagine?"

He turned back to me. "They live in a whitewashed world, like some politician. Shrinks are shrinks because they're all crazy – that's item number one. They wouldn't know how to balance their own checkbooks! That's item number two. And Moss doesn't have the staff and knowledge to handle anything, He's smart but, maybe too smart, but he's long past his prime. That's item number three. And so far as I can tell, those shrink people will say anything and make it sound like it was God's word and sensible and make me sound crazy at the same time! And the fucking Bank – they think

148

everything has to be done professionally which only mean they do it their way. They have to hire experts and all that just to cover their hind end. All that means is that they avoid liability. That's all they do. Avoid liability! Experts know nothing! Can you imagine? Banks want agents to take the heat. You think any one of those numbskulls could make the same fortune I have? Well, they couldn't. Professional, my ass! And they're not too smart, besides." He finished with a flourish. "This Whitson girl is supposed to have a boy just about Frankie's age – so they can relate!"

I interrupted, "Ann Whitson's kid is seventeen. There's nothing in the world a seventeen year relates to except maybe Superman and Dolly Parton's tits. So, let's talk reality. Who is going to be you lawyer in this? Harry can't represent her. In conflict with you."

Sophie returned with a tray of cups and silver decanter of hot water and Jasmine tea bags and poured two cups.

I waved the cream and sugar, bounced the tea bag in the cup and took my time. He was right. Something was fishy. "Bullshit," I said.

"It's all bullshit. Now I gotta go get another lawyer to deal with my lawyer? Bullshit is right!"

"Wheeler…"

He got up. His hands clenched.

I stayed seated.

"You with him?"

"Listen," I said very softly, "it could be this is Harry's way of insuring the smooth and proper administration of the trusts, that the guardianship business is all perfectly sensible in these circumstances. Just keep it all in the family, so to speak. Close at hand."

I took a sip of my cold coffee. Case going in wrong directions. Decided then that Wheeler was the butt of the problem – but maybe not the perp.

"I'm his grandfather. That ought to be enough!

"I don't need another damn lawyer! It's all because of those damn doctors up at Mara Bay!" He turned slowly and gazed through the French Doors to the trimmed green angular perfection of the rear yard.

He sat down again on the edge of one of the blue satin couches.

"Now Please, dear, you have to stay calm, Really." She turned to me. "He has pressure problems, you know." She smiled a condescending smile which she flashed around – teeth like a florescent tube.

"Please don't patronize me, Soph, I know you mean best. Maybe that boy of yours can help. You know, Ace, he's a graduate of Cornell. But there's nothing wrong with me that some sense in this world wouldn't cure. Now, I'm just telling you, Ace, what we want from Harry. You go to him. You are

149

in the hot seat now. Right? This had become your hot potato. That detective fellow said you wanted to take over but they were concerned about it. You're the alternate in the trusts. John insisted. So, you're in the middle whether you like it or not. Everyone involved probably knows that already. Harry's very efficient that way. But this guardianship nonsense has got to be changed. Don't they have to have a hearing on it?"

Sophie's fingers twined themselves together and slowly twisted as Franklin spoke. Sophie had a worried look which was not about Franklin and which was another first impression. I finished the tea. And a cookie.

"Tell me what John's actions were the week before this all happened? There might be something you noticed or something he said."

He waved his arms and started all over again. "How can that Whitson woman know anything about Frankie? "I ask you, how? Goes to show you. All of them figured, even Sophie here, that someone else was better for Frankie than me. You said that, Sophie. You shouldn't have."

"I didn't say any such thing."

"You did. Harry came here to get all the stuff signed. With that girl and her notary stuff. That Whitson girl. That's what you said. Someone the boy can relate to. "Can you beat that?"

I let the dust settle for a minute. "What appears certain," I said, finally, "Is that if someone controls Frankie's estate, Frankie's trust, they control John's interest, too…so they basically control you. Right?"

"Over my dead body, Ace! Now, my own lawyer is betraying me. Where do I go from here?"

"Obviously another lawyer."

"I don't want to think about it. Harry said the hearing on the petition to be guardian of Frankie's person is coming up in three weeks." His palms opened up.

His shoulders jerked upward.

"Not of the trust. The guardian makes all the decisions? No fucking way!"

He shook his head. One thin strand of hair fell into his face.

Wheeler began to walk in agitated circles again, head down as if watching his empire crumble at his feet.

"There are things pending. No one else knows how to get it done. The highway property is ready to go. I've zoning and highway issues, and stop signs, and parking headaches. You think Harry knows what to do? I don't need this crap."

"Mr. Wheeler, I don't see how Moss can file a petition or make recommendations against his client – which is you. That's clearly a conflict.

Are you certain this is what he has suggested and is it really what he is trying to do?"

"Quite positive, Ace. Quite positive. He says it is what's best for the child and is exactly within the law. I say he cannot do this." He looked at Sophie.

She remained still.

More than still.

She was a statue staring at nothing.

"I don't really know how I can help," I said. "You need a lawyer to get rid of a lawyer. They're like super glue with each other. Perhaps Moss has perfectly legitimate events in mind. Maybe he believes what he says. "But I think you need a non-local firm of lawyers to deal with this. You don't need me. But I need you. John was assassinated. Remember?"

"Nothing. I saw nothing, except when John and Harry came over and we signed all the papers. And Sophie said, something like maybe its best. I know what's going on..." He snickered to himself as though he had just busted open a quark. "It's Sally. She's got together with all of them."

"Oh, Franklin. Please," Sophie said. He ignored her.

"Go ahead. Don't pay attention. Just like always."

He wasn't having it...not going to contend with her. "Listen, Ace, the worst way to fight a lawyer is with a lawyer Trust me. They don't like anyone telling them what is ethical. Everything they do is ethical. Just ask one. Or a judge. They can't force this down my throat. I'm the best thing for Frankie. I'll do it my way. There are ways –"

He pointed a finger at my chest as if that was the last word on the entire subject. "There are ways."

"Look, Wheeler, I'm trying to tell you, this is not my kind of thing. It's terrible story and I'm sorry as hell for all the misery you people have had. But I'm just a bystander really. I have my own agenda and it's not this. And you're not helping me find Frankie right now. Anything more that was said, or done by John, or anyone before this happening that might help me."

"You say I'm not helping. I've got the management of the trusts to worry about, and a secretary with power over things she knows nothing about and you tell me I'm not helping." His voice grew into a snarl. "You have a damn lot of nerve."

"That attitude won't help. I'm trying to help."

Sophie came over and stood behind Wheeler. Her hand went to his shoulder. Her fingers squeezed.

"That's enough, Sophie. I'm fine. Mr. Ace isn't going to be trouble."

I took a chance. "Did you trust John? Completely, I mean?"

"Totally. Totally. Totally. We did, didn't we, Sophie? He and Sally had a couple of years of idyllic married life. Before…"

"Not that long, dear. But she was in good spirits when John decided to call it off."

"I thought she had been committed by you or John to an institution in Mara Bay? How could that be idyllic or she be in good spirits?"

Wheeler looked up at his wife searching for an answer. She straightened and said, "She was simply under the weather. Tired. Exhausted. The strain of living John's sort of life was too much and she needed…she needed a break. Dr. Simon suggested this place and it was nice."

I, of course, knew that Doctors were not immune to the needs of life, of the requirements of their practices.

"The doctor suggested she be institutionalized?"

Wheeler held up his hand to stop me from more. "Enough, Ace. She was sick. She had to be put into someplace. She had to."

Sophie's face hardened. Her eyes narrowed. "Tired, Franklin?"

"Just tired. That's all."

"And then she died. Suddenly."

"She was sick, Ace. Dammit, Sophie. Tell him. She was unbalanced. My own goddamned fault. Spoiled. Totally spoiled."

That's not what she died from. They were holding back. Or, one of them was. "Was there a Coroner's report?"

"I don't know. I asked Harry about that. He just told me there must have been one. And that was it. She was cremated within a few hours of her death. I couldn't handle it. Sophie handled all those details. There was no fuss. Glad Sophie managed. Don't think you're getting it, Ace." He poked a finger into one of the blue cushions. "You're just not getting it. I got off the track – you're not here just to listen to me carry on. I agreed to see you to help save Frankie—"

"But, Mr. Wheeler, I'm the alternate Trustee, like you said. Like Harry said. I am in charge. The 'it' guy like you said. Someone to take care of Frankie is not a threat."

"You aren't too bright, are you? Don't you know that what that boy says – when he is found and that's what you are going to do – He said, 'No.' What he says goes. So, that's your job, Mr. Ace. That's why I said to Sophie, 'bring him here' when you called. You find Frankie and make a pretty penny in the process. Listen, this doctor they're shoving at me; the shrink who thinks he knows what's best, he must be some kind of charlatan."

"Right? Harry says he's got a big reputation. Name's Evons or something like that."

"He's the head honcho at the Bright Paths Institute, that kid's division they have. Everything for kids is separate there. My Foundation donates money to that place. That place has been washed clean. They are on the up and up. Sophie just seems to go along with whatever some doctor says." He threw a thumb in her direction. "She believes all that stuff."

Sophie blushed and turned away but I caught a look of disgust on her face at the same time.

The afternoon sun suddenly reflected off a window at the back of the house and shot a beam across her face. It was a soft face gone hard, carrying secrets. She quickly moved out of the sudden light. Wheeler's head dropped. He was haggard.

But he wasn't beaten. "Getting John out of the way may have seemed smart to some people, and maybe... Well, just maybe." His head rose slowly and he stared at me, pointed and growled, "Find my grandson. Find him!"

Franklin Wheeler was a significant force to contend with, even though at the moment he was older than his chronological age and beaten down. "The school people, they have to be behind this, too.

I'm strapped down by lawyers and doctors and I feel like I can't make a move," he said, quietly back in control. "Not something I'm accustomed to, Ace. There's no legitimate reason for Harry to go along with this guardian nonsense.

"Something's not right in Denmark, if you know what I mean. This is not right. Not right at all. Who put them all up to it? Who told them?"

"Oh, Franklin," Sophie murmured, soothingly, "you're getting yourself all upset just because you don't agree with the doctors. I'm sure they want the best for him. I'm sure that's all it is."

"Now, Sophie – I told you, I'm not in the old folk's home yet. I'm not cuckoo. This Mrs. Whitson," he leaned close to me, "doesn't she sound a little...off base...that she would do this? For Harry or for anyone? Sort of adopt a little autistic boy? It doesn't fit, even though the Trust must pay her plenty. And I can't set her fee. I guess the Court does. Or, what about you? You're the alternate. I'm telling you, Mr. Harvey Ace, sure as I'm sitting here, I'm their target. There has to be more to their plans. Get to me through Frankie."

My tea was cold, but I sipped and listened. It all sounded like the usual family fight, but it wasn't usual. Everything about it leaked deceit and suspicion, yet might likely be completely innocent – and paranoid – at the same time. Why didn't Harry tell me about this? About Ann? Why didn't she? He warned me to watch out for Franklin as though the old man was going to pick my pocket. What about Ann? Would she lend herself to this without severe pressure or some other involvement?

"This is where you come in, Mr. Ace. Finding Frankie is first. Then I need ammunition against them...or..."

"Who?" I insisted. "Who do you need ammunition against?"

"Who? Harry and that Whitson woman! That's who. They have designs on my entire estate. They're in cahoots with the doctors who have been treating Frankie. Known Harry for years but can't afford to take chances. Not for a minute."

"Maybe he just needs the money. Harry, I mean. But I can tell you, there's something funny going on. Control of Frankie means all of them could get effective control of John's trust assets. And Sally's. It's the first step in their plan. And John's position in the Foundation, control of that, too. Control of that trust in the wrong hands, as well as John's trust and my personal trust will ruin me! No question. A good portion of my stock holdings in FK Wheeler Construction are also in that boy's trust. I need to stop them. Need to know everything about them. Every move they make. I want to know whenever they are go to the bathroom. And what they're up to. And who is involved. There has to be big money involved. Assassins don't kill for fun. Who? Deposits or checks or something."

"Oh Franklin, please," Sophie soothed again, "Mrs. Whitson is to have only control of the person, not any of the trusts. Franklin, you're upset about nothing. Not good. The doctors told you. I don't see how that Ann person could hurt you. She's a perfectly nice woman. I've known her for a while, too. I got her the job. And I don't know what money you mean."

"Today the person and tomorrow the whole damn ballgame. That is what you don't see."

Sunset rays bounced off one of the blue vases into Franklin's eyes. He put a hand up shielding himself and moved in his seat.

"Why do you want me?" I asked again. "Remember, it was Harry Moss who asked me to come here in the first place. He seemed to be worried about you. I can't believe he will represent Whitson in a Petition against you for control of the boy. Even though it is only as a guardian for the boy, it's a conflict. He'll be suspended, or disbarred."

"He must know that. So, it means he has something else up his sleeve. You figure it out."

"I can't.

"He's got more to gain than his useless license. He just thinks he's smarter than I am. But he isn't. No one's getting control. I don't want Ann Whitson or anyone else to be Frankie's Guardian. I'm his grandfather. That trumps all. Transferring all those assets into those trusts and to the Foundation seemed the right thing. Harry's great idea to beat the IRS. I had confidence in him and in John. Harry has wonderful credentials. Did you know he was an IRS agent for ten years? Yale Law School. But it's all baloney, isn't it? Just baloney. And now, John is gone," he finally muttered, "even Sophie is against me."

He didn't look at her.

I did. She was dead panned. Her face was set in granite. Cheekbones tight. A distance rolled into her eyes. They grew dark. She was not with us – in a world of her own. Neither of them had considered the possibility that their Grandson was dead. The idea was too painful.

Franklin wiped his face and closed his eyes.

Franklin's right hand reached up to Sophie's. But when she looked down at him, it wasn't with love.

She straightened. "Franklin, I'm asking you not to make trouble. That's all. I didn't tell you to go along or agree to anything. And pursuing all this about John is useless. The police can do it very well and I'm sure will. I really don't want to hear all this wrangling. You need not agree to anything. I don't want you to be upset...all this wrangling."

"That's not the way you said it yesterday."

"That's the way I meant it." She stretched for a ceramic-jeweled cigarette box, extracted one, and held it angrily in the two fingers of her left hand. She lit it with an ivory lighter and blew the first puff right at Franklin. "I don't smoke anymore," she said turning to face me, "really, I don't, but I still grab a cigarette lately to still my nerves with all this wrangling."

A phone ring interrupted and rang several times in the background.

I heard a Latin voice answer.

"I don't mean to berate you, Sophie, really, I don't.

"But you simply seem to contest everything I say about what to do and what is right."

"I'm sorry, Franklin.

I didn't think I was. Honestly, dear. I'm thinking of you. Didn't seem to me that having a guardian of Frankie's person, a nice woman, a trusted person, was a reason to be so upset. That's not good for you. I just think we should wait before we take any ill-considered actions. What we decide may be dangerous, too. Putting Mr. Ace in the middle may be dangerous...for him and perhaps for us, too. We don't know yet." She touched his sleeve.

He shook his head again in a sad slow shake. "You're not listening. Not listening. Sophie, sitting and twirling our thumbs solves nothing!" He sat back and fixed his gaze on me, just as the sun was swallowed into the

155

western horizon and got lost in the Pacific. A lean and dark aging tiger at bay. "Sally's out there. I know she is."

I wanted out of there, too. I was in the middle of husband and wife bickering about family affairs.

However revealing, it was, it was not the place to be. "Well, I appreciate your confidence," I said to Wheeler. "But except for knowing more about what happened to John, and why, and hoping to perhaps be of some help to the authorities in finding Frankie, I don't think I'm interested in trust affairs or family feuds. I'll find the boy. For me. And I'll find John's killers and whatever additional debris is in the way. But I don't want to be involved in these family things."

"Things? Things? You don't want to work for me? That's it, isn't it?"

"Not at all, Mr. Wheeler. Nothing to do with it." I rose. Time to get out of there. But he was going to make an offer. It was hard to avoid hearing it. He knew that part of me wanted the assignment. However, for reasons of experience and the heartache that comes of family affairs, especially with children, I sensed the unhappiness that was in store for all of us, that the path would be twisted and tangled and would involve me in the family business, which was always a bad idea. I also knew that either Franklin or Sophie or both would be on my ass every minute. On the other hand, as they say, everything in life is a negotiation, a balancing act. We have all gone through periods of self-enlightenment. The last few days were mine.

As I listened to Wheeler, recollections crowded my head. I recalled my father saying, "You don't want to do that for me?" He was thunderstruck. Astonished that his son would refuse him. Didn't remember what it was but did remember that I didn't want to do it. He was a man who was sought after by a different company every couple of years, a glad handing, gambling and boozing ladies' man, thoroughly charming, as he charmed his way up the ladder. He had an ability to find a business weakness, poke it, reveal it, and "thin the ranks" as he called it.

And he had a near desperate need to look down on the world instead of up to anything, resulting in my strong desire to stay put, in my neat beach condo, in my familiar environs, with my habits, friends, forego booze, keep my socks in color order, and t-shirts separate from shorts, to leave nothing on the floor. In short, I wanted every tomorrow to be the same as every yesterday, except I wanted Sarah. And I needed winners. I told myself it would all work out. It would.

Sarah would come back and say she was sorry. The sun would shine and we would all be happy to stay put. My filly would win the Derby. But my reflective inner self said, hey, Ace, maybe you are full of shit. Maybe you're just afraid to invest instead of gamble. Staying out of family affairs was a good idea.

"Mr. Wheeler, there are a dozen people who could handle this. I am only the Executor of John's estate. I want to locate Frankie and find who killed John as much or even more than you do but it's essentially police work. Maybe, I'll just watch from the sidelines. Just let the police handle it."

Getting involved with the Wheeler's would be not only a pain in the ass but also dangerous. I rose and gave Sophie a slight bow and started towards the entrance.

Wheeler took a step toward me. "I didn't tell you what I would pay," he said. "Look," he smiled, showing all those teeth and pink gums holding on to a secret surprise. He picked up a bust of a male figure decorated very lightly in blue and gold cap trimmed with a faded red wash over the gold. "Han Dynasty – 1496." Wheeler was instantly transported to a time six centuries ago when, a person in his position could snap his fingers and his will would be done.

"Very beautiful," I murmured. But I don't think I want to know what you will pay. You don't seem to understand what I'm saying, you have to advise the police and give them specific reasons and evidence of illegal stuff. I'm going to do what I'm going to do. And it doesn't have anything to do with you…unless…this is a game you are enjoying."

"Minimum retainer ten thousand," he interrupted. Queen Sophie blurted, "Franklin, no."

. "Hundred dollars an hour on top," He said. Make it one twenty-five. Plus, expenses. Get ten in front. Find Frankie and learn everything about John, Harry Moss and that woman, the doctor or anyone involved. Good or bad. No preconceptions. I know about you. I know you can do it. You beat the police to the punch every time."

After a moment of internal math, I said, "I don't beat them to anything, Mr. Wheeler. Really. Let me give you some free advice. And you know what that is worth. Number one, get a different lawyer. You don't need me for that. Contrary to popular opinion, they're not all bad." I kept moving towards the door.

"Number two, try to recall every minute of John's life and yours this last couple of months."

Franklin pleaded, "Just do this for John, for the boy. You have to do it for them." He almost said please. "You're already involved with the estate, Mr. Ace. You have to see Moss now and then.

"It's a perfect fit.

"He wouldn't suspect."

I shook my head. "Intrigue between the principles.

"How about getting a larger investigative group involved.

"Maybe Golden Investigations. They could do this."

"I know what you can do. I know all about you. I'm sending you a check. And you're in the middle now anyway. You're stuck in the middle. You can't just turn me down like this." His eyes grew thin. He reached for my sleeve. I thought for a moment he would cry. But he steeled up. Chin out. Ten years younger. "Maybe you're in cahoots with them. Maybe that's it. Right?"

I waved my hand. "Forget it, Mr. Wheeler. You're barking up the wrong cahoots. Thanks for the tea and conversation." I nodded at Sophie Wheeler. Franklin's hand dropped, with noticeable tremors. "I'll call you tonight, Ace. I don't intend to forget it!"

I left him at the doorstep of his very large house, muttering to himself – justifying himself Sophie was silent, withdrawn, no smiles.

My sense was that Franklin Wheeler seldom understood anything about other people. I suspected that very successful people, super successful, do not really care what is in the inside of others except when it suits their purposes. Caring was superfluous.

I climbed into my car and sat for several moments contemplating what ten thousand dollars and probably a lot more could do for me and wondering if I was an idiot. However, the prospect of dealing with the Wheeler family and Moss and Ann Whitson and the lot of them was not in my Futures Book. Then I drove south to the Fremont Street exit at Olympic Boulevard, except I had forgotten that it had long since been closed to automobiles.

I turned back and headed for the Wilshire exit on the north.

The exit was dressed in ivy, a few tiger lilies adorning the top.

Sophie waited at one of the stone pillars, blue dress, smoking fiercely, with hard gray, unblinking eyes.

She waved me to stop.

Stood right in front of the car. And came to my window.

"I have to speak to you. Please."

I nodded.

"Please."

"OK, climb in."

I said nothing and drove east a few blocks on Wilshire and then back to Olympic to a local used car lot along the boulevard and parked. Advertising banners fluttered in the breezes. We were in the middle of Koreatown which spread along Olympic Boulevard and cut a straight line directly to the new Staples Center, the Convention Center and all the new and upscale condos just south of the Civic Center. East to the #5 Interstate Freeway. It was hard to find a commercial sign in English along Olympic until you reached Staples Center in the heart of the south end of downtown LA.

I asked Sophie to toss out her cigarette which she did.

"I thought I quit. But this has been too much. This is all too much."

She had a red knitted scarf around her neck. "You probably won't believe this, but in spite of what appears, Mr. Ace, I am very fond of Mr. Wheeler.

"Even though we snap at each other now and then, he has been very good to me.

"Even with his strange family as well as with mine, he was always thoughtful. I want to keep him well and happy in spite of all this misery.

"And I'm not sure I know how."

"Just agree with him."

"Yes, that's one way.

"The way of wives of yesteryear."

"And you're not one of those."

"Correct. I'm not one of those. Never. But the reality is, and you probably won't believe this either, the reality is that the ghost of Sally Augers is still haunting us. Franklin feels it very strongly. And I think the possibility that she is actually alive scares him. I think –" she hesitated, looked at me long and hard in her sharp way. "Don't get me wrong – anything is possible. And he is guilty. Very guilty. He feels it every day."

I put on my listening face. A belief that Sally Augers was something more than a memory by Franklin Wheeler was intriguing.

Maybe Moss was right, the two of them, father and daughter, were unbalanced.

Perhaps time and trouble had taken its toll. Maybe when she was a child... But there seemed to be nothing unbalanced about this person in front of me.

Calm and purposeful.

"I know it sounds strange," she said, "but I've had this feeling that she's close by. Waiting and scheming. I think she's real, too. Strange, isn't it? Actually, it's more than that." She looked at me as if expecting a dismissing frown.

"Feelings start from facts, Mrs. Wheeler. You have to have more than a feeling. "After all, dead is dead. You were the one who arranged it."

"I told you it sounds silly. "Sally and I were close, but that was at the beginning.

"She was very unfortunate and inherited and very bad gene from her mother. She was unbalanced. That's what it was – unbalanced. And very devious. You know, the way Franklin set it up, she would not get control so long as John and Frankie were alive. She would not. She would not control those trusts as well as a lot of other assets. Now they're dead and gone. Didn't Harry tell you that? Franklin's scared out of his wits by that possibility. So am I. Not for my sake, mind you. We'd all be in serious trouble if that were the case. And she hated him. An insane, livid hate."

"If he loses control, seems to me you lose, too, Mrs. Wheeler. In this hiatus time, I'm going to do what's right about everything. But I need to know, are you asking for help for yourself as well as your husband?"

She sighed. "My life depends on him."

Her carefully designed nose came close to me as well as those determined eyes and uplifted breasts.

For a moment, I thought she would punch me or kiss me, but all at once, she sighed and her shoulders collapsed and she became quite vulnerable. Her face grew into a troubled darkness. Her eyes narrowed and darted away. Everyone has their own agenda. The world is full of private agendas. I gave her another rundown of the facts. "There was a Death Certificate. Harry made it quite clear even though he never got it recorded. And there was a medical report, and perhaps a coroner's report as to the cause of death. That's a lot of people to be involved in a conspiracy about Sally's death," I said. "And why would this ghost hang around?"

"I'm not crazy," she replied, as if reading my mind.

"I really do care for Franklin.

"And he and I have to think of Frankie, that poor boy. In spite of all his worries, I don't want Franklin to go into his last years a lost old fool believing he had not done his very best in terrible circumstances. He's not at his best right now. And for him not to be in control of his own fortune, under whatever situation might exist, would be a tragedy. Yes, my life is tied to his. Utterly. Like chains. His fear is real."

"You had her cremated. She is dead. That's that. All this hocus pocus is nonsense. Unless..."

"Unless what?"

"Didn't answer than. But said, "Franklin should ask me directly...ask me to find her if he believes she's still out there?"

"Figure it out for yourself."

I did. The possibility was strong that Franklin was behind the kidnapping and didn't want the boy to be found. "She murmured what I was thinking.

"He doesn't want anyone to find her. If they did, he believes he is cooked. He would be in Sally's clutches. She would control. She needs to be dead. We have to find Frankie. We have to control. If anyone tries to take over in this hiatus surrounding John's death and Frankie's disappearance, I can assure you, Franklin will just mow them down. He's getting ready. He's lining up people and banks and brokers. It will be a terrible fight. We need your help to prevent all of this. The Will puts you on the Board of the Foundation. You have to find the boy. Franklin doesn't believe in letting public servants do his work. He never has. Private. Not government. He wants you. So do I." She reached into a small purse and started to extract a cigarette and changed her mind. "She leaned her head back and closed her eyes. "Maybe Harry is behind the whole damn mess."

"Killing and kidnapping? I don't think Moss is our boy. He isn't very relevant in his world anymore. Just as Ann Whitson told me, he is an old horse with tired talents. But anything is possible. Frankly, Mrs. Wheeler, I can't help. We need facts. Everyone involved has a motive."

I examined her cold, quiet countenance carefully as though I would find a false note in her eyes. Age lines spread out from the tips of those piercing orbs. "What can you tell me?"

"I saw her," she whispered. "That willow tree on the property, near the driveway!" she said, "Late one night. She was there, in the middle of the falling branches and leaves, hidden but quite clearly there. It was only for a moment as if she wanted me to be sure. And then she was suddenly gone…but she was there."

"If true it means that the mortuary didn't do its job. What motive do they have unless someone else got to them with money before you did."

She closed her eyes. Sophie had arranged the cremation of Sally yet claimed she saw her recently. Big time liar or another nut case in a long line of nut cases in Wheeler's life."

Her chin down to her chest. "I saw her. She's real. I know you won't believe me. You can't say anything to Franklin except to agree with what he says. She's quite real. I know." She pulled a slip of paper out of her bosom.

"Here's my check."

She handed me a folded green check.

"Use discretion. That's all I want."

"You want me to investigate the lawyer I'm working for?"

"If that's where it takes you."

"I don't want your money."

"This won't work. I'll go where the facts take me."

"If that's a problem for you, I'm sorry. But I don't want your money."

She pushed my hand away. Shoved the check between my legs.

"Take the money. Discretion, Mr. Ace, Discretion." She kissed the tips of her fingers and placed them on my forehead, thought a moment and leaned over the gear handle quickly and kissed my cheek and her hand squeezed my

161

thigh. "I'll call you," she whispered. "You can be sure." She slipped out onto Olympic Boulevard. We were about three blocks from her home. There was a slight wind tossing her hair.

"I can't leave you here," I shouted. I leaned to the driver's side window and called again into the breeze. "I haven't agreed to do this!"

She waved back and mouthed the words, "I saw her."

People are crazy. Sophie and Franklin Wheeler could be proof positive. I shoved the check into my jacket. I would send it back later that day. I thought of a line from H. L. Mencken… *To every human problem, there is a neat and easy solution – and it is always wrong.*

Chapter Twelve

My filly was big. As big as colts. Deep barrel chest, as if a Beverly Hills plastic surgeon had worked his wonders on her, white blaze in a triangle down that chest and inquisitive brown eyes. She looked like burnished gold. Pulpit progeny were often big. Big isn't always good. Native Diver wasn't big. Determine wasn't big. All champions.

However, if you're well conformed, big is better. Longer stride. Less stress.

Citation was big and majestic, and Round Table and Man O'War and Silky Sullivan, who was among the prettiest of the lot, satin gold reflecting off his coat. He was, however, perhaps the laziest of the lot. Citation was definitely the most elegant. Perhaps the best of all. Nineteen wins, though the English stallion, Noor, beat him 4 times. First two times with almost twenty pounds less at a mile and a quarter and only by a whisker. I was standing at the rail in the infield and was no more than ten yards from the finish line at the first of Noor's wins. Citation was as elegant as a king. The famous lady horse of the era, Ruffian, was not big but the best of all the ladies up to this date. She had the courage of a dozen lions. The ladies were always the toughest and the most ferocious in protecting their dynasties. Her heart never gave out but her legs did, in the middle of a mile match race in July, 1975, against the Kentucky Derby winner of that year, Foolish Pleasure, they raced head to head from the very start. Ruffian on the outside. Into the backstretch, they were still head and nose to nose. Neither was about to let the other get more than a nose bob away. Suddenly, Ruffian went down…legs mashed and broken, joints smashed against one another and into a pulp, suffering greatly. It was a miracle she got as far as she did. She euthanized right there on the track behind screens as is always the case when such tragedies occur. She was the ultimate athlete, giving everything for what she loved, contrary to most humans.

Years ago, during the racing day, I watched Citation do a mile workout at Santa Anita in the middle of the racing day – all by his lonesome. He came out and arched his neck and pranced and the crowd stood and cheered.

Citation acknowledged it by dancing on his toes as though he were a new recruit showing his stuff at his first major league game. He was close to twelve hundred pounds but with legs the size of a baby's wrists. Thoroughbreds know what they are supposed to do. The good ones never forget it, never give you a second-rate try unlike maybe 90% of the people in the entire world.

Trying is everything. Maybe not winning. I sure as hell didn't always win. Winning is merely score keeping. But trying, giving it your best, that's what counts. End of story. Winning Silks gave a person a sense of confidence. You believed she knew what to do and damn well was going to do it.

Big, bright eyes with a white spot off center above her left eye. An affectionate, nuzzling creature that wouldn't let another horse near me. Jealous as hell.

No claiming races for her. When she retired, she would travel by hired limos to wherever she wanted. Silken handmaidens to shovel her poop. She could have the best seats at Broadway shows and first row at the Oscars. She was my ticket. And my friend.

I flashed my card early the next morning and walked past the guard and into the "backside" city behind Santa Anita. Rows of barns squatted adjacent to the towering grandstand, dirt street, hot-walking circles, wash down areas, feed bins and sheds, miniature goats and shaggy dogs and lots of cats, and smells like big sky summers on a Kansas farm, and trainers and owners huddling together, exercise boys and stable hands murmuring in their own languages – and flies. Horses love goats and attract flies. Even when it was cold, it seemed to be hot and steamy around the backside. Horsehide and shit, and nervous athletes. There was nothing lovable about it – but it was a special world made for risk takers, one and all.

***

Everyone develops a sixth sense about danger as years pass. Mine was on high alert. After meeting with Wheeler and Sophie, I had the distinct feeling that I was not only in the middle since John's death but I had the kind of legal control that made everyone nervous and me a target.

I stopped one of the stable hands.

He was small and bald and had that illegal look on his face.

They had a furtive look a looking for the exits look. "*Senor, donde esta Senora Wiseman, por favor?*" As I spoke, I gazed up and down the dirt street. There was still a uniformed officer wandering around.

I had been told that there would be observers who wouldn't be apparent. Yellow eyes of black cats contemplated me. "No immigration," I said, "no. Just looking – *para Senora Wiseman.*"

His eyes inspected mine thoughtfully. His natural suspicions told him to get away from me fast and disappear. He shrugged and backed away. I asked another stable hand.

He shrugged too.

No one on the backside answered questions.

I assumed that they believed that every Anglo unknown to them was an INS agent.

Especially one who kept looking over his shoulder.

I stopped one of the workout jockeys.

"Donde esta Senora Wiseman?" She pushed her helmet higher on her head and smiled a thin smile hiding her out of kilter front teeth with straight closed lips like Billy Shoe used to do as a younger man – before he got his new set of teeth. There was a large smudge on one cheek.

"I ain't no Mex."

"You know where Miss Wiseman is?"

"Down at the end. She might still be there."

"How many mounts so far this week?"

"Two. Just two. No one likes girl jocks. Probably won't get more'n a couple more all week. Chauvinism. Bunch a white guys in suits. I just need some of those old farts to gimme a good ride. And I don't mean belly to belly.

"Go all the way down to the end of the street. Then to the right a few steps.

"It's where they try to hide the lady trainers. Even ones with a rep like her."

I waved a half salute and found Gertrude a minute later.

She wasn't ready for the grandmother role. With a red bandana around her forehead she might have been the sidekick of the Lone Ranger.

"Got a good runner ready to go?"

She shook her head. Wagged a finger. "Not until Thursday."

"Got John in your craw?"

"Right."

"One minute here – I see him down the street, still pissed at him, and the next minute, no one to be angry at."

I said nothing. Words don't replace people. We sat on one of the benches in front of her first stall. Finally, she got up and said, all business, "If you're waiting for a tip you know I don't tout gamblers, Harvey."

"We're all gamblers in this business, Gert."

"Wrong. We're all players. Not all gamblers. I'm not guessing when we're ready to run. I am guessing when I think we will win. There' a big difference."

She rose and then sat down and again, repeated it several times while we talked – small talk, all the while keeping her eyes on a dark colt attached to a walking tether. "Nice one," she murmured when we had run out of talking about nothing, "gonna make us some money."

She sounded exactly like my dad who took me to Santa Anita, after the war, in the late forties. That's what he used to say. "Gonna make me some money."

The old man and I were at Santa Anita in a nice box seat on a sunny Saturday when Artillery and Cee-Tee-Cee, two sprinters, were hooked up in a feature race.

He came back to our box after betting and said, "I'm gonna make me some money."

I wanted Artillery.

I was sixteen and wanting to know everything about everything. He got up and went back to the window and bought me a $2 ticket on the horse but wouldn't tell me what he had bet. Then he went to a different window and bought another $5.00 ticket on Artillery.

His Dad's brown fedora was tilted and he was a little flush with one too many highballs. He was loud when he had been drinking. And he was different. And I liked him better that way. He smiled more when he had a couple. Without a couple shots, he was a sullen son of a bitch.

The seven eights of a mile race began way out in the chute at the northeast part of the track.

I held my breathe when they were loading the horses into the starting gate. The bell rang, the gates opened and our two horses got a good jump out together and were in front neck to nose all the way around the far turn. They left the rest of the pack ten lengths back. They did the half in 46 flat. Pretty good time for seven eights. At the far turn, Artillery on the inside had the other horse by a neck, but as they came into the stretch they were nose and nose again and I started screaming because of my $5.00 bet on Artillery at four to one.

My dad started shouting too. They were 56.2 at the five furlong – good numbers. My father started waving his arms with the Daily Racing form in one fist. At the middle of the stretch, they were clocked at 108.3 for the three quarters, which was very fast. They figured to fade. Dad shouted, "He's gonna get caught. Dammit, dammit, dammit!"

Three dammits were usual for him. Crowd noise became a roar. The noise of more than fifteen thousand. Normal Saturday in those days.

The sound rose like thunder. It reverberated in the grandstand. The horses were still nose and nose.

Arms waved in the infield, – a mass of arms reached for the blue sky. Our box was about twenty yards before the finish line halfway up. My dad always loved getting a box right in the middle of the blue noses. We would now and then meet someone he knew and he would tell them how beautiful or handsome they looked; he loved telling everyone how great they all looked! The he would turn and wink at me. None of them looked great to me – just old.

The horses were nose to nose into the stretch.

Neither could shake the other.

The only thing each had left was courage. The track announcer was screaming into his speaker system. It was Harry Henson. He had a nasal sound. Whips were out, jockeys deep into the manes of their horses. They came to the quarter pole, noses bobbing together, legs high, reaching out in perfect unison like Siamese twins.

I wanted them both to win. How could you not want them both to win? They approached the wire, heads bobbing with each stride, not an inch between them, far ahead of the field.

Eye to eye.

Nose to nose.

Heads bobbing together. I really wanted to win.

I don't know why, but it was a visceral, deep necessity. Like they say, you had to be there.

The horses hit the wire. And silence suddenly fell on the entire crowd. The photo sign went up and we waited.

And waited.

I remember that wait, like waiting for a bomb to drop. Not with anticipation but with dread. Couldn't go anywhere. Couldn't scream. My Dad held his tickets in one hand but I couldn't see the numbers. I clutched my five dollar yellow ticket on Artillery. The sound of waiting was silence. Finally, the sign came down and another went up:

"Dead heat!"

I Jumped up. Flush with victory. Waved my ticket. I got it! I got it!"

I screamed at my dad who sat in a heap on his chair almost sobbing. He looked up, younger than he was – I asked what he had.

With an exhausted smile, barely touching his lips, making me realize that winning this time had been really, really important to him.

Tears streamed down his face. Why? I remember that lonely lost grin that had suddenly found a saving light at the end of the tunnel. He needed that win more than I could imagine. He wiped his eyes with his sleeve and pulled out two tickets, $50 exacta box with Artillery and $50 to win on Cee-Tee-Cee. His last dollar. No going home broke again. It was a good day. One of his few. The best day for me.

I didn't know it was his last hundred and he had to go home and face my mother's temper if he lost and all the questions and the why of it. The misery of it. I wanted my mother to be happy and solicitous but that was never going to happen. "I don't have to tell her anything now," he said. "Neither do you. Because you're a winner, too. You are always going to be a winner, kiddo."

***

I took Gert around the shoulder and said, "I need to hear the John story. The whole story. You have to let go."

"You think?"

"Yeah, I know."

We sat on a bale of hay in front of Sam's Song's stall. A pretty good allowance racer.

"It's an old and stupid story," she said. "You know most of it." She poked a knotted arthritic finger onto my knee. "But let's deal with your filly first. She interests me."

She pulled off her bandana and shook her head and fluffed her hair, looking younger, a raw edged kind of good looks, sort like you can't ignore her when she walks in. She grinned at a well-dressed fellow as he waved a finger and walked by.

"Right now, I want to talk about John."

She fumbled around in her pockets and extracted a Kleenex and wiped her eyes. "Always so damn dusty here. Bad business for allergies."

"Ice. You put ice on the eyes. It helps."

She nodded, considering the thought. "C'mon, Gert. I need to know about John. I have to find the kid."

She studied me. "Sometimes you look like a regular human being to me. Not just a gambler."

"That's all I am. A regular, dyed in the wool ordinary human being."

She smiled well aware of the fact that I could be the biggest liar west of the Mississippi. She was silent, one of those insecure silences. She shrugged as though what-the-hell. Took a breath.

"All I know is that Johnny was involved with the Wheeler family. Big time. The old man's daughter is a ghost right in the middle of their family, and now it seems prophetic somehow that all is in limbo because Frankie is missing. And I know that Wheeler and Johnny were often at one another's throats." I don't know much more."

"That's it?"

"I'm done."

I waited. There was more.

"Ace. You must be getting paid pretty good. People who want to know about John come from richer parts than I do."

"Somebody else has been asking?" I pulled out an old, wooden chair from the confines of the shady eaves nearby. I turned it backwards and sat. Gertrude waved at her worker and a pony was untied and she went to it, shooed the flies away and handed it a cube of sugar. The colt's lips pursed gently out and took the cube and shook its head and came back for more. "Hey, hey – you're in training, fella. That's it." She scratched between its eyes and patted the colt like he was her lap dog and told the walker to wash him down good and said, "We'll work him a half tomorrow and then I got him a good conditioned race next Wednesday." She turned to me. "Thinking of nominating your filly for the Pasadena Handicap late in the season. Hundred fifty grand, eighty-five to the winner."

She poked a finger at me, "I'll need a couple thousand for the fee."

I pulled out a thin checkbook and wrote the check.

She said, "Thanks, we'll get the nomination in today. Yes, somebody must have asked one of my stable hands about you because he asked me and he wouldn't have had no reason to do that on his own, would he?" Her use of double negatives grated my English 101 genes.

"He asked about what?"

"You."

"You don't know who it was?"

She shook her head. "I know you gotta be in the middle of something, or no one would be asking."

"Not in the middle of anything."

She laughed. "You are a first-rate con artist, Harvey. You know that?" She had a soft, almost accepting grin on her face. The wrinkles diminished. She wasn't as tough as she wanted the world to believe. "And you don't even know it."

"OK. Whatever.

"So, now, tell me the rest about John."

She turned, thrust her head out, "Guess it's not fair to hold out anymore. Couple years ago I wanted to kill the son of a bitch, that's all. He fucked me out of the best thing I ever had. You can quote me."

I coaxed her into the rest of the John and Gert story. *Arise* was a Bold Forbes filly.

Her dam had no special winning record. The owners of the dam, however, were willing to pay the stud fee which was like $50,000. Arise was compact yearling, with a long stride and a chest like Jane Russell, maybe Jane Mansfield – no one remembers Jane Russell.

Gert and John were close.

"We went to the auction," she continued, "at Ocala in Florida for the yearling sales one year. I had two hundred thousand I could offer. Maybe more with a phone call. In those days, that was a lot of money. I wanted that filly. I begged, borrowed, and nearly stole to get that pile of money together. John knew it.

"And he saw what I saw. She was going to be a good one. But behind my back, he got to the auctioneer and she was pulled out of the auction. He bought her direct from him for the exact two hundred. Big time money. Front page in the Daily Racing Form. And then, he ignored me. The son of a bitch paid the handler maybe ten, twenty thousand, on the side, probably in cash, to pull her out of the auction and then he went directly to the owner and paid him the big ones and had her shipped before anyone knew what happened. I know they all do it.

"But we were sleeping in the same fuckin' bed, while he was still married to that nut case Sally. Named the filly Arise." Her face flushed. The tissue went to her eyes.

I let her anger settle. She loved him and hated him. Not unusual in the annals of humankind. "That *Arise* filly could gallop two miles and barely work up a sweat, Harv. She was made for the big races, the mile and a quarter handicaps, the Breeder's Cup. The Oaks, The Del Mar Juvenile. And she won them all. And that's the story. He fuckin' stole her from me."

"Maybe it turned out for the best. You didn't have to sleep with him anymore."

"Very funny. Harvey, You're a regular Jack Benny. Don't you know women? That's not the way it is. You have no sense when it comes to women, do you? I didn't figure the whole deal out till later, anyway. *Arise* won those races and Debutante and beat the colts in the Hollywood Futurity. She was beautiful," she murmured. Bay colored. And I was still fuckin' him and callin' him darling. I almost killed the sonofabitch when I found out. I sure wanted to."

She pulled out a chair from the corner of the shed and joined me. "This is a cutthroat business, I know that. I'm not educated like some of these fancy trainers but I think you're born with integrity. If you don't have it, you can't go out and buy it. I know that even good guys get stretched out and cut corners. I can cut corners. Life makes it so. But this was too much."

She signed and continued. "Then Arise broke down in a grade two handicap against the boys at Aqueduct. Four good colts against her and she had them beat, had them good.

"And bam, just like that, her right foreleg gave way, halfway down the stretch. It was terrible. Like Ruffian. Jockey went flying. Terrible to watch. Just horrible. They put her down then and there."

"John's dreams went with her," I said.

"And so did mine.

"She would have been a Grade One winner."

She wiped her nose with another tissue.

"It wasn't like John."

I answered. "Maybe something else was on his case. Something heavy."

"I know all of that, with that wife of his. And with Wheeler as an in-law. Had to be heavy. But he hurt me bad, Harvey. And we was close."

"Did you know that first wife?"

"Sally?"

Gertrude's watery eyes grew even darker. They darted about my face as if each crevasse in it would speak to her. "I knew her, sort of. Died young. I actually met that Carole lady.

"Was Sally as off kilter as they say?"

"Not gonna name-call dead ladies. Why dig up her memory?"

"Her spirit keeps intruding into a bunch of unhappy lives. I'm trying to fix the misery, get rid of the spirit and find the kid."

"You can't fix the past."

"I've done it before."

"Don't wanna argue with no numbskull womanizing gambler who thinks he can replay the past. Especially one named Harvey Ace. Can't believe your chutzpah. Johnny used to claim that people would call him at night. He said it sounded like a young person or woman threatening him." She leaned back and stretched. "Thought he was joking at first. But he wasn't. Tried to trace the calls. Refused to call the police. Said it was family business. I know he called Harry Moss a couple times. Look, this is getting us nowhere. It was Sally. Crazy lady. Whad'ya say we just talk about the filly. All this other crap is not my business. Don't want to talk about the dead. Don't think anything I say can help you. Talked to that Sampson fellow. Smart fella."

"However, Gert, don't you think it's time to bury Sally all over again.... put all of this to rest?"

"Enough, Harvey. Don't be stupid, I mean it." She stood up and set the chair back under the eaves, pursing her lips, almost talking to herself. She ran her fingers through her thick hair.

I started to repeat myself but she waved that same suffering finger at me.

"There's more, isn't there?"

"There isn't."

"OK. We'll deal with my filly. Tell me, will *The Silk* take to the gate and the crowds?"

"Let's see. It's Saturday. She's had her gallop for the day. Make it Tuesday morning early.

"I'll see you at the head of the stretch. We'll see what's really there."

"You going to be at John's funeral?"

"Half the track will be."

She stuffed her bandana into her pocket and began to walk away. Then she stopped, did an about face, suddenly somber, great deep-set eyes which seemed to understand the worst of human frailties, and said, "You know, Harvey, I'm telling you again, you shouldn't be getting mixed up in the Wheeler history. It ain't healthy. Wasn't for Johnny. Do yourself a favor. All these people are dangerous. They get what they want. And they don't look back and don't care. That's the thing—these people don't care. Look what's happened to everyone involved with them. It just ain't healthy."

"C'mon, Gertrude. there's more."

"See ya Tuesday morning."

"Gert, hold on. This whole damn history wants someone to end it once and for all – some tragedies have to be physically buried. They don't die on their own." I followed her as she strode to her office door and held the screen. "Tell me one thing. C'mon, Gert –"

She put a hand on her hip. "Last thing, Harv. I'm not kidding."

"When was the last time you heard from Sally and where were you when you did?"

"I never talked to her."

"I know you must have." I was insistent. I heard my voice rise. It was strangely unfamiliar.

"Who have you been talking to?"

"Never mind. Just tell me."

"Alright." She looked at me quizzically. "She called me from Tucson, Arizona, then once from Mara Bay, up the coast."

"About what?"

172

"About John, of course."

"She was lucid?"

"Not always. I have to admit. But she was this time – those times."

"So, OK, what did she say about John?"

"Said he's in trouble. Big trouble. That's it. Told you, not talking anymore about the dead."

***

"Hey, *Senor*, over here." The stable hand I had spoken to a few minutes ago turned away.

"No, no, no. No immigration." I flipped a ten-dollar bill in the air. "*Dinero, mi amigo.*"

"*Dinero.*"

It's amazing what money can do...unless it's not enough. Everyone has a price.

The stable hand looked around as if checking escape routes then sauntered over but no closer than about six feet from me. He gazed at the money as if it was a leaf of good grass. I added another ten-dollar bill.

He reached out. I pulled back. He got closer. "*Primiro, informacion. Comprende?*" He nodded. His long straight black hair fell into his face. His shoulders went up, he became an inch or two taller. "I'm quite able to speak perfect English, *Senor*. My name is Walter Rodriguez. Your accent stinks by the way. You may call me Walter. Not Walt. Not *Senor*. I graduated from Birmingham High and Los Angeles City College, East LA. Been here since I was eight years old. Make a better buck here than most places and I stay safe. Some of us work here by choice and do not wish to be hassled by the immigration authorities. Or to see friends with questionable status hassled or deported."

"Sorry, Walter, I assumed –"

"As you all do."

"I'm sorry again." What he said was true. Put a yellow or brown face in front of you and you begin to speak loudly and slowly figuring it's the only way to be understood. "I just want to know who saw what happened to John Augers? There has to be somebody around here who knows something. Who saw it? Who else was on guard that night? Who else was around?"

He opened his hand and smiled. I leaned and put the bill into his palm.

His fingers curled a silent and slow three times signaling more. I stuck another ten into that palm. "You drive a citizen's bargain."

He smiled and nodded. He understood that there was more than one way to make a living. "Who was here that night? Besides Herman Barnes."

"Rashid."

"Who?"

"Rashid. Rashid Jefferson."

"Jefferson?"

"You can't hear me?"

"I can hear you. Keep talking."

"There may have been others but I didn't see any and don't know about any."

"Was he official? Or just hanging around?"

"He lives here. Hangs out wherever he can cage a meal or a bed. Helps out here and there."

"Just hangs around?"

He was impatient with my reactions.

"You need help, don't you?"

"All I can get. Where can I find him?'

. His finger pointed at the ground. "Right here. Like I said. Right here. But you have to find him. He hides. Like a shadow. Sort of. But he is here all the time. If you can find him." He laughed. It was not a laugh. More like a dismissive grunt. "Just keep looking."

"Thank you, Walter. When is the best time I'm likely to find him?"

He looked at me like I was something out of a comic book. Or someone ready to stick him on a skewer and barbeque. "Don't know more."

"C'mon. If he knows things, I'll make it worth his while."

"And me?"

"You already got paid, okay? You don't want to help find the guys who have the kid…killed John? Just forget it. I don't want to keep paying every time I talk to you."

I started to turn away. He kept his eyes on me, took out a brown cloth and wiped his forehead. He smiled and called out. "After the eighth race, come on back here and start looking around. He's a black guy, tall and thin and wears sort of a uniform. Gray uniform like a janitor. With a stripe down the side. Made money as a singer, usually singing or humming. Deep voice." He walked away like I was a bad omen.

There was Carly Klein and now Rashid Jefferson.

I leaned against the weathered green side of one of the barns and watched horses lazily tramping by, being led by backside grooms and walkers. Between the barns, horses were hitched to automatic machine hot-walkers, around and around and around they went like a tether ball.

Sunshine struck the shingles of the shopping mall to the west of the track just above the rooftops as it decided to grace us with its golden rays. I knew I should tear up Sophie's check. I knew I should be squeezing Wheeler's neck about Sarah and her whereabouts. I reminded myself that whatever they say about Robinhood, it was at least six to one he knew that money didn't have a conscience – from whoever it came.

Chapter Thirteen

Sophie's check was for ten thousand. People are crazy. Totally convinced. Sophie and Franklin Wheeler are proof positive. I shoved the Sophie check into my shirt pocket. I expected Franklin's check in the mail. I drove to my condo and parked on the narrow street just in front and was tapped on my shoulder as I got out.

"Hey. Kiddo, having a killer day?"

He was tall, dark, and looked Italian because he was. Hard eyes the color of the Pacific late in the day, tough jaw line that protruded a little. We attended the same kindergarten. Ate dinner at one another's house, and played ball in the same empty lot or in my back yard. He wanted to be a cop way back then and every month since. We were in the same junior High school and LA High until my dad shipped me off to University of Pennsylvania. Wharton school of Business. Who knows how he got me in? Paul Sampson ended up at UCLA, and graduated near the top of his class, then a Masters in Government Administration. I was a haphazard student as I was already an addicted gambler. But I graduated. I didn't attend my graduation, as I knew no one who would be there anyway.

Paul had a wife and one disabled child suffering from ALS known as Lou Gehrig's disease. His care was expensive even with the LAPD's health insurance hard to imagine how they managed on a cop's salary. Unfortunately, there seemed to be no cure for the boy. A matter of time. Like all tragedies they are right there in front of you, but most of us refuse to see what's coming.

Paul went up the ranks pretty quickly, became a lieutenant, homicide detective, jaded yet persistently surprised at the depravity of humankind. He had been offered higher rankings and office command jobs but contrary to good sense and the harping of his sensible wife, he opted to stay where he was because he liked it. He told me often enough, "In spite of the shit, now and then you do something, get somebody who is really bad, fix something, save someone, and you realize that you actually did something special and worthwhile."

Of course, he was right.

We met regularly in our younger years until time and circumstances weighed us down. But we remained close in spite of his disapproval of my life style. Over the years, he threatened to institutionalize me, or kill me, and kept telling me to get married, get a dog and settle down," whatever that meant. I reminded him that dogs were not allowed in the Turf Club and wives would never adjust to the hours.

"Well, grab that Sarah girl and get a dog. You can change."

Bull. I tried that. I didn't tell him that Sarah had walked out on me. Unfortunately, Paul had been assigned the Augers Affair.

He knew I would be involved in searching for answers to John's assassination and young Frankie's kidnapping. "I knew you would be in the middle of it."

I shrugged. Offered to take him to dinner.

"Can't, Barbara's night off. We trade off whenever we can."

"Even with a Nanny?"

"Not the same. You know that. You had a half dozen Nannies as a kid. You like it?'

"We weren't always rich…just most of the time."

"Lucky you."

"Not so sure." There we were on Wilshire Boulevard in Santa Monica so I climbed into his Crown Vic. And he put on the siren and we sailed to the local *Dennys* in about one-minute flat. "Siren was for my benefit?"

"You deserve the best."

"I ordered an omelet; he ordered two burgers… For the price of one."

Over coffee, I told him about my meeting with Moss and Wheeler. I made it as detailed as I could. Impress him with details like the shaking of Wheeler's hands and the sweat on Moss's lips as we spoke. He had similar impressions. After a patient listening, interrupted now and then by, "I'll check that." He leaned back, held his hand up. "Enough, I got it. I know you want to do the right thing, but we will start tripping over one another. Better to just butt out. Go make an honest unfulfilled living as a gambler, with a Federal IRS gambler's number."

I searched his face. Maybe he was kidding. He wasn't. "You know better. I'm not stopping," I said, "Just go check with the Wheeler Foundation books and records. They're public as a Charitable Trust. Check on the books of the Wheeler trusts if you can get to them. If you can't I might be able to. Like they say. Follow the money."

I hoped it would keep him busy and out of my line of fire for a few days. "Now it's your turn."

"What you didn't know and don't know, Harvey, is that John Augers was in debt up to his ears. Smothered in debt. He owed trainer's. He owed the track. He owed his owners, he owed Wheeler over two hundred thousand in winner's purses he never turned over to the stable account. The Racing Board threatened to boot him out. They said he came up with the money only a day before they voted. But he always had money."

"Hard to believe. Never saw it. How could that be? The trusts? And Wheeler took care of Frankie's doctors, plus everything else..." I thought a second. "Maybe Sally and her costs. Maybe the old man gave up on her"

"Unless he didn't." He looked at me as if expecting me to add to the facts.

I added nothing.

My guess is that Paul knew everything and was testing me.

***

When I came back to California after graduating from Wharton, I could not get a job with my degree in Business/Employee Relationships. No one cared about Employee relationships in the 70s. In fact, most employers thought there was no such thing. They wanted someone who could sell whatever they wanted to sell. I couldn't. So, I started to hang out at Aqua Caliente the racetrack in Tijuana, Baja California. I took a bachelor apartment in San Diego and made the drive every day.

The drive was pain but the gambling was successful. I got involved with a young Aureliano Mondozo, the son of a mucho rich and well-connected Mexican family. It was during one of those summers while the track was still operating that I found Aureliano passed out on the floor of the not so nice Men's Room at the track with two kids rifling through the pockets of his jacket.

They were the usual pickpockets and vultures of the city. I chased them away, got the young man on his feet. He was small and light and I shoved his head under the water at a basin, patted him down, straightened him up, talked to him, and suddenly had a best friend.

Through murky mumblings, I understood enough to take him to a box in a special section up high in the stands, and holding him tightly was introduced to his father, Miquel Mondoza, a shortened version of his name, who rose to shake my hand.

I told him what a nice boy he had and that the poor young fellow had been shoved and pushed to the ground which explained the mess he was in. I nodded and smiled at the short bald old man who was surrounded by two very large fellows who had black t-shirt under their black jackets and who had muscles on their muscles.

I don't know how they were connected but people in the boxes surrounding them deferred to the old man, nodding and smiling whenever he moved even a little finger. The Mondozo culture was to repay kindnesses with overwhelming responses. A person would become locked into a cultural debt. I became a regular at their small five-acre ranch just outside of Tijuana.

When I would visit them, Mr. Mondozo would whisper urgently with Aureliano's brothers and they would march off to carry out one of his orders. Aureliano's brothers and father were always in corners whispering. I was a guest who never heard anything except *Hola*, and *Buenos Dias*, and what would I like for dinner.

Dinner was held in an enormous dusty colored dining room, the same color as the desert expanses outside, surrounded by murals of great long horned bulls each of which seemed ready to attack. Impressive in size was the mahogany table and the wood chairs, which were uncomfortable but fit the room.

I suspected they used this room only to impress guests. The first dinner with the family was spooky. Papa Mondozo asked about my family and every head shook in unison when they learned I had no brothers or sisters. It was a matter of concern that I had no family. "Ahh, shame, shame, shame...my boys are my how you say, my phalanx, my long arm."

He shook his head and again everyone followed suit. "No brothers, sisters? Children?"

I told them a lie about Kim, that she was in college in the east and doing well. It seemed wise to tell them as little about me as possible and still be appropriately sociable.

That first time I was invited, no one else offered a remark or question except the old man.

Senora Mondozo, sitting at the opposite end of the table, merely smiled a strikingly beautiful, long lashed smile – black eyes, however, not smiling. She often two-fingered her thick hair behind an ear and offered more of their perfectly barbequed steak.

"From our own ranch outside Ensenada, *Senor* Ace. You know where that is?" Smiling.

Checking with a quick practiced glance at the old man. They never stopped smiling.

Aureliano and I became buddies. At Papa Modozo's unspoken insistence, we met at Hollywood Park and Del Mar Race tracks often and I spent many nights rescuing him from women and drinking binges. But, in spite of becoming close, he was not from the old school as his father was. He reciprocated when he had to, which is when his father insisted. Otherwise, I decided it was best not to turn your back on him.

There was a mean streak in Aureliano. If someone didn't please him, he would shove whatever it was away – man, woman, or dog, and usually had someone close by to help.

One day, surprisingly, sitting at a table at Hollywood Park, he leaned close to me and asked me to find the mother of his then favorite girl, Zoe Hersch. The mother, who was known as Zoe Mantilla had suddenly disappeared.

Didn't take long to find out the mother's maiden name was also Hersch. I found her and Aure was grateful. Money was the only thing he knew but I refused, it was nest to keep him in my debt.

I did. She was the daughter of a well-known screenwriter, Walter Hersch. I didn't know at the time there was such a thing as a Jewish Mexican person or that there were well-situated Jewish Mexican families mostly in Mexico City and generally people who had run from Hitler with money in their jeans.

Zoe turned out to be sensuous, sullen, and quick-tempered.

She was also susceptible to monetary inducements. She was shacked up with a handsome bit player, one of the persistent hangers on who never recognized his lack of talent but got by with looks and charm.

She did everything not to return to Mexico, including wanting to pay with her body but I was the soul of discretion—and happened to have a terrible cold at the time. With her help, we concocted a great story of why she disappeared – she traveled to San Diego County and checked with various Juvenile institutions to help lost and abused Mexican kids who managed to get across the border.

When I found her at dinner with a tall, dark, and handsome bit player in west Los Angeles and convinced her with a promise of a thousand bucks cash which made her willing to be brought back to Mexico City I met Aureliano's father, Miguel Cervantes Redon Mondozo, for the second time and he was more lavish in his praise of me than ever before.

Senor Mondozo was, however, one of those people who gave me big knot in my stomach each time we met.

It was clear that he was a family man solely because it was family, people with his name and connected to him, that created and maintained his status in society and not out of love or respect for any of his progeny, brothers, sisters, cousins, second cousins, uncles, or aunts.

Every year after that, I had an invitation for their Christmas dinners. The integration of Zoe into the Mondozo family was not in the least strained.

They smiled at her and she smiled at them and everyone was smiles. As far as I could tell, I was a family favorite.

Strange, but about a year later, Zoe disappeared again and no one asked me to find her.

I was occasionally involved with Aureliano after that. Miguel always hugged me tightly when we met, making certain I wasn't carrying a weapon.

***

The phone was ringing when I got home. Stuck it to my ear just in time. "You know, we've got your girl. Shut up and listen. Here she is."

It was Sarah's voice. Hysterical. "Harvey, I don't know where I am! These people...they came and grabbed me from Josie's place! Harvey!" Muffled half screams.

Then a disguised voice. "You do what we say. Or else."

Chapter Fourteen

Instructions were that I perform at the Foundation's Board Meeting this Saturday." It was Thursday. Saturday was a thousand years away.

The first call after that was Paul Sampson. Told him about Sarah. We agreed. All roads led to Wheeler. He said he would get right on it. But Wheeler's possible guilt was like a child's Jig Saw puzzle. Too neat. "But having a suspect is better than none."

I could go straight to Wheeler's home and beat it out of him.

"I know what you're thinking, Harvey. Go to the damn Board meeting and do whatever they say. We'll have a task force just for finding the two of them. Do whatever he says."

Later on we were sitting in my dining room which doubled as a small library.

"From here, I go to the Wheeler home," Paul said. "We may pick him up on some charge and see if we can get anything out of him." He was intent – on the trail of killers and kidnappers and was wound tight. An involuntary twitch appeared on his left cheek just below the check bone. It was a familiar twitch all through his life. "We need to get in the middle of this as soon as possible," he said. "Your lady is in deep shit. The phone was a throwaway."

"The Foundation meets Saturday. Let's see what he wants, what's up for grabs. Take all you shares under that will or as John's alter ego and do whatever the old man wants."

"That's not a game the police can play. They told you plainly vote his way. Right? Think maybe that's the time to arrest him. On the spot."

"Mistake. Paul. Don't do it. Call them off. He might not even come to the meeting. If he is the guy, he knows about the threat to me. He's probably sitting in his China room and already discussing the scenario with the Director. His director."

"Walter Christakos."

"Right." I was emphatic. "Call them off. Let that old man hang himself. Let the case put itself together. They won't harm her... I don't think."

"They won't. Guaranteed.

"Except for the trauma of it. There's no big pay-day in it. If this is all about money and not revenge or some genuine craziness, then their percentage is to get her to force everyone to cooperate. She might call you…their way of to make sure you understand."

"Count on it. And she'll ask you to just do what they say."

"Harvey, we sit on that old son of a bitch in an interrogation room, move him from station to station or keep him in a car, and keep driving and we find her and the kid at the same time. He knows where and the why of the whole thing."

"Except what have we got? And if he is not the guy?"

He shrugged. "He is."

"Why would he grab his own grandson. Take a chance on hurting him?"

"Votes. People like that don't give a damn about anything but power, keeping it. That's their mantra. That's their job, their livelihood. You are replacing the guardian of Frankie as a practical matter."

"The guardian is of his person, not anything else. Ann Whitson does not speak for the kid. Harry's Petition is nothing until they have a formal hearing and get an Order of the Court."

"Exactly. Until then, she can't complain or get in the middle."

"Don't think she wants to."

"You are in charge. That's the point they are making. The hearing is a couple weeks away. If you don't show up you are next in their kill scenario."

"I'll vote their way. I'll record it…I'll do what they want. But they have Sarah so we need to bring this to boiling quick."

"For the next twelve hours, hold on, it might come to a head at the meeting."

"I'm not sure. Harv. If it's Wheeler why would he wait?"

"He is sitting right in his own wheel house."

He pointed a finger at my nose. "Anyway, Harvey, don't be a wise guy."

"We'll know what to do after the meeting. I'll let the old man know that Sarah has to be released unharmed within a couple hours along with his grandson."

He sat for a full minute staring out the window at the darkening sea. "You're a pain-in-the-ass."

"And you are that pain's best friend."

"OK. We'll set you up with a wire."

"OK. I'll go there and I'll vote with them – whatever they want me to do. Somebody will clue me in. That should tell us who's who involved and what's next. And I'll let them know that there is a price for my vote."

He nodded. Sighed. Paul had been at this detective job for more than ten years. I could look at him and tell he had had enough.

But he was four years shy of retirement. Twenty one years was enough. They all said the last few were the hardest. They drank, they swore, they hated, the complained, they often wanted to kill, and then each of them went home and fed the baby and helped do that final load of dishes, hugged their wives and took a pill to sleep. Paul's hand ran through his thick black hair. Pulled his long hands together and entwined them closed, fingernails obsessively manicured, about which I always chided him. "Money is all it is. Don't let him fool you." He had long since grown tired of the rules of his job, of the niceties of civil rights and what is good for the goose is good for the gander. He never believed good guys could ever be a gander.

"Money is the root? What's new about that, Paulie? He is not what we need to worry about now. He's not going anywhere. We need to find the kid. Find Sarah. He might not know himself. He isn't going to personally lead us to either of them...and suppose he doesn't bend?

"How can you hold him more than a few hours? He'll have ten lawyers on the doorstep within an hour. And a half dozen lawsuits and the Chief will turn you back to a beat cop and maybe less."

Sampson instincts were to grab and hold and not let go. He was a cop with a good suspect. Good cops are just people. Bad cops are more than evil. They chip away at our best institutions. But even the best cop gets excited when their quarry is just a first down away. Paul was one of the good ones. He would put in his time, give the LAPD his best shot, then head home to his Barbara and his unfortunate son, Daniel, and act as if it was merely another day at the office, an insurance office, a brokerage, a buying office, whatever. But he would never betray what he was feeling. If he did, the horror of his many years on the job would attack and he would be useless to everyone. He admitted to me often enough how he came to hate his "Bad Guy" adversaries and some of the brass in his own department. There were bad guys there, too. He knew this.

Thus, he managed, relegated his feelings to his back pocket. Just do the job, no matter what. Then to hell with it all. Forget. Shove it away to that back pocket. He would find a way of keeping absolute tabs on Wheeler whatever it took. It was his personal measure of success. Hard not to understand and at the same time hard to understand when cops grab onto a case and cling like biting roaches convincing themselves that the innocent are guilty and that the guilty are all evil and need to be destroyed, and that whatever a cop does is proper, forget about legal. They just needed to get their guy. They firmly believed that no one would get hurt except the bad guys. They would make it legal. At least close enough. And, if not, so what.

Harvey watched his friend move into that space of denial, a calmer state of being.

Paul knew he had his man. "I'll get the sonofabitch. The whole bunch."

***

It was Friday, just after dawn. It was the best of times for seagulls; fish were jumping. And small ballets of whitecaps brought hordes of sardines to the top.

An occasional halibut came along out of the deep for the ride. A small cloud of seagulls screamed and dived. The wind carried them back up into the blue and wherever they wanted to go with a mere tip of a wing. Sunlight reflected out to where the earth curved away from sight. I had arrangements to meet the people responsible for my position as lacky to Franklin Wheeler after the Foundation Board meeting. With another untraceable phone call, I got a location to make the deal for Sarah and Frankie.

Called and got Paul out of bed, moaning and bitching and told him, "The Grove. Third and Fairfax. That's what they want. Hundreds of people on a Saturday afternoon. They get lost in the crowd and you can't shoot and can't chase very well."

"Won't do. Impossible to command the space. We'll find an exchange location – if and when it's required. If anyone contacts you, tell them no. They'll not agree but tell them that's it. I'll call you."

"And if they do it their way in spite of what I say?"

He shrugged. I opened my glass door to my fenced patio leading to the beach and tossed off my sandals, went through the gate to the damp sand and jogged a couple hundred yards to the Marina, to the Del Rey stone breakwater that protected the yacht harbor and path to the sea. I climbed onto the rocks and searched the ocean for answers to all the questions I had as I often did and found none.

I never did. But you never know.

Wheeler wanted his way and would have it his way with his creations or not at all. There was no other conclusion. Except somehow, Wheeler as a subject was way too obvious – and he was not a slow-witted man. The perpetrators of all of these events had other goals and special purposes. Perhaps there were purposes in the facts that even he did not know about. After all, he was a very good target. I would find out before Sampson and his leagues of gray suited lieutenants with guns.

185

A slim forty-foot sloop coasted under minimum power along the inlet toward the breakwater and the open sea reached only on the south side of the break. A young woman, working alone, wet orange halter over perfectly molded breasts and a black something about the size of a Kleenex covering the rest of her, was at the mainsail untying it and shoving it out into the wind. The sloop was too big for one person but she seemed to be in charge. Sail clips on the forward sail banged against the metal mast. The wind came harder and changed direction. All at once it brought her bow aiming directly at the breakwater.

She hurried to the wheel and stood very straight and still for a glorious snapshot made for Travel and Leisure. Then she turned, almost as if posing, head back, hair flying, turned her wheel –the wind grabbed and she stiffened and the self-conscious poses stopped. Her little sail boat began to slip away from the breeze, heading north by northwest. The sail fluttered, losing the frivolous wind. The clips for the remaining sail started banging at the metal mast. The young woman turned her body into the wind and the stiffening breezes, and reached out with one hand as if to scoop up drafts of that frivolous wind and bring her bow to the correct direction. She shoved her motor handle all the way down and the little motor dug into the sea like a burrowing dog. The burst of energy was not enough. The inboard/outboard was doing the best it could but the wind was now its master. The young woman struggled with the wheel, she shoved her body into a right turn. Then the wind changed again. Her beautiful boat was not responding, her beautiful body was in trouble. She pulled the motor handle up to lessen its power and flipped the wheel all the way over to the opposite end and then shoved the motor handle back down all the way and I could hear the engine dig and assert itself once again and saw the sloop come about and suddenly catch the air just right. What a feeling that must be for her. Its sails blossomed and the beautiful young lady, standing tall and triumphant ay her wheel was now in control of her destiny, her entire body outlined by the wind. She commanded her boat, and she sailed majestically into the glistening blustery sea.

I sat on the rocks all the while watching the flood of small boats begin to struggle with the mischievous breezes, struggled with them as they fought the wind and watched their kids and wives scrambling about to make whatever they were sailing obey them. In a while, I jogged back to the Condo and found a message pasted to the window facing the sea. "FORGET AUGERS! NO COPS!" Black felt pen and uneven.

Someone knew my every move. There was an eerie sense of lost power that came with the note. I searched the beach, though knowing whoever it was they would be long gone. Too early for the volleyball players and the mothers with their strollers. Some foot traffic on the pier nothing I could pin. I searched up and down the "boardwalk" and finally carefully folded the note into an envelope on the chance that there was something about it that Paul Sampson could glean. I showered, shaved and dressed, did a quick Cary Grant in the mirror, and saw worried eyes and a forehead that was growing, not a lot, but there it was, then stood with a coffee staring out to the beach just in case there was something, anything that would strike my foggy brain. Of course, there wasn't. I pulled out a tie and started to tie it on, then changed my mind, I didn't need the tie, unbuttoned the top shirt button and hurried out into the world hoping there would be something in the day that would take me closer.

I had visions of Sarah tied, bound, and gagged sitting next to Frankie on some damp warehouse floor somewhere in another town. Mara Bay was all that came to mind. The meeting of the Foundation might provide some answers. So I hoped.

My set up was already taped to my belly and the small of my back. I was a walking recording studio. It was quite marvelous how they had taped me. I had had it done before but each time the equipment was smaller and better and they claimed more reliable. Nothing could be seen. Flat, growing hot against me. Microphones not much bigger than the size of a pea but flatter.

Sarah could not be helped at the moment. The unfortunate boy would also have to wait. The opposition now had the power. But they needed the kid alive and presentable should the Judge want to talk to him. Whoever it was had enough professionalism in them or him or her to know that dealing with Sarah roughly was a useless enterprise, that, although I would comply, they still had two live bodies to deal with. I would hear from them again.

***

There was one more thing on my plate before the meeting. I drove to the address given to me by Harry Moss, the one Moss described on June Street, in Hancock Park. I had to get this interview done and off my agenda; meet this Carly Klein woman and satisfy myself about her involvement and perhaps lead to a better understanding of John Augers and his – how do they say it? – his facockta personal life. Perhaps there were happy things in the house, memories that might come alive. Just going through his space would help. If I found anything, I intended to give it to Frankie when I found him.

Hancock Park was midway between the ocean and downtown LA, about eighteen miles from one to the other. It was before Beverly Hills was Beverly Hills, just after the early Los Angeles mansions moved westward for about two miles from what was now the Coliseum and the University of Southern California Campus. As the mansions came and the area grew in population, west Beverly Hills grew, as did the Cheviot Hills developments – rolling hills, expansive properties, imitation castles, grand stairways. Hancock Park however, was the original location of those who controlled and made Los Angeles the center of the west – in spite of San Francisco's claims.

The lawn at 2215 June Street had already grown a trifle sad, English countryside neglect. It was a brick two-story home, entrance surrounded by four skinny swaying palm trees, and tall stately cypress at each side of the door. I dug out the key Harry had given me and shoved it into the door when the door all at once opened pulling my hand with it directly into the belly of a rather handsome woman. "I beg your pardon," I said, and automatically turned to look at the address again. "Don't worry, this is the place. You are either the broker Harry hired, that sweetheart of a devious man, or Harvey Ace, the executor he described. Which is it?"

Chapter Fifteen

Sophie's check was for ten thousand. People are crazy. Totally convinced. I can't figure out what they want or how they want it. Sophie and Franklin Wheeler are proof positive. I shoved the Sophie check into my pocket and promised myself to send it back. I expected Franklin's check in the mail. There's line from H. L. Menckin that always comes to mind at the beginning of a every case: *To every human problem, there is a neat and easy solution and it is always wrong.*

I drove to my condo and parked and was tapped on my shoulder as I got out.

Paul's flat azure eyes, tough jaw line stuck out. He told me often enough, "In spite of the shit, now and then you do something, get somebody, and you realize that you actually did something special and worthwhile." We met regularly in our younger years until time and circumstances weighed us down. But we remained close in spite of his disapproval of my life style.

Over the years, he threatened to institutionalize me and kept telling me to get married, get a dog, and "settle down," whatever that meant. I reminded him that dogs were not allowed in the Club and wives would never adjust to the hours. I didn't tell him Sarah had walked out on me, as he had high hopes for that situation.

Unfortunately, Paul had been assigned the Augers Affair.

He knew I would be involved in searching for answers to John's assassination and young Frankie's kidnapping.

"I had a nice day. I'll take you dinner."

"Can't. Barbara's night off We trade off whenever we can. S, at least we see each other."

"Even with the Nanny?"

"Not the same. You know that. You had a half dozen Nanny's."

"We were rich most of the time. That's what rich parents did. Shove us off."

"Lucky you."

There was a Denny's near Olympic and Western. I climbed into his Crown Vic. He put on the siren and we sailed to the Dennys in about a minute flat. "That was for my benefit?"

"You deserve the best."

I ordered an omelet, he ordered two burgers... "For the price of one."

Over coffee, I told him about my meeting with Moss and Wheeler. I made it as detailed as I could. Impress him with details like the shaking of Wheeler's hands and the sweat on Moss's lips as we spoke. After a patient listening, interrupted now and then by "I'll check that." He leaned back, held his hand up. "Enough, I got it. I know you want to the right thing, but we will start tripping over one another. Better to just butt out. Go make an honest unfulfilled living as a gambler, with a Federal gambler's number."

"You know better. I'm not stopping. Just go check with the Wheeler Foundation books and records. They're public as a Charitable Trust. Check on the books of the Wheeler trusts if you can get to them. If you can't, maybe I can. Like they say. Follow the money."

"I'll remind you – John was in debt up to his ears. Smothered in debt. He owed his staff trainers. He owed the track. He owed his owners' he owed Wheeler two hundred thousand in winner's purses he never turned over to the stable account. The Racing Board threatened to boot him out. They said he came up with the money only a day before they voted."

"I'm surprised. I thought Wheeler took care of Frankie's doctors, plus everything else on John's table."

***

When I came back to California after graduating from Wharton, No one cared about Employee Relationships major. Employee Relationships in the 70s didn't mean diddle. They wanted someone who could sell whatever they wanted to sell. I couldn't. So I started to hang out at Aqua Caliente the racetrack in Tijuana, Baja California. I took a bachelor apartment in San Diego and made the drive every day, through the visa gates.

The drive was pain but the gambling was successful. I got involved with a young Aureliano Mondozo, the son of a mucho mucho rich and well-connected Mexican family.

It was during one of those summers while the track was still operating that I found Aureliano passed out on the floor of the not so nice Men's Room at the track with two kids rifling through the pockets of his jacket.

They were the usual pickpockets and vultures of the city. I chased them away, got the young man on his feet. He was small and light and I shoved his head under the water at a basin, patted him down, straightened him up, talked to him, and suddenly had a best friend.

Through murky mumblings, I understood enough to take him to a box in a special section up high in the stands, and holding him tightly was introduced to his father, Miquel Mondoza, a small pudgy little man with sharp black eyes who rose to shake my hand.

I told him what a nice boy he had and that the poor young fellow had been shoved and pushed to the ground which explained the mess he was in. I nodded and smiled at the father who was surrounded by two very large fellows who had black t-shirts under their black jackets and I was sure had muscles on their muscles.

I don't know how they were connected but people in the boxes surrounding them deferred to the old man, nodding and smiling whenever he moved even a little finger. Mr. Mondozo insisted on repaying kindnesses and I became a regular at their small four-acre ranch just south of Tijuana.

They would whisper between themselves at the ranch. Aureliano's brothers, and father were always in corners whispering, using a kind of bastardized Spanish that only the family understood...I was a guest who never heard anything except Hola, Buenos Dias and what would I like for dinner.

Dinner was held in an enormous dusty colored dining room, the same color as the desert expanses outside, surrounded by painted pictures of great long horned bulls around the walls each of them ready to attack. Impressive in size was the mahogany table and the wood chairs, which were uncomfortable. But fitting. I suspected they used this room only to impress guests. At that first dinner, Papa Mondzo asked about my family and every head shook in unison when they learned I had no brothers or sisters. It was a matter of concern that I had no family. "Ahh, shame, shame, shame...my boys are my, how you say, phalanx, my long arm."

He shook his head and again everyone followed suit. "No brothers, sisters?" I did not tell them about the existence of my daughter. It seemed wise to tell them as little about me as possible and still eat their food and enjoy their hospitality. They treated me like a new-found son. However, I felt I could trust them as far as I could throw the big guy who sat just behind him...not eating.

That first time I was invited, no one else offered a remark or question except the old man. *Senora* Mondozo, sitting at the opposite end of the table, merely smiled a striking beautiful, long lashed smile – incongruous hazel eyes, however, not smiling. She often two-fingered her thick hair behind an ear and offered more of their perfectly barbequed steak.

"From our own ranch outside Ensenada, *Senor* Ace. You know where that is?" Smiling. Checking with a quick practiced glance at the old man. They never stopped smiling.

Soon Aureliano and I were buddies. We met at Hollywood Park and Del Mar Race tracks often and I spent many nights rescuing him from women and drinking binges. But, in spite of becoming close, he was not from the old school as his father was. He reciprocated when he had to, which is when his father insisted. There was a mean streak in Aureliano. If someone didn't please him, he would shove whatever it was away – man, woman, or dog and usually had someone close by to help.

One day, surprisingly, he leaned close to me and asked me to find the mother of his then favorite girl, Zoe Hersch, who had suddenly disappeared. Mother was known as ZaZa Mantilla. Didn't take long to find out the mother's name was also Hersch, first name Rachel.

I found her. Took three days only.

She was doing business at the Border Motel in San Diego, a half-mile from the border crossing. She was drunk. Made her presentable. "Oh my God, I can't wear that. I need clothes. You don't know those..." She stopped and grimaced, not knowing which side of the fence I was on when it came to the Mondozos. Cost me almost six hundred dollars just to get her in shape to be returned to her daughter.

Within a week, Aureliano asked me to take Zoe and Rachel to LA and deposit them at the apartment he kept for Zoe on Detroit Street and Eighth Street.

He assured me he was forever indebted to me. Yeah, sure.

Chapter Sixteen

I was at the John Augers House in Hancock Park. June Street. The door opened quickly.

"You're either someone from the Harry's bank, or a broker. In either case you are wasting your time."

"I'm not a broker." Gave her my name.

"Good thing, because I'm not selling." She stuck her hand out and gave me a firm shake. "I'm Carly Klein. Which you probably guessed." Her lipstick was one of those bright red almost luminous colors, pale skin with faded blue under her eyes. She had rich, dark hair falling to her shoulders and a light bump in her nose. Her tan blouse was buttoned only at the waistline and tucked into a pair of short denims with a fashionable shredding at the bottoms. I had the instant impression that I had seen her before and told her. She replied, "Never. I don't travel in your circles, or any circles...or travel."

I smiled my most winning smile – which had never gotten me anything. "Just a homebody."

"Just."

She backed up and I entered the foyer and faced a circle staircase with curved mahogany railings. "I have to make it clear to you," she said, leading me to the sparsely furnished hollow living room, stucco fireplace at the far end, "I don't care what the estate problems are, or your problems, or your health, or Harry's problems. Nothing gets me out of this house. It's mine," she laughed, "All of it." She looked me up and down, "Not bad, but you aren't big enough to move me. I can handle two of you." Again a small laugh that was a little like a child's giggle. "You can sit over there," Mr.? Sorry lost the name somewhere."

"Ace, Harvey Ace."

"Like an Ace of Spades?"

"Like an Ace of Hearts." I sat and settled in.

"OK, Mr. Ace, you go tell that Harry Moss what I said. John wanted me to have it. It's all I have and all I have of him. He didn't give me money. He gave me this house. So, I'm keeping it." She pulled a tissue from a box next to her and dabbed an invisible spot on her lips.

"OK with me, lady. I'm just doing this for John because we promised one another, so, I'll just take count and report it to the Court and get out."

"I don't get why anyone is interested. There's nothing here."

"Miss Klein, John was assassinated. You know? Killed. Murdered. A kid who had nothing to do with anything except to have a very rich old grandfather, is missing. You get all that? Murdered. No need for attitude."

She contemplated me for a moment. "Still don't get it." She sat next to me. Put a hand on my sleeve. "Still don't understand. My banker says you are all rubber stamps. Just agree with anything you want. Are you a rubber stamp?"

"Who was that clever lawyer?"

"Not your business."

"Hold on, here. I'm just doing John a favor. I signed up for him and he signed up for me. That's all there is to it."

"If Moss said this house had to be sold. He is way off base."

"Lady, your claims are not my affair. I just do an inventory and get out."

"Don't trust any of you. He double crossed everyone. Hot walkers, grooms, that sleazy Mexican rich kid – unless you slept with John you didn't know him, and we were together for years. Not going to let him do the same to me. Even though we were together for years." Her eyes faded off into nowhere as spoke.

"Sounds like love…for a while and then something else…and then he is gone. Did that Mexican kid say anything about getting back at John?"

"No. Just that the kid was mad as hell at him and wanted a load of money. Don't know why. And Johnny just told him to fuck off."

"And the name of this kid?"

"I don't know. Johnny just called him, the kid. John had this way of being superior but it pissed that kid 'cause he was supposed to have bunches of money."

The obvious came to mind. Aureliano knew about the trusts and cooked up some scheme to latch onto the proceeds as they were doled out.

Maybe he used Harry Moss as a tool to get to John. Or threatened Carly Klein. Or she was part of it.

"Miss Klein. I'm just a bean counter and all I want to do is count your beans…I mean the stuff…"

"Relax. If you count my beans, you'll get lost after number one."

"Cute. But let's get on with it."

"Everybody is a wise guy." She shook her head and a half dozen wisps of hair fell into her face.

"In any case, I'm harmless."

"Funny. You don't look it." This time her laugh was a chilled giggle.

"Let's just go through the place and I get out of your way."

"Not much here. To tell the truth, we made love at my place. This is just an expensive barn...which I think I can make into something special. We talked about it. Johnny and I."

"I have question."

"You have a lot of them."

"How did John have time to deal with Sally, Carole, you, Gert and God knows who else?'

Her face turned slowly sour as if her lemonade had turned to lemons. "Would you like me to kick your sorry ass out of here? He was my guy. Not those others. They weren't even real. Made the old man happy."

"Tell me about that."

"Nothing to tell. I think you should leave."

"Not going. We have work to do. My little notebook supplied by Harry. Gotta fill it up."

She made a move toward me and it was surprising.

"Miss Klein. Not sure what you are doing. But don't try it. Please." My tone was soft and careful. I had enough on my hands and what do I know about serial lovers? Or anything to do with women?

I had a record of failure.

"OK. Back to business." She gave me a smug smile and she pointed at the staircase. Second floor had the usual bedroom accessories. I entered each on the notebook and started to go through the drawers.

"Hey. None of that," Klein interrupted. "Everything in the drawers is mine and it's private."

"Not until the Court says so."

"Wrong.

"There is no court order about anything private as of now...and there won't be. So just stop right there.

"They don't need to know about my underwear."

I agreed. If there had been diamonds and gold and Rolexes, they would be gone by now anyway. I followed her onto the upstairs balcony overlooking the rear yard. It was enclosed on one side by a wire fence and one stately Eucalyptus tree in a kind of forlorn semi-nude late fall condition jettisoning leaves as we watched, patches of Bermuda grass in scattered clumps fighting to stay alive until spring. In the northern corner of the rear was a small, perhaps ten by twelve, garden tool shed.

There was dirt pathways, gardeners' pathways, ways from the shed to the house.

"Doesn't look like anyone really lived here, does it?"

"Told you. Neighborhood is four million and up. They occupy the space but no one leaves dishes in the sink."

We went through the second upstairs bedroom and she waved a hand over the twin sized bed and one bureau in the corner and said, "No love lost here," I said.

"Go through anything you want here. Never spent time in here. Kept a bunch of junk in here. Horse racing stuff. He had these moods, you know."

There was an old oak rocking chair in that corner. Big bed, no bed covers.

"Tell me about those moods."

"Not your business. And stop asking questions." She had a way of turning when she spoke as if not caring if you heard her. She closed her eyes leaned her head on one wall and her shoulders heaved. I stood away. Better let her cry it out. In a couple minutes, she swerved back toward me, all smiles, a different person. "We had wonderful years. Yes, we did. Great memories."

"His moods?"

"What moods? There were no moods. We were lovers. That's all."

"Won't argue the point."

How could those memories all be wonderful? He was dealing with a sick wife, a sick kid, FK Wheeler and his wife, and an anxiety ridden business? And a series of lady friends?

I found a three by five framed image of a troubled child of about six or seven years of age, inscribed with a fancy scroll of "Frankie." Pulled out another photo with browning edges of a smiling women with light brown hair, low cut blouse, black slacks, well put together, and seeming to dare the camera but half turned away, avoiding something. "This Sally?"

"Wouldn't know. Never met her. I don't know her or anyone like her. Never did."

"Take a closer look. See what John was dealing with."

"Put it down. Dammit. She doesn't look like anything. You finished?"

"Sort of like you. I'll keep it if you don't mind."

"Who cares? No one cares." But she reached out for it suddenly and I pulled back. She stood there with her hand out all at once insistent about seeing the picture. I handed it to her. She stared. "Strange looking creature." She dropped it.

"That wasn't nice." I picked it up.

"Nice was not my intention, she replied.

"Did you know Carole? The second Misses Augers?"

"A little. Not nice lady. The past is past. Dead. No need to dig her up again."

"And the two of you? How did you get along if at all?"

"She was…she just was…we had no relationship. Nothing. No connections."

"Not even with the boy, Frankie?"

"She was not good to him. Pretended."

Her voice sharpened. "That's not what you want to know, is it? You want to know who shoved her, who attacked. Was it me? Which is crazy." And you keep looking at me funny like."

"No. We're just talking. I'll look the other way if you want."

"You are a sarcastic son of a bitch, you know that?"

"Been called worse. But you knew her. Carole?"

"Not well enough to kill her." She laughed and again, suddenly, that little girl's giggle was in the moment.

"Says who?"

I thought she would hit me. She leaned back, fists clenched, and then said, "I already told you what you are. Do you know what your voice sounds like when you ask questions? What you look like? Your face screws up and you get creases in your forehead. I know guys like you. Digging. Digging." Then she smiled a cunning smile. "But maybe you're different. Yes. Different. Bright and happy like…you know, happy people. Not many of those around, I thought. I could see wheels and bells going around in her head.

"Maybe you're not one of those people with questions all the time. No more questions. Drink your coffee. You want me to warm it up?"

She was bright and cheerful again. I held out the cup and she poured. I said, "You seem in pretty good spirits, not like a few minutes ago. I'd rather have you high than low."

"I'm neither, Mr. Ace. Really. Can't you see that? Don't like all your questions. Don't like questions at all. Just remembering John, and how we were. There was a movie like that wasn't there? I never saw it, though. Just drink your coffee and go home.

"I can see what's in that beautiful head of yours. You feel like talking, don't you?"

"Just drink your coffee. I told you." We sat in her kitchen, green and yellow tiles on the walls along the sink and the stove.

And old house, past its prime in a neighborhood that was always in its prime. "You think John was some kind of philanderer, or kook, don't you?"

"I'm a listener. Not a judge."

"We were in love. He gave me this house. That's about it. Told me that Wiseman lady was trying to steal a famous horse from him. You have to get all that stuff about John out of your head. Unless you're dumb like most guys. He just needed money. Racing costs money... That's what he kept saying."

"Miss Klein. I feel like you are not understanding. "John was murdered – murdered. They shot him several times. And his kid was kidnapped and another person was kidnapped. They are all in danger. What am I missing? What's in there?"

She lifted the canister and poured herself more until the canister was empty. The steam curled into her eyes. "I think you better just shut your mouth. I'm not one of those people that hang around racetracks. "John and I were going to be married."

"Both of his wives are dead. Or they are supposed to be. Didn't that give you a little worry?"

Silence. She did not look at me. Pretty clear to me I wasn't getting more out of her, "You should leave, Mr. Ace."

"OK. That's fine. But I'll ask my friend, a homicide detective to come by and talk to you some more."

"Go ahead. Do that. Maybe John needed to be saved from that terrible Sally woman. Everybody said she was crazy but maybe she wasn't. Maybe it was time to save him from that old man who controls him. Women do that, you know. Save men. Maybe this time it's an old man." She ran her fingers through her thick hair. "I've done that. Carole was a big mistake. He said so. He loved mmm... Sally. Sally was his love. He could have just walked away from her. But he didn't. She walked away from him. Sally, I mean. Or Carole. He didn't hurt anyone. That was the trouble. You're saying he might have arranged to kill her?"

"Go on."

That's not true. Johnny was wonderful."

"I'm sure." Her hand went to my sleeve. "They called her crazy. Didn't like that..." Her hand went up my sleeve. "You like that? I got more."

"She was institutionalized."

"Forget that. She was better than they say. We have a bed, Harvey. Let's just go upstairs."

"Whoa, Carly. Slow down. No thanks." Her hand crawled further up my sleeve "This is business. Not monkey business. You know where all the money he made went. You know that.".

I pushed my cup aside and got up and started for the door. "If you're not willing to talk, I can't bother anymore." She jumped in front of me.

198

"This won't do, Miss Klein…" I shoved my notes under my arm.

With a mischievous smile not quite fully formed, she began to pull her jeans down. Then she reached for me.

This was not going to happen. I asked about Carole, "You knew her?" Her pants were in a puddle on the floor.

"I hated that Carole. She kissed the boy's baby ass. Coddled him and then screamed at him. Mean." Carly shoved herself into my body, arm around my back. "You're just like all of them. Right?"

"Not like all of anybody." I warded off those hands. Panties were almost to her knees. She couldn't move and I could. "Men are not too bright. C'mon, Ace. C'mon. You scared? That old man offered her money to get out of John's life." She put her arms around my neck, and began crying. "Why are you holding out on me?"

"Listen to me, Miss Klein – it looks like John played you and all of you. Some scheme of his maybe to get around his father-in-law. Whoever killed him and Carole and took his kid and John, killed everything left of John's past life…" I took her naked body and pushed her back and held her at arm's length.

"Stay. I need you."

I extricated myself and managed to get to the French Doors that opened to the back yard. "Stay there," I said.

A blue Jay dived at a squirrel and missed. A lesson in how to prevent attack the squirrel scampered up a tree to the underside of a large branch. There was a Gardener's shed in the corner of the yard. The grass was already brown and scrubby. An elm tree in one corner was as nude as Carly Klein in the September Autumn.

"OK. Tell me, if you know, who that bear was that shoved Carole off the cliff?"

Her eyes widened. "A bear?"

"That's what they called the creature." I got to the front door.

"Get out of here!" She grabbed her panties, wiggling just to get them back on."

"You better get yourself a lawyer. You know more and people will want to know."

I slammed the front door of that hollow house, the house that was so precious to Carly Klein. I couldn't fix her or anyone then, or anything. But I knew I had to go back and check out that gardener's shed. Seemed like all these large places had enough land that they needed these sheds.

I called Paul Sampson and asked if he had enough time get with the Klein woman. "We'll get to her. Meanwhile, LAPD has a fund for this and have a reward out for young Augers and for your Sarah. You want to add to it?"

I added another twenty-five thousand. Sophie and Franklin money "Any news. Any at all?"

"No. Maybe the money will talk. Did you all her roommate in Denver?"

"No help. All their schedules are messed up with Sarah's disappearance. She is working double time."

"I'll call her. She might know more with and tell me and not some cop."

He was irritated but said, "Alright. Go ahead. Enjoy yourself. What about the Foundation, Wheeler's Foundation?"

"Going there tomorrow."

"Give 'em hell."

"Ha Ha."

Chapter Seventeen

The FKW Foundation had offices on the top floor of a twenty-five-story black tower on Avenue of the Stars, Century City. It sat at the north edge of the development closest to the intersections of Santa Monica Boulevard and Wilshire Boulevards and the busy side streets of Beverly Hills. I parked in the belly of the building and walked to the correct elevators and was followed by an expensive blue suit and stripped red tie. Mr. Blue Suit smiled and nodded and hit the 25 button before I did.

"You're a member of the Foundation I presume," I said, as sweetly as a person could.

He grinned and shoved out his hand. "Right. Jack Gordon. You?"

He had a round face, golden tan, and curling black hair. His nose was perfect. I forgave him. This was Beverly Hills adjacent, married to Hollywood.

Gave him a firm handshake and my name. "Joining the group for this one time."

"Group? Oh, yes, the Board. You must be the one George Jacobi told me about. A friend of John Augers. Coming in cold. Too bad about John. Any news?" He smiled.

Smiled? It was not a smiling question.

"You're supposed to be voting a lot of shares. We have lots of news." He hesitated, "But not for publication."

I nodded.

We stopped at the eleventh floor. Young lady with close-cropped blond hair, holding a fabric briefcase close to her bosom.

"You know what we do at the Foundation?"

"More than most. The Foundation was a public Charity and there were records in the State.

Young lady exited at sixteenth floor.

He shrugged. "Good for you. You know Alex?"

"Like a brother."

"Very funny. He has no brothers, sisters, or anyone, I don't think. No one quite knows Alex." He smiled again as though he had swallowed the western world and which agreed with him. "You know that girl who just got off?"

Shook my head. "She is the CEO of the very large advertising agency. Hard to believe she is more than twenty years old. But she is. They do forty or fifty million a year. See her all the time and she seem to be running away."

"Or running to. Such people seldom run away."

"Suppose you're right."

The twenty-fifth floor opened to a comfortable reception space, framed nautical prints, and straw papered walls. Deep red upholstered chairs, gold and red Persian rugs, two small couches, matching olive shaded lamps…all designed to make one feel at home and in the lap of important people.

Blue suit existed with me and walked straight past the receptionist who nodded and said, quietly, "Good afternoon, Mr. Gordon."

He mumbled a response and disappeared through the double door into forbidden space. It was obvious he didn't know the receptionist's name even though a placard with her name appeared on the desk. The young lady, earphones attached to her head, looked at me, and knew what I was thinking.

Just to the right of the receptionist was a glassed-in conference room, large enough for more than a dozen participants, end was with books in shelves which had never been read or even removed, a blackboard set into the surrounding books, and a far wall of glass overlooking Century City to the South and West. I could almost pick out my Condo from the vantage point.

I was advised that Mr. Alexander Christakos was the President and Vice-Chairman of the board. "I guess he runs the show."

"Maybe not." She smiled reached for a package of gum in her desk drawer. "They'll be tied up for a few minutes. That's what they told me. No smoking here. So the gum helps. Mr. Wheeler would have a fit if he saw me smoke or chew. He doesn't do anything that isn't perfect, you know."

"Mr. Wheeler is here today?"

"Oh, yeah. Been here a while. Don't know what they're doing but it must be important. Not a peep out of them."

"Probably in a gin game."

"Mr. Wheeler playing gin?" She laughed, barely showing teeth. "Guess not…ummm." Stopped. Stuck the gum in her mouth, checked herself in a pocket mirror, wiggled a little, and looked at me. "You're not married?"

Shook my head and sat in the deep cushions of a red chair. "Well, you know what they say."

Phone rang and saved me a conversation about marriage. She flipped her mouthpiece back to her mouth," Foundation, who can I connect you with?"

I closed my ears and gazed out the glass enclosure to the ocean, thin line of dark green at the horizon.

"Nice view."

"You know the Board?"

"Everyone."

Three minutes later, Miss Johnson motioned and pointed at the door. "Now."

Wheeler sat at the end of a large glass conference table, the spread of Los Angeles to the south, an airplane from LAX arriving just as another was leaving in the opposite direction. Jack Gordon was on one side of the table smiling easily at me, and on the other side Mr. Gray Suit, pin strips, a satisfied look on his narrow face and prominent chin, figured to be Christakos. I hoped I had the name right. Gordon was next to him. I supposed Jacobi was the one across from him and two more I didn't know and wasn't introduced to flanking them.

Wheeler stuck out that small hand of his, "Hello, there, Mr. Ace. Good to see you gain. Guess you found your way." He didn't get up, meaning I had to go to him to reciprocate the extended hand.

"I usually do. How are you?"

"Very well, thank you." All teeth. His eyes fluttered close. "Well, I assume you know what we do here. Problems and such?" His eyes squinted open. "You know we have to find my grandson. Have to stop all this guardian nonsense. Figure there's a motion before the board on that." He surveyed the group and each smiled and nodded. "Spent half the day yesterday with some police lieutenant. Got my lawyers sitting all around that bunch. They are setting up a reward money for the return of the boy. Fifty thousand from us. I understand you have been asked."

"I have and did. Same as you. Might do more." How could a person resist one-upmanship just then?

"Right. Right. Calling Harry later to make sure it's done right. Then I'm firing the son of a bitch." He looked around the table to make sure his comments had been absorbed. It meant he had the power to fire the bunch of them but my guess was the PR would be a problem. His faced settled into a mask of determination. Or hate. Hard to tell the difference on that face. "We won't rest until we find the boy and that Sarah whatever."

"It's a package deal," I said. I didn't care about secrecy or not making the deal clear. I figured every one of them knew exactly what was going on in my life.

"Deal? What are you talking about?" Wheeler acted surprised. "don't understand any deal here. That Sarah lady is a Finkel. Finkel? That's a Jewish name, isn't it?"

"Don't play games, Franklin. You know it all."

There was silence. No one ever called him Franklin. Doubted if Sophie ever did. Someone in the room stifled a laugh. Franklin looked around, searching, seeming to be bewildered.

"You heard me. You don't like the name Finkel? Probably Finkelstein at one time. A good name." I was getting close to losing my cool and realized it in time and pulled back. Wheeler humped a couple of times. Gordon looked at me and his hand indicated a damper on the exchange. "Let's get on with it, what say?"

"Right. Right," Wheeler intoned. "We have an agenda to get through. First is the reward money. Fifty thousand to join with LAPD funds." A dozen nods of assent.

Wheeler waved and Christakos rose and took over. He was almost scrawny – about a hundred and forty pounds and five eight, a light black suit and no stripes and plain black tie over a white shirt, the collar of one tweaked over. His black smooth hair was receding.

Christakos made a note about the missing John Augers and Harry Moss and other voters, "Missing some," Wheeler added. "John, who we all knew well. So, let's proceed."

Christakos went to the blackboard at the end of the room and pulled down a white board with a list hand printed on it with a felt pen. I wondered why there were no notes or recording devices.

With nothing to lose, I asked, "Do we have a method of recording these proceedings?"

"It's being recorded," Christakos said. "Don't worry yourself."

"More than one tape?"

"One is enough."

"Which only you or Wheeler possess?"

"Take it easy Mr. Ace," Gordon piped up. "Not to worry."

"Except I do."

"This is a public entity. We have to abide the State rules," Gordon said.

"Good. Then for the record, I want a copy of this meeting. OK with you Gordon? Jacobi?"

I thought I saw Gordon wink.

It occurred to me then that all of these people might be enemies of one another, angling for some prize that was not apparent to me. In any event they were not friends to me.

"Well, Christakos said, "Have you met George Jacobi formally?"

A younger man reached out for my hand and we shook, and he said, "I assist Mr. Christakos."

'I know. I've reviewed your history. I didn't want to come here unprepared." Jacobi leaned back as though he was done for the day.

Wheeler added, "Well, we certainly know all about you, Harvey Mr. Ace."

"Doubt that Franklin. Never really know about anyone, do we?'

He didn't like that I talked back, or that first name business, and harrumphed and pointed at Christakos who rose quickly and pointed at Item one on the white board and requested a vote. "Let's get to it."

The item was a $35,000 grant to the YMCA in West Los Angeles. Everyone raised their hands and voted yes, and I did the same.

"Mr. Ace has voted aye and so it will be recorded along with the representation by him of the principles who own the shares. Note, he is not the owner."

"I represent John Augers, Franklin Augers, and Sally Augers. I have, as I understand it, however, control of voting the entirety of their voting rights," I said, "According to my interview with your lawyer. And that should be recorded Somewhere. I will need a copy of the notes and minutes or recordings."

They all stared. Golden nodded, then Jacobi and then Wheeler, finally Christakos.

Wheeler said, "Yes, yes, you're made yourself clear. Let's go on."

Second item was the contractor approval of the final contract of the project on the 101 Highway near Mara Bay. It was a five hundred thirty-million-dollar contract. The Foundation owned one third of the project. "Franklin, I believe you own the a third of the project through FKW," I said, "and I control the remaining interests. Is that true? Subject to any bank loan, of course. You have big plans, don't you?"

He waved his hand, "Move along. Move along."

I knew that the remaining trusts owned a third. "Just make that note, please. For the record." I enjoyed the power I claimed to have. However, who knew?

"Move along. Move along."

Motion was made to approve the contract and I interrupted again and asked if competing bids and investigation of the Contractor had been accomplished and where are the documents demonstrating it. I asked if the materials and designs had been approved earlier and if there were architectural approvals with the City and County.

No one spoke and I added that I wanted to see the contract. They assured me the contract would be available when necessary. It wasn't available at the moment. Wheeler interrupted and said he had a copy and Christakos added that he had a copy.

"Do you have a copy with you?"

"Move along. Dammit," Franklin repeated. "We don't need to slow us all down. There is no trouble between any of us here. Do you understand, Mr. Ace?"

I smiled and persisted and wanted to know if there was a Foundation copy. "There might be some trouble. People are missing. And dead."

Wheeler waved his hand impatiently at the Director who went immediately to the next item as if I wasn't there. The next item was approval of the ingress and egress maps to the property in question, and the County approvals. I knew that Frankie's trust carried the exclusive rights to approve the County permissions and grading.

Harry had made that clear. I kept my mouth shut. But raised my hand in approval.

Christakos tried to explain that all trust and real estate rights had been bundled, something like a real estate mortgage bundle, and thus it wasn't necessary to deal with all of the approvals piecemeal or with the specific rights of each trust. I said I doubted that such a vote was valid.

"Like you would know," Christakos said, voice dripping with silent laughter.

The vote was called for and though I hesitated just to let them know it was not what was really in my mind I voted with Franklin again. Everyone smiled and relaxed and we went through the list one by one, me voting for whatever seemed like what the rest of them wanted, with Gordon once interrupting to clarify the commencement of construction and the amount of the Construction bond. Christakos seemed impatient but answered the questions, looking at Wheeler each time.

We got through the list and every person raised hands and bellowed "aye" to every motion, Jack Gordon sometimes a little hesitantly. Maybe he was a quiet ally of mine.

Turns out, Gordon was the Prime shareholder and CEO of Border Oil who was the distributor for some of the brands of gas and oil in Southern California. And the primary supplier to all trucking asphalt and oil contracts of the new Mall. Mucho bucks on this own. One time when the group was voting on the limitation on the proposed Mall, Jack Gordon held up the vote objecting to the limitations proposed. He wanted the access roads to carry truck weight and the others wanted auto weight access roads only, cost being the issue. More room for home and apartment construction. But Gordon was right, and he won the argument.

Now, he had another beef. "I also don't want the little shop squeezed out. The big guys can take care of themselves as you've seen – but these requirements on shop size, the types of retailers, is too restrictive. Shouldn't be in the Deeds."

The silence could be sliced. They called for the vote and Christakos drilled Gordon with a set of very black Greek eyes and a scowl. He stood as tall as he could and said, "Mr. Gordon, I think you do not understand retailing."

Golden said he did and they wrangled for a while and managed to get to a vote and I went along with Wheeler and the Director. Golden was perplexed. He believed I was a genuine independent voter, but he was catching on.

I shrugged and the motion was passed as Wheeler wanted. I looked at Wheeler making it clear that he owed me.

There was one more item on the list but Golden got up and said, "Fuck it," and told them all he had to leave. He gave me a hard glance as he left. Wheeler was smiling.

They passed a couple other motions about financing with what was a Wheeler Savings and Loan. I started to question but kept my mouth shut and wished Gordon left.

I shook everyone's hand at the end, asked about a copy of the minutes or the recording and Christakos said I would have one delivered to my home with twenty-four hours. Just mail it."

"Everyone gets it delivered."

"I won't be there. I can't sign for it and it shouldn't be left on the doorstep. Mail it, Alex." At his name, he stood back at though slapped.

"I can't accommodate your circumstances.

"You must accommodate for this company. Unless you want to resign?"

"It gets delivered."

"I suggest you be careful who you send to deliver."

"I might send several people."

"If they all want broken noses, do just that. I guarantee it. Mail the fucking notes and I expect them to be correct. California is tough on monkey business in charity groups. Attorney General is always interested." I laughed at myself as I left quickly. They were too smug for me. Gave them another reason to want me out of the picture.

I turned quickly and left, paid the aggravating twenty dollars just to park there, and drove quickly to the Wheeler Mansion. I sat for a minute feeling shitty about raising my hand like a schoolboy and approving every motion at the meeting. Not a great feeling to be that helpless. But it was nice to toss a little, very little, monkey wrench into their machine.

Sophie greeted me at the enormous mahogany door with surprise registering all over her, widening her eyes with short breaths as she hemmed and hawed and asked what I wanted, He features seemed to have narrowed. She told me that Franklin was not there. "I know that. I just left him."

"He won't be home. He is expected in Santa Barbara County to speak to County officials regarding rights of way and various such things. Has a car taking him from his office. I don't expect him back tonight."

She was perfectly groomed. But she was not the same. A forehead crease. She must comb her hair every hour and apply lipstick every half hour. Not a wrinkle in that lavender dress. I couldn't imagine her in slacks, or in anything but a proper dress. She had the damn-est look in her eyes. Almost disjointed. They widened and narrowed as she spoke.

She did not ask me in but she wasn't about to stop me from getting in. I didn't push her but I swept past her and started shouting, "Sarah! Sarah! It's Harvey! It's me Sarah. Call out! Can you hear me?"

All the anxiety of the past few days regarding Sarah and her walkout that Sunday morning and my part in it and her disappearance came out.

Maybe it was uncharacteristic, but I was frantic. Whatever my behavior, I didn't want to lose her. Not this way. I didn't care about my behavior.

I kept shouting. The old lady kept trying to pull at my jacket and I would jerk away. She was squealing.

Sounded like two utterly mad people in the wrong situation at the wrong time. She reached out as if to shove a hand over my mouth. "Stop that! Mr. Ace, stop that! There is no one here but Estella! No one! Are you crazy?" She punched me. Tried to trip me. She seemed extraordinarily strong. Pushing her away was not easy.

I ran through all the first-floor rooms, the closets, bathrooms; banged on walls for hidden places, ran upstairs and started the same process. Every corner, shouting, "Sarah! It's me! Bang your feet, anything. Let me know you're here!" Sarah was in that house. I knew it. Twenty-five years of searching and finding people and dealing with nut cases told me she was there.

Sophie was with me every step. Breathing short, heavy breaths like it was the end. I looked at into the expansive yard, leaves gathering, winter brown and dry. Gray sky began its slow waltz into night. There was a small garden with stunted white azaleas. And a shed in the northeast corner. Just like the one at Carly Klein's.

I ran back down stairs certain Sarah was somewhere in that great old house. If not at Wheeler's, where else?

Hurried to finish the inspection of the kitchen – leaned down once more to inspect the areas beneath the sinks and in the cupboards with Sophie dragging on me. Suddenly, the world went dark and my head felt like it had been split open.

***

I was on the lino floor in the kitchen. My head was the size of an overripe melon. No one around. I could hear myself groaning.

Got up to a sitting position. Then saw Paul. Standing above me.

"Took a bad fall, huh?" Smiling. "Mrs. Wheeler said you fell on the stairs and then stumbled into the kitchen table here you were in such a mad rush. Hit your head there."

"Where is she?"

"Mrs. Wheeler?" Paul helped me up. "She left. Big hurry. Nasty cut back there, Buddy. Probably bounce your brains around and make everything better. She will probably file a big-time complaint for busting into her house."

"How'd you get here?"

"I had an appointment with the old lady."

"Take a look at the stairs. See if there is any hair or blood there. Quick, go take a look."

He came back in a few minutes while I took a dishtowel hanging at the side of the two-basin sink, soaked it, and pressed it against the back of my head. I sat in one of the kitchen chairs. Still dizzy.

Paul shook his head. "Nothing there. Nothing. How'd you get into the kitchen? If it happened on the stairs?"

"I must have stumbled here. I know I wanted to look under the sink and cabinets. I was about to do something. Something I hadn't covered."

I rubbed the spot on the back of my head with the wet towel. Still oozing small amounts of blood. Went to the fridge and found ice and wrapped the towel with the ice and flattened it against my head. Felt better almost instantly. My brain was coming to. "I was about to do something. On my way…" I moved the ice pack to my forehead. Paul waited. "I don't know how you got into the kitchen," he said. I think we got here just a few minutes after you fell."

"Was Sophie here when you came?"

"Yeah. She told me you fell, pointed at the stairs and ran off. She was gone by the time I sat you up. I'll get to her. Don't worry. We can hold her but had you on my mind at that moment. I can hold her and charge her if you make a complaint. And, you should know, we're going to bring in Wheeler and ask him a few questions."

"I can keep tabs on Mrs. Wheeler. The old man will be out of your hands as well. Best to leave her alone. Let's find out where she goes."

"OK. That's fine, but if there is a weapon here somewhere that has your hair stuck to it, I'm picking her up."

"Probably an old frying pan. Still wobbly. But I remember. I was headed out back to the shed, that gardener's tool shed in the corner in back. That's when it all stopped. Better check it now."

"Game playing? Hide and seek – like one of those kid's games?"

"Paulie," I said, irritated. "Shut the fuck up. Just help me. Sarah had to be here. Assuming the Wheeler's are involved somehow."

"You really think she was here?"

"If they're it, she was here."

"They have help in the house?"

"A maid. Maybe gardeners. Is Mrs. Wheeler's car in the garage?"

"Everyone's gone. We'll follow up on the maid. We'll get ICE to see what they have."

We went through the rear kitchen door to the now dark, empty yard. The cool fresh air helped me get my balance.

I opened the shed. It was about ten feet deep and probably eight feet wide and dark. Tall enough to stand in.

Paul flashed his small light. I climbed through the gardening debris. I felt the walls and stumbled back to the rear corner. Paul moved the light to each corner. "Take a close look, Harv."

There were piles of old pillows stuffed into a small bundle, and the corner wasn't cold. The walls were almost warm. "It's not cold back here. Somebody was here. Flash that light closer."

"Harvey, look, down there just to your right. See it? An earring, or something like it. Can you reach it?"

I put my hand over the spot and pulled the object to me and held it out into the light. Sampson said, "It's an earring alright. Little circle of diamonds."

My heart sank. Felt a wave of nausea settle over me. "That belongs to Sarah. She was here. I knew it."

"She's a smart girl. Left it for us."

***

I had made Franklin Wheeler happy with my votes, even though I made sure he knew I expected a return on my votes. I ran out of the meeting before they could start pinning me down about selling my rights or assigning them to Wheeler. That was going to be the next avoidance hurdle.

I couldn't keep caving in but would have to confront the situation sooner or later. Had the sense that Jack Gordon might be helpful. He kept smiling at me.

I thought of calling Kim all at once. I needed some connection. About all understood right then was that three to one paid eight dollars and that was better than a bank. Good rationale for gambling except who was I kidding? I was an addict. It was about Sarah. *I'll send for my things.* And what will I be doing ten year from now? Sticks in my throat. And my belly. And I didn't have an explanation as to why it hurt so much. I was a big boy. I had a life. Damn. It hurt. Time was ripe for a serious discourse on the nature of my life. Forget all that my father had insisted… *Winning is everything.* Just win. Remember what I say, Harvey. No one loves a loser. This history led me in a strange way to an understanding of Franklin Wheeler. He couldn't make a connection with her early in life and now it was fear and fear only. And he had no intention of becoming a new loser.

I'm was in the car planning. I needed to win. It had caught up to me. *The Silk* was running. Two hundred and fifty thousand Dollar San Diego Handicap. Big move up for her. And I had to do was to take a look at Palisades Park along the promontory above Santa Monica Beach where Carole met her terrible end and Frankie went into his silent gear. And I had to deal with John's funeral and the Mortuary where Sally was cremated. I had complied with the demand that I vote the way I'm supposed to vote. They didn't need Sarah or the boy any longer. Let them go, dammit! I called Paul again. Didn't worry about bothering him. I wasn't worrying about how it seemed to him…that I was being an amateur…or something. "News? Any news?"

"We're working on it, Harvey…we got to the Mortuary yesterday. Your Sheriff friend, in Mara bay is working on that end. Not sure what to think of him."

"He's good. Not to worry. Any real news? Location. Something."

"We're working on it. It will work out."

"Dammit! Paul, that's not good enough! I need her alive! I need her! Don't tell me that anymore!"

***

The letdown after Paul's explanation that he was *working on it* left me frustrated and angry. Last time I was angry at Paul we were about fourteen years old after he whipped me on a one on one basketball court after school.

I had to get a message to the powers that be – whoever they were. I would cooperate, let Sarah go. Seemed the best way was a direct approach. The maid answered the phone at the Wheeler mansion. "You Estella?"

"*Si.*"

"*Donde esta Senorita Sarah?*"

"*No se. No se.*"

"Very important message for *Senor* Wheeler. *Comprende?*"

"Si." The voice trembled.

"Tell him I will continue to cooperate. I will continue to cooperate. *Comprende?*"

"*Si. Si. Co-op per ate.*"

"You speak English?"

"Yes. I do. Born here."

"Why didn't you say so? Why the act?"

"White folks like us to be half dumb."

"Give that message to him. Give it to him. I know he has her. He can let her go. Or else."

"I understand."

"Repeat it, please." The line went dead.

***

The mortuary was halfway to Mara Bay, just north of Santa Barbara before the tunnel up to Solvang in the interior. The proprietor was a fellow named Herrara Pillar, Indian or something according to the mortuary Association for the State and the State records.

Chapter Eighteen

The persistent fable is that all gamblers eventually get beaten and die broke and on the streets. It's a monstrous fabrication, created by neglected families and losers. Gamblers founded the West, believed in the great beyond, built ships and sailed around the horn to settle the lush valleys of the lands beyond the great river; they piled cement to a thousand feet in new places, flew airplanes that traversed oceans in one hop, built a dam to hold an entire inland ocean.

Indeed, gamblers were the future. They didn't always win. Of course. But I was one of them and believed that I was destined to win. Maintain my equilibrium and I would be just fine. I was ahead of the game. And it was a game. Just like life, it had a hundred rules and rules for the rules, which you couldn't foresee. We all hated the RULES. We found ways around them. Legitimate, and otherwise. It was life condensed. Sit five gamblers at a poker table and one would win more consistently than the others.

I knew my histories, my numbers, but not algebra, not calculus. The calculus I knew was that three aces had already appeared on the table and I had the fourth, with twin Kings. I knew that light bends, that mass and speed were one calculation, and that everything, absolutely everything had an end... except the universe. And I had a sense of why people lose... it was because they didn't believe in themselves. They didn't believe that they could be right and everyone else wrong. It was not arrogance, although that is what "they" want to believe. Fact is, I believed, absolutely, that Sarah and I would end up together, and that, at the end of the day, my destiny would be what I wanted it to be, what I needed it to be. However, I could be wrong.

I had fourteen hundred and thirty dollars from yesterday's winnings, and Sophie's check for ten thousand and money coming from FK Wheeler, both checks for the same reason –find Frankie.

My table at the Santa Anita Turf Club was squeezed in – like all the other tables – I was next to Doc Lee, and to a rotating bunch of ladies on my other side who were there every Saturday. For some reason as I ambled toward my table, sitting above the finish line, my hands were trembling, my breath short, and a knot at the back of my neck. Vague acquaintances remarked on the bandage at the back of my head and I waved my hand that it was nothing. I felt tired as I sat down, as if I hadn't slept.

I had the feeling that I had to win, but at the same time that I should be doing something, anything but what I was doing. Go figure. I should be back in high school paying attention instead of fucking off and thinking I was smart enough. Instead I was sitting in a vast luxury hole in the ground with a Caesar salad in front of me, conjuring up scenarios about murder and Sarah and Frankie and John Augers and that silent ghost of Sally Augers. And sitting near to Doc Lee who never stopped smoking. The most likely suspect of the various crimes was a rich old man sinking slowly into dementia and needing desperately to get his way about almost everything. Paul Sampson had already decided that Franklin Wheeler was his man, the culprit. He told me he had been having "conversations" with Wheeler at his station in Parker Center when a bevy of lawyers showed up and whisked him away. "And we found what hit you. An old frying pan, just heavy enough to damage and heavy enough to kill unless that wasn't the purpose of the hit. We're running fingerprint matches now. None are Sophie's."

"Tell me about Sarah and the kid. *Something.*"

"Nothing. But all stops open. Rewards. Bulletins, every cop in the west is looking for them. Pictures everywhere. We found the mortuary who did the Sally cremation. Up in Mara Bay, just north of Lompoc. The Mortuary Director is a guy named Herrera Pillar at the Eden something mortuary. Sits out over the ocean. Your old friend Joe Dowbrowski is the chief up there and he has his people on it, but it's not much. We have people there, too. Don't bother to find them. You won't."

I ordered coffee from Joey Sendank, former jockey, now chubby waiter. He gave me one of those, "That's all?" looks. I waved, "No tip today. None!" Which he knew was not true. We were all afraid to get on Joey's bad side. I settled down. Racing form in front of me but mind not on it. All of those calculations had been made.

Not sure of where to aim my next foray into the mess of the Augers family. I had to focus, get a direction. Mondozo was one, but it was not *the* one. The Wheeler mansion was another but certainly the LAPD had searched the place and Wheeler was in their sights. Harry and Ann were another, considering their petition to take over Frankies position in the trusts. The connections with Sophie and Ann was interesting as was the fact that Sophie had a son.

I looked at the San Gabriel mountains, the white tips of Mt. Baldy, rising just above the late morning cloud cover. Wheeler was not in his box, Gert was just walking to her box below me and caught my eye and tossed a tiny wave. I did the same. Juan Gallegos was with her along with Sammy Riddle, another trainer who was friendly with the Augers/Wiseman group.

All the stuff bouncing around in my head reinforced the need to win and to find the bad guys and kill them. Killing them had settled in my mind and stomach. It was absolutely what I decided to do. Not talk. I would execute the sonsabitches. And I would find my Sarah and Frankie and be gloriously happy and I would never gamble again. And I would find a house with a white picket fence and my daughter would answer my calls and that would be that.

Billy Fitzer came to my table. "Your tie is in your coffee. Idiot. You have a hot wet tie. And you're wearing a black sock and a brown sock. Did you know that?"

"Color coordinated."

"You need a lady. Listen, Harvey, I know what you need. Even though it's not possible. You are not settling down into a regular life, a regular suburban existence. Give it up. Go find a different mountain to climb."

"Go away, Billy." He was wearing one of his horse blanket jackets, squares and swirls in red and black.

"The LAPD will find her and the Augers boy. Stay out of it."

I didn't answer.

Winning Silks was in the next race. She was four to one, second favorite to a two to one shot. I was ready to place my bet which would alter the odds.

"Why aren't you down in the saddling barn and paddock with Gertrude?"

"I stay out of her way. She gets upset when I'm with the horse and jockey. I tend to interrupt which is the last thing they need. When we win, I'll go down to the circle with her."

The race was the two hundred fifty thousand Handicap 6th race, The *San Diego Handicap,* "Gertrude said it was just a beginning. Thought she had a great chance. Worked a 59 flat just the other day, coasting."

"So you're making a big bet." It was not a question.

I shrugged. "Probably."

The race was for three-year-olds, most of them brand new three-year-olds, as their age changed at the first of the year irrespective of

215

when they were born. It was January. The skies told you it was January, sharp and chilled, gray wisps over the mountain which were so close and clear you could settle underneath one of the trees and touch the TV towers at the top. None of the owners and trainers really knew if their horses were ready for three-year-old open company at a full mile. Most of them had done well as a two-year-old, being quick for five furlongs and some for six furlongs, three-quarters of a mile. But a full mile was a different story and required a horse that was a genuine winner, with toughness of spirit, and who would be a contender through the year, given no injuries and good health.

As I rose to go to the betting window, Billy said, "Put twenty on it for me."

"Use your own money this time."

He pulled out a twenty and shoved it into my hand. "OK. OK."

The Pari-Mutual windows stretched down the length of the great betting room. A dozen windows on each side. I looked for Helen, my favorite and lucky ticket seller. But no Helen. Got in the short line at Fred Wallins' window. Asked where Helen was. "To the dentist. Taking a couple days off to get all of them fixed. Big deal. So you're stuck with me." He had a clicking sound when he spoke. Sort of a nervous tic.

"She should look great when she gets back."

"Which means you have to trust your dentist. Which I don't."

"She will be fine."

"We'll see. You betting *The Silk*?"

I gave him my bets – five hundred to win on number seven, my girl. Another five hundred to place and another five on the late pick four, and two combinations with *Winning Silks* for a couple hundred each with other horses in the race at good odds that had a chance to be close at the end. Fred's eyes widened. His eyebrows raised a couple of creases in his brow. "This is a make the month bet, right?"

"Not your business. Just gimme the tickets. You can ruin the odds by spreading the news."

"Not saying anything to anyone, Mr. Ace. Honest." His hands went up. "She must be ready."

"Lots of very good horses in this. Boys and girls. Remember?"

I knew that Fred had two kids and a stay-at-home wife and that he was a gambler. He punched out twenty-dollar tickets so that I could redeem them separately and at different times without having to sign IRS reports of the winnings. I noticed Fred punched out two extra win tickets and shoved them in his shirt pocket. "Shouldn't do that, Fred."

"It's my life."

I could hear him thinking, *Stay out of my addictions.*

I stopped on the way back at Doc Lee's table. He crushed out his half-smoked cigarette. And coughed. "Your girl's big day."

"We'll see."

He pulled out another Marlboro and flipped his lighter. I don't think I would have recognized him without a cigarette decorating his lips. "You can't sit still, can you?"

I waved at him and turned and went into the Grand Lounge of the Turf Club. I sat at the fifty-foot curved and polished mahogany bar under the art deco ceilings and copper chandeliers. The thick carpets crated a softness to the noise of the losers and winners and the buzz from outside. I got a glass of Pellegrino with ice and went back to my table and asked for a couple of corn beef sandwiches on rye for Billy and myself, "Hot, Joey, hot."

"Relax, Mr. Ace. I know your filly is running. You'll end up in an emergency room."

Doc Lee leaned over and said, "I recognize the symptoms of acute stress."

"I'm fine."

"You're not, but that's OK. Normal for the circumstances. Any news? About your girl?" He knew the story.

"Nothing."

"Sorry. I liked John. Though I grant you not many did."

"Let it go, Doc."

"None of it goes away, does it? You hide from it but it's there. We all hide from the real stuff. Let it be, Harvey. Just let it be." He coughed again and took out a handkerchief and coughed again into it, and then again. His face turned blotchy red. He finally stopped, gathered himself and shoved his handkerchief back into his pocket. His skin was like splintered plaster, veins and lines everywhere.

"You're telling me to let it be! Just the way you deal with suicide smoking?"

He laughed a thin laugh, his face drawn. "As long as I don't pick up a scalpel any longer, what is the harm? I rather be here than on a couch in my living room, wasting away. That's the bottom line. Listen, Harvey, don't you know, smoking is the way of all Protestants, eating is the preferred suicide track of all Jewish folk, and drinking is the way of the Catholics ... and Anglicans. To each their own. By the way are you really going to win today?"

"Yeah. You're right. To each his own. And in a word. Yes. No more losing."

Nails snuck up to the table. Nails Nirenstein, holding his nails like treasure in his hands. He was half black and half Jewish on his father's side. He couldn't work because of the obsession with growing those fingernails. They were always painted a meticulous bright red. His eyes were set into enormous bowls of blue and brown. He started out in his young days as a simple, well-known safe cracker, hired by the best criminals. After spending three years in Folsom State Prison he was smart enough to realize there had to be a better way. So he grew his nails and thus could not crack safes anymore. And worked now and then for TV shows as a curious creature who permitted obsession to rule. He always assured the group, Larry, Billy, and myself, that he was not obsessive or "off his rocker."

"I'm not crazy, you know. I just have to take care of my nails." But he was crazy. His father was a successful liquor store owner, owning two stores in the northeast Valley out Pacoima way. Both parents appeared to be "normal." All of our parents seemed to be "normal" yet we were all off-base, more or less – some more, and some more than more.

The sandwiches came and I ordered another for Nails.

"It's not the same, you know," Doc added. "When you have a scalpel in your hand. You are the God. And you must always win. Never lose. Death rides all the losers." He crushed his cigarette on the table. "Let the kids operate... A little luck and sticking with your filly, and I'll last until the money runs out."

Joey leaned over and whispered in my ear, "Sumthin's wrong with these people, you know that?"

The track announcer came over the loudspeaker system, "Horses are approaching the starting Gates."

Gertrude Wiseman was pointing at the horses as they approached the gate nearly in front of her. Juan sat immediately in front of her. Another groom sat with her. She turned and waved at me.

Santa Anita was a one-mile track, thus the starting gate and the finish line were close to one another. *The Silk* had a lead pony to guide her into her slot. She went in without a hinge, the result of Gert's going through the exercise with her about a dozen times over the last week. My mouth went dry. I had to win. This girl horse had to save me, along with that lady trainer who looked like my sixth-grade teacher. Losing would be more than a disappointment – it would drain what was left of my resolve and energy. Winning is the validation of your total self and losing was the opposite.

218

Especially now. Recent workouts showed that there were a couple of front runners, quick from the gate and for the first half mile. One of them had a recent 58 flat for the five furlongs and was touted as being the "sleeper." There did not appear to be any real "closers" from the meager information on these babies and there was no buzz about any of them in the Backside. These youngsters were trained by the best and ridden by the best, and would not be in the race if the connections didn't think they each had a chance. I knew *The Silk* could run a 24 for the last quarter in a three-quarter mile race. A couple of the fillies hopped and danced at getting loaded into the gate.

They 're all in the gate now – flag is up, waiting for number three, Lans Dans to settle down. I checked the board. My girl, number seven, was nine to two. The bell rang. The gates slapped open. Eight horses at about eleven hundred pounds each leapt forward. A good start, seven horses, no tumbling and veering heavily into one another which was a frequent problem in these young horse races. My girl got a good spot behind *Maximillian, No holds Barred* and *Pete 's Choice. About Right,* the suspected "closer" was right at the heels of The *Silk,* just away from the rail. One king-sized blanket would cover the first four. As they hit the clubhouse turn, *Lans Dans* cut toward the rail and took a half-length lead. I was hoping for a quick 23 for the first quarter which would give the closers a better shot in the stretch. *Pete's Choice* went up and kept close to the leader. All the pack kept reasonably close, not wanting a front runner to get away from them. Donna kept a firm hold on *The Silk* as instructed about five lengths behind the leading two runners. The quarter was accomplished in 24.2 slower than I had hoped. They pack moved a little faster through the backstretch straightaway. I focused my binoculars on the jockey riding *Pete's Choice.* He was easing up on his mount keeping close but trying to conserve for the stretch run. *Lans Dans* kept to the rail and the lead. The half was timed in 47.3 a decent pace but still not as fast as I had hoped. Billy was standing, arms raised high like a boxer after a win. He kept mumbling, "C'mon baby. C'mon baby." ANNOUNCER: *Lans Dans and Pete's Choice, a half-length to the side are right there keeping the rail to themselves. Half mile to go. Restraint now making her move and coming around the outside and settling in with Bargain View: Winning Silks at the rail just behind looking for room.*

Nails started screaming something indecipherable as they came into the far turn. Doc Lee started coughing again, standing then sitting and coughing.

ANNOUNCER: *Now into the turn, Winning Silks moving up past Maximillian and Bargain View moving at Pete 's Choice and Lans Dans.*

Winning Silks still looking for room. Into the stretch. Winning Silks up next to Bargain View inside. They are at Lans Dans and Pete 's Choice now, both fading and now Baargain View and Silk nose and nose moving past Pete 's Choice. Now it's Winning Silks by a half-length coming to the 16th pole, Bargain view right there. They are pounding down the long strength neither giving an inch. The front runners are through. Bargain View coming at Silk again. They are heads apart. But Silk is hit once by her jockey and she is moving away from them, by a length, now moving out by two, tail waving. The jockey on Bargain view was whipping his horse furiously, trying to keep *The Silk* from taking over. *Coming to the finish line Winning Silks by two now three lengths, and it's all over folks, she is widening her lead and hits the line almost four lengths to the good. Impressive run.*

"You got 'em! You got 'em!" Billy screamed. Nails began jumping up and down holding his nails for dear life. Doc Lee was in the midst of a coughing spasm and I stopped and took a step to him and held him up. He felt like he was collapsing and then he looked up and gave me a pained and unhappy smile and put his hand on the table and eased himself down. He waved at me insistently not to bother with him. He started to reach for his cigarettes but I pushed his hand away. The crowd was slapping me on the back and shouting congratulations. I sat down, done for, just then realizing how tight and breathless I had been for those moments just before and during the race. I reached for the water and took a sip, put it down, took a breath, and closed my eyes knowing this was more than a mere winning race for me – and for Gert. The control of my own life had slipped away and now, at least for this moment, I had it back. Doc Lee reached over and patted my back and lit another cigarette.

I hurried down the stairs to the winner's circle and almost knocked Gert over as she was doing the same. We hugged fiercely. We got to the horse and to Donna Camina and hugged them all and waiting while Donna grabbed her gear and weighed out. I couldn't stop kissing *The Silk's* nose until Gert pulled me away to pose with Juan, and two other grooms, and Donna, back in her saddle, for the winner's photo. A TV reporter stuck a microphone at Gert's head. She shook her head and said, "All I can say is that we have plans for her."

A minute later the official sign went up and the payoffs posted. *The Silk* paid $12.40 to win, about thirty-one hundred for my win bets. Plenty more for the remaining bets, and the winner's share of the purse which came to about $170,000. Carve out Gert's share and Donna's share and the assistant's share as well as the grooms and the IRS and I still had enough for breakfast... in London or Paris... and I had what I have always wanted, the sense that I was not just a gambler. It was more than a win. It was a kind of justification for my existence to that point. I went into the Men's room and threw a handful of water on my face. Billy was behind me. He understood. "Who are you now?" he said as he put his hands into the water and squeezed out soap onto them. "Do you know?"

"I'm... I'm... I don't know, Billy. Not sure what I'm feeling. But it's more than winning and the money. It's more than that. I assume you all won, too."

He nodded.

"I'm in the racing business. I own a winner."

"And?"

"Yeah, I know. I have to find Sarah and start over with her. And find that kid."

***

I didn't go to the barn with Gert to watch as her staff washed the girl and checked every inch of her as if for her annual check-up. Gert would report to me in a while. When I got back to my table, Aureliano Mondozo was sitting there, poking at a grab salad. "Get the fuck away from here," I said, bitterly.

"No chance. We've got money coming."

Just then Georgie Saltos came over to me and told me that there was a call from the LAPD and to follow him. Apparently, there was some big news.

Chapter Nineteen

It was Paul. "We may have a lead. Take it easy and we'll be in touch."

I wasn't going to stay out of it. "What can I do?"

"Sit tight."

"Fat chance."

But that's what I did. I had no leads of my own.

***

Next morning I hit the damp sand out on the beach just the moment the sunshine first hit the quiet surface of the Pacific, making it a vast undulating silvered skate ring. Wore a T-shirt and short denims and a cap to shield reflections, hanging one of those striped canvas chairs on my shoulder which I struggled to unhitch, finally succeeding. I stuck my nose into The Racing Form, checking workouts, adding numbers adjusting to track surface, arguing with myself about whether or not to revisit Ann Whitson. I knew it would be more than a visit so I nixed myself. *Stay away, Harvey, stay away.* I knew Ann was in the middle of a mess. And there was still news about Sarah I was waiting on. But I didn't want to take on another one.

Twenty minutes on a quiet beach was like a couple hours in church. At peace with the numbers in the Racing Form, marking with a red pen a very good five to one shot in the third race at Santa Anita on Friday, a life held at bay for just a while. I had hot dollars in the bank from *The Silk's* win. And an urge.

Feeling lucky I called my daughter again. Just not that lucky. The same response – not at home. Leave your name and phone and number and I will return the call. She had to have an unlisted number. Kept the one I called to fend off dealing with me. Not fair. Nothing kids did was ever fair to their parents. But who knew at the moment of conception? At least I always got Kim's voice and not some automated one. My instincts told me she had to be involved with some guy or something else important to her and couldn't be bothered with me. Perhaps she's getting ready to marry or got a promotion (to what I didn't know). Perhaps one day I would catch her. Perhaps she would actually want to talk to me. After all, I took care of her all those years rather nicely; paid the bills, showed up at recitals, where her mother would sit on the left side of the hall and I would sit on the right side; talked to her first-grade teacher, took her to Dodger games, to the Lakers. But that was nearly twenty years ago. How was she to remember or understand? She closed ranks with her mother when I left. I told myself it was natural. It wasn't but it was reality. Besides, feeling sorry for myself was sort of comforting.

I called Jimmy the Mummy a couple of times, not expecting an answer. He didn't have an answering machine. After ten rings I hung up.

I knew my next move and that it must be relatively quickly. Jimmy seemed to be a sort of fulcrum in the whole Frankie situation. Find him and the rest of the secrets would unfold. He had been certain someone was following him. I discounted it. Somehow Jimmy was in the middle. It was not that I knew he was involved – I didn't, but experience in the misery business is worth something and Jimmy was in the middle. I would have to start digging all over again using the Mummy as my lead. Meanwhile a nice late winter sun was warm and not so mysterious and mine for the taking. I closed my eyes.

Two minutes later I heard a familiar voice, "Hey, Acey, Ducey, looks like we got a winner." Aureliano Mondozo sat down next to me on the sand, gray slacks, white silk shirt, diamond cuff links, and thin black tie, all suntanned and fresh and fashionable; tassels on his shoes, tie slightly open, hungry eyes. Hair glistening. Slick. He was definitely slick. Polished and smiling, ready to strike. His face had attack written all over it. Sammy Glick with slicked hair, a thin grin and a tan. When your family was worth something more than a gazillion, you could afford to have a smile plastered on. "My filly did great, don't you think? You can keep the win money, Harvey, this time." He laughed. "This time." He pointed a finger and pulled the trigger.

I shaded my eyes. "Ahh, there he is, my famous friend from south of the border. This is a nice surprise. Tell you what, Auri, I'll keep whatever I want, including the filly, and you don't have to sell me your lovely house for ten dollars. I'll sacrifice. Just tell me how the family is. Dad, Mom?" I did the finger trigger routine and got to my feet, lowered my voice, "Now, you can turn around and get the fuck out of here." He had well-dressed companions, straw fedoras and concealed armor. "And take them with you."

"My father would like to talk to you."

"Don't think so."

"You will. Trust me. Never mind the family. We're changing trainers on my filly," he said. "Thought you should know. Like to keep things clear between us, you know."

"You don't own a horse, Auri. At least not *The Silk*. She's mine. Lock, stock, and big Dolly Parton chest."

"Oh my, gee whiz and golly gee, Acey, Ducey. You definitely will talk to my father. He is waiting." His face was narrow, hair perfect, altogether a wonder to behold. He tossed his jacket over his shoulder. He was trying hard to be dangerous. But he was just a spoiled, rich kid trying to make it without his father. However, because of his family, he was indeed very dangerous. And at the bottom of it all, he knew he was nothing without his father. However, when he smiled, he was very dangerous. He wouldn't do things as smartly as the old man or the rest of the family, but he was more likely to do something like kill a person and worry about it later. "I have the papers here. Just needs a signature." He pulled out a sheet and a pen, still smiling. Slowly, as if to emphasize his meaning, he pulled the top from the pen and handed it to me. I sat up.

"You definitely have the wrong person, my friend. The name's Harvey Ace."

He blinked and turned away from the direct rays of the sun. "That filly. She's mine, you know. I bought her before you knew she existed."

"Not true. But it doesn't matter." I measured him. He would be easy. Taking on the other two might be harder, but doable. They had to cover about ten yards in polished Nunn-Bushes and deep sand. I calculated my moves. Then I said, "You own nothing, Aure. Nothing. I want to be helpful. I really do. However, not really."

He definitely wasn't as smart as his father as he grabbed at my wrist with his free hand. It was not a good idea to let him think he could control anything.

I said, "Auri, you have hurt my heart. So let's just call it a nice morning at the beach." I jerked away and tossed a handful of sand in his eyes, hit him hard right on the button, and he was gone just as his hefty but slow army got close. I threw sand at them, shoved my canvas chair at one, and jumped the other right at his feet and pulled. There is no solid footing in the sand and he went down. But the other got me good in the belly. I turned and pulled at his legs but the other one of "good fellas" recovered and started to reach for his piece resting in his shoulder holster. Big mistake. Gave me plenty of time to bring a hard right into his kidney. I wheeled around and gave the rising and blubbering Mondozo a smack across his nose again, hoping to break it. Was not enough – I got a hit somewhere on my skull and that's the last thing I remembered for a good ten/fifteen seconds. The one that hit me started chuckling, like we were all in an asylum. He must have scared the small crowd as they had faded away like a melting Milky Way. When I came out of it, the big one had a trickle of blood oozing from his right ear. There was another bigger trickle down my forehead and into my eyes. He said, "You are fuckin' crazy, man. You know that? This is big trouble for you." He reached for Mondozo. His eyes squinted as they measured me. "No fuckin' reason. You got trouble coming your way. *Estupido!*" He spat the words out. "Could've worked it out, man. Easy like. *Estupido!*" He shook his head like he was dealing with a confused gorilla, thinking of me as a genuinely pre-human being. He held Mondozo and shoved a handkerchief over his nose. "Trouble, man. Plenty trouble. You are a major asshole."

He pointed and directed me back to the condo. "Go on inside, *estupido.*" He led the still dazed young prince of the Monodozo family away from the crowd and motioned us into my home. I leaned toward the second guardian of my former friend, who was getting his bearings back, and whispered into his ear, "I'm going to kill you and your boss. Remember. When this is done, I'm going to kill you if you get within a hundred yards of me. You're dead. A dead man. *Comprende?*" His eyes squinted into slits in the sunshine and he laughed. He had heard it before. I scared myself more than him.

I smiled at the two older ladies and a stroller with a kid, each frozen in place, too frightened to move. "We were just playing games. Old friends." I smiled a bloody smile at them and grabbed my chair and tried to put it back together, gave up, smiling still, "Just a game," I shrugged, wiping my eyes.

I followed the group, two of them holding and guiding their damaged prince.

Sitting at my dining room table, surrounded by my books and bric-a-brac was Miquel Cervantes Redon Mondozo, fat face split ear to ear with a satisfied grin, fat fingers entwined. "My dear Harvey, dear boy, let me get a cloth for that cut. Nasty. Nasty." He went into the kitchen, came back with a wet paper towel and dabbed at the cut on the side of my head. He stuffed the towel in my hand and pressed it against my head. "Hold it tight there. Aure, you foolish boy. How did you do this?" Then to me, "We should take you and Aure to the doctor. There is an emergency room at the hospital just five minutes down the boulevard."

I declined. "But thanks for the ice."

"His nose! To the doctor!" he growled and they took Aureliano out, obedient soldiers with their bleeding boy, leaving one sentinel behind. Miquel Juliane's white shirt was open at the collar, flesh creeping over and touching the gray sheen of his suit coat. He was the boss of bosses. His fists clenched and released, clenched and released.

We stared at one another. Finally, he said, "See? Harvey, dear boy. I have no weapon. I have only me. Old and fat and still fond of you. We should not have problems."

"I appreciate that."

"I knew you would." He closed his eyes, and sighed.

"Miquel, I appreciated the greeting by Aure, too. Out on the beach. With guns in the nice sunshine and among the children and old ladies. A nice surprise."

"It's TV, Harvey. They watch too much TV, but you must not mistake me." He tapped the side of his head. Brushed his non-existent hair back. "Someday Aureliano grows up. But he is a nice boy. My youngest. Girls love him. But me? I am not Aureliano. Which you know." He stared at his fingernails.

"You were always nice to me."

"I was paying a debt. A family debt does not have to do with nice or good, or bad. Do you understand? You took care of my boy. I took care of you. Understand?"

"I do now, Miquel. But your boy. One day someone pops him and he doesn't get a chance to grow up. It won't be me. But someone."

He tossed a hand in the air, "I have more boys. And you? Do you not pay your debts?"

"Always."

He shook his head thoughtfully and turned to his fingernails again. I waited.

"It's a business. We are in business, Harvey. We are a family. There is required honor among us. Required."

"So, what does that mean, Miquel?" I tried the familiar. Perhaps I would be safer on a first name basis. "Does it mean you get my filly, Miquel? That is not a debt for a debt. Doesn't add up to me."

"You are correct. Debts are even. We pay you three hundred thousand for her. You must sell at that price."

"No, Miquel. I cannot. She is not merely money. You must understand this. She is me. I call on your lifetime of wisdom. She is part of me. She is her babies, her future. Her wins. She is my door to somewhere."

"She is money, Harvey. A big lovely animal. Talented. But an animal. And money is money and family is family."

"Wrong." I was not sure that was the best way to deal with this boss of bosses. I never heard anyone speak back to him. But I went ahead. The entire

226

matter had meaning to me that he could never understand. "She is a life, Miquel. A new life. A future. She is not merely an animal that makes money. She is my future. New breeding. New wins. Grade Ones. New highs. A reason to exist. I think you must understand this."

There was a long pause as he inspected his fingernails. The air around us grew icy. He did not respond. There was no way to guess the best approach to this man.

"No one can have her, Miguel."

"Hmmm, you were very good to my boy in years past. We repaid you. Took care of you. Gave you money to gamble with. The debt was paid. We are even. Now we start from where I wish to be. Even. You understand this? We need our stable to grow. I want the horse." He looked up. One eyebrow went up. He whispered. "I want the horse."

It was growing dark. Lights on the pier began to flicker on. They flickered red, blue, yellow.

I pulled my chair closer to him. I wanted to reach out and touch his hand but dared not. That left-over minion of muscles standing nearby might very well simply shoot me and all of them disappear into the rare air of a Mexico that belonged to the well-bred, careless, safe and rich.

"It is difficult to find genuinely good stock. We bought the colt that came second in that race. What was it, Georgia something? Sounded like a girl's name. We gave a fair price."

"C'mon, Miguel, A broken head? Maybe a threat to the owner's wife? I know what you do when you want something. I've seen it. I know it now. But the answer is the same."

He sat back quietly and gave me that smile again. "Three twenty-five."

I shook my head.

He rose, placed a corduroy cap on his head and leaned over and patted my cheek. "Too bad, Acey-ducey. That's what we used to call you. Right? You remember?"

"Long time ago. I am grateful for your kindnesses. I am. Truly. I want you to know this again. But I am not selling my future. That's what she is. You have to understand. My life is changing."

"Oh, my benevolent God, Ace. Santa Maria! Gamblers do not change. What do they say? They go gently into the night, broke, falling into pieces."

"Too old to go gently anywhere."

He took a step toward the door. He sighed a waspish sigh. "Three twenty-five. That is the last I will say. I will do it in cash." His small, rotund body, blue light stabbing his face, turned and he gave me a spread-eagle smile, pulled the brim down on the cap and said, "You will sell. Trust me. And maybe you don't get three twenty-five."

***

After I showered and dressed and stuck a bandage over the cut near my right temple, I dug out my small .32 Cal, checked to make sure it was loaded and stuffed it into my pants. It could kill but wouldn't likely. However, it would hurt a lot and dissuade. And it was small and concealable. I knew that sooner or later, I would have to confront the situation and somehow end it, perhaps with Miquel Cervantes Redon Mondozo himself. How and when? My dad used to say, 'You'll know when it happens.' He had a saying for everything and a shot of Wild Turkey for most things.

I found him one summer when my mother said he had not been home for a couple of days. I was home from the University of Pennsylvania for a short visit and restore my capital from the family troth, maybe eighteen years old. I found him sitting on the floor of a large shoe store in Long Beach. He was slumped, head on his chest, belly protruding, thin hair in his face with a Long Beach uniformed cop standing over him. "You going to take him in?" I asked.

"Not if I can help it. Lot of paperwork for an old drunk. You take him outta here. He can't just stay like that. Got a call from his area supervisor."

"He's the area supervisor. He does that. He calls and gets himself taken in. But, OK, I'll take him. I'm his son. Help me get him up and I'll get out of your sight."

He did and I did. We were in my car. I said to my father, "How do you get into these messes – time after time?"

His eyes rolled and he grinned. "Easy. I drink."

"Mom's gonna kill you."

"Yeah," he mumbled. "We'll know it when it happens."

He was wrong. You know it long before. Especially in my universe.

When I finally got into my car, heading for the track, I dialed into my answering machine and listened to messages. One from Sampson and from Joe Dobrowski. That was when each told me about Stanley Simon.

Good old Stanley was obliging a sinister pattern by getting himself killed by a hit and run driver outside his office in Mara Bay. Paul told me that Simon had apparently tried to fend off the death vehicle by aiming his closed umbrella at it, like a matador trying to skewer a runaway train. It happened about nine p.m., not more than a few hours after I left him. His office had been ransacked, records taken, files missing. One entire drawer.

228

I called Joe. "The '93–94' drawer is missing entirely," Joe said. "Now we're stuck. We can't even find out who his patients are."

"You can, Joe. Small town. Subpoena them and don't take no for an answer."

"Maybe. We'll have to reconstruct from the receptionist's memory."

"Life is tough. That's death number three and still a missing boy. This killer or those killers are getting desperate. But I don't know why."

"Maybe they think you're getting too close. It happens."

A passing sudden rain all at once tumbled down under low gray skies and then passed. It left a sky looking like it would fall, and we would need another Noah. The rain would last intermittently all through the day along the southern coast. Drivers would curse and bump fenders, gutters would overflow, and school kids could never find their rain shoes.

When I called Sampson back, he was abrupt. I told him that I would try to see him as soon as I could and would call. He said "Now." I said, "*Tut, tut, tut*, Saint Paul, no temper. I'll see you when I can." I did not tell him about my fun and games with the Mondozo clan.

The next morning I was at the track and felt safe. And I did quite well – it was one of those days – two very good winners and a couple of *Tri-fecta* combinations. But I was looking over my own shoulder – feeling generally miserable and guilty. Guilty for not making enough headway in finding Frankie – and Jimmy, and feeling a little "*estupido*" like the man said, for precipitating a physical altercation that I might have avoided with a modicum of finesse. I always thought finesse was my forte, but it wasn't. I was a regular impatient klutz.

I left after the seventh race and headed for Larry Flynt's Hustler Casino in the Southeast part of the Los Angeles industrial section. It was set between a metal fabricating plant and a large parking lot. I had to get rid of my misery. It felt good just to walk into the place. A different world. Warm colors, soft lights, clanging machines, people not paying any attention to you, the smell of booze and sound of chips and losing groans. Great. Lights, action, start the cameras!

Flynt was a smart guy. He gambled with his life and kept winning. He taught us lessons about what was worth fighting for. One time, however, he didn't win and got shot right in the belly. No walking for him after that. But he was alive, and still smart and living life as best he could. Big office at the corner of Wilshire and La Cienega mid-town. Nothing half-way. I played poker, lost a sizable portion of the day's winnings, and had no one to blame but myself. Two old ladies took me down. Two smart old bitties. They kept smiling across from one another at the table and kept upping the bets and raking in the pots. Had no idea when and if they were bluffing – absolutely couldn't tell. One had a lace collar around her neck and a quiet dark blue dress and the other, more fashionable, wore a black nylon thing with two strings of pearls. She used very bright red lipstick and had diamond studs in her ears. The other wore a muted pink lipstick and no adornments. Each would smile at the other as they swept in all those chips. They winked when they won and winked when they lost. They laughed when they won and laughed when they lost and laughed when the cards were dealt. The false teeth in the one with the string of pearls kept clicking when she laughed. I was making the clicking and the clacking and the laughing all possible. How do you tell a couple nice old ladies to shut the fuck up? Problem was they were having a good time and didn't give a damn whether they won or lost. Which is why they won.

No one at the table, except the two old girls, remained in a gambling mood and most left after a half hour or so. I didn't. I kept trying to beat them just for the sake of beating them. But they kept upping the bets, first one then the other, well-oiled old machines. They had me. And the River always seemed to be the crucial card for one or the other. I had trouble concentrating. That was my excuse. What did those records stolen from Doctor Simon contain? Was the instigator of death in those files? Was Sarah hiding in there? By the time I conceded defeat to the two nice old bitties it was nearly three am. It was their bedtime. And mine. They kept giggling as they followed me to my car, expecting, I suppose, to protect me from myself. I was happy to crawl into my own bed an hour later. As my eyes closed the damn phone rang. One of those nights.

It was Harrara Pillar. He told me he was on his way out of Mara Bay and that it was important that I see him before he left and as soon as possible, that he had something he wanted to show me. I agreed and we set up a meeting date and he gave me an address. Same one he gave me earlier.

***

Chapter Twenty

As though it was ready to slip into the sea and disappear like an old turtle, a half mile down from a modest peak which dipped to the Coast Highway, sat the old tilted village of Mara Bay. Like everything else along the California coast, Mara Bay was in the process of being gentrified. How anyone or anything can gentrify an old turtle remains a mystery. "Gentrified" usually meant that the local grammar school had a new principal, and a new traffic light at the most significant intersection: as well as a new bakery and a coffee house with neons that invaded the main street from seven pm whether still light or not.

Sid's Restaurant was still there, small sign in black on white like a not wanting to offend. Still had leather booths and languid lighting and my friend Max the Muscle as the new proprietor. Most local shops had to move to the outskirts of Mara Bay as the rents went the way of the world, and the new principal of Greeley Grammar School believed that no kid should ever lose. No one should lose bet, or a friend, or a game which seemed to me to make games pointless. Talk to me in twenty years, let's see how that idea works out.

The Rocky Beach area was in a marine wind pattern northwest to east, and its salty dampness clouded windows and corroded whatever was exposed and neglected. The salt wind was the one single thing that controlled the nature of life along this section of the Pacific coast. Breeze Street is in the middle of the damp, old end of Mara Bay, right against the northwestern expanse of the Pacific. I was leery about any meeting anywhere except his office, however, Hararra Pillar, his voice urgent, and the stranger's note insisted I meet him and perhaps find Oritha Durden at number 39 Breeze Street. The number and the mystery created a memory of the thirty-nine steps movie, Robert Donat and Madeline Carroll. Harrara said it was important. If he said it was important, I figured it was. He was the guy who was supposed to have burnt Sally to a small pile of ashes. He had to know a great deal more than he had revealed in our call.

Breeze Street was a block from the beach, rimmed by rotted wood bungalows built in the twenties and thirties, set between narrow streets and dangerous alleyways leading part way up the surrounding hillside which spread out with flowers and green lawns and neat bungalows painted into a half dozen colors. Sort of Copenhagen without the tourists.

The alleys down off Breeze Street had garbage cans that were open or ajar. Automobiles vintage of the 60s and 70s disintegrating in the sea air littered the area like discarded tin cans that could not be salvaged at any price. Bony dogs roamed. The place had obviously been kept together by repeated applications of juicy fruit and Elmer's Glue-all. Bicycles abounded and seemed to be the favorite mode of transportation in the area. Windows were covered in graceless battalions of red oleander. Half dead geraniums peeked up in disconsolate comers like a child desperately trying to survive the unfriendly environs. Elaborate graffiti markings decorated the sides of some of the dwellings – modem hieroglyphics, to be translated a thousand years from now by some scholar who would attest solemnly that the markings were variations on Einstein's mathematical equations codified in accordance with long dead local dialects. In short, some scholar would find a way to make a buck on the discovery using pure nonsense while stroking a scholarly beard, or, in the case of a woman, tucking in her stomach and speaking as if to her kindergarten class.

Prices in the area for the untouched dregs of tiny bungalows close to the Pacific had sky rocketed so that only computer and engineering analysts could afford to live in them, therefore there were dozens of FOR SALE signs and many were vacant or inhabited by those who shouldn't. Bankers didn't know what to do with these foreclosed properties and no one in a bank takes a chance on doing or saying anything remotely sensible. They have protocols to which they must abide. Renewal is not in their lexicon. It is not the conventional wisdom to break the protocols or bend the mold.

A mere two blocks away, new four-story condo complexes with security garages and color coordinated copy-cat entrances rose in a sort of modernist's grab at a better and brighter history – and a stab at pride lost.

An old Ford four door, vintage late seventies, was parked at a wire fence through which I could see in to the empty rear yard of the address Pillar had given me. I went to the front, leaned against a no parking sign and waited. I was not going in without first observing. Yellow streetlamps struck abstract shadows through ocean mists. I could hear the thump of disturbed Pacific waves against the shore. I checked the clip in my little .22, shoved it back into my trousers, buttoned my jacket, and after ten minutes of nothing walked from the car in front of the address around to the opposite side of 39 Breeze Street. Great title for a new movie. I waited under a naked streetlight as house lights dimmed and the misty darkness grew, waiting for someone to do something, maybe shoot me, or hand me a twenty for sexual favors. There was no one within sight, in any direction. Enough waiting. I went around to the rear, pulled out my pistol, shoved my way through the half-decayed fence. Twisted hose, beer cans, and bottles littered underfoot. I overturned a galvanized bucket which polluted the night with unholy noise, righted it, stood on it, and peeked through one of the dusty windows. Maybe a couple nude dancing girls. But nothing.

One of the other windows was ajar. I slipped my fingers beneath it and pushed. The smell of mold and assorted dead things made me pull back. As I did, I suddenly felt intruded upon. I turned quickly and leaped off the tub and crouched, my pistol searching the dark. As I turned, I saw a man on crutches gazing at me from the alley on the other side of the wire fence, silhouetted, immobile, bearded, cap tilted away from his forehead, great hollow sockets where his eyes had to be, every bone breathlessly still, hanging onto one crutch. In the reflected light I could see only his outline and the whites of his eyes.

I waggled the gun. He whispered in that sea-misted darkness, "Go ahead. Do it! Pull the fuckin' trigger." He sounded like a rusty saw.

"Go away soldier," I said, "I can't help you now."

"Do it. Kill me. Go ahead, kill me! Lived plenty long. They couldn't get me back in 'Nam. No one could get me then. I had an aura. You know what that is? Didn't get touched and should've. But you have a chance now. Right now." His voice was pleading. He meant it.

"Go away."

"Someone is already dead in there. I heard it. Why not me? I shoulda died back in '64. I shoulda. I'm dead anyway. A thousand years old." He pointed at my pistol and shaking a finger, "One squeeze. Just one. You would be saving me. Retribution! Retribution for all those dead guys and the smart generals! You're my savior."

"Save yourself. For God sakes go away." I insisted. He looked at me for a long time. "I hate this life."

I went back to him, pistol still in hand. His face was deeply crevassed, gray beard about an inch long covering the whole of his face. He smelled of stale cigarettes and bad wine. His wrists were as thin as a sick child's. I dug into my wallet and handed him a couple twenties. He started to reject it but I squeezed it into his hand. "Sorry, man. I can't fix it. I can't fix you. I can't fix anyone. But this is enough to take away the pain for a couple days. Go away."

233

He stared and I stared until he gave up and with his crutch backed off into the mist and darkness. He turned and screamed, "Should've killed me, asshole!"

His voice echoed through the alley, bouncing like destruction off the crowded bungalows.

Too much misery in this life and not enough twenty-dollar winners. I turned away quickly and, in a quick fury, jammed my heel against the back door and finished the job with my shoulder. I pushed the unhinged door open, gazing into the dead inner blackness.

**

There was a groan, as if it had been waiting for me. I crawled over the floorboards through a short hallway, until I reached a body. Still warm. The floor was covered with cold slime.

Everything smelled stale, but there was one scent that was familiar.

The groaning kept on. "Please... help me."

"Pillar?"

"Help." It was a plaintiff thin plea.

I found the torso. My hand slipped across the floor. Warm blood. In the terrible dark I could, nevertheless, make out the person's head, his thin dark countenance and black beard.

"Who is it?'

"Oh, God mother... come to me... help." Pillar's voice gurgled, barely audible, but fervent. "The records. They have the records..."

"Hold on. I'm calling an ambulance. Where are you hit? Where? Show me."

He pointed to his right side.

"Tell me... who? Who did this?"

I ran back to the car to retrieve my cell. Called 911 as I and rushed back into the house, I started to quiz Pillar again but he was barely conscious. I held his hand. "Who? Tell me."

"A monster woman!" He cried, wet choking sobs. He seemed to stop breathing. I pumped his chest. Sirens pierced the night. I leaned close to Pillar, his breath on mine. "Talk to me." His face twisted, lips barred, tobacco teeth. He coughed blood. I put my face next to his. "Talk to me." But his hand fell, suddenly limp. Then a big sigh. One eye opened. "Pillar!" I began pumping his chest again. "The boy," he said in a bare whisper. "The boy. I had him."

I listened and kept on pumping. And he began to breathe.

234

Chapter Twenty-one

I sat in Joe Dobrowski's sparse office. One desk, two chairs. One picture of wife Hedy on his desk. Joe was long and bulky, bigger than I was, and moved as slowly as a sleepy cat. Not an ounce of fat anywhere on him. He reminded me of my uncle George Nicholas, on my mom's side, who was also a big guy, spare, sharp edges, with hands like shovels. Uncle George had a violin in his closet which he pulled out now and then. With those big hands and that bulk, the instrument look like a toy. He would spend a few minutes tuning it, thumbing the strings trying to get it just right, and then scratch out a few atonal holiday tunes letting us know that his closet violin was proof positive that the family had "culture"; he would murmur under his breath, "I used to be able to do this." He reminded us that his side of the family was a cultured one every time we saw him, on occasional holidays.

Joe sat me down at the opposite end of his metal desk and wanted every bit of the story – twice. We talked old times first. He told me about his marriage to Hedy and how he relied on her as his deputy to keep his office organized. She was a whiz at it. He had two other deputies, mostly checking up on domestic calls and issuing tickets for sliding through Mara Bay's two red lights and one stop sign. We met when Joe was a deputy in Santa Barbara running for the Mara Bay job from which his father, old Joseph Prince Dobrowski, was retiring. No one would or could explain how he got the Prince added to his name. Joe the Prince, had run a money machine on tickets issued by his deputies for jumping the lights in his town and for speeding on the Interstate 101 Highway.

It took three long hours to give Joe and his deputy – the deputy was his wife Hedy – an extensive statement. It started with my phone call to the mortuary looking for Pillar and then my inquiries on the phone about the night he cremated Sally. And then Pillar's insistence that I meet him at an offsite place which turned out to be the Breeze Street address, the seedy part of town. I tried to think kindly about Joe and our past during those minutes, but it was hard. The light was too bright, I was done in and he didn't have answers as to why Pillar had been killed, But. I could tell, he wanted to tell me more. He had to have records, asked to see them and was turned down. *Ongoing investigation.*

Told him to check the Pillar mortuary for them. I couldn't add to Joe's knowledge and he couldn't, I suspected he wouldn't, add to mine. "You're holding out on me, Joe. You know what goes on in this town. Including every last complaint coming out of that Bright Paths Institute." Just finish your story and forget about what I know, Harvey. Stop trying to butt into stuff."

I shrugged and went on to explain that I had earlier called Bright Paths and the night orderly said that no one was in except the night shift which came in at about five o'clock. No one since then except Dr. Ebrons, the Institute Director, who was often there until late. He had an office and received had several calls during the evening. Chief Dobrowski was one of them. "That's all I know. He spoke to Dr. Ebrons." Told me she sort of remembered that Sally person; She had this horse of a friend. Durden. Remember her and that name 'cause the doctors had to shoot her up now and then."

Joe and I agreed that the house where Pillar was found was the place where Frankie had been held for the last several days "Easy call."

He told me he would turn over the crime lab duties to the County Sheriff s Department which would go over the place carefully. Joe added that Sampson and LAPD were doing the same. But who was in charge? Joe didn't know. I was sure Sampson wasn't going to lose this case to small town cops, or the Sheriff, even to our friend Joe D. Joe, on the other hand, was happy to relieve himself of the Augers Affair.

We stared at each other for a couple minutes, nothing left to say. Joe wasn't a talker and I was even quieter. He unwrapped that bulk of his and shut the light and exited with Hedy and we all went into an inner office that Joe kept, furnished like a Waldorf Lobby, though smaller. For a big guy he had a whispery voice. "Hedy did this. Pretty neat, huh? She thought I need to get away from the phone and my two other deputies now and then."

One leather Chaise Lounge, one table with four drinking glasses, apples in a carved glass bowl, a small fridge just beneath the table, and two more leather chairs big enough for me and whoever. "You know," he said, after reaching into the small fridge, pulling out, and pouring himself a Mountain Dew, "I'm thinking the boy, the girl, and your friend's murder is part of the same merry-go-round. It's one person…"

"You're thinking of the old man. Everything heads in his direction. My voting, John's control of too much, Sarah's disappearance, Sally's sudden death, taking Sarah from me, Carole's strange death, and all that power falling into the hands of the only Augers grandchild, an autistic kid at that."

"Pretty obvious. Which means that the bad guy is definitely someone else. Yessir, someone else. You know the Nuthouse has another place in the Arizona desert. They transfer people when they get too loaded here at Bright Paths."

"Yeah. Billy called them, too. Of course there's also the theory that the obvious one is, in fact, *the* one. And that's always the problem. You know?"

"Harvey, I know you. You will figure it out. But, listen to me. It really has to be someone else. Like in that Foundation you told us about. I'm telling ya'. It's someone else."

He pushed a button on his black 1960s phone and told responding deputy to call Paul Sampson. On the speaker Paul told us that that Jimmy Gaines was in fact missing, his car still in the garage. Clothing and household items untouched. I told him I would continue to do Wheeler's bidding so long as Sarah was still missing. But did he have any notion what happened to Jimmy. "I'll do what they want but these people better not be dead."

"He needs absolute control, doesn't he? He has to keep the Foundation in his pocket. But the petition for Guardianship of the kid is certainly not part of his plans."

We each hung up the phone knowing someone was smarter than we were, at least as of then. Called the Wheeler home. Sophie answered on the first ring. She was near hysteria. Babbling about Sally Augers. "I saw her! Sally! I saw her! Find her!"

I finally was able to tell her the news that Frankie was undoubtedly still alive, that Herrara Pillar had had him in his grasp. However, the torrent of words from her questions and accusations wouldn't permit anything to squeeze into the middle.

What about her grandchild? Was he in her thoughts at all? Did the old man know? Tell her? Was this a game of some kind they were playing? With Sally being the unwanted third party?

Called Paul again and told him the Sophie conversation. He told me that Wheelers had put together their eight and half million ransom in cash and were waiting for instruction as to where to deposit it and instructions as to how to obtain the return of Frank Augers. "That eight and a half number bugs me," I said. "Why that number?"

"Wrong speculation about the wrong problem. Meet me tomorrow, early. The usual."

"Are you going to get your forensic people into that house in Mara Bay?"

"Not our bailiwick. Joe and his Sheriff will handle it. See you tomorrow?"

Chapter Twenty-Two

In a small Spanish style bungalow, all arches, with desert shrubs surrounding the entrance, Sarah sat and stared at two men. It was all she could do. Hands taped behind her, aching from the lack of movement, fingers cold, feet taped together in a garden chair. The old house was on a non-descript street midtown Los Angeles, she had guessed was not further west of downtown than Western Avenue, by counting signals they had stopped at after she had been grabbed. It was on one of the straight-as-an-arrow north/south streets that comprised the Los Angeles Grid, cut in half by the Interstate 10 Freeway. Without the blindfold, removed just ten minutes before, she could stare at her captors and survey the room and the light of day or lamp light. The room was twilight dark, except one standing lamp in the opposite corner with no more than a 60-watt bulb in it casting shadows through the crumbling white shades. Two burly fellows sporting week old beards like those favored by baseball players sat in another corner, one on the edge of a folding cot and the other on a second garden plastic chair. They avoided her stare. Finally one of the men, uncomfortable because of her unblinking stare, said, "Close your fucking eyes, lady, or the blindfold goes back on."

"I prefer not to," she said.

"Then I'll close them for you." He rose, heavy bulk tilting to one side because of a misshapen foot.

She blinked. "Hit me again? Lotta marks on a dead body. Is that what you were told to do?" She wiggled her hands which were bound in tape trying to keep the circulation going.

"Shut that mouth!" the second man said. He was the one in charge. He stretched mightily. "Do like he says."

She closed her eyes for a moment. Then opened them and stared. "What are your plans? You must know. It's been two days... and nights. You can't keep this up any more than I can. Untying me and letting me hop into the bathroom and worrying that I will just croak right here. I see the way you act when my hands are loose. You are as frightened as I am."

"Told you. Shut up."

"You can at least tell me what you are going to do with me. That's the least you can do. You should tell me if I'm going to die here."

The man in charge rose and limped toward her, hand raised. She closed her eyes and flinched involuntarily. The blow didn't come. It stopped in mid-air. "You won't shut the fuck up, so the tape goes back on."

The fact that the fellow stopped meant something. She translated the failure to strike her again to mean they planned to release her sometime without obvious damage. Or perhaps smacking her around was wasted energy as they would end up killing her anyway. The man pulled out the roll of black tape from the lone cabinet drawer. He seemed as fidgety as she was. Much too long a confinement to be happy with continuing it. Instead of the tape he pulled Sarah to her feet and forced her to hop toward the bathroom. At the door he pulled off the tape from her hands and, pushed her into the bathroom and shut the door. "At least this shuts her up," he said to his mate. The room did not give any chance to escape. It was devoid of anything but a toilet, a wash bowl and one large rag used as a towel. "I'm coming to get you if you're not out here in two minutes."

She was out quickly, and he pushed her toward her cot, the one that had been her bed. He shoved her and she tumbled onto it and he tossed a blanket over her. The sequence had become a ritual for each of them. They all welcomed the interruption from the monotony of doing nothing. They each had a turn as they changed their watch every four hours.

"So, you are not going to kill me?" she hollered from under the blanket.

"You got that wrong, lady."

They both laughed.

***

Eden Rest & Mortuary was about five miles north of Santa Barbara, just off the 101 on the beach side, above a craggy line of rocks and waves and low rises above where the mortuary sat with about a football field fronting it to the 101 which had a barely paved off-ramp to the space in front of the building. I reached it from the turnoff sign that read, *Join us forever in peace* – black on white with an cherubic angel carefully rendered on one corner. Not a bad invitation if one was thinking about dying. It was two days since I found Pillar on the floor of 39 Breeze Street.

The field fronting the mortuary was hilly and rocky and wasn't big enough for sticking anyone in the ground. A long row of three marble walls, separated by avocado trees that had grown to enormous size, composed the places where the remains of cremation were stored. You could see the tops of the structure from the highway as you came off onto the access road to the mortuary.

The light was low in Pillar's office. He had a gold tooth right next to his left incisor and a black brush of hair that would not stay off his forehead. His large black eyes receded into small tea cups on a round face with a near eastern complexion. There was a bandage around his left ear. He seemed a little woozy when he motioned me to sit. A faint odor of formaldehyde hung in the air. Pictures of Jesus and angels were everywhere on the walls. There was a small plastic sign at the edge of his desk that said, *Rugs for Sale – Pillar Co. Santa Barbara.*

"You sell rugs too?"

"I sell very good ones. Persian and Turkish. Fine quality. I do whatever is necessary to support my family. And I sell good insurance, too." He pointed at his wall where a State Farm Insurance placard hung. "Their policies are the best. Oh, yes. The best service. You need a policy? Your car, perhaps?"

"No chance. I see you've recovered nicely."

"Oh, yes, oh yes. Hospital said I had just lost too much blood. Grateful. Very grateful. It is necessary for me to do all these things. Americans are not hardworking. They simply do not know." He slid on a pair of reading glasses, pushed them against his forehead and said, Lletme see, here. You asked about Sally Augers?" Squinting into a book dated February 12, 1996. "Long time ago. Such a long time. Ahh, yes. Here it is. Yes. present; F.K. Wheeler, and John Augers, her husband. The book was not signed, however. Names merely printed on the pad as relatives. And Sophie Wheeler. But, like I said, not signed by anyone except a scrawled Durden name as you can see." He held the book up. "Seems to be, Oritha, I think. Sloppy writing. Indeed. Like a child." His eyebrows raised. "You have to remember that not everyone signs the book. I am under the impression that there were more people here, but that is just a memory."

"Do you remember a Doctor Simon or one of the doctors from that Bright Paths Institution signing in or being present? Any document to that effect?"

"I don't recall, but do you have the date of death? That might help us find the death Certificate."

"You must have such records. I don't. You are required to, aren't you?"

"Hmmm, of course. Yes, records. Let me check." He pulled out a lower drawer of a cabinet next to him. There was large pistol in the drawer with files upright against it. "Ahh, yes. Good, Mr. Ace. Good. The certificate was signed on the 12th by…"

"Doctor Stanley Simon."

"Yes. Correct. And will that be all, now? It's quite late. And beginning to rain."

"Just one more thing. Were you working that night? You said you had a memory of more people than actually signed in. Was she cremated before the funeral service, or after? And, more important, did anyone preside over the cremation or say a few words for her?"

"No. I don't remember such. I think they all left but one. Someone stayed but I don't recall who. Can't remember."

"Did you see her body?"

A wind came up and the sycamores leaned against the exterior walls. An Agatha Christie sound. We could hear the thump of the waves hitting the rocks and shore line. A perfect night and place for an Abbott and Costello ghost movie.

"I don't always handle the final cremation. I have staff. Mostly part time from the area." He turned another page. "She was cremated and there is a memorial on the third wall, just toward the north end. Out there. You could find it. But, I'm afraid, one man's ashes are the same as another man's ashes. Did I see her body before the cremation? I do not know or remember, Mr. Ace. I was in the hospital for a couple days lately. My memory is ... how to they say? – off. As I said, the staff handles that and I am often busy with the family or other events. I do not have a special memory. Can't really..."

"You do recall, don't you?"

"Mr. Ace," he said, slowly, leaning back in his chair. "I am looking at you. And I see in your eyes the color of this room and that they betray you... you see what you want to see, you make guesses."

"Informed guesses, Mr. Pillar."

"Those eyes have seen more than they care to remember. You're sad, aren't you? Am I right?"

"Wrong. I'm fine. Good life. You check the bodies that come in, don't you?"

That is our practice. The ceremony, you know, the family must know what and where and when. They cry and carry on but they want to know they are getting what they paid for. That is often the most important thing."

"'May I see your book?"

"Of course not."

"What could possibly be secret about your record of her cremation?"

"The past is dead. I have told you. Resurrection is not my trade. There is nothing to see. And, you know, things went missing while I was in the hospital those two days." He sighed again, pushed back from his desk and closed his eyes. A tired wounded man. "I think we are done here. I have a family and it is late. And raining." He pushed up his sleeve. He had an enormous gold Rolex decorating his wrist. He replaced the book. "Our records, what's left of them, are kept private by State Law."

"I know you remember all the details of this particular event. I want to know why you won't tell me what you remember."

That look came over him. The money look. A small smile. Those born elsewhere than the USA seemed much more attuned to a negotiation than us lowly born natives. He rose. "Good night, Mr. Ace. Be careful driving. Perhaps we will talk again. I will gather my thoughts."

"Gather them tonight."

He shook his head. "I must go to my family. It is our ritual."

Money would do it. "I have money. I will call you later. We should meet again."

"I know nothing."

He shook my hand and slipped a piece of paper into it. Closed my fist and kept it there.

It was dark, rain had let up a little. On the way to my car, parked on the side of the building, a tall figure slipped from the drizzly shadows. The thin figure was outlined against the lights of the highway in the distance.

The stranger wore a Giants baseball cap and his pants had a light strip down the side. He came to me. Arms raised. I thought I would just tackle him midships and he would tumble down. I saw deep set cavernous eyes. He came one step closer and I started to go at him. But the sandy voice came at me, low and shadowy. I heard you lookin' for Oritha. I work here sometimes. They know."

I grabbed one hand and pulled it around behind him.

"Hey, you got no reason to do that!"

I pushed him toward my car. "Keep going. We'll talk out of the rain."

"She knows about Sally, so does that fella in there. Take it easy, you're hurting me."

I shoved him into the back seat and slipped in beside him. His hands were free. He put them up like in surrender. "Ahm tellin' you. Don't look at me like that. I ain't no thief. You can't even see me. Ahm like a shadow. Mostly can't see me. You heard of the Shadow? That's me."

"OK, Mr. invisible, tell me about Oritha. Take me to her."

"Big motha."

"Take me to her."

"No way, man. She and that Sally were close. I mean close. You best find that Oritha. she knows what's goin' on. But you gotta find her quick. An' I

242

can't help you. You gotta find her quick. And I gotta get outta here and pee. You unnerstan?' I gotta pee."

"Are they still together? Where?"

"Don't know! An lemme tell ya's, be careful around those ladies. Oh, yeah."

"I thought Sally was dead."

"Some people are dead when they ain't and some people ain't dead when they are. Now ahm getting out an' doin' my business."

"Your name."

"Rashid."

"Whatya doing here?"

"I work for that pain in the ass you just talked to – sometimes."

"You saw John when he was shot. You were there. Who was it? You saw it." I took his shoulders and shook him. "Talk, dammit."

"Ahm talkin'. You crazy? Ol' Herman was sitting outside the office and that's all I know. They got him good. I got low. Real low."

"Who? Who? Could you see?"

"Masks like the movies. An' hats. No, wore stockings – just like the movies. They couldn't shoot. But it was dark. John pulled out that horse from the barn. Climbed on and off they went. Off they went. They ran up. I was down at the end. They was just black shadows. Couldn't see who – just that guy on his horse and them startin' to chase. I stayed away from them.

"I could only see two shadows. There was maybe more but don't think so. Don't know why they didn't try to get closer. And one guy pulls out this rifle, long sonofabitch, and aimed and shot and that's all I know, except that fella got on his horse and off he went like the wind. Next day everybody said, they got im."

"You see them take the kid?"

"Kid was out in the street there screaming. The horses were jumpin' around and making noise and the grooms were whispering at them Those guys grabbed that screaming kid and they was gone. Like a flash. An' that's it – and I stayed down, man. Didn't move."

"And the boy. he was kicking and screaming? Alive?"

"No tellin'. Just wouldn't guess. Lissen, I gotta go. I mean, I gotta go."

He opened the car. I had let him loose from my grip and he was quickly out and dashing into the bushes across the field up a few yards from the edge of the highway which was raised a dozen feet above the mortuary space.

Sat for a while trying to figure out why a race track hander-on would be north of Santa Barbara. Hard to believe the story that he worked for Pillar. But none of it to this point was believable. But it all was.

243

Chapter Twenty-Three

Jack Gordon sat in an office of the Wheeler Foundation, on the second floor of a 1930s downtown LA office building on Fifth Street, the kind with frosted glass doors and script style names on the glass. It was vintage 1936. Wheeler owned the entire building and made money renting it to himself. He made a good purchase during the early nineties slowdown in real estate by threatening the then owner, Sam Jacobsen, that Wheeler's Foundation would vacate the two floors it rented and leave him with a lawsuit trying to collect the rent.

The owner, capitulated after the Foundation failed to pay the rent for two months and sold. He did basic 6th grade math and whichever way he turned he would lose. Two or more years of litigation and more than 20 percent of his income down the drain in that interim, plus two years of lawyers.

Jack was sitting in the "Lounge Room" of the suite, on a soft brown leather love seat, staring at Foundation President Ian Christokos. The lounge was dimly lit with only one standing lamp with a yellow shade covering its sixty-watt bulb. Wheeler liked dim light and everyone who ever went in the office made sure that the one lamp was the only illumination. There was desk lamp set into one corner of his desk with a genuine Tiffany lamp and shade that remained unlit, and a Liechtenstein original of the Great Cathedral in Paris on one wall and nothing else. He was proud of the way Sophie had managed to buy the art by advising the then owner, Norman Gilbert, that "things could happen." It was enough to convince him to sell.

Christokos said, "We can't just hold her indefinitely. We have to do something. Just let her go."

"Why do anything? I say we hold on."

"She gets sick, then what?"

"Relax. We'll take her to the farm in Colorado, or right here up in Monterey and let her loose. She'll wander around. It's thirty miles from anywhere. She won't know where she is. Won't know anything."

"She seems to be a person who will figure things out."

244

"Thirty miles from nowhere! Another few weeks we'll drop her off somewhere when the project is half built. That's a trouble free billion for you."

"And one for you."

"And three for Franklin. Or more. Might take a long time through. The project is enormous. A whole city going up. Two hotels, several office buildings. You saw the plans. Condos, apartments, a shopping mall." Gordon sighed. "She's very pretty, you know. I'd hate to have to kill her. I think I can do something about her. I really do."

"But if we have to, we have –"

"Won't be any killing."

"Got a better idea?"

"Definitely."

***

"I know I didn't call, but –"

"What on earth are you doing here?"

"Hard to catch you not at the office without Harry hanging around."

"You following me?" Her eyes were as wide and suspicious as a six-year-old starting school.

I shrugged. The kind of shrug that answers everything.

"It's nine-thirty!"

"I know. But I need your help. Sumner with you tonight?"

She opened the door just enough for me to barge in without knocking her over.

"Watch it. Take it easy, chum." She stepped back, arms folding over her breasts. "No, my kid isn't here. He's at his father's, a little two-week experiment. Just stay back there." Her hand went out like a stop sign.

"Experiments are good," I replied. Had to admit. She was luscious. Built like... only romance writers could put it into appropriate over-the-top words. "Maybe they'll discover the theory of fathers and sons," I added. "Or mothers and sons. Hey, maybe it's not too late to teach me." Lame nonsense, but the best I had at the moment. I was distracted by her see-through pink slip which stuck to her with static electricity like a second skin, nipples clear and not quite reachable.

"Stop giving me that high school salivating look! Turn around, dammit! Let me throw on something." She vanished reappearing in a few minutes, in a well-worn white terry cloth robe, left arm frayed, she pulled it tightly about

245

her, tied the sash and held on. Thick auburn hair curled around tired eyes, but her lips had been reddened.

"Relax. No problem. You just look fine to me."

"All females look fine to you, Harvey."

"It's a curse."

"Yeah. I know – the Devil makes you do it."

She was probably right. "Take it easy, Ann. Not here about that body of yours. Although…"

"Although nothing."

I put my hands up in surrender. Of course, wouldn't I know it? Sarah popped up in my mind. Listen, I said to myself in about two seconds flat, she is the one who walked out… fair is fair. "I Need your help," I said. Really. You know things that might save people's lives. We have to talk."

"We don't have to do anything."

"OK, don't talk. Suit yourself. But I'll be here tomorrow and at Harry's tomorrow, and the day after and so on. You have to help me. So, my feeling is that we make it easy on ourselves."

We stood and stared at one another. She tied the sash on her rose again. "Damn it, Harvey." She took a deep breath, a trace of a smile barely touching the tips of her mouth. I think it was a trace of a smile. Had to admit she was easy to like. "OK. Just don't go sneaking around or go to Harry. I need that job. Understand? I have responsibilities."

"Don't we all."

"And you stay right there, three feet from me at all times."

"Got it. You got a tape? Or how about like this?" I spread my arms.

"Don't move, Harvey. I'll make a cup of tea. Go sit down. Over there. I have that apple stuff. Decaf."

She pointed at the kitchen table. She flew into her small kitchen, about the size of a double closet in the Hancock Park home of Carly Klein. I followed. She made herself busy filling the kettle, pulling out tea bags from a shelf. Hard to take my eyes off that body. Is there such a thing as not being affected by a gorgeous woman? Not to want to touch? Such a thing exists?

There was no interrupting her and we contemplated the kettle until the pot whistled and she poured the bubbling water into the teapot and stirred it and then into the cups. "OK, now what? What's so Goddamn important, Harvey Ace?" Her eyebrows went up and once again – just the tip of a grin.

"First, tell me. What's so amusing?"

"Nothing. Well, you. Just the way you're looking at me. I see right through what you really want."

"Number one, you're wrong. Number two, you're wrong. And number three, there's a ten-year-old kid who may be dead by the time you decide to be human. I need to know about Harry and this petition he has dreamed up that's driving the Wheelers out of their minds. I need to know Harry's plans, and anything and everything else you know about this entire Trust and his petition mess. And voting rights – and that old man."

She sat across from me. Elbows on the table. Slowly covered her eyes. Shoulders sagged a little and the robe fell away from one shoulder.

"This is what I was told. Harry said this guardianship was the best for the boy. He's eleven or going on eleven. My kid could spend time with him. It was what the doctors wanted. All those shrinks that Harry calls at that place in Mara Bay. That Ebrons creep. Now you want me to be a mole in my employer's office? Find out all if it is all true. All of Harry's plans, which I never know about anyway, and then tell you? What he has his fingers into. Not very nice. Really, Harvey." She tossed a disapproving look sideways at me as she poured the tea into two cups and gestured at the sugar bowl.

"Don't move, Mister Ace. You just want some part of that action, don't you? All that money wherever it is coming from."

I put a half teaspoon of sugar in the hot tea. "Don't want money. The Wheeler's are handling my costs. I'm getting paid. I want to save that kid and the woman they are holding. Someone I know well. Her name is Sarah. And I want to find the assassins who killed a good friend. They chased him and shot him a bunch of times. Why is the question? What did John have?"

She waited. "That woman I read about in the news is a close friend of yours, isn't she?"

"Not relevant. You know that term. She is someone who is innocent and not involved in any of this. As is the eleven-year-old – an autistic kid who needs help. Whoever it is wants me to do what they say, whenever they say it, jump to their tune, or else. Whatever Franklin Wheeler wants. Vote with him. For him, kiss his ass. Play along. Cops think he is behind it all. And it certainly looks like it. But –"

"But what?"

"Too neat. Too plain. They need a link, though. A connection to make it real. Maybe you have it. I'm really not sure about the old man being it. His involvement seems so damn obvious though…"

"Might be different when Harry gets through with all of you."

"Might be. Depends on what he is up to. If anything. Harry has to be after control of these trusts through you. Why else the petition? What else is there? You might know. He needs money now. He has not been in the chips for a while. He wants and needs money now. Not in a year or two."

"We got paid. Cash. Never saw that kind of cash. In a small box, all bundled." She shook her head remembering the sight.

"Cash? ...who the hell sends cash through the mail or in a box? Where do the ordinary folks get that kind of cash? And did Harry deposit it? Or string it out?"

She contemplated the thought. "I just do the work, Harvey. Cable is the money guy. I'm a grunt. But I can't tell you more. I have to stay out of this. Not getting in deeper. Not just ethics and all that. I need this job. Harry pays the bills."

"Those two people are in deep trouble, Ann. Just a kid. Every other trust beneficiary is dead. John, Sally, Carole. Kid in danger and an innocent bystander. Maybe Jimmy Gaines is still around. Maybe dead. Doesn't that give you pause? If you go through with this petition you are next in line. You would have power. Or Harry would. And that is dangerous. C'mon, Ann, tonight is not the end of this miserable business."

She looked away. Her voice was almost a whine. "I just signed my name. I'm not next anything." But I saw that she understood. Her hand trembled as she poured the tea again and missed the cup then shoved the sugar bowl at me. I shook my head.

"I don't want to get more involved, Harvey. I don't. I don't. I have a good job. And a kid. All I did was sign this thing that Harry said was good for the Augers boy."

"You're involved. Up to your ears if you go through with this petition. Why did Harry create it?"

She wiped the spill with a paper towel then thoughtfully spooned a half spoon of sugar in her cup. "I would like to help that kid. and even that lady, but I have no special information. I'm an employee."

"You're in the middle now and if bad things happen." I pointed at her nose.

"I haven't done anything wrong, Harvey. Nothing." Her fists clenched. She poured more tea into her cup and it overflowed. "Shit."

I grabbed a cloth towel and tossed it onto the spill. I got up and stood over her. "Listen to me. It's not going to get better. You don't seem to realize how deep into all of this your mere signature makes you. By the way, did the mortuary director call Harry last day or two?"

"Harrara Pillar?"

"That's the guy."

"How'd you know his name?"

"I keep busy."

She did her own version of a shoulder shrug, bounced just a little from the waist up. "Yeah. He called. Three or four days ago. I've got the note. Seemed agitated. But I passed on the call and I didn't listen in. I don't know how this petition makes me involved. You say it but that doesn't necessarily make it true."

"Someone will need the kid's share of the trust, his voting rights. His parents are dead. I'm not gonna be executor for John forever. That leaves you. Just little you. There's more. Just tell me."

"Harvey. Just drink your tea and get out of here. I'm through. And I'm exhausted. My ex makes nothing easy. I'm not involved. Please."

"Bullshit. You're stuck with whatever Harry says. Or whoever paid him."

Tears slowly came to her eyes. Her hand came to my sleeve.

"I'm not going, Ann. I need to know what you know. Either me or the police. That's my next stop. And there are a bunch of police departments in this. LA, Arcadia, Mara Bay, I'm sure. They will make it worse than I ever could."

She stood up. Her hand kept trembling when she lifted her cup and realizing it put it down. "All right. All right. It's not a secret. Dammit, Harvey. He called the other day. I took the call, Harry wasn't in. Receptionist wasn't there. I don't know why. The guy seemed desperate. Couldn't find Harry and told the guy, and he didn't like it and that was it – that was totally it. Said he wasn't waiting. No – wait, he said he was mailing something, for Harry to watch for it."

"And?"

"Nothing yet, unless Harry got it first. He does that sometimes. Comes in early. Like before nine when I get here. Grabs the mail. Especially when big checks are expected. He doesn't want me to know. It's crazy I think. How can anyone operate like that?" She took a breath. "But he does."

"Has this voice on the phone had any past dealings with Harry?"

"I don't know, Harvey. He was just a voice at that time."

"OK, go on."

"Harry comes over now and then…"

"Figures. You have quiet dinners in hideaway places. When Sumner is with his father." I was building up an anger. Not sure if it had to do with her or me or John or what I expected her to say. The Augers Affair kept growing. "No more half-truths, Ann. Not going to work. Need the full story."

Her face fell, revealing small tidbits of age and disappointment. She began to talk, slowly at first. She explained how she came to where she was. That Moss was involved in everything Wheeler did. That Sophie kept needling the old man and he listened to her. Sophie could make him jump.

She talked about Carole and that shoving of her off the cliffs in Santa Monica. She thought it was possible that Moss had plans to ease Wheeler out of the Foundation. He had power.

"Pretty ambitious… and unlikely," I said.

She went on: Franklin had had done something to his daughter when she was a kid that put them all in jeopardy. She said that Sophie was friends with her mother in their early lives which is how she got her job. They were neighbors or close friends or something. Then, she added, as if in an afterthought, "You know, that Pillar has been to the office several times. Once with Sophie. I assume you will talk to him."

I nodded and she went on. Told me about the doctor who signed the death certificate; Stan Simon who called asking for the Wheeler home number. She said that money was not the only thing involved with the Wheelers. There were secrets. Past life secrets. Sally and John and the Mara Bay Institute they called Bright Paths, where Sally and Frankie were treated.

"Ann, you want to be mixed up in all that? Sally and doctors and shrinks? Get out of it. You're now part of any conspiracy that might exist between all these people – get rid of Harry, get rid of any threat to the Wheelers. Not sure how or who but…"

Her breath stopped for a moment. She looked down. It was plain just then that this person was not among those who dealt with pressure well. She had managed over the years to rely on her looks and a quick wit, and quick fingers on a typewriter and, apparently, her mother. This was the time to prod her, to keep after her. She rolled out more of the story. And as it came out, I felt a crazy kinship with her. I've been in her spot before. My life was something akin to hers; I had to cut through the crap and figure out exactly who I was/did I really want someone just for me, just me… someone for more than a weekend, someone to have secrets with, someone who makes faces when you tell bad jokes, to worry about the garden? You know – someone. Or did I want ME – as is, looking for those adrenaline highs, the big wins, the fantasy tomorrows. Adrenaline highs were one thing, feeling was another. Maybe it was why they all left me. Gambling required an absence of feeling. That was its secret. Would *The Silk* really make a difference?

"God, I've really fucked up, Harvey. I couldn't help it. You can call me every name in the book but it was the only thing at the time. Honest to God. That damn ex of mine, and Sumner. He wasn't always a six-two high school hero; just a little kid who needed me and needed a decent life. And not the macho shit his father represented. Kids love that. I had to stop that little boy from becoming like his father. So I did whatever I needed to do. I just didn't know. Really. I thought I was right."

My heart understood and felt what she said. It was true. That blame and recrimination was not what she deserved. I did the only thing I knew how to do. I grabbed her and hugged, and she struggled at first and then when she realized there was nothing to fear, she melted. We stood there together not sure of anything about ourselves.

Finally, I asked her where she and Harry met and about Pillar and Doctor Simon and if Harry had records on Pillar and Simon and where they were.

"That's at the edge, Harvey."

"You're not running for political office, Ann. Considering someone has been assassinated – understand? Murdered? And people are in very serious danger… and considering our friendship."

She leaned close, pulled that robe close around her neck. "Friendship? What kind of friendship?"

"What difference does it make? You have to do the right thing. You know that."

"No difference," she snapped, pulling away. "Nothing makes a difference to you? Absolutely nothing? I'm sure it never has." She couldn't look at me. "But I don't go over the edge with mere friendship, Mr. Ace."

"Then I have no choice," I said. "Relationships with strangers are not in the equation. I go from here to the LAPD. There's no time for late blooming morality."

"You are beyond miserable." She snapped at me, stood up. "I don't know more. You got it all."

"I want the institute information. The doctors." She had given me the name of a Doctor Ebrons and Simon and where they were, but that was all. I got up. Pulled out a five-dollar bill from my pants' pocket and dropped it on the table. "This is for the tea. And the company. Can't save Harry's neck or yours."

"I should have known. Just like all the rest. Damn, you are a real bastard."

"Yeah. You're right. A kid is in danger of getting his throat cut. Someone I know well is in the same danger. Innocents!" I stopped and lowered the level. "It's simply necessary, Ann. I'm going to find out the whole truth – and save your lovely derriere in the process."

Her hands went over her eyes, then through her hair. Tears streaming down her face smudging the lipstick she had put on, just for me.

"No one is exempt from what is going on. More than that – you have to consider that Harry's been targeted, too. Since he knows so much. Has records. If Wheeler is the bad guy, why not you? He hates you right now, Wheeler does. Why would the bad guys leave Harry or you out? Why would he leave you out? Have you been told about any votes or assignments of the kid's interest?"

"Harvey, the Harry Mosses of the world do not die or fade away. They're like that everlasting guy in the movies…"

"Dorian Gray…"

"That's the one. They go on and on, and when they're gone there are a dozen more." She looked up, a bunch of miseries in her eyes, "Dammit, Harvey, I thought maybe we had something, there was a chance with you. It was really stupid of me, wasn't it?" Her hand touched my sleeve. "I'm old enough to know better about guys like you. A quickie and a nice few words and maybe a nice few hours and then goodbye. That's the way it is. Smashed hopes." There was an ending in her voice, like surrender. "Smashed hopes."

Like so many women alone in a callous world.

I had heard the same tone in a hundred cases by women who believed themselves to be one down in a one up world – which, perhaps, they were. I was not inside their hearts, only privy to their fears and a sort of end-of-life-aloneness.

"Ann, I'm sorry. I've been pretty cavalier with you and I am sorry. But, presume I care, presume we've had a golden anniversary and are sitting by the fire with two of our many grandchildren, make that adopted grandchildren. Do those presumptions mean I stop looking for that lost kid, looking for the people that assassinated a friend of mine, that kidnapped a beautiful young woman? And consider that now you have become just another tool – just for their grubby dollar only purposes, all by people still out there? Not known but guessed at. Do I stop?"

That started the tears all over. They came rolling down her cheeks. Her full auburn hair plastered to her forehead.

"Don't be like a victim, Ann. Don't always be one down. Do what is right. Whatever it is."

"Stop, Harvey, for God sake, stop. Don't talk to me like that."

"Someone has to."

I could see that brain of hers sifting through all the possibilities. Bit by bit her shoulders straightened. She knew. She knew she had to "do what was right." She leaned over and dropped into my arms. Her knees buckled. Honest to God, I'm sorry. I'm not sure of anything with Harry and this mess with the kid. Not even sure of right and wrong." She held onto me tightly. I couldn't help but respond. "I can't take chances. Sumner's father will try to take him from me and he is all I've got. Kid is old enough so that I can't stop

252

him. I make a mistake and I'm yesterday. He jumps to his big macho father. I want him until he graduates then the asshole can have him. I want him, just until then. Sophie is my best –"

Sophie's name once again made me sit up. "Best what?"

"My best hope. My protector. She'll protect me. You know she got me the job."

"Run all of that by me, again."

She did.

***

Sky was cold and dark as I slipped into my car. Phone rang. "Leave her alone. We'll take care of all of it… stay out of it. Last warning."

I headed for the ocean…

Chapter Twenty-Four

Pacific Palisades is a strip of park land that sits a little over sixty feet above the Coast Highway and Santa Monica Beach, just at the terminus of Wilshire Boulevard. It is populated by Malaluga trees which snake their way along the ground then rise and attach to the local Palm Trees, and by the local homeless who arrive from the wintry east to the balmy west and think they are in heaven – even though they sleep in make-shift bunks of old clothes, blankets, and rags dug half way into the ground, protected by the Malalugas. Santa Monica sometimes holds food fests and feeds the whole lot of them to the chagrin of the Santa Monica residents who live on lovely shaded streets or tourists who visit and stay in the upscale hotels and stroll along Ocean Avenue and through the park to the gourmet restaurants nearby.

The city doesn't have much luck in chasing them away. Periodically the police roust the overnighters and dismantle their tiny homes and take away the stolen grocery carts. They move to all the other secret places they have for such inconvenient times and soon drift back to the green lawns, fresh breezes, and Malalugas.

I had to see how Carole Augers was killed. Was it merely a crazed homeless person attacking a wrongly perceived threat or was it planned by those who knew where Carole, John, and Frankie would spend a warm evening, ice creams in hand from a nearby Ben and Jerry's. It was usually a Thursday evening as Fridays around Santa Monica were too crowded with cars and diners and tourists doing the same. I started on a Thursday evening a couple blocks south of Wilshire Boulevard, the western extremity of which was at the park. The sun had just arrived at the tip of the ends of the earth and was turning red, (why it turned red, I don't know), late enough for the encampments to be in full swing, but light enough to see clearly for at least another hour. I approached one earthen bedroom after the other, smiled as best I could, handed out a dollar to each person turning over a blanket, taking a pillow out from their grocery carts, and throwing a couple rags over their shoulders; women with dogs, men with dogs, all tails wagging, all happy: women with a child, men with a woman and sometimes a child, all bedding down for the cool, misty night. I asked each if they remembered the time the police came in force about the shoving or carrying of Carole over the side of the embankment to the highway below. Every one shrugged and waved their hands to shoo me away. As I got to the last few earthen bedrooms, I stopped to catch a breath and one fellow tuned over, faced away, and pulled a blanket over his head.

"Hey, you don't want to talk?"

"Don't you do any of that hey stuff to me!"

"I have money. You want money?"

I could see arms pushing at the blankets which had rolled around him.

"Yeah, money," I said. "Just like everyone in the world. Good old money."

"Awright. Awright! Let's see it!" His right hand came out. The pinkie finger was missing. Probably the smallest thing about him that was missing.

"You're a regular politician. Come out. The money's right here. Have to look."

"You're a liar."

"Okay. I'm leaving. If you want the money, you have to come out."

The fingers on a crusted hand wiggled in a put it here routine.

"Goodbye. You lose. I'm calling the cops – you were the bear that shoved that lady off the edge. You killed her and almost killed the kid. I know it. I'll count to three. I knew that everyone around the park knew what happened to Carole – a close-knit community of derelicts. They stole from one another, cheated one another, and knew everyone in the park within a half mile in all directions."

I raised my finger to get to the count of one but I didn't get there.

"You sonofabitch! Wasn't me. You crazy or sumthin'? I was in Timbuctu!" Three-inch beard, face caked with the accumulation of not caring; shoes with the soles flapping with thick pad of paper stuck under the feet.

"Don't gimme any bullshit. You don't even know where it is."

"I heard." The blankets tightened around him. "See ya later."

"It was you, wasn't it? You saw who did it. You're my guy."

"God dammit! You crazy? You know it's not me, asshole!"

"If you want the money, quit playing around. Here's a buck. There's more. But you gotta sit up and start talking."

He peeked out. Checked me out with one squinting eye. "Shit. I don't wake up for a buck. You're crazier than I am! What's a buck gonna get me? Nothin'! You in the middle ages or sumthin'? Ten bucks or I go back to sleep. You bothering everyone here at Park Lucca."

"No. Bothering only you. You want to make money? Just sit there and listen and answer me." I pulled a ten out of my pocket. You remember when that lady was shoved over the side? Remember? Don't give me any crap talk now. I can see your eyes. You're no dummy."

"Two years at UCLA. Been a while."

"Answer my question, college boy." I held the ten out close to him but held it tight. "Who was it? The guy still here?"

"After all that shit went down that night she was gone. Somebody came in one a those stretch black things and he – maybe she – was gone. That lady got shoved? She's gotta be dead."

"So, somebody must've put him up to it."

"Told you. You deaf or sumthin'? It maybe wasn't a guy. Maybe a big bear of a female person, you idiot?" He coughed. Reached for the money. I pulled it back. The enticement of the money was better than a shot of Jack Daniels. "Didn't you know? –Fac' is they called her the Bear. Stayed here now and then."

"She have a name?"

He reached for the money. Ten dollars was just enough to keep him in cigarettes and beer for two days. He didn't need food. Cigarettes took care of his hunger.

"You're not done."

"Costs more to get me 'done'."

"Was this she person a regular here?"

"Sometimes. When it suited her. But she didn't talk. Never talked." He drew circles around his temples with a finger that was absent about a half inch of the tip.

"A name. Give me a name."

"God dammit you stupid ass… gimme a minute to remember!"

I brought the money closer to his eyes. "OK. Here's the ten. Talk."

"I want more."

"You're a thief."

He laughed a huge gurgle of a laugh and slapped the blanket in his lap. One of the other residents of the earth encampment lifted a head up. "Goddammit you assholes. Shut the fuck up!"

My guy put a crusted hand over his mouth and stifled a laugh. "What's new about that? 'Course I'm a thief."

"Name!"

"Ori… Ori something! Called her the bear. That's it. Ten bucks more please. You don't wanna cheat me, do you?"

"What else?"

256

"Long time ago. Nothin' else. Gimme the money!"

I held it back.

"God dammit! You're a thief!"

"I'm in good company."

He shrugged. A sudden big grin. No front teeth. An admitted thief was a nice surprise. Sort of like now we're all friends. "They walking down here with ice creams, just walkin' along, and bang that fuckin' bear came at 'em and the guy tried to save the lady and the kid at the same time. Didn't have enough hands. And over she went and that bear lady just ran to the curb and a couple seconds later boom she's gone. And the kid s screaming and screaming like the world was blown up and no one had arms or legs and then he stops. Just stands there like a statue or sumthin'. The man was crying and kneeling in front of the kid."

"Planned, wasn't it?"

"'fuck do I know? The ten! Gimme the ten!"

"There's more. Stick with me here." I held the money closer but held it tight.

"Yeah, yeah. I remember it. Then that black limo came down and swooped her up and away they went, south on Ocean. Gimme the fuckin' money."

I gave it to him. It was like feeding a hungry child. "Anyone else know something? See something? Talk to any of them?"

Pulled his blanket over his head again. "Get the hell away from me. I don't know you. Just let me die here and be done with it."

"Who else? C'mon."

"Ask, asshole. Ask! There's a dozen crazies here!" He pulled the blanket tighter around him and disappeared into his special darkness, but I could hear him repeat from within his hole in hell, "Ask, asshole! Ask!"

Most of blankets and people and dogs had silently dispersed. They wanted no part of me or my questions. I tapped the dropout's blanket. "I'll be back."

"I'll be dead."

The homeless along this Parkway were not all dumb but they were certainly emotionally shortchanged or a terrible set of facts had scrambled their emotions so that there was nowhere left but an alley, or a car, or a dirt hole in a park, in a corner away from sight, from the degradation of pity. I sat on a bench facing the street watching cars whiz by on Ocean Avenue. The avenue had lost a little bit of its luster. Everything seemed to have gone to seed, even when it hadn't.

The answers were elsewhere. That's where I had to be. I would find them. I was not meant to end up like my friend in a hole in the ground, still alive, but nowhere. Like Gertrude believed I would end up. Like Sarah was afraid I would and afraid that she would go down with me. Hard to come to grips with the fact of the depth of fear there was in being a part of my life. Perhaps I didn't fear it, but they certainly did. Everyone around me. It came to me that my father, the big man at the head of great industries, was simply fearful he might end up in a hole…so he drank to blur the vision – and drank to fulfill the vision, and bounced from one alleged success that was no more than a failure, to another, the same fear inside of him every time.

I added a big bear to the missing. However, it wasn't only a bear I was after. I was after the driver of that black limo… a bear and a limo driver. They led to somewhere.

***

Chapter Twenty-Five

Sophie Wheeler answered on the first ring when I called. She was near hysteria. Babbling about Sally Augers. "I saw her! I saw Sally! I told Franklin. He is in a terrible state. Find her! – Kill her! Kill her! I saw her! We have a note. You know, don't you? I'm sure I told you or that policeman. Not sure of anything except I saw her! Kill the bitch! She knows."

I finally was able to tell her the news that Frankie was undoubtedly still alive, that someone still had him. However, the torrent of words from her questions and accusations wouldn't permit much to squeeze into the flow of her hysteria. Her outbreak was shocking—and I thought I was beyond being shocked by anything.

Find Sally? Kill her? Almost guttural sounds. Not a word about Frankie. What about him? Was he in her thoughts at all?

***

Paul told me that Wheelers were in the process of putting together eight and half million dollars and were waiting for instruction as to where and how to obtain the return of Frank Augers. Alive and well.

"Hernandez says they might have something. Spoke to him early this morning. I'll let you know."

"What did Hernandez say?"

"Said he might have something. That's it."

"You know that eight and a half million number bugs me," I said. "Why that number?

Why not an even ten? And Sophie screaming about seeing Sally Augers. Are they all crazy or is it just you and me?"

"Wrong speculation about the wrong problem. Sophie Wheeler isn't crazy. Smart old lady. Meet me tomorrow, early." Paul said. "Usual place."

"Find out what your geniuses have on Sarah."

"Working on it, Harvey. I know how you feel. Just remember, the bad guys need her alive. I would like to charge that whole Wheeler Foundation

259

gang with kidnapping but we need a really good direct link on the charge. Otherwise their dozen lawyers will make us look silly. And the bad guys will be out in an hour and they'll know what we're up to. You cooperate with them and she stays alive. If there was anything, you know I would call."

"Pick up Wheeler anyway. Might shake him up just enough."

"And if he is not the guy?"

"No harm, no foul."

"And if he is the guy?"

"He gets his minions to get rid of the evidence. But, ok, do it your way."

Half hour later Billy called. "I opened the store today and sold a car within ten minutes. New record. And it's only Tuesday!"

"It's Wednesday, schmuck."

"OK, I won't tell you the rest because you know everything."

"Keep talking."

"Saw Gertrude this morning. Says that Mondozo kid is bugging her. Threatening her."

"Aureliano won't do anything. If it's the old man, then…"

"It was the Mondozo kid. He is as low down as they come. Don't be so sure about how low that boy can go."

"Yeah, yeah. Meantime, I'm arranging another meeting with that Mortuary guy if he isn't dead and Dr. Simon's secretary."

"Good luck with that."

'***

Pillar's records would be very revealing in tracing the who and when relevant to Sally's cremation. 39 Breeze Street was certainly the place where Frankie had been held for the last several days. It was also clear that whoever was behind grabbing Sarah, they needed her alive. She was the perfect pawn. Without the board-certified minutes with the entire Board in favor, they wouldn't get the variances they needed from the County. County wasn't going to take a chance on litigation. Neither was Wheeler. All or nothing.

I didn't understand what was holding up crime lab reports from Joe's County Sheriff's department and their forensic team. And, I was hoping for the same from Sampson. I figured Sampson wasn't going to lose the initiative on the case to small town cops or a local mid-State Sheriff's Department. Which was great with Joe as the Augers Affair was more than his four-man department could handle. However, in Joe's own way, he was playing it close to the vest. I recalled the last thing he said when I left, "All right, Harvey, if you need anything, just call me. If it doesn't require killing a cow, glad to help. Old farts have to stick together." His eyes were fixed on something in the distance when he said it.

***

Miss Deets, thin lips perpetually puckered, dusty hair, and horned rimmed glasses, significant bustline under a dark green cotton T, working hard at not being desirous to anyone, pointed at the empty chair, one of only two in the bland office, and gave me a form to fill out. With instructions to go to the second page and fill out all the personal information as well as my insurance information. "Miss Deets, Dr. Simon is dead. He was killed. You certainly know that about your boss. Aren't we wasting valuable time?"

"Makes no difference, this is what I must do."

She was creating a life for herself as though the doctor was still with her. I don't know what the psychologists would call it, but she needed the routine. It was part of her existence. And it was weird. But it was that thing that gave her meaning.

I obeyed and wrote that I was Clem Cadoddle with a nasty cough and a cash customer, all cash, and with a bank account in Los Angeles and a paid for automobile and handed it back to her.

"You allergic to anything?"

"I'm here to talk to you. Not a dead doctor."

She stared. I pulled out a pile of cash from my jacket pocket and flipped twenties in front of her nose. All impressive five foot ten of her, with a rear end that shimmed like someone's sister. Kate rose and disappeared.

Didn't take long.

She came back out as though she would guide me back to Dr. Simon's office.

"You don't look sick."

"Since I have cash, what difference? I am sure the good doctor would have been happy to help me and answer all the questions he could. Don't you think he was a cooperative person? Someone who cooperated with the authorities?"

She clucked and smiled and pushed a wisp of gray hair from her eyes. Oh, yes, the doctor was a stickler for doing the right thing." She put a hand over her mouth as her emotions rose and she stifled a sob.

"I'm really sorry about what happened to the doctor. Really. But I need help. A child is in terrible danger." I thought I might as well hit her with the whole mess and see what comes up. "I want to know what you know about

261

Sally Augers. I need records. And I have to know who hired the doctor to care for her and who ordered the cremation. You must have records."

I hit the right nerve. Her back straightened. She stared at something behind me. Into space. "Exactly who are you, Mister Cadoddle? That's certainly not your name."

"I am working closely with police to find poor Sally who might still be alive. And the boy"

Her jowls bounced. "Can't help you."

I put five twenties on her desk and spread them out. "This is what I would have to pay the doctor for his time if he wasn't you know, dead." Wrong thing to say. She sobbed. "Just tell me," I persisted, "who hired Dr. Simon? The Augers boy is autistic,"

"Eleven years old." She sat back and her chin sagged to her ample chest. She breathed heavily. Her lips were moving in silent private discourse. She wanted to talk. I could see it written all over her being. Trembling lips and hunched shoulders. She took her time. "Well, Doctor Simon treated the boy a couple times for minor things, Doctor Ebrons at the Institute sent him over. They wanted an independent look at what was troubling the boy."

"I thought they had a facility set aside over there for young people."

"I did, too. But that's all I know."

"Is this Ebrons the one in charge?"

"Far as I know."

"Why would he send him here?"

"Am I a suspect for something?"

"No, Miss Deets. But you can be a big help in finding that boy and settling the mystery for all of us. You want to save the boy, don't you?"

"I read about what happened."

"I also work with the police here in Mara Bay and in Los Angeles. You wouldn't want me to tell them you didn't cooperate, would you?"

"Listen here, the doctor certainly didn't do anything illegal. Believe me."

"I'll tell you if I believe you when we're done."

We eyed each other for a minute, me standing over her.

"What do you want to know?"

"I want to know about Sally and Oritha… Oritha Durden. How they got out of the institute. Where are they? Mostly, I want to know who ordered the cremation of Sally?"

She thought a long minute. "Mr. Ace, truthfully, I don't have time for this sort of thing, and I can't talk about patients. You know that. I can't breach doctor's oath, can I? Just because the poor man is dead? Ask the people involved. You have to ask them. I'm not the person you need."

"Listen, Miss Deets, this not a situation where you are a volunteer. The police from Los Angeles will certainly want to talk to you. Chief Dobrowski of Mara Bay will be here also."

"I can't tell any of you anything more. Get a warrant or whatever you need to make it legal. The records were taken... taken when the good doctor... when he was... I thought you knew that."

She started crying again, a soft sob which was highly contained.

"Don't cry. I know this is hard. But we need to save this little boy."

"I can't help you. The whole place was ransacked just last night. Took most of the morning to put it back together..."

Miss Deets looked ragged.

"Did you call the police?"

"This is not anyone's business. Don't you understand? The doctor would never let me permit private records get to the police or any public place." The lines on her narrow face deepened. Her age showed. Perhaps seventy years old. Working at staying meaningful was simply becoming too hard.

"I read the newspapers. And watch the T.V. We have all those modern conveniences here in Mara Bay, in case you didn't know. And I know what goes on. I know about that Wheeler big shot. He's got plenty. He wants records about his grandson, and the boy's mother. Well, how much would he pay? At least two month's salary."

"I would expect you to tell the truth and I will report all of this to Chief Joe."

"You didn't answer me. How much?"

"Stop this, Miss Deets. You said two months. That's good."

"That is not the answer I want."

"This is not a game. Thousand dollars. if I'm happy with the report." I pulled a chair to her desk. "Now that you know the money part – the rest of what I failed to tell you is that I will make a lot of trouble for you, Miss Deets. A lot. I need to know what you know."

"I'm calling the police."

I grabbed his phone, "Please do. Here."

She stopped. The air went out of her. She waved and pointed a crooked forefinger at me. "You said a thousand... dollars? Two?"

"OK. Two." She would be getting the bundle from Wheeler. What the hell.

Both hands came onto her desk and she flattened the palms against it.

"Strange person. That Sally was. Yessir, those two were strange. Doesn't hurt, I guess, to tell you... she. came to see the doctor first time several years ago when she had a persistent bronchial infection. Part of her problem was, of course, herself. Not eating, then getting fat and then not eating again. Catching a cold, then getting loaded with anti-biotics. Doctor kept shaking his head when he was dictating his notes. That Institute tried to stabilize her – Bright Paths, I mean. But she was, as they say, nuts. But," she shook that forefinger, "Not always. No sir, not always. With what Doctor Simon prescribed, the right medications, some of those new mood elevators, there were times when she was coherent. But she would clean us out. Grab all my magazines here and take them with her back to the institute. If she was home, somewhere in LA, she would need to dry out and start with the doctor again and some stuff that would make her hate anything that even smelled like alcohol. Then she would go back to the institute or home, wherever that was, somewhere in Los Angeles. We have an address somewhere. She would get a little better and the cycle would start all over. Then they got her that caretaker person." She wiped something imaginary on the top of her desk with her hand. Kept her eyes aimed at the desk. "That Durden lady. Treated her with a lot of vitamins, Antibuse, lots of water, some Prozac when it became available, sent her back to Ebrons with notes. Don't know more."

"Did she get any better during that time?"

"Getting that caretaker helped. She was like a bear. But, I must say, they stayed off of booze. She had company with this person who was like a watchdog."

"What else? What about her cremation? How did she die? The certificate says 'Thrombosis'."

"Well, from what I know, it doesn't take long for a person to die from such an event." She poked at finger to the table top.

"But she was in that Institute? I assume they could act quickly enough to clear that up?"

She shrugged. "I'm not the doctor."

"And what about Franklin Wheeler and his wife, during all this time?" "What about them? Somebody ordered the cremation of Sally. Somebody paid for the care, for the mortuary."

"Can't help you."

"Meaning you won't. No tickee, no washee."

"I'm telling you everything! There's no more to tell. There's no way I can dredge up the details of her treatment from the institute. Everything's gone. The doctor is gone. My life might as well be gone. Don't you understand? He was everything. He was my life. Can't do anything just to suit you or the Wheelers or anyone. I told that to Chief Dobrowski if I get a subpoena what good would it do? He was killed – the records gone. Please leave, Mr. Ace. Please go. I'm not spending another minute with you. Send me my money!"

"She died while in your employer's care. Someone ordered the cremation. Who?"

"Get out!"

Chapter Twenty-Six

Paul's voice was relaxed. He was frustratingly cool no matter what. I thought I had seen it all but there was absolutely nothing new in his book of memories. He was a brand-new patrolman when he was asked by his captain to count the wounds in Walter Emery's body after the Brentwood shooting that hit the headlines. He helped with the cordoning off of the area of the shooting on Federal Avenue in west LA near the cemetery where the graves of war heroes are marked over ten acres of precious ground. There were a lot more shootings but nothing cracked his cool after that first one.

"Well, we found something. Remember getting bopped on the head at the Wheeler mansion? I think we have a lead. Thought you might like to know."

"I still feel it. So, tell me. What'd you find?"

"Prints on the handle of that metal pan and a spot of blood near the stove in the kitchen, not yours. Don't know how that single drop got there. Lab is on it. But it's going to be another couple days. The bright guys at the lab say they are pretty sure it's a younger male."

"How do they know that?"

"They know everything… or they can figure it out."

"So, someone was with her all the time. In the house."

"Could be this someone thought you were a danger to Wheeler or Sophie and took you out and then ran. Question is, why did he run if he thought you were an intruder? You know, he hits you harder and you're dead. You know that, don't you?"

"Not on this head… anyway, Harry's secretary, that Ann Whitson lady, told me Sophie has a son, apparently a troublesome one."

"OK, we'll trace that. We need her DNA. Let's hope the smart guys can connect the dots."

"Tell me about Sarah. Found anything? Is there a missing report on her?"

"Yes, yes, and yes. We've checking on each of Wheeler's Foundation Board members. Some interesting stuff."

"What? What have you found?"

"When we confirm I'll call you right away. It seems their Board President, that Cotsokos guy, whatever his name is, was once involved with one of LA's biggest bookies. In fact he was one of them. Laid off his bigger bets on our famous Mickey Cohen. Don't know what that history means, except he is part of the gambling culture. Just like you. There were dozens of bookmakers in the 60s and 70s. No internet betting so it was a sort of accepted pastime. The bribes gave the beat cops a little extra money. Anyway, we're doing everything we can. The Chief put Hernandez and McCuddy on Sara's case exclusively. They're good. So, just sit tight."

***

I was on my Epson computer trying to get a fuller picture of Jack Gordon, the Board member of Wheeler's Foundation. He was too smooth not to be more involved with Wheeler than even the president of the Board. Everything I learned indicated Gordon made money in real estate by taking chances most would not. And, he somehow got great loans on real estate speculations, then made them work. Some of them were from Wheeler controlled banks and a Savings and Loan in Hollywood. He kept being right. Every time. Struck me that there was something wrong with being right all the time. No one is right all the time. Gamblers. Muscle guys that hurt people. Talked to Norma Gordon, his former wife. Found her number and called. When I mentioned my name there was a click and Norma was gone. I got bank statements for some of the loans. Just told them I was FHA and gave them a phony ID number. I was still digging when Billy called.

"Struck out so far. Can't find Jimmy anywhere. He has a sister in Florida, Millie Peneida. Lives in one of those Cuban old folks homes in Tampa Bay. She made it real clear that she was not close to her brother. And definitely didn't know where he was. And didn't want to know. Said he was one of those bad people with Cuban rough guys.

"Go on."

"Jimmy wrote a note. Very neat writing, taped to the back of a drawer. Says, *'Sorry to end like this but I don't want any Coroner cutting me up. Sorry again. Jimmy Gaines, age 83 on Sept 4, 2006.'* He must have pulled the plug and jumped off somewhere."

"No way. Jimmy is not a jumper. And why would he write down his age? Give the note to Hollywood Station. Make a few copies."

"Okay," Billy added. "You know. He lives right in town on Detroit up near Melrose. Walked right in. Not locked. Looks like there was a fight. Spots of blood. Specially on that big brown chair of his. This has to be part of this whole fucking mess you're in. Jimmy said he know something he doesn't know he knows. Doesn't fit anywhere except connected to you. I've got Larry and Nails looking in all the low places. All the places he hung out. Don't expect much. Call Paul?"

"Just finished speaking to him. For God's sake get to the Hollywood station and give them the whole story. Jimmy lives not too far from that station. Give them the note. Tell them the whole story. Blood and all. Be sure and make a copy of that note. Meanwhile, let's keep trying on our own. Maybe we buy an ad in the Daily Racing Form. You know a missing person thing. How much does an advert on the TVG racing channel cost?"

"Three grand tops depending on time. Twenty seconds is plenty. Couple thousand – that's my guess. Get us a picture and description and maybe we get it ESPN news. Use that photo we had a few years ago when Jimmy got jail time for shooting at that doctor."

"Yeah, I remember. The doctor got it in the shoulder and they ended up charging him, for malpractice causing the death of Jimmy's wife – sent him away. Jimmy got bubbkas. I'll call the papers and place the ads and get something going at the Hollywood station. And charge the costs to you."

"Naturally."

"Don't think an eighty-year-old can put up much of a fight. But the place was a mess."

"Don't kid yourself. Jimmy is as tough as steel bar and he is not going anywhere he doesn't want to go. I'm sure he caused some damage."

"Where you headed now?"

"For a talk with a bunch of doctors at Bright Paths Institute and some doctor named Ebrons and whoever shows up."

"Got armor? You know those psychiatrists types."

"Not to worry."

"Receptionist at Bright Paths, a young lady, whose voice sounded much like a five-year-old with a cold, told me a female fitting the Sally description was there but didn't remember the name and no record of when except she thought it was a couple years ago. She told me that the Sally lady had a friend. Sort of a caretaker. Big mother named Durden. Told me maybe Sally went to their other place in Arizona that is owned by the same people as own this place. Said, 'That Durden has gotta be a gorilla in disguise'."

"Anyway," I told Billy, "can't rely on any timeline. They have shitty records. But I managed to get her to show the commitment document. The file was sitting right on her desk like someone had just finished looking at it. It was signed by Doctor Stanley Simon and prepared and co-signed by someone named Analee Whitman."

"That's a familiar sound, isn't it?"

"Yeah, yeah. I know."

"Seems like you're back to Harry and Ann, and they answer to Franklin Wheeler, don't they?"

"Who does Wheeler answer to?"

***

An hour later I was on my way to my first stop, to Max Saliera's restaurant in Mara Bay. It was a road less traveled at that time of the evening and as I drove over the winding interstate coastal route I dictated into the recording device I kept in my car. Saved a lot of time and gave me fresh recollections to replay that would otherwise be forgotten.

A red neon in Max's window flashed OPEN on and off. The scent of garlic greeted me, and the feel of an old-fashioned leather booth steak house in dim lights struck me.

***

Max Saliera was one of those cops who liked being in a black and white, roaming the streets in downtown Los Angeles. No one in the known world really liked it. But Max was happy in his day to day routines. He had various partners who always managed to get transferred out to different stations. He would ask me, seriously, "Am I that hard to get along with?"

He enjoyed the monotony and the sudden adrenaline part of being a cop when something serious happened – death, armed robbery, or gang bangers shooting one another. There was always something –   he actually liked the idea of saving people from violence. Los Angeles was too big to bring a sense of community even in the geographically enclosed neighborhoods, like Culver City or Pacoima. He even liked the misery of the homeless camps on San Pedro Street and up through 1st and 2nd street in downtown next to the north/south boulevards of Alameda and San Pedro. With danger in very cardboard tent and down the middle of every street he would spend a minute with the anger of the homeless and just listen to them. Max knew that listening was a gift for the talker and the recipient. Mostly, the homeless were sick and looking for a way out. He would find at least one person to save every week and he kept count. "That was twenty-two, Harvey. Got her into the Wayside Housing Group, Catholic Charities, Jewish Charities. A little at a time and we'll clean it all out."

It was a foolish hope. He knew it – it was like ice on a broken ankle, wouldn't fix it but took away the pain for the moment. And he got free tacos from all the street vendors with stomach cramps that go with the territory. He learned how the small vendors and the small restaurants in the area worked. How they cooked and how they kept their books and poured their drinks, how they ordered and argued with the delivery people. When you looked at him in his uniform, he looked about ten feet tall and six feet wide and no one argued with him. When he retired, he was invited north by a former partner who had years earlier created and owned *Sidney's Restaurant and Bar*.

Sidney Billings knew Max had become a good cook and had learned how to be a good operator. Max worked for him to start with, a little extra dollars during his off times. Sidney eventually gave Max an interest in the restaurant. A small one, and then died two years later. Max was sure Sidney knew he was dying. He had no relatives. No one ever came to visit him and no one called. Not one person – an entire life essentially alone, thus no one complained when Max took over. He added a couple of upholstered booths, put some old pictures of resting dogs and sailboats on the walls, cleaned the place top to bottom, added lights, cut some of the junk stuff on the menu, added a ribeye steak and a sliced brisket sandwich, a butter fried halibut dinner, a Mamma Max's hot-air fried fries, and a couple of appetizers and doubled his gross income within a year. He handled the bar for a while until he found the right guy who stole the least of the several he tried, and he became a very successful restaurateur. He even won prizes for his brisket sandwiches and write-ups in the San Luis Obispo paper and the Mara Bay Record, the local throwaway.

When I walked in, he did a double take, threw up his arms, and hollered, "Whoa, Nellie! Look who's here! Harvey Ace, great finder, intrepid detective! How the hell are ya?"

We hugged and carried on a few minutes, the few customers at 11 AM smiling at the roars of grown men. "Congrats, Max. Sid would be proud. Place looks like a regular restaurant. Nice flavor. That's a photo of Will Rogers over on the wall, isn't it? Right next to that big old Sailing Ship. Can you get that gang of yours to cook up something for me?" I sat at a corner table. "Lemme make a call and then we'll tell some lies about old times."

"I never lie, Harvey. It's possible I exaggerate a little." He hit my right arm playfully which rattled my teeth.

I called Paul. "News?"

"Getting closer."

"How close?"

"Close enough that we'll find her soon. We will, Harvey. We will."

"Dead or alive? Just tell the truth."

"We'll find her. She won't be dead."

"Promise?"

"Don't be foolish."

I stared at the phone. I know there were no promises he could make. Finally took a breath and said, "I'm in Mara Bay, in Max Saliera's restaurant. Nice place."

"Punch Max for me and tell him we miss him."

Max motioned and I moved to a newly set table, white table cloth and large white plates.

A wooden bowl was placed on the table full of the proper salad ingredients and Max started to pour dressing into the bowl and then peppered it and then squeezed a lemon into it, more olive oil, and then squeezed an anchovy paste against the wall of the bowl, tossed in a couple of anchovies, dusted it heavily with parmesan, and whipped the whole thing up. "Whoee, Harvey, that's a Rembrandt."

It was. We stuffed it down then sat back and contemplated one another. "Nice to see you, buddy. Even though it's been, well, I guess more'n a year."

"I'll make it more often. I promise. Hate to tell you but I need a favor."

"Old times were not that great anyway. Shoot. All ears."

"I need to know everything you know about Stanley Simon. Local doctor."

He looked at me suspiciously, creased on his forehead and his eyes squeezed together. "Doctor Stanley Simon?"

"That's the one."

His shoulders relaxed. "Hey, I'm suing my last doctor, but not that Simon guy. See this foot, how it's swelled up?" He grimaced. "That doctor Willie Williamson didn't set it right when I broke it. He just fucked up. Then another guy broke it and reset it a second time. And it still hurts. I'm a strong guy but this pain persists and gets me down. Really does. I sued the fuckers. Think I got a good lawyer. But those doctors, they don't even tell you when they messed you up. Anyway the first guy set the wrong bones together. Imagine that? They had to take it all apart. But never mind that. I'll get them. Don't you worry."

"Brains don't always come with knowledge, Max. Facts are one thing, brains another."

"Now tell me. So what's this about Doc Simon?"

"He was responsible for caring for this lady I am looking to find out about, and thought you might know something. Your place here had got to be a place that information is spread around. She was in *Bright Paths* down the road a little."

"Yeah, I know him. He's one of the few independent doctors that stuck around the area. Kept to himself. Think he would have been promoting, joining the Rotary and all that. But he didn't. Bought a little property around here now and then. I see the signs his realtor puts up. Ate breakfast by himself at *Gillies Donut* place just down the street. Bottom of the hill."

"Clientele just local?"

"Well, guess I can talk about the dead. Did some follow up with the institute's patients when they are released. See them around town. I mean the patient and Simon walking around when its sunny."

"What else? Anything about the Wheelers. Anything at all about treating Sally Augers, old man Wheeler's daughter? And Johnnie Auger's wife?"

He pulled back. "You getting involved with that family?"

"No. Just asking, Max. I'm in the middle of it and not sure about anything."

"Yeah. Yeah. Nutty lady. Used to skip around town like she just got out of prison and scare people. Old Franklin owns a lot of property hereabouts so Joe never arrested her, just put her in his Sheriff's car and gave her a ride back to Bright Paths. Been a while, though. You know, you can't forget some of these people. Sad and spooky at the same time. She's been dead a while I think."

"As far as I know."

There was a rustle behind us and we saw someone standing at the rear door which led to a balcony overlooking the Pacific. He was dark against the light, long arms and legs, like an elongated rag doll in its last days. He waved a tired two fingers at Max who flashed a returning signal. "Just a second, Harv. Got a friend who needs attention."

He hobbled to the door, reached into his pocket, and pulled out a half dozen bills and peeled off two of them, grabbed the fellow's hand and shoved them into it and clamped it shut. He leaned in and gave the shadow a quick guy's hug. One of the waiters handed Max a bag which the dark figure eagerly grabbed, and like a weary soldier, saluted Max, turned and left. Max closed the door behind him and stood there a moment as if contemplating the state of the world and came back and gave me a "But for..." look and grinned.

"I know. Could have been any one of us. Too much booze and it gets out of control. Gave him leftovers. Better than wasting it."

"Back to business. You know the Wheelers?"

"Yeah, sort of. Big wheels around here. Used to see Mrs. Wheeler when she came in town now and then. See that Doctor Simon or buy something. Your question sort of brings it all back. Simon was the guy the Mara Bay cops tried to interview when Sally died. Don't know how far they got with that 'cause he left town."

"I talked to Joe but didn't get much."

"Well, Simon was the doctor, if I remember rightly, when that Wheeler's daughter was cremated. And then he just closed shop. Let his nurse go, that Deets lady, and took off. A couple months, maybe a little more, he was back and started all over again. I'm sure Joe got to him. Used to see Mrs. Wheeler go to Simon's office. And a couple times over the years they came in here, both of them, to have dinner. They didn't mingle much, not with an old cop like me. But they were polite enough. Never actually met her. Had Georgi wait on them."

"That's where she came to visit – Simon's office?"

"Seemed like it. Not my business so didn't pay much attention."

"You've heard about Augers' assassination and the missing kid, haven't you?"

He smiled, "This isn't Appalachia. We have T.V, even radio and newspapers. Have you gotten anywhere in tracking the boy? And I heard someone else is missing. A lady? Someone."

"Yeah, year…a lady someone. I'm getting closer, Max. Trust me. I'll get them. That lady you just mentioned was close to me. Or me to her, I should say."

"Don't know who to chase after first?"

"I'll get everyone and everything. And maybe kill them twice."

"Harvey, I know what twice means to you. Twice might not be enough."

***

I was walking out of Sid's place. Paul called again.

"Forensics tell us the ransom note seems to be reliable. Eight and a half million for Frankie. No mention of Sarah. Actually no mention of any name… just eight and half million. Plain white paper from cut outs, no prints."

The abrupt announcement by Sampson took my breath away. (Could be the hunch I was holding onto war a good one)

"I'm here. How the hell do they pick that amount? Do they have it?"

"That's what they have in cash, but it takes a day or so to put it together."

"Someone knows the nature of their assets…"

"For sure," he interrupted.

"Check with all the bank managers, the brokers, all the guys who have to deal with it?"

273

"They're clean. You know damn well we checked everyone upside and downside. The labs and the new computers have been at it a while. Takes time to check them all out."

"What about Sarah and Frankie –?"

"Note said wait, more instructions coming. Gave the Wheelers twenty-four hours to get the money together. We have the money now. We set up an exchange. Money for the kid and Sarah. Somehow the bad guys will get their instructions to us."

"That's where I come in."

"Right. You're the man. You give them the money, you get the kid and Miss Finkel—at that's the plan, anyway."

***

Billy Fitzer was smart. The crazy picnic blankets he had especially made into jackets didn't make him crazy, just made everyone think he was crazy. He prided himself on being a real help to me when I had a case. Sometimes he was.

He was on the phone. "Talked to the reception girl at *Bright Paths* this morning," he said. He repeated that she couldn't come up with records. "They had 'flown away' she said. Just plain lying to me. Apparently, this Sally lady and the something looking like a small bear left town. That's all she would say. I asked about Frankie Augers and Sarah and described them and she clammed up and told me she had answered all she was going to. Anyway, I've got the phone and the address of this Arizona rest home where they might have taken both of them. The Augers woman and her gorilla friend. What I want to know is how this Sally Augers ghost ended up getting dead and cremated in Mara Bay all the way from Arizona. If that's where she was kept. Maybe it never happened. The Cremation, I mean."

"Or the trip to Arizona. The timeline is screwed up."

"And Simon getting knocked off like that."

"Have to leave that to Paul and the LAPD. They may have already served subpoenas on the right people."

"You don't happen to know if anyone heard the name Harry Moss or if it appears in any of their files?"

"Got nothing, Harvey. There was a nurse, helper or something, for Wheeler's daughter."

"Well, ok. I'll figure it out. Thanks, Billy. What about Jimmy? I'm still in Mara Bay."

"LAPD has scoured the place. Ask Sampson."

"And Sarah?"

"She will turn up, Harvey. She will."

"She is in the middle of this because of me. If something happens to her, more than what has already happened, I should be shot. Never thought for a minute that anyone close to me would get stuck in the middle like this. I've just got to make it up to her. Get her back. In one piece."

***

Sitting tight was what I couldn't do. I stepped outside into my patio, watching seagulls wander the skies in a darkening bluesy night. My cell phone rang and gave me a start. Phones ringing late at night were bad news. It was when kids were rushed to the emergency rooms at local hospitals, when people with feeble hearts died; it was the hours of violence. It was the time when people like me get terrible phone calls.

Which I did.

***

Donna Camina whispered, "Meet me at Gert's barn. Please, you gotta. I'm in deep shit."

I figured Donna was too small to get into really deep shit, but a half hour later, I trotted up to the entrance of the Backside. Guard Jackie Summers nodded. "You here late, Mr. Ace. Sumthin' wrong?"

"Don't think so, just couldn't sleep. Want to check on something."

"Must be sumthin' wrong. Must be. Not happy when you come round so late. Sumthin's wrong."

He followed me as I stepped gingerly down the unlit side street to the main row, avoiding piles of hay and left-over puddles of water. I turned, "I can handle it, Mr. Summers. Really."

He reluctantly withdrew, murmuring, "You're all the same." Meaning all the rich guys.

Large patches of grass and occasional rose bushes filled the air with the scent of Kentucky fields, missing the salience of fireflies. In the empty silence I could hear our local nasty flies, the occasional screech of an annoyed cat —and the blubbering of sleeping horses that had been exercised and hot walked and washed and combed and wrapped and God knows what. I could hear the faint thump of a nervous hoof, the cough of an ailing horse, could see the golden eyes of black cats that kept me in sight and smiled as I emerged onto a dimly moonlit main row, stables on each side. I wondered what those cats knew that I didn't.

Further down the street was a light pole with a 60-watter under a green shade streaming its solemn unhappy beams. A dog began barking a low old man's bark and I had the same dread that John Augers must have had during those last few moments – searching a thousand shadowed places, fear for his son and himself, at the end of a thin knowing rope.

I came to the corner that turned onto a side street and stepped back into semi-darkness to confront Donna Camina. She motioned to me to follow. "Over here." Hushed tones.

"You look like you've been in a fight. What gives?"

"Please, c'mon."

She was shivering, wearing light blouse, short denim pants. She led me into one of the barn areas and pulled me into one of the stalls. "Keep quiet now, Mr. Ace." She let a canvas sheet roll down which enclosed the stall in complete darkness for a moment. She reached for a flash and flipped it on. "There."

In the faded stab of light I saw Harry Moss propped up into a corner like a dark doll, blood about his face, trickles of blood streaming down the back of his neck, bald head shining like a lost light. His eyes were closed, mouth half open. "My God, is he dead?"

There was blood on her hands. "Oh, God, Mr. Ace, I sure as hell hope not," she whispered. Her voice came between heavy sobs. "I didn't know who else to call." She fell into my arms shaking. Her body was young and delicious. "Oh, God almighty. Don't know why he acted like that."

"OK OK, hold on. Slow down. Just tell me what happened?"

Her words came between shivers. "He's been on my case. He's been here on and off for a few days… like a crazy man. But I don't know why. I don't. Didn't know who to tell. Ms. Wiseman would kill me if she knew he was like this. She would blame me."

"What do you mean? He's been here the last couple of days?"

"He's been staying here. Gertrude is hiding him. Said he was a lost soul who could use a friend. He has a gun. I don't have the slightest damn idea why. Sometimes I bunk in number 46 on the next street, when I have a few early workouts. But he's been after me." One small singular cloud stayed beneath the moon and the world below, our world, darkened.

She didn't finish. "Oh, God. I'm done for." She kept sobbing into my shoulder. I grabbed the flashlight from her. "OK. Stop crying for a minute." I bent down and touched his neck. There was a faint irregular pulse. I looked at the back of his head and came to an enormous gash on the left side just above the cortex. "How long has he been like this, Donna?"

276

"Since I don't know. I came in to get another blanket a couple hours ago and there he was. I mean I didn't see him at first. Just the hulk and I leaned over and there was something wet. I didn't do it."

"You haven't called anyone?"

"I was afraid. I didn't know what to do! I didn't do anything, Harvey. I have this blood all over me – tried to wash it."

"He could be dying. Dammit." I flipped my cell and called 911 then ran to the gate and told Jackie Summers to call the staff vet who would call for the nearest doctor. I didn't care if ten doctors showed up.

Donna told me the story of how she would see Harry sometimes at night, that he would be in one of Ms. Gertrude's barns or another. She repeated over and over that she just found him like that and panicked. "Should have called 911 right away. Who knows what they'll think now?"

"Don't worry. Tell it like it is. I'll be on your side. But you have to deal with this straight up. You know you shouldn't have waited for me."

"You're the only one who would believe me. Don't you understand that? No one around here is worth a damn. Just a bunch of game players. I didn't do anything. They'd arrest me and then what? My life goes fuckin' down the drain."

Then I saw the shovel tossed aside, blood on the back side. "You hit him with that shovel?" I pointed. "You did, didn't you? Why tell me a stupid lie?"

She pulled away. "I don't lie. He was crazy, goddammit! Crazy! He attacked me! Pulling his pants off! Grabbing me! He kept saying something about Sophie. Then that old man came. That big shot guy. Harry called him FK. Please, Harvey, I called you to help me. We should get out of here. Shit, if you aren't helping me I ain't waitin'. I'm getting outta here. I shoulda left. But I called you – you're the only one. I stayed around just to give you this. I should've gotten the fuck outta here." She shoved a small white slip into my shirt pocket, "No one here will believe me. There's no way I can come out on top. The old man said to shove the note into your pocket, make sure you got it. Gave me a bundle of fifties to do it. Then he left. Real quick like. And then Mr. Harry came and then he grabbed me and pulled me down. I hit him with my fist. Didn't stop him. He was weird, Mr. Harvey. I'm telling you. He had these wild eyes that were like death warmed over. My boobs aren't that big, but he got holda one and twisted and hurt me."

"What did he say? The old man? Did he give Harry the note? How the hell did Harry come here and the old man follow?"

"It's like they had it figured out beforehand. Oh, God, I see it coming. Just – never mind. I gotta go. I didn't anything. The old man. He did."

"You stayed just to give me this?" But she backed away, slipped out into the dark backside street, getting lost in the night. Chasing her wasn't my job. She made an instantaneous decision. Being chased was the way she might end up living her life. I remembered what Gertrude had said to me a couple of eons ago. "The girl's good all right. But she talks the talk and doesn't always walk the walk."

The scribbled, nervously written note said, "Don't trust Sophie. It's all a conspiracy against me. I told you not to bother about Sally. But you better find her before I do. And you better think…" The initials FKW were scribbled at the bottom. The last sentence was not finished. Seemed clear that Harry and Franklin arranged to meet where there would be no witnesses.

I dialed the always open line to the track vet who maintained an apartment on the track grounds. A few minutes later Noel Van Ritten, one of the track vets showed up. Less than ten minutes later the police and fire department medics arrived. Tried to tell them that it had to be someone who could swing a shovel. Not likely anyone around *the Backside*. I called Sampson. "St. Paul?"

"Go away, Harvey. For God sake, go away," he said in a hoarse sleepy voice.

"I'm not going away. Wake up."

"It's two A.M.!"

"Just listen –" I explained what I knew. Told him that Donna was a victim. "My guess is she grabbed the shovel as a last resort. Listen to her. Don't jump to conclusions."

"Is she running already?

"At the moment she is."

I didn't stay around for the hours of interrogations that would automatically ensue. I called Ann Whitson and told her I would be there in an hour. Anyplace in a storm. Didn't give her a chance to object. Said nothing about Harry and ran to my car, waving at Jackie Summers, the gate keeper.

At Ann's front door I said, without hellos, "You have to come clean and tell me everything you know. Your boss's life might be over. I figure he had to be saying something about Wheeler or Sophie. There's a ransom demand. A kid's life is at stake."

A white terry cloth covering not much was wrapped around her. –. She said, loudly, "What do you mean Harry's life is over?" She pulled the robe tightly about her. "I've already done what I could, Harvey, you can't come here and start with stupid stories! What is going on?"

"Just tell me if Harry has heard from Franklin Wheeler in the last twenty-four hours. Just tell me."

"No, he hasn't."

"And you?"

"No. And Harry's been gone. Don't know where. What's this about Harry?"

"Did you resign that petition?"

"Yes." She did an abrupt about face, leaving the door open.

I called after her. "He is in trouble. Make a cup of coffee. We have to talk."

At the kitchen table her resistance crumbled. She pulled the robe over her knees but it seemed to surrender to its age and slip away. I sat across from her. "There is some heavy stuff corning, Ann. So, just listen until I get through all of it."

She turned the knob on the stove. Sat back down, pulled the robe tighter and reached out to me. I put my hand on hers and held it there. I spoke slowly and carefully about what had happened to Moss. He kept pulling her hands away and putting them over her eyes. She grabbed a paper towel and pressed it against her eyes. I told her that Donna Carnina had fingered Sophie, possibly Franklin Wheeler as the culprit with a note apparently from Franklin.

"It may not turn out to be anything. I'm really not sure if the note was real. I told her it seemed that her boss was the person behind the rehab or retirement homes that sheltered people like Sally Augers and Oritha Durden and youngsters in trouble like Frankie Augers. "Frankie is likely to be in Mara Bay, somewhere. Her robe fell away again. Or she nudged it, revealing most of her special parts. However, I felt as closed up as King Tut's tomb.

In that moment each of us understood: I had lost the ability to trust her and she had lost the ability to trust me. Until something changed there would be a dead space between us.

"Why did you agree to be a guardian of anything? That's the bottom line," I asked, quietly after she had absorbed the news about Harry. "Something more than money was involved in that decision. Tell me that there was something more than money involved."

"I already told you everything. When it comes to things that count, you are not too bright, Harvey. Guys never understand. What makes you not see what people have to do to exist? Can you tell me all the things you've done to merely exist? It wasn't just money. And don't give me any bullshit that you've always been a good guy, moral and upstanding every minute of every day. You've been protected by all those nut cases that surround you – and money. You've been protected by the nice clean world you were born into. Even if it wasn't clean and not nice, it was better than almost any other life

279

born. You're in the fast lane. I'm not. My life isn't gambling and racehorses and bullshitting and mothering a bunch of weirdos. Real life is not your life."

I wanted her to stop, but there was no way that would happen.

"You've always lived in a goddamn insulated world," she went on. "I did what I did because real life is seeing past the shit. I had to see beyond the Harrys of the world. I had to see over them. My real life was and is just getting through the years and getting through the weeks and earning enough to raise a kid and one way or another, try to live a decent existence – getting through the goddamn day. Sophie helped me. She and Harry helped me get through the goddamn day! But he had conditions. Everyone has conditions. Sophie was my angel. Sophie Wheeler. You want me to deny her? And then Harry turned into an animal and I had to go along and do what I did. Actually, I don't give a damn if he is dead!"

She wallowed in her miseries and doubts and the difficulties about what her next step would be. "This is all I'll tell you," she finished. "You can believe any damn thing you like. I quit him! Yesterday! In spite of good sense, I quit him. He wanted me. They all seemed to want me. See this body?" She opened her robe and closed it quickly, "That's what they want." She pulled the straps of her night gown. It dropped, falling like lost threads of life. "Now what do I do with this? What, smart guy, what do I do? It's just a body!"

'Just a body.' It was a **body!!!** She looked down, suddenly a little girl, trapped into a life that had been shoved at her, never being able to object, or express, regularly surrendering to what was required.

Sophie Wheeler seemed to be everyone's angel. Moss was everyone's fall guy. Franklin Wheeler was unhappy with his riches and the spidery web he had woven. He was trying to get out from under what he had created.

Took her hand in mine. "Do what you're been doing. Take care of yourself,"

"I will. I am. You do the same."

As I walked to the door, she said, "Maybe sometime?"

Chapter Twenty-Seven

It was nearly 9.00 am. *The Egg and Omelette* was already full. Sampson was waiting, leaning his chair against the enclosing wall catching some sun. His dark hair, slightly too long at the back, was receding at the forehead, leaving a fading widow's peak. A shadow cut his face into a black and white mask. Orson Wells at his best.

As I approached he had a sardonic, suspicious look, as if unwilling to believe in the good faith in any human being, especially me. Not what I remembered from his untroubled kid's face when we were growing up. He had one small earring in his left ear, left over from when we were about fifteen years old. We both thought it was a nice defiant gesture but one I was afraid to make with him. He dared me then but I chickened out which I was always sorry about until we reached forty and his ear got infected and had to be nipped a little by a "cosmetic" surgeon. "Always late," He said.

"Sorry. I can't park just anywhere like you can."

His eyes assessed everything, moved computer-like, catching your entire demeanor in an instant as well as the lay of the land. A policeman's habit. He had a movie star nose, but severe wrinkles crevassed his forehead and eyes when he frowned or smiled that fleeting big grin of his. How could you not like him?

I turned and headed for the men's room and scrubbed my hands for a couple minutes. I always did that in a restaurant. Almost always.

Then sat next to the muraled wall in the open patio.

I said, "I hope you have something useful to say."

"I do. And you?"

"I do."

"You first."

"Food first."

Valerie was on top of us. She leaned over, boobs first, "I know you don't know what you want but they're bringing coffee anyway."

"Egg beaters scrambled and hash browns and bacon, crisp," was my order.

Valerie gave me an eyebrow lift. "You think you can beat the cholesterol odds that way?" Her horned rim glasses fell to the tip of her nose. She had that deliberate lean over system, I thought, presenting an enticing cleavage down to her belly button. Loved that girl.

"You're showing off again," I murmured.

She didn't blush. "Lucky for you. Good for both of us. Anything else?"

"The same."

Sampson nodded and said, "This is the girlfriend you've been telling me about?"

"One of many."

Valerie poked a light finger at my forehead. "You should be so lucky."

He put two teaspoons of sugar in his mug and sipped and nodded. I took mine black.

"Okay. I'll tell you what I know," he said. "But you are definitely not going to like it."

"That keeps your score intact."

"Jimmy the Mummy Gaines has not and never has been Jimmy the Mummy Gaines. The line jumped again below line goes here. Except to fool his friends and enemies. His real name is Hyman Monkosh Garfein."

Held up my hands. "Whoa!"

"More. His father was a Garfein and mother a Monkosh."

Took me time to absorb the news. "Hyman Monkosh Garfein? You gotta be kidding."

"Believe it. Believe this, too. He was indicted for murder way back in '81 in Chicago for killing a restaurateur who had the temerity to refuse to use the disposal company Hyman shoved on him, fronting for a local gang which, as fate would have it, controlled the entire South Side garbage contracts for the city. Indicted, but no trial and no conviction. Somehow there were no witnesses left to testify and no bullets – and no anything, including the restaurant which was blown to smithereens about a week later. The only thing left were pieces of four people, three that were cleaning up late that night and one that owned a piece of the restaurant action. Jimmy was implicated in a half dozen other murders of politicians, gang members, of Joey Maronato who ran the casino at Winston Towers in Miami. Cuban Florida was his real beat. In short, Harvey, you good friend was, maybe still is, a hired killer. Except no one has anything on him – not even a parking ticket." He waggled his hand. "Maybe sort of semi-retired – and a little long in the tooth, but you never know. Never know about people like Hyman. Anyway, Hyman got married. Which may have cooled him off. The old Cuban mobs are essentially dead. Chicago is different than it was. The new gangs, young fellows, didn't need him to do their drive by killings of one another, which is probably OK, because if the civilians can stay out of it, then I say let them kill each other."

I slumped into my chair. "My Jimmy? Parkinson's beginning to affect his hands? That Jimmy? The Jimmy who lost his wife and cried and has barely enough visible means to survive? The one I paid to get his hernia operated on? The one who hangs on me and needs someone just to stay alive? How could that be?"

"You ask very good questions. However, I am informed by unreliable people that you're the smart detective. You tell me. I will simply tell you the rest – if you're ready."

"Start."

"He has a sewer full of money, Harvey. How he acquired it, I can only guess. You have to figure it out. The IRS is after him. They'll get to him sooner or later. Probably sooner. Did you look in his freezer in that god forsaken room of his?"

"No. Had no reason."

"He has a dozen frozen Omaha New York Steaks, frozen mashed potatoes from Whole Foods, frozen Daiquaris, a nine-millimeter and a huge forty-five resting comfortably in the freezer with the food and booze. And about twenty-five hundred in twenties. And a bank book with little notes, little precise, hand-printed notes. In short, dear Harvey, the keen observer of men, the guru of character, the collector of strange people, your friend Jimmy the Mummy was happy to bleed you of money and sympathy while he had a gazillion of his own shackles, six hundred thousand and maybe a little more, and had no sympathy for anyone whatsoever. He was devoid of emotion – at least that's my take on him. I suppose we could pick him up for possessing those guns. If we could find him."

"Where was it?"

"You mean the money? In the goddamn bank, off shore naturally. Bahamas. Why not? He was a legit citizen. The old guy had the gall to register to vote. Just a little old to be very active in his chosen field. Six hundred thirty-two thousand dollars and twenty-one cents in different off shore accounts and nearly another million in two and half percent short term CDs in Taiwanese Banks! Taiwanese! And thirty-one thousand in a local Wells-Fargo. The IRS will get that for sure. Census records were very helpful. Jimmy had a younger brother. We found him in Miami. He immigrated there with Jimmy as a baby. Parents were from Odessa, Russia, and were active against the Russian Czar. They escaped the Reds in 1924. Jimmy became Herman Garfein and got work in Havana, Cuba, which was easy to get into in those years. He started out there with someone named Anotia Lozano who operated under the protection of Mickey Weisberg at the Paradise Casino in Havana. Then Herman became James Gaines and shows up with his brother in Miami. Tried to get in the Marines during 1942 but was refused. 4F. Records indicate very flat feet. We got the information from the FBI – that was like pulling teeth. It's taken the IRS and the FBI weeks to pull the information together which we would not have gotten except that he is a murder suspect. They had to respect that. As to the money, Jimmy would call a local rep and roll over the CDs every three months. He has a safe deposit box that we haven't gotten a Court Order or Subpoena to open as yet. Must be hordes of cash there. He's a collector, Harv. He collects money like bottle tops or stamps. It doesn't seem to be in it for the comfort or ease it might give him. He never spends it. He collects it."

All I could think of was that it couldn't be. Not *my Jimmy.* The person who was fearful and shaking, who was an incipient Parkinson's patient. "You're sure about all of this?"

"I'm sure."

"He's gotta be worth a fortune to some movie-maker for his life story."

"There were busloads of immigrants to Cuba just before the war and during, if they could get there alive, they could get here. Had a bundle of money when he arrived. He just bought his way in. He lived quietly until he was picked up in Vegas right after the untimely death of Joey Gallardo who was boss of the Old Pirate's Cove casino in downtown Las Vegas. He was like a special event terminator. Here, then there. Almost never charged with anything. Mickey Weisberg migrated from Havana and took over that Casino along with Tony Firense. Figures that Jimmy was Weisberg's boy. Which may explain the money. Mickey died about a year later as did Firense. Apparently, Jimmy was a bad manager and when he got married, he and his new bride shook it all off and came to LA – that was about '84 and both actually registered to vote under the name Gaines. That helped find him. So there you have the short story of *Jimmy the Mummy,* your good friend. There's more if you want it."

I wrestled with *"the story"* for a couple minutes trying to fit the pieces. "Why would any of the Augers' story have anything to do with him? What's the connection? He was afraid of something the last I saw him. Genuinely afraid. Can you be that afraid of the IRS? I thought it was just an old guy with a touch of paranoia."

'The friggin' IRS, Harv, is very spooky. They have investigators. Big guys just like the movies. Had to be the IRS. All the old bad guys are dead. Chicago is not the same. Cuba is not the same. Can't get out of XCuba or into Cuba without at least an outboard and lots of gas. Jimmy, the fucking dear old Mummy, hasn't paid taxes for God knows how long. He made a mistake a few years ago and started buying Well-Fargo CDs. He had a talent for timing and moved things around to prevent the IRS from finding it and grabbing the money. First a local bank for a week or two, then the Caymans, then Switzerland, then Taiwan. He is probably the smartest crooked Jewish boy on the block. We can trace where some of it went, but he was just a step ahead of the slowpokes. He was a brilliant crook. Very intuitive and fastidious when it came to timing and witnesses. As far as John Augers, well, I'm not sure what fits or if anything fits. But he certainly fits *somewhere.* We're checking ballistics on his pistols now but don't think we will connect anything to the guns. He's too careful. So, you're the genius – you figure out the connections."

"Why is it when the entire Los Angeles Police force can't figure something out, you think I can?"

Sampson's dark eyes had that knowing, weary look. There was nothing they hadn't seen. Mysteries were child's play. Another day at the office. But this one bothered him. "I'll tell you Mister Harvey Ace,' he continued, with an edge, "something you may never have figured. I'll give you another little tidbit, although I hate to do it. It's called respect. It's the only reason I stick with you. Like when we worked on the Willa Katt case. Also, because you've never asked me for a real favor. A real one. And my old supervising Sergeant, Jake Dibetta, good soul that he is, had that kind of respect for you. He's a good guy so I have always figured, you must be. Then you have that entourage of yours. Those nut cases. Nirenstein, Lowenstaff, Fitzer, even that Doc Lee fellow. Nutcases. Everyone. And you still take old Joe Dibetta to the Dodger games he tells me, though he can barely walk anymore. And, I'll say this, I know that you wouldn't screw me or lie to me... very often, that is. But," he poked a finger at my nose, his eyes flattened to their cop position, "it doesn't give you the license to interfere with police Department investigations. For God sakes, Harvey, just let us handle this. We'll get the bad guys. We'll find Sarah."

"How long do I wait? And won't they get me or be done with Sarah before you get them?"

He ignored the question and sat back. Closed his eyes. He was calculating his words as though interrogating a suspect. I counted a full sixty seconds before he opened his Italian eyes and said, "You know, it occurs to me… you can chew on this… think about it… as far as the Mummy story goes, my guess is he thought that you, his good friend, was getting too close to something he was involved in and didn't want to kill you. The son-of-a-bitch didn't want to kill you unless he had to – so he kept bothering you and staying close so that he knew what you knew and when you knew it. Maybe he wasn't trying to be done with. Maybe everything he did was a pose, maybe he was just a bad guy laying low until the last few years when age began to get him. Age does that, doesn't it? That's my guess." He gave me one of his grins. It wasn't a guess. It was what he had decided.

"Was it really him in the blue Chevy that almost shoved you off the road on the way to Mara Bay that you barely mentioned a week ago?"

"Didn't seem like anything but a bad driver." I mulled the facts over. They actually hurt. "Well, St. Paul, seems like I never meant anything to him. Our past doesn't mean a thing. I saw his old blue Chevy recently. Didn't register with me at the time. It was in the wrong place. At Bright Paths in Mara Bay. What does that tell you?"

"Tells me he's at *Bright Paths*. Holed up there. But, too logical for my tastes. Bright Paths? A nut house?" He mulled it over. "Whatever. Like to get hold of the car and check it out. Can't be sure but he may have been the one to run Dr. Simon down. We haven't gone to the DA yet. This is all just for your ears."

"Still doesn't tell us the connection."

"No," he mumbled. "And no motive. I hate to say it, but I may have to rely on you. I want the car without the fuss. No fuss, no subpoena, no search warrants, no chance to clean it or junk it. It's up to you. And I want to get into that institute and search every corner without tipping them off. Whoever *them* is."

"Suddenly I'm desirable." I took a bite of my muffin.

"You don't get in my way and I won't get in yours. Unofficially, of course; the institute could use some sniffing around."

"Agreed."

He folded his arms and looked at me with unblinking black eyes. You are going to tell me everything, aren't you?"

"Maybe."

"Start talking."

I did. I told him everything including my brief episode with Carly Klein. Between breaths I sipped coffee. He told me that he had been there to see her and understood that she was going to fight for the house but that it seemed to have nothing whatever to do with the series of deaths that had

286

followed me. I told him **everything** had to do with this Augers Affair. Sally, old man Wheeler, Sophie, Carly, and Jimmy – I just didn't know how.

Finally, I said, "You know, the way Sophie screamed, 'kill her' and not a word about her grandson – and she gave me this hush money. I don't even know for sure what it's for. Told me to stop everything. I told you that, didn't I?"

"Not a word. Not a fucking word."

"So, OK. I translate it to mean she's not worried about him or she knows he's dead and no longer part of the equation. That somehow she knows where and how he is. Not sure how that could be and I could be completely wrong. Although I'm never wrong. The strange thing is I have her money with a bunch of conflicting instructions to find him. Find Frankie was the first instruction. Now, it's morphed into find Sally and kill her. Then it changed to 'get out of the way,' and then, back to kill her."

"She wasn't shy about telling me that she and Franklin both had hired you."

"She told me. They both think Sally is alive and kicking. Which means the Quantum Principle is alive and well."

He stared at me. "What?"

"Never mind. Just a famous physicist's principal that says that nothing in the whole world is as it seems. Nothing goes in the direction it is supposed to go. You aim east and your bullet goes north. And the space between the stars is more important than the stars. His name is Richard Feynman in case you're talking to the boys over a beer."

He shook his head in that slow way he had. "Anything else?"

"That's it." I did not tell him about Ann Whitson. He gave me that straight hard cop's look again, "Did you fuck her?"

"Who?"

"You know who."

"Very crude, Saint Paul. Very crude. What would your mom say? I thought you were a well-mannered person, a nice proper fellow."

"With my wife and kid and that's it. I'm a cop, remember?"

"I do not discuss my love life. Carly Klein *is* interesting, though."

"Doubt if she is anything in this mix. The mystery is not that horny lady." We sat a while sipping coffee.

"So?" He looked up. "Give me the conclusions."

"Look, if Sally is alive, like they all seem to think, and she is still a rational being, she will be the boy's guardian and therefore she will control Frankie's Trusts and John's estate and therefore a significant and worrisome piece of everything old man Wheeler owns. Including a seat on the Foundation Board of Directors as well as a piece of it. However, the other tack is – suppose Franklin's capacities are diminished enough for someone to take over, then Sophie might, through Ann, her good friend, end up with everything. Franklin never figured on any of this. He was just trying to be smart and arrange his estate like good lawyers do, and save inheritance taxes, income taxes. Harry obliged. Just doing his job – which is what he wants us to believe. But if Sally isn't alive, with Whitson in the mix, looks like Moss has been scheming all the time. And then he is our guy. He operates through Ann and Sophie. Complicated. Ann is Moss's proxy and maybe Sophie is the proxy for all of them. Then there's the ton of cash sent to Harry. Why? And who? He may just be a lackey, but it all begins in Harry's office. He did what Franklin wanted... or did he? This new petition to appoint Ann changes everything. Motives are clearer seems to me. Harry steps in."

Paul responded, "Seems to me if Franklin's brain goes south, Sophie takes effective control of her husband's affairs. Not Ann. She and the Whitson woman would be antagonists then."

"So why kill John?" I asked.

"With his powers over several trusts, he threatened Wheeler. Even a threat to Sophie."

"So either would have a motive to get rid of him. Sophie claims to have seen Sally or the ghost of Sally lurking about."

"Nonsense," he almost snorted. "Let me finish what I told you about Jimmy..."

"More?"

"Yes, more. We got blood samples of Jimmy from his deceased wife's doctor. He was going to give blood for a transfusion for her. But wrong type. The blood at his apartment was, in fact, Jimmy's. And it appears that he might have been dragged away. Wasn't very apparent but the lab boys said it's possible."

"So he is dead or in someone's cellar wasting away. You won't find him," I said. "I might. But not you and twenty cops descending on possible locations. If he is not already dead, he will be. If there is any story about John Augers to tell, Jimmy might be the one to know. I'll find him before you."

That Jimmy was a bad guy, was hard to swallow. But not for Paul Sampson. If Stalin had been a CIA spy he would have said, "Seems about right. Shoot him."

I left bills on the table. He grinned and said, "I can pay my own way." He touched my sleeve, then dropped a ten spot on the table. "I heard about the Mondozo incident. Front of your condo. Don't look shocked. There are life guards with glasses watching out for such things."

"Nothing to it. Rich kid's tantrum."

"And the old man? They want your filly. Right?"

"Three hundred twenty-five thousand worth."

"You're fucking crazy. Guess it pays to be good for nothing."

"I'm not, but you're entitled to such thoughts. You have a pension. That big girl is my ticket. My pension. I don't think people with a regular job can understand that."

He shrugged. Closed his eyes. "It's your life, Harvey. Strange as it may be. There's one thing I want you to remember and to promise."

"Name it."

"Do not mix business with pleasure. Sarah is still out there. Mix it all up right now and you'll be sorry."

"Then, Paulie, I'll make sure that whatever I do is not a pleasure. But I should point out Sarah dumped me. I didn't dump her."

"Okay," he sighed. Business and pleasure. Don't mix it up."

"You just don't get it."

"Okay. I know nothing about relationships. Just married nearly fifteen years. Just remember, don't mix pleasure with business and don't mix gambling with anything – especially with your Mexican friends. And... take his fucking money. And don't get killed... By the way, one of the doctors at the institute got shot. Someone tried to assassinate him, too."

Chapter Twenty-Eight
Ebrons

Gert had two winners the next day. They were both coming off layoffs of a few months. Both fresh. Both eager and ready. Horses are like that. They want to run, they want to feel their strength and speed. They are bred that way. For the last couple of centuries. Problem is they can't tell you if something is wrong, if something hurts. Gertrude understood that you can't be short-sighted in the care of successful horses. They can't be ratcheted up with two or three weeks of grinding workouts aiming for one race and expect to get more than that. Or expect to maintain a healthy animal. The trainers who worried day to day about money didn't give their horses a chance. In the end they were the loisers. Money screws up a lot of beautiful horses. Get them hot for one race then not again for a while as they wore down. Run them when they hurt and they break down. Money is the goal but only through consistent and healthy stock.

Gert knew everything about her stable. She knew how to conserve a horse. Use it when it was feeling like it *had* to run, like it was their time. She knew exactly how much each animal ate every day, how much water each consumed, when to use laxix, the chemical that eliminates excess water from their systems; she knew how restless or cool each animal was. She got consistent races from each of her stock. Consequently, she was always fearful of the claiming races. She believed fervently that class counted. A fifty thousand claiming horse was simply not fast enough to make money in good handicap races Claiming races meant you could buy the horse for the claiming price announced for the race. It was a buy and sell business and that was the part she didn't like. Claiming races were the depository for owners who required these races for the need of money or to trade way less promising stock. Place a ready animal in a claiming race and hope he or she doesn't get claimed and wins.

Anyway, I bet her two horses, combined them, ended up with an $1150 day. It would have been more except that all the while I had Frankie Augers on my mind, wandering to the bar in the Turf Club and wondering if he was still alive in some deep dark cell.

Frankie was the white pawn in the end game. There were no white Knights or Bishops covering his flanks. An invisible someone had a black queen, a bishop, and a knight surrounding him. The black queen hovered. He was a pawn alone. Wherever the white King was, was dependent on this lowly pawn. It would eventually decide the issue.

I phoned John's tack room at the track. Wheeler answered and simply grunted a hello. His voice was vague, as if he was in the middle of a very long string of worries. I could hear his exhaustion. One's voice was a tell-tale sign; its timbre was hollow and resigned. Exhaustion brought the brain to a near halt, made the business of *thinking* bare and hard. He told me he was ready to go home, that he was checking on his Gertrude trained stable. He said, "We're waiting. Just waiting for the instructions to come." I asked him where Sophie was and he murmured – at their "Farm" just north and east of the Danish village of Solvang. It was wine country and horse country. Rolling hills—grape orchards. You could hear the veiled whispers rise out of grassy fields with their fireflies flashing come hither specks, come into the fields; lazy happy horses munching in the dewy greens, and dirt paths and deep green fields that were often used in movies as a substitute for the English countryside. A person could feel themselves joining with nature after a while in these fields. Wheeler kept his brood mares and studs and their babies there as well as his resting or recovering horses.

Franklin gathered himself. He straightened up and his tired eyes brought him into the moment, "Sophie is not doing well, Mr. Ace. Moss and that Whitson girl are the cause." His voice trailed off once again. "Frankie is my family. That is the bottom line in all of this. He is my family. What's left of it. This is a fearful place to find myself in. Fearful. I could lose everything. Lose control." He coughed and harrumphed and then began to ramble on about family and about *"that woman"* and about *"them"* trying to take Frankie away. About Sophie and her sickness, about his dead daughter. I did not interrupt. I knew the gift of listening. Paid dividends. Finally, he said, "The amount has changed to eight point six million. How they came by that number, I don't know. There was a note. Gave it to that Sampson detective. But it's every dime in cash we have and it leaves us almost dry. Joe got a note – left at his Mara Bay office. Why there I don't know. They are trying to take over, Ace. Ruin me."

"That's the exact amount of cash you can lay your hands on?"

"Right."

"You have millions more."

"Can't get more millions in a day. Can't do such things. Even if I borrow from my own Savings and loan, it takes a few days to go through the required banking processes." Then, the line went dead as if something pulled him away.

Why not ten million, why not twenty? Or seven?

***

When I got to the midtown hospital in Mara Bay, where Dr. Ebrons had been taken, I was surprised to find him in pretty good shape, sporting a wry smile. "Bullet went through the edge of my right side. Clipped the skin next to a rib. Hurts like hell, whole side looks like a purple sunset but nothing vital messed up. Should be out of here in a couple days. Told that Joe Dobrowski everything. I don't know what I can add." One unruly eyebrow hair curled down nearly into one of his fierce black eyes. I wanted to push it away but it annoyed me more than it did him. His hair needed trimming as well as his short wintry beard. "What do you want with this poor wounded creature?"

"I need the whole story. Not just pieces. You have problems."

"I don't have any problems, Ace – none whatsoever. No wife, no kids, folks living in Florida, and healthy $46,000 in the bank, and a decent job. That ought to cover it."

"Maybe I ought to remind you, you are the connection to Harrara Pillar. You are the connection to the Wheeler boy and to Sally Augers. You have a connection with Harry Moss, too. You went with Pillar or followed him – he got his ass beaten, you didn't. You had the boy in your possession, at least for a little bit. So, maybe you knew where he was to start with. Someone had the boy at Breeze Street. You ought to get over all those nice grins you're giving out and make it easy on yourself and tell me where the boy is. I can't arrest you. But I can get the Mara Bay police to," I lied. Joe would never do something anyone asked unless it hit the money on the head. "You can talk. You won't incriminate yourself with me. But, I would venture a good guess that you know damn well where Jimmy is. And where Sarah is."

He flashed a grin. It passed in a second. Nevertheless, it pissed me off. "Number one, I don't know. Number two, I don't know. Number

292

three, you're full of shit. Number f o u r, I don't know. Number five, I didn't know. I told you the police have already asked me, both LAPD and that slow Dobrowski guy from Mara Bay. Number s i x, you are full of shit. I'm a doctor who treated the boy. Naturally I wanted to know more. That's it. I have no axes to grind. Those LAPD people spent two hours with me. They got every little detail. Get it all from them, or that Mara Bay Sheriff."

"Listen, Ebrons, someone you know got that boy to the Breeze Street location. Got you there, too. Seems to me that it's a cats-out-of-the-bag kind of thing. You must have told Joe and the others who that was. Dammit, Ace, I don't know. I told them, I'm telling you. A voice, a muffled voice, said the kid needed me, would recognize me, and not be afraid, gave me the address and then bang, gone, hung up. No forwarding number. Nothing."

"Go on. You went to Breeze Street thinking Frankie was there to take care of him. I'm supposed to believe that?"

"It's the truth. Only difference I was late. Came after you."

"You were not late. You saw Pillar there and figured this was not a place where you ought to be and also figured the boy was with Pillar and safe. So you ran. Out that alley. Then what?"

"He was afraid. I got the same story. Pillar seemed to think it was all a mistake. I asked him if he knew the person who called and he wouldn't answer. Or couldn't. Then everything was chaos."

"Speculate."

"You can guess just the same as I can."

"And you?"

"I don't know a damn thing and I'm not guessing, Ace. I got out. I got some money and did what they said and got myself shot. I was right outside Bright Paths. Told the police what I'm telling you."

"It wasn't just 'some money.' You got a very large deposit into your account, more than the thirty-six you've described. Mara Bay police already know about it."

He began to grin again, one of those sheepish grins that everyone is stuck with when they have been found out.

"How much?"

"Ten thousand in a brown envelope sitting on the floor of my office."

"So, OK," I said, "you did what you were told. Money was in plain brown wrapper and you went traipsing off. You and Pillar went to the same place at slightly different times. The money makes you an accessory. So just tell me, your guess? Who was it?"

293

His head fell back onto his pillow and he closed his eyes. "You're wearing me out."

Smiling, I said, "Happy to oblige."

"You're an asshole."

"Takes one –"

A nurse came in. She had a red ribbon on her breast and curly hair tucked into her hat. She pumped the attached blood pressure wrap on his arm and looked serious. Ebrons laughed. "It's gotta be 160 over 90 right now."

The nurse did not smile. "Doctors are big pains," she said, and left.

Ebrons continued. "I told the police and I'm telling you –I got a call to my office, check it out, didn't know who it was, guy said go to the address, be there at ten the next night and I got a package with money. I went there. All I can determine is that the money was left late that night. I was told I will find the Augers child, that the kid needs help. That's what I told the police. I think they must have traced the call by now."

"And you didn't tell anyone before you went?"

"Of course not. Why the hell would I?" He put his arm over his eyes. His voice had a new defiance in it. "I think you better get out. You can't intimidate me. I told the police everything."

"I don't believe you. I figure you are in a conspiracy with the kidnappers. You're in the middle of this. You might get away with it for a little while but the LAPD won't be gentle when they figure it out."

With a rattle deep in his throat, he said, "Fuck off. I'm trying to help. An autistic kid can hardly be helpful, Ace. Even if I knew where he was, he can't tell you anything."

"You know that's not true. That's why I know you're lying. Kids like that can and do talk and improve substantially, depending on their care. You know that. Your car wasn't at the location you were picked up. Explain that. How exactly did you get to the location?"

Either Ebrons was lying or Joe and his minions were not doing a careful job. Anything more than basic competence was hard to come by. "This is too much right now," he said. "I don't want to spend my life dealing with you and the police and the sick and the stupid all at the same time. I don't want that anymore. I did what I did. That's all." He reached for his calling buzzer. I closed my hand over his. It was a long thin violinist's hands, like Paganni's must have been. But not strong. You know people by their handshakes. Some squeeze just to prove just how manly they are in spite of the truth, some linger a moment or two to let you know they "really mean it." Most are perfunctory. Ebrons' shake was simply flaccid, "Do not try to push that

294

button, Dr. Ebrons. Not yet. Disabuse me of the idea that you are or were involved with Harry Moss, that you know who called you that night. I can assure you, I'll find out about your calls to and from Moss's office, which, you dumbbell, everyone has undoubtedly already done."

"OK, OK." He held up his hands in mock surrender. "There were calls, but so what, they are grandparents, concerned about their grandson. I got the cash from someone unknown and deposited it. Sheriff Dobrowski gave me all sorts of papers to fill out about where it came from. I did the whole number with him and the LAPD."

"You were taken to the Breeze address."

"I told you. Picked up. Sat in the back. Guy had a like a cape over him and his head. He was not about to be known. Voice on the phone said I'd get thirty thousand and they'll pick me and take me to Breeze Street and I should take care of a boy who had a fever and then told me what to do afterwards. Didn't recognize the voice muffled, but pretty sure it wasn't Moss. I couldn't tell who it was."

"And your driver was an old thin man."

"He never spoke. Swaddled in that cape-like thing. He didn't seem thin or fat. Just stuffed with clothing. Seemed sort of woozie. Came and went. Ten-minute ride."

"Did you look at his hands."

He looked up quizzically.

"You can tell age by hands, doctor. You know what I want."

"I didn't look to see if he had gloves. I don't remember. Why the hell should I? It was a lot of money. I was going to earn it. I was going to get the kid. Take care of him. Under what seemed dangerous circumstances. They delivered the money, dammit. So, I went. I have a hole in me to prove it. No one has a legal right to take it away. I was doing the right thing!"

"And there was Pillar."

"It was dark, smelly, moldy. Place was empty. Suddenly this Pillar fellow came in the same door. I could see his eyes. Like he suddenly realized he had been tricked. They probably gave him money too." He tossed a hand dismissively. "Pillar sort of jumped and turned and gave a half scream. He was frightened out of his wits. Then someone I thought was the driver was suddenly there and he shoots this Pillar and I'm running out the door while this shooter with this funny whine, I remember that whine, like a banshee or like he's coming off something, then he turns on me and I keep running and that's it. I told the Sheriff all of this."

"But not about the money."

"So what? It's mine."

"It makes you a suspect. You are one dumb doctor. You took a bunch of cash to set someone up. Pillar. They wanted him out of his office. You played the fool. You're sure the voice on the phone was male?"

"You sure aren't smarter than a two-bit gumshoe gambler."

He had me there but I persisted. "So, did you guess at who it was?"

"No way. Bundled and covered. Could have been big or thin or anything.

"All right, now where is Moss? Harry Moss?"

"Don't know the guy. Never met him directly. I know he's a lawyer for the Wheelers. They give Bright Paths grants every year. They paid some bills for their grandson through Moss. But that's all I know." Tiny bubbles of sweat broke out on his upper lip. "I don't know anything about this whole damn mess."

"Don't bullshit me, Ebrons. You dealt with the Wheelers about Frankie and their daughter, Sally."

"That was my..." The door opened. As I turned I saw a smile on a wide face, a Latina woman holding a pill cup. She was clearly enamored with tortillas and beans. She ignored me and fiddled with an IV hookup. Pulled out a thermometer.

"I'll be back," I said to Ebrons with as much menace as I could muster. It didn't quite reach the same level of foreboding as that of the Terminator... or maybe Little Orphan Annie.

"I'm holding my breath," Ebrons said.

***

"Harry, we got it. The records. Oritha Durden and guess what, James Monroe Garfein, just like you said. And, get this, he has a daughter, says right here, as a kid he had a daughter. She's gotta be full-grownd by now." Larry Lowenstaff s phone voice was excited, triumphant. "But don't know where she is."

Larry wore a brown corduroy cap. It covered his thinning gray remains of hair. He grew up in Santa Ana, California, in the middle of Orange County and remembered hanging out in the little park of the old town square with its red courthouse, which was still there. His father, William Lowenstein, was a buddy of John Rousselot, the Congressman who was in the big time witch hunting business with the John Bircher Society in the 60s. William Sr. managed to get *The Last Temptation of Christ* kicked out of some of the libraries and had great success in enforcing the perceived dictates of Joe McCarthy until William Sr. was caught with his same sex lover in a motel in Oceanside. Larry denied being born Lowenstein or in Orange County and insisted his father's name was George and that he never heard of William Lowenstein and never stole anything from his house to finance his gambling. Never did such a thing. He was, however, convinced that Orange County was inhabited by red devils in the disguise of gentlemen farmers, bank managers, and TV preachers. According to Larry, Elmer Gantry still lived in Orange County.

"We used Doc Lee's business card. What a kick! Walked right in the main building of that *Bright Paths* place about nine that night. Night attendant at the desk led us to Ebron's office like we owned the place. They hire nincompoops. The doc's business card with the Hoag hospital in Santa Ana on the card was like magic. I wore a suit and stethoscope."

"What about your cap?"

"Stuck it in my pocket. Told the attendant we were meeting at Ebron's. I guess they figured he was there. We walked right in. Anyway, we got them."

"Any trouble?"

"Bull necked youngster named Arthur, about as wide as a house came in and was ready to throw us out. He knew Ebrons wasn't there and wouldn't be. I think the kid lives there. Told him to fuck himself and Nails waved his nails at him and snarled, just like the moving pictures, like that guy, you know, Friday the 13th. The fellow jumped and hollered and said he was gonna call the police. I handed him the phone and told him, 'Please do.' He backed off and then all at once he went at Nails, who I gotta tell you, was about as menacing as Bugs Bunny. I hit Arthur with the phone and then we just grabbed the files and got outta there. Arthur came after us and Nails started snarling and screaming. I'm a killer! I'm a Killer! Watch yourself!

"N a i l s is a killer like I'm Dillinger." I pointed a pistol at the kid. That did it. And off we went. Had a hellava good time, Harv."

"Joe will be looking for you."

"We won't be here. But he'll be happy we got the files. We cut through the legal bullshit, you know, there's another home there – for kids, disabled kids. Out around the side. A whole hospital like place."

"I know. You get in there?"

"Harvey," Larry said, "we are high class professionals. We don't do half a job. Of course we got in there. Went to the front desk and I pointed a pistol at the gate girl who was half asleep and she opened her file cabinet and I grabbed everything with Augers, Wheeler names – not much, but got what there was and here and we are alive and well."

"You got any more tapes?"

"No. We got files, not tapes. What exactly are you looking for?"

"I want to see a name we don't know, something that tells me who is holding Frankie Augers. It's possible that Sally's cremation was fixed."

"She is dead, Harvey. Plain dead. As to all the rest. I don't know."

"We'll see."

Through it all there was a missing Jimmy, someone I thought I knew but didn't, a dead doctor Simon, an unfilled Death Certificate of Sally; Harrara Pillar's protestations, missing files, the Ebrons connection, Frankie Augers, and mysterious phone calls. I had the strong sense that someone wanted us to believe that Sally Augers was alive – but that the same someone was aiming our noses at Wheeler. Maybe Sally was dead. But, hell, maybe not. Put it all together and I figured Sally was alive and probably armed and dangerous and with two things in mind – the death of her father and those around him and control of the Wheeler fortune.

Chapter Twenty-Nine

"I'm still waiting, Joe. You were supposed to be here at eight this morning."

"Sampson and his gang will be at my office in a few minutes. But how come you're there?"

"Just get here. Like now."

"Okay, Mr. Ace. If you say so, we'll jump to and salute..."

"'Bout time you recognized your superiors."

"Fuck you, dear boy. Anyway, I'll see you soon, got some juicy news about Doctor Simon."

Sampson brought officers Eddie Dupree and Tom Wiley with him. We met and nodded and entered the lobby entrance of *Bright Paths*. Joe showed up alone a few minutes later. Paul dropped the subpoena on the receptionist's desk and asked her to step outside. When she reached for the phone he touched her hand, waved a finger, and pointed at the door. She took another chew of her gum and obliged. We waited in the entrance foyer with Eddie while Tom Wiley's thin frame moved anxiously like a squirrel looking for his dinner.

"I used to come and see my father in a place something like this. Couple months before he died," I said. "One of those places where there were only a few like him. I guess you would call them patients. Small homes with supposedly better care. Everything smells the same, though. Looks the same."

We began inspecting the units thinking it would be tough to hide a human being. Especially someone like Jimmy. We finished sixteen of the forty-two units. Every ten steps was another depressing trip to hell. People slumped in wheelchairs, dying slowly in front of us, perhaps too slowly for most of them. We kept coming up empty. One corner and then another. We looked for anything that seemed out of place, for any stray paper, unexplained empty cup, anything that might help lead to Jimmy or Frankie's whereabouts which I believed had to be within a fifty yards of where we stood at any given moment in our search. Sampson was sure we

would find nothing. "There's nothing here, Harv. You wrong. As usual."
But we kept at it. Bathrooms, beds, closets.

Tom Wiley began pulling bedding apart. He was quick and was nearly
through with a room by the time Sampson and I arrived. I suggested that
we were looking for a human being and weren't going to find him stuffed
into a small mattress. But Wiley said, "What the hell, we're here."

"Where's Eddie?"

"In front of us."

We pounded walls, medicine cabinets, employee's lounges while
patients and employees set their chins, ground their teeth, and grunted
objections. Wiley, Dupree, and Sampson ignored them.

St. Paul was not saintly that morning. He was dour and muttering to
himself as though he harbored some grudge against the whole situation. He
kept shaking his head as if touched by some unseen hand pulling it back
and forth. "Your dad and my mom," he finally said, "spent time in a place
just like this in Culver City. Same smell, same towels on the floor. Not as
nice as this, really."

"If you remember, Paul, my mom didn't know up from down, was
out of it. Didn't matter where she was. Kept painting lipstick on her lips
over and over forgetting each time that she had already done it. Wondered
who I was, thought maybe I was her father. The only thing she remembered
was my phone number, not a damn other thing —sometimes she would dial
me as much, well, one month it was a hundred thirty-one times. Over and
over. No one could figure out how she remembered the number. And then
she didn't know who she was calling. The line would be dead, and I would
shout into it and after a while I would just scream into it and then I would
just hang up or take it off the hook. I added a new number but was afraid
to change the old because I thought she needed that outlet. She needed to
pour whatever was left into something. And then she died. Ten years of not
knowing anything about anything. She was a good person, did whatever
she could for me."

One room after another, one vacant stare after another, one dirty diaper
piled in a corner after another, now and then coming across a complete
human being, bright-eyed and happy to be disturbed and who would try to
engage in conversation. One lady, terribly frail, faded thin orange hair,
sitting in a comfortable white cushioned rattan chair with a maroon caftan
over her knees, said, "Have you tried their G.I. issue *'shit on a shingle'* for
lunch?"

Each room had its own details, colorful pillows, portraits placed around
the walls and on cabinets; relatives or friends unhappily forgotten. Now and

then, we found a room bare of anything except a bed and a chair and a lamp and a human being who would rise and stare hollow-eyed at us from a corner as if preparing for an attack. Several of the rooms had fresh flowers in them in the same blue vases, financed by relatives and delivered every few days by a florist owned by the management. Almost all of the walls had a large calendar in large letters and numbers, which each day marked off as if there were some triumph as each day was passed and marked as though being closer to the end was desirable. It was actually a social worker's attempt to define the day, month, and year. But it was marking the march of death. They also marked the calendar about dinner meals, whether it was meatloaf, beef stew, or creamed corned beef on toast for dinner, another attempt to stay in the realm of reality. I thought it was all a reminder that each day was the same as the last. But what do I know? Experts know everything. Just ask them.

After finishing the inspection of the first floor I told St. Paul to get the attendant, Arthur, in a room alone with us along with Eddie Dupree who was as big as the Griffith Park Observatory. Arthur's full name was Arthur Loyd Laffer, the namesake of a silly and discredited economist who was the champion of Vodoo trickledown economics, which was actually Econ I for billionaires.

Arthur was the institute's strong arm who could manage it only because of his size. But he was also just a kid, basically a slightly dim bulb trying to hold onto a job. Unlike his economist namesake who could fool an uncomfortable percentage of the people most of the time, but not all of them all of the time, young Arthur could not fool anyone even some of the time. He was pale as his attendant's jacket, sat wide-eyed and tense in a straight back chair in the office. Paul Sampson stood behind him and Eddie Dupree in front – me in a corner. Files were piled high. Sampson went around to the secretary's desk which was pushed into a comer and held a pile of files and said, "See these, kid? See these files. I've read every damn one," he lied. "Understand?"

Arthur nodded blankly.

"They say an old man named Garfein or Gaines is here and that you are hiding him. I know he is here and I want him. And a kid. Franklin Augers. If I don't get them I'll get you. Rather Eddie here will. Understand?"

Sampson used a lawyer and prosecutor's trick, which was that he knew everything already. "These files tell me everything and it tells me that you are the one I have to blame for everything. You're the one going to jail. I'd say it all adds up to about fifteen years in San Quentin. Wouldn't you say so, Mr. Dupree?"

Dupree smiled, "About fifteen and a couple more years just because." He leaned into Arthur's face. "Maybe more. We could put him in with the Crips. They like his sort." He smiled and slapped Arthur on the back. Hard. It sent a tremor through the boy as though he were an "F" sharp tuning fork looking for high "C." Arthur started to cry. Big guys cry – little guys snarl. Eddie put his fist about the size of Shaq' s shoe in front of Eddie's nose. "If your face is broken and they stick your head into a toilet in your cell and they ask you to eat your bread pudding, howr' ya gonna eat and breathe at the same time?"

"Please! He's here! I know he's here," Arthur babbled.

"Who, Arthur, who?"

"Gaines. That old man. Out of it, just plain out of it. Dr. Simon. It was Doctor Simon! Came every day – they told me to shut up. I ain't gonna stay shut anymore!"

"OK, when Arthur. Exactly when did he get here? What did he do?"

"You're not gonna beat me up, are you?"

"We love you, kid. You are the man."

"They shot him up. Full up. Didn't know what hit him. That's all I know. That's all I know. I didn't have anything to do with it. Nothing. I swear! They used the other guy, Tank, Tank Rigers. He's a regular nurse. He's as big as Mister, Mister..." he pointed at Eddie. "They used him."

Eddie's fist went to his nose and touched it very lightly. "What did I tell you a minute ago? Below line goes here don't start telling those little lies, Arthur. What would your mother say with that nose all pancake style? Who? When? Yesterday? Last week?"

"Doctor Simon, honest. Then Dr. Ebrons and then – I don't know. I don't know. Honest –"

There was a knock at the door. Joe came in, holding a small thick man by the neck. "This one tried to sneak out the back. Exit on the side. Told him, nicely, not to try such things. He wants to tell you something. Now, don't you, Tank ol' buddy?"

Tank shook him off but kept an eye on Joe's pistol.

Arthur said, "He knows where. He knows! I don't even know!"

Tank fit his name. He was a shorter and wider Arthur, about five foot five and about five feet wide at the shoulders. Close set eyes and two-day beard. Near two hundred pounds. There was small cut alongside his right eye. It was swelling as we stared. "This kid's name's Tank Rigor Mortis, or something like that," Joe finished and stepped away. "You want me to kill him?"

"Later," Sampson said. "Looks like he must have fallen."

"Must 'av."

"Take us to him, Mr. Tank Rigor Mortis. You know who. Right now."

Black eyes, deep set, beneath a crew cut, blinked. He nodded. Eddie took him by the neck. Joe stayed with Arthur. By this time Tom Wiley had gone through nearly thirty units. "Shit," he said. "Gonna kill myself early. No way can I deal with this. Nothing, so far."

We followed "Tank" up the circular stairs to the second floor. He didn't speak. He went into a kitchen area and Eddie shoved him hard at the wall next to a stove. The wall, which was inch thick of pine, turned on a hinge just like the wall that hid the monsters in the old black and white ghost movies, like *The Cat and the Canary,* with Bob Hope, or one of the Abbott and Costello films, the ones where the monster crawls slowly closer and closer to poor Lou Costello, pointing at the monster and Abbott ignoring every muffled scream. The opening took us to a stairwell and we took it to another stairwell to one of the turrets. Bright Paths had too many corners that weren't bright. We turned into another dank hallway, and then up four more stairs, turned right for another few yards and there he was, Jimmy the Mummy, as close to be a Mummy as a person could be, cowering in a chair in a corner, naked to the waist, gray soiled cotton sweat pants over his legs, wisps of faded red hair, very pale and very limp, cringing away from every movement.

I went to him. When I touched him he began to shiver. His eyes were severely dilated. He pressed his face against the brick wall. The next earthquake would bring down the whole structure. Instinctively Jimmy tried to cover himself with his soiled blanket. I grabbed his arm and pulled the blanket away. He had needle marks, back and blue misses, scabs up and down the whole of the inside of the arm, yellowing with age. "Who did this, Jimmy?"

He shook his head, glanced quickly to see who it was, registered recognition, then checked quickly to see who was with me. When he saw Rigors, he snarled, like I imagined a cornered rat would. His arm and finger came out and pointed at Rigors again and he made indecipherable sounds. Wiley grabbed Rigors and shoved him out of the room. Jimmy's voice rasped, phlegm flowing down the side of his mouth. It sounded like he said "time." Then he began to shiver and clutch his stomach, clearly in the midst of withdrawal symptoms. "Time. Please."

"Shit," Sampson said, his voice deep in misery. He did not like suffering. A twenty-year cop who was bothered by suffering. Go figure. "I'm calling for a nurse. We got to get him out of the pain, Harv. Get him a shot. Get him something. Then maybe we can talk. Get him something to eat, too."

"They don't eat much when they're like this."

Sampson barked instructions into his phone. He leaned down. "Gotta keep you alive, Jimmy. Need you to talk to us."

Chapter Thirty

Before turning fifty, and during the several years after that big event, my life had been pleasantly symmetrical. Winning was not predictable but winning and losing was my business.

Habits were my forte. Come hell or highwater, big win, big loss, death, or lost love, I rose at 6.30 am, showered, scrubbed my hands in a separate ablution, dressed, toasted a slice of rye, poured a cup of my cherished Amaretto French roast coffee. On Friday evenings I would call my daughter. That was always painful. Something was wrong. I left from her very angry mother when she was about twelve. Bad timing. I suppose there is no good timing. They moved east. A couple of Friday nights a month it was the same. There would be no answer. I would check to see whether I called the right number. I would call again and when the machine picked up I would leave a message. Each time I customarily drove to the local Larry Flynt Casino in the Southeast part of town and drank too much and listened to the sharp women players gossip about kids and lost loves, all dressed up like they were going dancing, and played poker until I lost my limit and my eyes no longer focused. Then, I wandered to whatever local track was in session, on time for the early workouts, stood at the far turn and talked to whatever trainers were available, watched the workouts, visited tall, grey, impeccable Jim, the Maitre D' at the outdoor cafes at both Santa Anita and Hollywood Park, added to my coffee intake, read the Racing Form. There was always talk about Hollywood Park ending up in a heap – the talk persisted, but who knew? By noon I ended up in the Turf Club at my perpetually reserved table.

Many nights I would head home, take off my shoes, and walk out onto the beach and climb out to the end of the jetty that formed the entrance to the marina and I would stretch and breathe deeply and wonder about the process of aging. I would try to pick out the most distant stars and wonder how it was that the light that my eyes gathered had left those distant places hundreds of years before I was born. And I would walk along the edge of the sea and wonder if I could get myself "normal" – something about traveling and square dancing and checking out the latest movie and such – I didn't really know what "normal" was. And now and then I would think about sex – perhaps more than now and then. And, of course Sarah…

Billy would sometimes say to me, "Get a life. I've got used cars, a regular business, what do you have?"

The last couple of days I felt almost high. It was lack of sleep, forgotten meals, depressed blood sugar, a minor touch of age. Minor.

Lately Billy would say, "Find Sarah. Or kill yourself. You're beginning to lose big time and you don't even know it."

"I have to find her. And the kid."

"And when you find her? You have to do something about that."

"Make a list."

Ann Whitson called. I thought for a second it was Sarah. I have to eliminate this jump in my heart. She said, "I'm coming over."

Can't say no to that. So, I didn't. Within the hour she had me surrounded, hair flowing across creamy shoulders, wisps of it tickling my nose. She sported a loose gold bracelet on her left wrist and one around her left ankle. And that was it. I wanted someone. She was certainly someone. She called out my name, not calling me but enjoying the sound. She rolled it around in her throat. Underneath the sounds was sense that the moment was contrived. She promised never to leave, never to move, to cook ten thousand meals and live out ten thousand sexual fantasies, and spewed a delectable stream of love words, fanciful and lovely to my ears. One of them was "forever" which was a very difficult word for me. I was already in the middle of a guilt trip. But I didn't throw off the covers and take a shower. I perspired. We did everything slowly, like small bites of *Haagen-Daz,* or *See's* dark chocolate.

At four-thirty AM, while Ann slept, I looked out toward the sea. Eased myself out of bed and parted the curtains and searched the Pacific. A white spinnaker in the quiet gloom of pre-dawn, halfway to the horizon, a thin brave sheet, tilted away from the barest breeze, testing it. When I turned back, Ann was gone. I whispered, "Sarah" as if it were quite proper for her to be there and to respond to my call.

But there she was again, a rather gorgeous, apparently devoted Ann Whitson, quite naked, with a dish of poached eggs on toast and a slice of honeydew at its side. "You say something?"

"Not a word."

She slipped down next to me and spooned the eggs into my mouth. The process was deliberately sloppy. The entire concoction dripped onto my chest. She kept spooning and dripping and keeping my skin clean of the drippings wherever they fell. She put the crescent of honeydew over my eyes

305

and continued the torture. I let her have her way. How I suffered. At last we fell back to sleep.

When I awakened she was holding the morning LA Times over her bosom with one hand and a fresh cup of coffee in the other. She asked which I wanted.

I reached for the coffee.

"Enough," she said.

"Not enough."

"You're not thirty years old anymore."

"Yes, I am."

We made love again midst the melon remains and empty egg dishes. When I was deep within her she stopped suddenly, held me at bay, and said, "This is interesting."

What it meant, I don't know, but I'll remember the phrase and moment for a long time. She turned out to be right. I wasn't thirty anymore.

She reclined next to me, eyes closed, looking precisely like a Roman idealized sculpture, slightly tanned. In a while I returned to reality, picked up the paper and after the headline stories I looked up and said, "Do you have a license to carry that big pistol of yours? The one that scared us half to death?"

"How could I know it would be you and that Horse Blanket fellow? I was going to open the safe, like you asked."

"Now that you have them, what will I hear on those tapes?"

"I don't know."

It was there in those unblinking eyes. She was lying.

"Did you resign as the proposed guardian of Frankie?"

"That's the plan. I'm going to. I have to see Sophie and tell her."

"I would like it if you were out of it by the time of the court date on the petition."

She shrugged. "I don't tell Harry what to do."

"You don't need to tell him anything. You simply need to resign." Same shrugged response.

"Tell me, how often do Harry and Sophie talk, on the phone or otherwise?"

"I'm not sure they do."

"I'm sure they do."

"You know everything, Harvey Ace." Her voice dripped in vinegar.

"You don't love me anymore?"

"Don't make fun of me, Harvey. Don't do that. I thought we –" her voice cracked. "Forget whatever I said to you."

"Sorry. I take it back. But I know they talked." She ignored the question.

The guardianship had been planned, carefully, and timed to perfection. It was not concurrent with the kidnapping or John's assassination. "I think the petition by Harry is too well-planned not to be part of a larger scheme. Where is Moss now?"

"Does this inquisition have to go on? I can't find him. I told you. He said he was going to Tucson. But I don't really know where he is. The State Bar is calling. He dropped a pleading date, an answer to some complaint, representing a regular client on some nothing case. I get no answer from his cell or the house. I think Wheeler is behind the State Bar letters, too."

I wasn't surprised. "Meanwhile, I have a date with your mentor. The Lady Wheeler. I'll tell her you're out as guardian."

"No, you won't. I will. It's not up to you to decide my life."

"OK. I won't try to decide your life. But Harry has no right to make you dance on the edge of right and wrong. You have to resign. On your own hook. You have to decide right and wrong."

"I know what's right and wrong! He and Sophie saved me and my mom. You have no right to criticize. I have a life now. You're not about to give me a different one. Are you? This was all for the moment, this day. This is about a forever thing. I'm right, aren't I? You don't have to say it. People like you never end up with people like me."

There was that word again. Forever. She rolled away from me. "I know I'll never see you again… like this… I know it. I thought, maybe for a few days…"

"Perhaps you will. Maybe. When you quit Moss and get out of the entire Wheeler affair."

"I told you I would."

"Telling me is just telling, not doing. When you do, call me. You're right, this is very interesting."

She had a sudden desperate tremor in her voice as if she read my mind.

"Don't cut me out of your life, Harvey. Don't do that." It was the end of the morning. I couldn't put a voice to any response. I shrugged. And smiled.

I opened my sliding door to the patio and to the ocean. The sounds had their usual effect.

My head stopped banging. Still naked she handed me a sheet of typed paper.

February 23 After violent outburst, non-explicable. No apparent physical cause. Spoke to Dr. Simon and he suggested Tucson rest care Palace. Family agrees.

March 4, 94. Patient has managed to leave this institution, disappear, without notice to any person. Called police. Called Arizona to see if she checked in. No one checked in. Suspect assistance of Durden, or Mrs. Wheeler. Cannot reach Mrs. Wheeler. Father stated that Mrs. Wheeler does not approve removal.

March 11 – report that patient finally entered Tucson Rest Palace.

4/ 0 Ebrons

***

Ann handed me the tapes. I stuck one in my player. It became clear that Ebrons was bowing to either Franklin or Sophie Wheeler and Doctor Simon or all three. The tapes were two and three years old. Simon was their doctor-do – whatever. Then I heard something that was startling but upon reflection not so much. It was about Sophie Wheeler by an admissions person at Bright Paths.

September 21, 91. Mrs. Sophie Wheeler brought here by Sheriff's office. Incoherent. She has not maintained her medications. Husband Franklin Wheeler has insisted that she be institutionalized under the California Health and Safety Codes along with daughter, Sally, who resided here in past. The admissions were facilitated by Wheeler Attorney H Moss Esq., Franklin Wheeler insists he was threatened by daughter and one Oritha Durden who maintains friendship with S. Augers. Received written authorization from Dr. Stanley Simon and =Appropriate Order served by said Attorney Moss.

Sept 23 – She has been a patient of Dr. Simon for several years. Obtaining records – if and when released, she will be released to the care of Dr. Stanly Simon.

Chapter Thirty-One

If you charted John Auger's life, it ended up looking like a bicycle wheel with Franklin Wheeler and Sophie at the hub, Frankie, Sally, John, Moss, Whitson, Ebrons, and Jimmy the Mummy as tarnished spokes out to a punctured tire. Carole Augers and Carly Klein were sort of serviceable spares. Each of the spokes was wired to John's mysterious death.

I headed out a less traveled road toward what had to be a source location.

Tucson had jagged black peaks to the north, everything else was as flat as mama's frying pan. Only auto available was a little Nova, top speed about sixty which took forever to reach pedal to the metal. I checked the maps and tried to memorize my route, kept turning south into the desert in which the lights diminished one by one except for an almost lost yellow moon, and a star nosing its way through scattered clouds. My last turn was onto a friendless narrow road which seemed to be heading nowhere. All along the way I was certain I was being followed in a desert that grew larger and darker until it all was midnight blue, anemic moonlight obscured now and then by those filmy clouds. I kept checking my rear-view mirror and I would catch a glimpse of the following car again and again. Finally, I stopped at a dusty shoulder, got out and pulled out my map and shone a pocket light on it and pretended to pour over it while I kept checking behind me. I saw nothing. But it had been there.

Out on that flat expanse to the west distant lights flickered. People carried on their lives behind curtains and shades, listened to music, watched television, did the dishes, locked the doors, got into bed, did things, while I hustled my little Nova over that desolate road to nowhere.

The *Tucson Rest Palace* was not a Palace, merely a coffee-colored flat roofed one story building about seventy-five yards in length, about twenty yards wide, with an overhanging roof line and dry desert brush beneath the windows and Joshua trees reaching up to find the sun and the stars, creating monster shadows in the melancholy light all designed to frighten children and old ladies. The parking lot was directly in front with white markings painted at an angle. From a distance I stared at the building and then, with the lights off, glided into one of the parking slots and sat for another few minutes, watching. Whatever or whoever was following me had simply disappeared. Each room was divided into two windows, with the entrance on the inside corridor. There was an entrance at one end, a tinted double glass door. Melaleuca trees snaked around each side of the entrance which was two steps above ground level. A large ramp for wheelchairs had been added.

An orchestra of cicadas and an occasional *gru-u-mp* of a frog, along with the whispering of a breeze, greeted me as I opened the Nova door and slid out.

I walked to the rear of the structure which was exactly like the front, except the windows were sliding doors fronted by tiny patios, cement slabs outside each room, some with plastic chairs and small tea tables. Haphazard Birds of Paradise, shaggy and unkempt, stuck up like wizened sentinels near each room. I checked the doors and exits and terrain that surrounded the place. Except for a copse of cottonwood trees next to a damp creek about thirty yards to the east, anyone wanting to walk away would have a long hot trip over several miles of unrelenting desert in all directions.

One side of the front entrance was open. All convalescent hospitals, care facilities, smell the same, are painted the same tan glossy color, have the same pleasant Monet country scenes prints decorating the walls and have the same lighting fixtures on the ceilings – fluorescent blue, with occasional blinks from fading bulbs along with art deco wall sconces encasing yellow 25 watters. Several of the lights were out, like an occasional cripple in a crisp line of old soldiers.

I turned into a tiny office and introduced myself. Marie had a round white Caucasian face like an overripe cantaloupe – covered by thin disappearing wisps of uncombed sandy hair, gray at the roots. She smelled like Pine Sol. Her head narrowed ever so slightly at the top decorated by a tiny nurse's cap pinned precariously to her thin crop. She wore layers of mascara and had enough fat from her chin to her collar bone to deep fry a couple dozen chickens. Her arms bulged from her short sleeves. One of those overhead fluorescent fixtures gave her skin the color of a frosty vanilla cone, all of which encased a serious bulk of muscle. She came in at around two ten at about five foot seven and maybe fifty years old. When you couple this vision with two perfect circles of *Heartbreak Hot* red rouge on her cheeks and buck teeth that almost crossed over one another, I could see how inmates might go completely bonkers when she favored them with a cold sponge bath, or, God forbid, an enema.

She looked at me up and down, gazing slowly at every part of my torso, beady black eyes half hidden by those layers of mascara. "Don't know whatchur doin' here this time of night. They all just had dinner. Can't be callin' on anyone now. So you'll have to just leave and wait until the morning nurse gets here."

"I'm from the Federal Government." I reached into my inside jacket pocket to extract a badge that usually worked. She jumped up. "What're doin'? Hold your hands there. I ain't got no money –"

"This isn't a robbery," I sounded like Joe Friday. "This is a badge. Sit down. The U.S. Government wants to ask some questions about a patient. There are Benefit claims. Social Security claims. We have to investigate."

Her hand went to the top drawer in the desk.

"Don't be reaching for anything there. Don't do that. I just want to ask you two questions."

She stayed on her feet, suspicious and ready to pounce or scream or do whatever overweight wrestlers might do if threatened. "So, go ahead. What's the question?"

"Sally Augers." I spelled it. "Has she been here this last year or two?"

"We don't have any Sally Augers here."

"I said the last year or two."

"Not here. Don't know."

"You didn't look."

"I know everybody we've had."

"Your name please." I lifted a two by three pad and pencil and wrote a note.

"Name's puttin' tame. What's yours?"

"That's what I'm putting down in my report. I know your boss will love that you're not cooperating with the Federal Government. If there isn't anyone here by that name then there's somebody is cheating the government. Got to be a lot of trouble for you."

"Whad'ya want?"

"Told you. Not gonna do this again. Give me a name."

"I tol' you."

"OK. Puttin' Tame it is. Now, just look at your roster two years ago. I have to report to the Claims Department of Social Security tomorrow."

"Never heard of such. Why'nt you do this when you were supposed to?" Her eyes had small flaps of skin dripping from the lids creating two slits where I was certain eyeballs existed. I tried a warm Harvey Ace smile. "Not enough money and not enough time. Government's broke. You know that."

She nodded warily.

"Just look," I repeated.

She gave a dismissive glance. "I been here a lotta years and she ain't here. Never heard of her."

There was a groan from down the hallway and then a little cry. "That's just Missus Walker. She misses her son. They're all crazy. This one cries every night about this time. He comes here alla time but she don't remember. He's unhappy, she's unhappy. Which is what you're heading for. I know those people who came here last week. They stole things. I know they did. You're one a them, I bet."

"Who came here? What people?"

"He wouldn't tell. He had a badge, too. Smart ass guy with half a head a hair. Buncha crap. I shoved his ass out. Got nothin' from me."

"You probably did the right thing. But I'm just doing' a job. OK? I have ID if you want." I reached into my pocket and pulled out a card with the same official looking emblem on it and the name of Harold Stassen. I had several of them. Some of them in the name of Tom Dewey, Eleanor Roosevelt, and Wendell Wilkie. "Now, if you never heard of the Augers person what about Oritha Durden?"

She stopped. Searched my face, looked at the card. "Never heard of that name." She blinked. The light caught a quick angry look. "You sure you're a Government fella? 'Cause if you ain't –"

"Twenty years. Never heard of Augers, Sally, or Oritha Durden?" I showed her Sally's picture again. "Forget the name or the age. You remember anyone like that? Look close now."

She pushed my hand away. "Told you. Not gonna say it anymore."

"How about I take a look at your books. Investigators will be all over this place if I don't give them a full report. Especially if I tell them you didn't cooperate."

"You're fulla shit, mister. You ain't getting' nothing."

"She's here now, isn't she?"

She squinted up at me. Red and black eyes. She leaned forward taking most of the air space in the little room, elbows on her littered desk. "I knew that guy was up to no good. You wanna see somebody, call a friend."

"I'm just going to take a look myself. Don't bother showing me around."

I backed into the hallway and turned down the longest corridor and opened one of the doors before she got to me. I was expecting it. "Get otta here!" She tried to grasp me about the shoulders but I shrugged her off, turned and pushed and down she went – hard.

"Tell me about Harry Moss," I asked calmly. "Harry Moss, Sally Augers. Oritha Durden. Where? "I reached a hand down to help her and she pushed it away and struggled to her feet. She was silent except for her breath. It came in short heavy bursts. "Just wait," she growled quietly, a continual sort of animal rumbling. "Just wait." She faced me as if to attack. I was not sure I could take her. She backed into her office and shut the door and turned the latch leaving the premises to my care. Her retreat was welcome but I didn't think it would be permanent. I could hear her using the phone and then her voice became muffled. I poked into # 101. The occupant was sitting quietly on the floor in front of her bathroom door, naked, angry. "No one can piss in my pot, hear that? No one. Go tell 'um." I tried #103 across the hall and saw an ancient half of a face, nose peeking out from the edge of the bed covers as if imitating Kilroy. I went from one room to another, each more depressing than the previous. Old was not a good thing to be. Old and sick was worse. Old, sick, and mentally gone was the worst of all. The horror of wasted end years, of an awful insistent fear that the hearts of these *inmates* must feel. The misery had to be deeply felt whatever their circumstances. They were alone. There was no world for them. No life, anywhere. Solitary confinement and open doors. It would never happen to me. I could stick a gun up my nose and fire. Over and out. I was ready.

When I got to the end of the corridor, I heard a rustle behind me. There she was, pistol in hand, puffed up as if after a session with a hundred-pound weights. I wasn't ready for death. I told whatever God may exist that whatever I said in the past about how life sucks, I had been kidding. I was kidding. Honest.

"You think you can fool me. You think that? Fool with me? I've been there!"

I knew it then. This woman was Oritha Durden, and she was going to kill me. She had graduated from patient to caretaker. If alive, Harry was likely there, too. Perhaps Sally, too. Hidden away, either in a back room at Bright Paths Institute or this lonely desert outpost. Oritha knew all the answers; it was part of the history of the Wheelers and the Augers. But she wasn't going to talk. She would rather kill. In short, she was in a perfect spot. Moss had to be part of this equation. Maybe he was there right now, pulling the strings. Wouldn't put it past him.

Her door was unlocked. Meant she would talk. I opened it slowly. "Oritha, dear," I held my hands low and smiled, and in a voice something like Frank Sinatra whispering, I added, "You are going over the top again, dear. I'm trying to protect you. You know, Mr. Moss was coming here to fire you, put you out into the street. I will stop him. You know that, don't you?"

"You aren't fooling me, mister, whoever you are. No one is firing me. No one. Not that old shithead Moss or anyone else! You got that?"

"I got it. But does *he* get it."

"You won't care 'cause you won't live to know. Just like –" She stopped, realizing she was talking too much. She motioned me away from the door. "Move."

"Oritha, wait. The others were trying to hurt you. I'm not." Still smiling. "I'm here to help. I'm going to get rid of that Harry guy and everyone who is trying to hurt you. They are all trying to hurt you. You know that, don't you? Sally, Franklin, Sophie, Ann –" I had no weapon, unless I pointed a finger and cocked my thumb. As usual, I left it in the car. Words would have to do. "We want to take care of you."

"Sally isn't here. Sally isn't here! I'm taking care of all of them." She began an incantation, "All of them, all of them!" She began crying and wiping her eyes with the back of one hand, spreading mascara over her face like the maddest of mad clowns, and slowly squeezing the trigger at the same time, with the muzzle pointed at my belly. "Now, Oritha, dear, we have to work together – how're you gonna get rid of me? How? Where are you going to stuff me? I'm trying to help."

Her thin hair flattened against her forehead, mascara running down her throat onto her uniform, sweat oozing from her armpits and creating a large wet oval around her arms and chest. She hesitated.

"Oritha, we'll take care of you. I promise you. You won't ever have to worry again. Really. Never again. Just tell me where she is. It doesn't make any difference now, does it? Tell me." What came to my mind that instant was that I wanted one more night with a piece of flabby pizza and with my daughter at Dodger Stadium, and one more night with Sarah. For whatever reason Ann Whitson had skipped out on my emotions.

The growling in her throat began again. The heavy lids of her eyes made them into tiny clouded pools. "She's not here," she said calmly. "Not here." But the sound continued. The tears came pouring down. The bullet was coming. My life didn't flash before my eyes. I had been at the wrong end of a pistol before. No, what came to me was the picture of my daughter at about twelve years of age tossing a hardball at me and practically knocking me down. And a pastrami sandwich on rye and an egg roll and that same overwhelming desire to have one more night with Sarah Finkel. That Finkel girl who was unhappy with me, who had given up. Go figure.

Oritha came closer. A big mistake. An amateur's mistake. She came closer, ready to shove the pistol into my gut and pull the trigger. I decided to take my chances. I took a breath. They say if you get shot exhaling it reduces the target area of the heart and lungs. That's what I was thinking. I exhaled and braced my legs. She looks like Ozzie Osbourne at his painted best. The inmates had come out and gathered behind us, murmuring, fearful.

Oritha twitched. She was heavy, powerful, but slow. I was fast. I saw her finger begin to squeeze as if she was enjoying the moment. I slapped my hands together, on the extended pistol, one hand in front of the other. It was a police trained movement. The pistol flashed a bullet into the wall off to the side. The sound reverberated throughout the hallway. I shoved my shoulder into her midriff, came up, and smashed the heel of my right hand hard up against her chin and she crumbled and dropped. Like a ton of oily rocks.

I kicked her pistol to the side. I heard a voice. "Get outta there! Don't touch anything! Go!" Staring into the darkness, searching for the form, any form, and not finding any. "Get out!" the voice in the dark screamed.

***

I did not leave. Not about to leave empty-handed. Whoever called out wasn't going to kill me. I stepped around the hulk of Oritha Durden, looked around and found no one even remotely suspicious. There was a murmur behind me. I switched off the corridor light and the faint hallway lights died. Gleams from the office thrusting into the dead space were all that was left. Murmurings from the darkened hallway continued. I entered the office quickly. Sounds grew. I fluttered through desk drawers, there was a clatter of whimpers and cries. None of it was my problem. I continued to dig, first under the "A"s then under "D"s. I found Durden and within it a treasure packed in a large accordion file containing a half dozen legal-sized files not all starting with "D." Durden groaned. Her eyes fluttered.

The chatter grew; noises at the door like a puppy dog crying. I opened the door intending to slip out with the stack of files, only to face a human being, breathing lamentations, eyes lost in terror, one arm about the size of a banana, who whispered, "Mommy, mommy – mommy."

Behind this person was a nude woman, breasts that had given up their purpose in life, heavy lipstick smeared across her face, the applicator in her hand, who said, "Dancing," over and over. "Dancing." There were eight or ten people staring at me from behind these two, then more, and then more, milling about and stepping over Oritha Durden's now stirring body.

I wiped everything in sight. "Mother is coming." I kept saying. "Everybody, Mommy is on the way." And pushed myself through the congregation, to the light switch and wiped it as best I could. I heard another, "Get out, dammit! Out!" Suddenly, someone began to scream. A long scream that would tear anyone's heart out and chew it up. I ran. I couldn't help them.

God knows, I couldn't. I couldn't make them better, I couldn't make their fears disappear, I couldn't fix their arms, their eyes, their despair, I couldn't do anything except try to turn the clock back for all of us and that was another couldn't do. I ran.

About four miles south sirens came at me and past me. Someone had called them. Someone cognizant.

I headed to the airport as fast as my little Nova would take me. On the plane I began pouring through several years of notes. Ebrons' notes first. He was everywhere.

***

I opened the first file: **Sally Augers** – *1993*

Move the italic text up a line November 19 – S. Simon, MD. Visited at the home of patient's father, Home from Mara Bay a month ago where she lived with a companion. She complains of being very tired. Fearful.

Nervous. Barely able to move. Fever diminished. 99.2. One day of Tetracycline remaining Anti-depressant (Equanil-or similar). Commencing Lithium. Avoids answers to personal questions. As if mute points at picture of father, becomes agitated.

November 25 – Ebrons, M.D. Patient in distress. Complains of severe headache. No fever symptoms or muscle aches. Was able to tell me she is expecting visitor later in day. Distress grew when questioned about daily routines and diet. Nervous about expected visitor. Questioned attendant as to whom was to visit. Attendant Rafilo did not know. Grew very agitated when questioned. Father arrived – was upset and refused to leave. Created greater problem.

Administered small valium dosage to patient intramuscular. Father has asked what best to do with her on permanent basis. Patient had developed very close friendship with a certain Oritha Durden who has become a regular part of patient's life. Durden was also a patient at this institute and released three months ago. Advised Father call me before visiting.

January 21, 94. Bright Paths Letterhead – Ebrons MD. Patient comfortable. Spends time with Step Mother. Nurse noted lengthy withdrawal type symptoms, as if on drug withdrawal, after visit by her lawyer. Maintaining Lithium. Recent medication Prozac. Will follow studies on Prozac. Dr. Stanly Simon requested her Medical file. Received authorization from patient and permission to forward information from step-mother, Sophie Wheeler.

March 3, 94. Bright Paths Letterhead – Patient removed from care at this institution after violent outburst, not explicable. No apparent immediate cause. Spoke to Dr. Simon and he suggested Tucson Rest Palace. Family agrees.

March 4, 94. Patient disappeared this evening at about 10 pm with Durden. Advised family. Called Arizona to see if she checked in at Rest Palace. No one checked in. Suspect assistance of Mrs. Wheeler or Harry Moss. Sophie Wheeler had been ah patient earlier. Father states that he does not approve removal from this institution. Father does not want police report. Mrs. Wheeler states they will handle.

March 8 – Report from lawyer Moss that patient entered Tuscon Rest Palace.

I pulled the Oritha Durden file. Simon was their *doctor-do-whatever-the-money* demands. Then I read something that was startling: an entry by an admissions person at Bright Paths about Sophie Wheeler.

September 21, 91. The admissions were facilitated by Wheeler Attorney H Moss Esq., Franklin Wheeler insists he was threatened by daughter and one Oritha Durden who maintains friendship with his wife. Mrs. Sophie Wheeler brought here by Sheriff's office. Incoherent. She has not maintained her medications. Husband Franklin Wheeler has insisted that she be institutionalized under the California Health and Safety Codes along with daughter, Sally, who resided with her in the past. Received written authorization. from Dr. Stanley Simon and husband, Appropriate Order served by said Attorney Moss.

Sept 23, 91. – When released Mrs. Wheeler will be released to the care of Dr. Stanley Simon.

Chapter Thirty-Two

"Nails, I need you. Just this one more time."

"It gives me a fever when you say that, Harv. Makes my stomach go on a ride."

We were at my table at Santa Anita. Two tables down the same lady with the pink hat was still screaming. As always, I couldn't tell if she was winning or losing. A Baffert trained horse had come in at four to one. Big odds for one of his brood. Some trainers trained hard and fast, figuring it was the best was to get a horse ready to win. Baffert trained them comfortable like. But he did push them judging when they were ready to be pushed. Gert Wiseman did the same.

Winning *The Silk's* first race reminded me never to let a leading trainer or jockey go un-bet at six to one or more, except in a major stakes race. Some horses trained fast and easy. That was when they were ripe. I was the of the school that none of the rules applied except the nature and speed of workouts, the ones you knew about.

The day was a Southern California day. The air was as clear and sharp as Italian crystal. The San Gabriels were not only all shades of green and violet but, to the east, still had their left-over Vanilla toppings from last week's stormy cold front. Sometimes you could catch a glimpse of the mountains from the west side of LA, looking east from Olympic Boulevard, and they would rise like armless, senescent sentinels guarding the flatlands beneath.

"There's a house in Hancock Park. Four-thirty-one June Street. Lady named Carly Klein lives there – for now. I don't think anyone knows or cares whether she's actually there or not."

"I know," I said. Nails settled back, rested his heavy hands on his lap. "Go on."

"Larry got as much as he could from Ebrons' office, so I figure…"

"That was an office," he interrupted, agitated, "not a private home in a fancy neighborhood where they have patrols and nosy citizens."

"They patrol only this office every two hours. I checked. You can do the whole thing in a half hour."

"They come irregularly. Why aren't you telling me that?"

"But they actually don't. They just say they do. Anyway, you're the expert. You can do this. Cut the nails short. They will grow back quickly and better than ever. Nothin' to it. There's an old safe on the shelf where they keep the coffee. In the kitchen. I want the safe or its contents. If something happens to me before I figure it all out, give everything to Paul Sampson."

"Harvey, I can't do it. You know all of us have some sort of loose bolt or screw or something. Ever think about that? You're a shepherd to a bunch of loose bolts, lame goats. We're gamblers. Sort of defective calculators. Not actually real people. I can't do this."

"Hey, Nails, I'm not defective. I'm just stuck with my addiction. But I don't think you are. You have family and things like that. A real past." I took his hands with their curled nails painted deep red, "Listen to me, these are just things – these nails are not an extension of you. They're your diversion from what is real. My pistols are an extension of me. Understand? But now you need to be real. A *real* person. You can do this. Count Vienns D' Viens. That's you. Someone special. That's what you always say. You're Royalty. This is a job meant for Royalty." Refrigerators in Alaska was my specialty.

He was disconsolate. "Unfortunately," he murmured, "I know what I am. And I ain't no Count, Harvey. Just sounded good. I liked it." He took a breath. "Listen, I have fingernails that are in Guinness Book of Records. I'm famous. I can't do your job without cutting them. Now can I –?"

"Nails. You are the best. The best safe cracker, the best thief and loyal accomplice there ever was, that means something, doesn't it? Cut the damn things."

"I just can't do it."

"You won't help." It was not a question.

"I can't."

"What were you like before the nails?"

"I was a messed up fucking safe cracking crook. An obsessive nut case. My mother didn't even want me. My father gave up a long time ago. No one gave a shit."

"That makes you special? You know I want you. We want you. Doc and Billy and Larry. And now?"

"This is not the issue."

"Are you going to help me or not?"

That same damn total silence that I hated. "Nails, with real hands you would be David Nirenstein again. Regular guy. Like I said, a real person."

"Safe cracker. That's what I was. I don't know, Harv. Maybe I can't be David anymore." He pulled himself up, stretched his ten inch nails out and

319

grabbed a white baseball cap and managed with two tries to get it on his head. A half inch of extra skin drooped from his jowls. His eyes were red. His arms carried his nails as one might carry a child.

"I need the contents of that bureau in the upstairs bedroom also. I can't get a handle on this Klein woman and I need to know whatever there is to know about her. And there are things in that safe that are likely to be important."

In spite of his protestations, I knew he would do it. People change. I tell myself that people change in spite of substantial evidence to the contrary. Maybe even yours truly. I told him the address once again and crossed my fingers. "If can get it for you. I will. Harvey. I promise."

***

Jimmy was precipitously close to the down side of staying alive. Paul's words were the bottom line. We had to keep him alive enough to talk. The EMTs arrived at Bright Paths. Joe was able to lift him to the gurney carriage and roll him into the wagon; sirens blaring, it aimed at the Santa Barbara County Hospital. Paul said, "Think that old sonofagun said 'KID' a few times. Did you catch it?"

Dupree and I shrugged. Either way the knowledge was useless. Thereafter, the dynamic duo of Wiley and Dupree and Harvey Ace, the third wheel, spent more time with Tank Rigors.

Sampson stayed outside the room. He was a cut above and he wasn't going to get involved with our methods. After further "discussion" Tank directed us to a nearby room with one three drawer filing cabinet. We ended up a fistful of files each of which was marked "Dead."

I opened the first file: *Sally Augers – October 17 1993 – Back from village a month ago where she lived with companion Durden. Admitted to intensive unit here. Fever 102.*

Uncontrolled anger regarding father. Next to catatonic. Equanil. Antibiotics administered intra muscular.

November 19 – S. Simon, MD. She complains of being very tired. Fearful. Nervous. Grinds teeth. Says she must leave. Fever diminished. 99.2. Asks for Oritha. Patient had developed very close friendship with this person who has become a regular part of patient's life. Originally retained by patient's father.

November 25 – Lithium appears to help. Patient in less distress. Complains of severe headache. No fever symptoms or muscle aches. Was able to describe expectation of a visitor later in day. Distress grew when

320

questioned about daily routines and diet. Becoming more nervous about expected visitor. Attendant Rafilo did not know who patient was expecting. Patient grew very agitated when presented with questions about father. 3 PM Father arrived – was upset and refused to leave. Insisted on attempting to interrogate patient as to where she had been. Created greater problem. Administered appropriate valium dosage to patient orally. Father has asked what best to do with her.

Durden was also a patient at this Institute and released three months ago and now remains at the Tucson Rest Palace facility supported financially by FK Wheeler. Advised Father to call me before visiting. Ebrons, M.D

December 10. No change

December 16. No change same fear of agitation about Father. Repeatedly asked if her father was coming. Asked for Sophie, I believed her to be Mrs. Sophie Wheeler.

December 21. Bright Paths Letterhead – Ebrons MD. Patient comfortable. Spends time with Step Mother. Nurse noted lengthy withdrawal type symptoms. Visited by person H Moss who she claimed was her lawyer. Maintaining Lithium. Recent medication Prozac. Will follow new studies on Prozac. Dr. Stanly Simon requested her Medical file. Received authorization from patient and permission to forward information from patient to step-mother.

January 17. No change.

February 12 – Feb 21. No change. M Ebrons

March 3, 94. Bright Paths Letterhead – Patient removed from care at this Institution after violent outburst. No apparent immediate cause. Shouts her father's name. Spoke to Dr. Simon Distance might help. Family agrees.

March 6, 94 Report from Tucson Rest Palace that Patient has disappeared at about 10 pm with Durden. Advised family. Asked not to call police. Father does not want any report to police. Mrs. Wheeler states they will handle situation.

March 8, 94. Found both Mrs. Sally Augers and Oritha Durden at Greyhound bus Station in Downtown Tucson and returned to Rest Palace.

March 12, 94 – Report from lawyer Moss that patient unhappy. The question then became – what is Moss doing in the middle of this? There were several more entries. With OK from Paul I sat in adjacent office and read files. Durden's file was part of the mound of the pale-yellow stack of files. As I read it became clear that Ebrons did not seem to have any medical power over his patient and was over-ruled several times by either Franklin or Sophie Wheeler and sometimes by Doctor Simon.

Then, at the bottom of the stack, another file labeled Mrs. F. Wheeler. contained something that was startling: an earlier entry by an admissions person at Bright Paths about Sophie Wheeler. It was the second time I read this or something similar.

Sept 23, 91 – Mrs. Wheeler has been a patient of Dr. Simon for several years. Obtaining records – Upon instructions by husband – when released she will be released to the care of Dr. Stanley Simon.

Chapter Thirty-Three

Wiley and Dupree left shaking their heads, but promising to get lab information back to me. Paul stayed with me a moment murmuring his recognition that Jimmy Gaines meant something to me and adding, "You weren't the only one fooled. You have to recognize that he was a clever and bad dude. Just deal with it."

"Maybe, he can come out of it and give us the bottom line on the whole damn business. Tell something about Sarah."

"Lot of time before that."

After I got home, I settled into a chair gazing out at the dark Pacific and plopped in another tape. It was like a bad soap opera. I listened until after three am, immersed in the misery of the Augers Affair and finally dropped off with the player still droning on, repeating the miserable stories. My mind retreated back to the beginning of the string of events that lead to John Augers' death and the kidnapping of Frankie. A heinous dream was upon me, In the deep dark of dreamland Dick Tracy, in black and white, was fighting with bad guys in the back seat while his new La Salle with its thin, elegant nose, which dived over the end of a high cliff – me and Tracy in the front seat trying to apply the brakes. Downward we went to the cement below – falling without end. Falling. Holding on. I have no idea if either of us survived. Then Flash Gordon, in the clutches of the evil Emperor Ming the Merciless, was being thrown into a huge meat grinding machine – down, down, he goes – and then the screen goes blank.

Suddenly Doctor Stan Simon with a syringe of the size of a baseball bat comes on the scene hovering over Sally Augers. Or was it Sophie Wheeler. But, he changes direction and descends toward me. Suddenly he is struck and flung into the air. He smiles as he sails to his death. I'm left with emptiness, still falling in the old La Salle. And a longing for Sarah and a settled life.

***

The phone rang. I fumbled with the receiver and finally managed a greeting. It was Gert Wiseman. She said she wanted me at her barn at Santa Anita immediately if not sooner. The sun had not yet risen above the pale sand and sea. I climbed into my car and headed for the 10 freeway east. It was still too early for heavy traffic, but there was enough that I couldn't let myself shove the accelerator too heavily. Turned onto State highway 110, which was the first of the freeways built in 1941, and then over California Street east through stately South Pasadena, the campus at Cal Tech, and then, when the sun was beginning to clear the morning dew, I reached the fragrant city of the Santa Anita Backside, over the soft dirt padded by ways to Gert's barn.

Dr. Gil Bochner and Gert were bent over a prone *Winning Silks*. They were in the Track hospital, an expanded version of a normal operating room – two-inch hoses for the anesthetic, gleaming oversized scalpels, and sponges, a large horse-sized movable table that rose and lowered with a touch. Two of the barn assistants stood at the edge of the stall, next to buckets and wet towels. They were in green clean gowns. The room smelled of disinfectant. Every few minutes the assistants exchanged the wet towels on the filly's head. *Silk's* eyes were wide. Gert grabbed my hand. "She didn't come out of that race too well. Thought she was OK at first, then yesterday – yesterday afternoon. Wouldn't eat and that's not *The Silk*. Head down, no life in her. I stayed here and her temperature grew and I called Gil about three am. Pretty sure there's a blockage in the large intestines. And she developed a bad infection as a result. Never know how these things start."

Bochner explained the nature of the obstruction and then I leaned down and whispered sweet things into *Silk's* ear. "C'mon, baby. You can beat this. We're a team. Sweet *Silk*. My girl." Whatever the particular sound of your voice horses know when it is a good sound, a comfortable and safe sound. Their athletes muscles unwind and they sense safety. They are highly trained athletes and this need such small comforts after straining every muscles in the bodies, gasping for more and more air, trying to beat that other animal, to meet their destinies as best they can. And they feel it when they dominate another animal, when have won or lost. That is the kind of kinesthetic brain with which they are endowed. They possess the power and strength of a movement. It is not intellectualized – they don't know they have won, but they feel it.

Gil Bochner finally said, "I don't know, Mr. Ace. I don't know." His glasses fell from his forehead to his flat nose and he shoved them back again. He had a deep crevasse in each cheek.

"How bad?"

"Not good. Fever is not getting better in spite of pumping her full of Tyelenol and some cold compresses. We can't keep giving her more Tylenol."

"Get an X-Ray?"

"The X-ray will be here in a few minutes." Hochner got off his knees and shook his head. "She's a strong filly, but this has got her good. It must hurt terribly. Totally blocked. If we can better locate the blockage, we can get in there and relieve it. Take a little of the intestine." He had a wide brow, the wrinkled skin of a smoker, thick shoulders and a belly that hung about an inch over his belt His head was shaved.

Silk whinnied with a heavy breath.

I bent down again and sat and patted her and cooed. "Get that machine here and find out, now."

"Take it easy, Harvey. It'll be here in a minute or two. The pictures take only a few minutes and then we'll know. The hospital is set up and ready to go. We've got a surgeon on his way."

"Who is it?"

"Dr. Faramina. Moshin Faramina. He's a good one. Among the best we have."

"You sure?"

"Take it easy, Harvey," Gert soothed. "You know this business. A heartache a minute."

"This is not business to me. Where is he? This Moshin fellow. Doesn't he have to see the X-rays?"

"Everything is being done as fast as it possibly can," Hochner replied.

"You're pale, Harv. Running out like that and nothing in your stomach." I felt a trifle faint.

"Get any sleep? Lean down. Head down."

"I don't need any 'head down' bullshit. Dammit, where are they?" But I sat down, head on my chest.

A truck arrived. A half dozen attendants hurried in and I was ushered out. I waited, Gert by my side, her arm entwined in mine. We stood together, quietly. It was good to have her next to me. She was as good a human being as one could find. Her features were drawn, her voice hoarse. "I remember when I was told that my dad was on his death bed," she murmured. "I went to the hospital, St. Lukes over in Altadena, and, as I got out of the elevator, my uncle said, 'Not sure. Not sure' and I dropped right there. Out. Didn't remember a thing until five minutes later. Happens."

"Not to me. *The Silk* will recover."

"Hold the thought."

We walked up the street and down the street, goats and cats and dogs lazily eyeing us, the scent of hay and feed and manure and the pungent air around sweating blubbering thoroughbred horses back from their workouts, getting hosed down and rubbed and combed. The sun rose. Within twenty minutes, Hochner came out and said they confirmed a blockage in her small intestine, which they needed to get at quickly, as it might become gangrenous. Maybe it already was.

"How does that happen?"

"It just does."

I waited. Gertrude told me to go on about my business as we wouldn't know anything for several hours. I didn't. My cell phone rang. "It's time, Harvey."

"For what?"

It was Sampson. "You have to carry the money."

"The ransom? Not me. I've got an emergency here. Besides, I get paid big time to get killed."

"Get real. Who you gonna leave your ill-gotten gains to?"

"Your son."

"Thanks but no thanks," he said. "We'll have an army backing you up. It's at Pillar's mortuary. That's the chosen place." His voice had that sound to it – that *or else* sound. Not loud, not urgent, but low and deliberate and enormously clear.

"I don't get it."

"They want you. The Wheelers do. I do, the bad guys do. Captain Rawlings agrees on you even though he hates you and the ground you walk on. And he doesn't even like you."

"You know what he can do."

"Doesn't matter."

"This sounds like a set up."

"If it is, we're stuck with it. But we have the army, they don't. And we pretty much have to go along with it."

"Don't you think they've figured on that?"

"We're doing this, Harvey. That's that." He voice was weary. He was weary – of the violence, the bureaucracy, weary of the necessity of subjecting himself to others who reach exalted positions by an unrelenting obsession to be first, to command people, often of lesser abilities who simply worked harder. "I'd rather be home," Paul said. "Promised my kid we'd go on a small walk in the park. He needs to walk. He needs help but it keeps those muscles alive." I understood that the boy's muscles were failing and he needed to keep them going as long as possible, alive enough to support the half a hundred pounds of his eight-year-old body.

"I listened to entries, medical entries about Sophie Wheeler and Sally. You have to hear them."

"Not now, Harvey. Honestly. Not right now. We need to get the Wheeler boy back or his grandfather and his whole world will descend on us. This is a now item. We'll worry about the rest later."

"She's very crazy, you know."

"Who?"

"The whole damn bunch of them."

"Not relevant now, Harvey. We're on our way. Head back to Pillar's place. I'll clue you in as to exactly where and get you the details and the money before then."

"And if I say no?"

"Stick you in a nice jail and keep you away from a phone for three or four days. Try me."

"Can't do it, Paul. I can't help. I've got a very sick person being operated on. I have to wait for the results."

"There is no 'no' here. That boy needs you. We're expecting one more instruction. Should be specific about exactly the time and precise method. I'll let you know. And this time damn the speed limits no matter where you are. Meanwhile, stay alive. Don't let that bogey man Mondoza get you."

"He is the least of my worries. I'll bet the nappers give you a time and then change it at the last minute. They always do."

"We'll have to deal with it. We all hope to get the kid back alive. You have to do the job. Eight point five mil to be delivered as per instructions. You're chosen. Joe will be there, too. He is backing up. By the way, this might interest you. It's about Harry Moss?"

"What about him?"

"Gone."

"What do you mean, 'gone'?"

"Gone. Like gone."

"How do you know?"

"Don't know anything for sure. Except he's gone. Disappeared. Been gone for last two days without an explanation. I just figure he's dead."

I didn't like Moss. He was fading old lawyer with not much left in the tank except cunning and, I was certain, a desperate need to secure his future. Nevertheless, I was concerned. I wanted him alive and well and looked forward to forcing him into confessing his involvement in Frankie Wheeler's kidnapping and taking over the Wheeler fortune.

"My guess he is somewhere in Arizona."

"At that Rest Home?"

"That's the place. Send someone. How long do I have before I have to be at Pillar's place?"

"Probably soon. But no specifics yet."

"Okay, Paul. I'll be on my phone."

It wasn't much later that I sat outside the operating room of the track and opened more files. I don't know anything about praying but I said a few for *The Silk.* The revelations of the tapes and files was getting me very close.

The exchange of money for hostages was set. I was the fall guy.

Chapter Thirty-Four

Sally Wheeler Augers might have died and been resurrected – but I only in Franklin and Sophie's mind. We create these parables of resurrection to give meaning to our present unholy need to last longer than life, to exist in a forever place that permits a return. Maybe it's all simple, we're resurrected each day with a new question – "What Now."

I kept thinking about Frankie Augers resurrected, happy and healthy, of Paul's afflicted son with new legs and arms, of Sally suddenly appearing and caressing her child's brow and becoming a real mother. It's the resurrection business brought down to neighborhood level. I am, however, too cynical to believe that resurrection parable is the way this story would end. But who am I to determine resurrection?

I drove home and washed my hands for the fifth or sixth time that day. An idea that had been simmering in my mind for a couple of days struck again. Ideas are a dime a dozen, right? But, ignore them? No way. I called Al Socher, a friend out of yesteryear, who was some kind of big shot for a local brokerage house and asked him to see what was going on with the publicly traded shares of FKW Construction. Didn't take more than a minute and he was able to tell me that the shares had risen from about 17 to more than 23 dollars in the past two weeks, and then it had suddenly plummeted back to 14. He said there was only a minor blip from the company about its interest in the Mara Bay development planned by the company in partnership with the Wheeler Foundation. I asked him to check on who was buying and who was selling if that was possible. He said he might be able to tell from large volume buys. His brokerage firm made a market in the stock and insider transactions were always reported. Told him it seemed a lot easier to understand a "Pick Four" at the races and certainly a lot safer than figuring the stock market. The only thing I knew about the stock market was not to pay attention to the daily nonsense, but to watch the hundred and two hundred day trend lines. That made me an expert. I waited on the line for about three minutes and he came back and told me that the offices of Jeff Malin, an attorney for several of the local professionals as well as Dr. Stanley

Simon, located in Montecito, which was an upscale neighborhood just down the road from Santa Barbara, had been a heavy buyer. Socher didn't know if he had been acting for someone else as he wasn't able to find any significant value in Simon's other stocks and bonds to explain the purchases. The shares were bought primarily from one of the only sellers of the narrowly held shares – Franklin Wheeler, who was not only the largest seller, but what remained made him the largest owner of the publicly traded portions of the stock. "Whoever is running the Wheeler interests," he said, "ran it up by buying heavily and then dump it. The public came in when the stock began to rise. Over two hundred fifty thousand shares already. Then it stopped. Nice way to make a living. I'll refer it to my managers, although I'm not sure they care if it was legal or not as long as we got the commissions. I can't give you any information about Malin and anyway, don't have any."

What a fine business! All these people were making a profit going in and coming out. They pay *Monopoly* for real. Wheeler or his trusts would be receiving cash from the sale of FKW Construction Co. stock and Malin in the process would have acquired a ton of it. Malin couldn't be buying for his own account. He was a probate lawyer for Stan Simon and that was all. A couple of phone calls made it clear Jeff Malin made a nice quiet living in the probate business, dealing with the estate accountants and other representatives. He had dealt with Ron Cable in the past. But Malin was small fry in a big ocean and would never have enough of his own money to explain the large purchases and sales. As long as he paid taxes on the gains he was in no trouble with the feds.

I left a message on Billy's answering machine at his used car lot hoping that he had not gone to the races and that he would meet me later at Glenn's on Sixth Street. I pulled out my binoculars and went to my upper porch, leaned against the rail and searched in all directions for anything on the beach or the pier that might upset my stomach. I kept thinking of Wheeler's last shout out. But also, burrowing his way into my concerns was Aureliano Mondozo. He was too nasty and macho a character to fail his family and simply disappear without machismo winning the day... and beating me, at anything.

Just south of my condo was the Marina Del Rey breakwater. I searched that with the naked eye trying to get a broad view. Then I glued the glasses to the end of the breakwater and drew them painstakingly over each massive boulder that comprised the construction. Damn! There it was! I knew it! I wasn't immune to whoever was behind this Augers Affair. It was a tiny thin nosed something pointing out of a dark hump, pointing directly at me. I couldn't see a hand or a head. A damn phantom pointed a damn rifle at me, waiting for the propitious time.

I dropped the glasses and shut the blinds and slipped on a pair of running shoes, grabbed my 357, stuck it into a holster, and sped out toward the breakwater. It wasn't more than two hundred fifty yards from my window. I was running in the sand around a few stragglers, early sunset fires and roasting hot dogs. I was winded by the time I got there. A piece of a red sun hung like on a string at the horizon. I dashed over the rocks. A late afternoon breeze sprayed me with malevolent lips of the sea. The sky changed from red to a variety of faint blues. The stars began to reveal themselves. A fucking beautiful night – and maybe my last? I started screaming like a banshee, "Dammit, shoot! Shoot already!" I scrambled and stumbled over the rocks. "Where the fuck are you?"

Nothing. Nothing but the fading sounds of my screams. I could see the point of the weapon fifty yards ahead. Only the stars would witness my death. I held my pistol high enough to shoot quickly and ducked into crevices as I approached. I moved as fast as I could. I was in the mood to shoot first and ask questions later. A lone fisherman saw me coming, big pistol in front of me, as if I were a maniac on the loose.

He jumped into the cold channel to escape my approach and stayed under water until I had passed. He was smarter than I was. A motor craft, perhaps a thirty-eight footer cruised in from the sea, heading home, with someone aboard who must have spotted me. It suddenly roared into deep-throated inboard motor action, whirled nearly in place and headed back out towards the descending night and distant film of darkening clouds.

Nothing shot at me. Absolutely nothing was responsible for the anger and anxiety in me. A thin piece of innocuous galvanized pipe barrel about the size of a rifle lay on the rocks under a rigged blanket. No one in sight. A set up to get me out here. Searched the area. There were a bunch of apartments off to the left, winking lights just coming on, people busy within. Life goes on in spite of my miseries. No one cares. Not sure anyone ever cared.

Pedestrians strolled the frontal cement walkway along a hundred yards down along the beach. But this was too cleverly placed. Someone wanted me here. The pipe had been carefully aimed, blanket on top and tucked under the pipe. It was a threat. Stay out of this damned Augers Business. Or away from Wheeler – or something. What did they want? I sank down and contemplated the sea and sunset and the deepening sky for a few minutes. I wasn't sure of anything. Why was I a target? They needed my vote. The message was stay away, lay off this damn Augers business. This threat was the warning before the storm. Like a rising wind. Fuck 'em! Fuck 'em!

The fisherman who had jumped into the water came up for air. He sat on the rocks, shivering, his eyes riveted angrily on me. He wasn't quite sure which one of us had gone mad.

He stared and finally said, "Asshole." He limped away. Dripping like a soaked rag.

I rose to look again out to the sea. Perhaps that was where the answer lay. Suddenly I felt a terrible crash on the back of my head. I could feel myself slumping slowly to the ground, then lights out.

***

Curtains, white clad women and young men bustling back and forth and peeling my clothes off, light glowing in dazzling dances. How am I feeling? Same question ten times. "Follow my finger."

"I'm am following the damn finger!" I croak out.

"How are you feeling? See my finger?" There was Sarah in the corner. Tried to get up and fell back down, reached out and she was gone – there was no Sarah. "She was here," I said. "Right?"

"Follow my finger."

I had to be dead.

Doctor shoved his glasses down his nose. He was twelve years old. Took my pulse. Hummed a little, said, "Better," and left.

Nurse came in with a tray of something that looked like blood. "Tomato juice," she said. She really had big boobs. Imagine carrying those around all your life. "How can you deal with those things?" I started to laugh.

She looked at me as though I was mad as a march hare. "Are you OK? How do you feel?"

"That kid who came in, the local high school – is he a doctor?"

"He's the doctor on duty this shift."

"Lean closer, sweetheart. That's better. Closer. You know you have...?"

"Shut up." She put a hand over her chest. "I'm up here. Look at me. Up here."

"I am. I am. But they're..."

"Shut your face."

"OK. Tell the truth. Who was that kid?"

"He's your doctor."

"Go on. You gotta be kidding. He's still in middle school!"

"Shut up and stay still. Best if you don't move your head."

"Closer, sweetheart. I promise, I'll close my eyes."

332

"They said you have to stay still, very still, a couple of days. Real concussion. Otherwise you'll be a dementia patient by the time you're sixty."

"Never last that long." Closed my eyes. I managed a sort of breathless, "You don't have a ring. So, whad'ya say? Dinner at eight?"

I opened my baby blues. She grinned, beautiful teeth and jade eyes. "Doctor said, if I'm on top, it's OK. I control, but not for a couple days."

"That's a sin," I replied. "What does he know? He's twelve years old!" Couldn't keep my eyes open. "Had to be three of them that hit me. Too many goddamn enemies," It was the most I could come up with and then dropped off into sleep.

***

The next morning no one was there. I figured I had hallucinated for those few moments when I thought Sarah was there. I asked a different nurse, tall and skinny, if I had any visitors yesterday. Or whenever I was brought in. She said some man had called 911 and an ambulance came and that the man who called was soaking wet all over but left no name or message. She didn't remember any other people involved and I had had no visitors. They couldn't find my shirt or pants for a while. Not sure they were looking. Very busy. Seems there was a brief gang bang that night in the nurse's lounge. Or something. Finally, by the middle of the afternoon, someone dumped the clothes onto the bed and told me I was free to go, take it slow. Lots a rest, baby. Pulled out the IV, bandaged the area, helped me into a wheelchair and wheeled me out. "You just dumping me?"

"We called a cab."

When I got back to the house, the door was open. My condo had been ransacked and the Moss and the Ebrons tapes were gone. I had been suckered. Get me away from the house and take whatever they wanted. Some smart detective I was. Since they took only the tapes I figured the bushwackers were not a connection to the Mondozo conglomeration. Unless they were just making trouble. Still, Paul Sampson must have some of the tapes or all and must have made copies from them.

I flipped the gas under the tea kettle, pulled out a mug and a tea bag and then the doorbell buzzed. It was one of those, angry old-fashioned buzzes, nothing light and melodious. I moved slowly and dragged myself to it.

Wouldn't you know it? That damn Aureliano Mondozo, with his smug grin, pushed his way in, gently. The black limo was in front. One of his "men" slid in with him and stood in a comer. He was the size of Eddie Dupree.

"Take it easy, Harvey, old buddy. Not here to make trouble. Just get what I'm entitled to. I'm sure they told you not to get excited. Just here and talk. Old friends. I know you're hurt."

"How do you know tha'?"

He smiled. "You can't piss without me knowing it."

"Aure, If I get to my gun before you kill me, I'll fuckin' blow your head off." Mine was already coming off. And I didn't know what happened to my 357. Just remembered it.

"Relax, Harvey. Relax. Just talking. Honest to god. That's all. I didn't have anything to do with all this mess. We were not near when you got it. And I was on the way here to wait when I saw the cab come up and you get out. You looked like shit, like you could barely make it to the door, so I stopped the cab and we talked. Told me you came from the hospital. You're in a real mess, aren't you?"

I poured out four orange Ibuprophens from a bottle on the sink, poured the boiling water into the mug over the tea bag and sat down. "I'm thinking you made this mess, Aure. What for?"

"It is a mess, all right. But it wasn't me. On my life it wasn't me." His black eyes were serious. "My father talks serious but he isn't that bad. But I'm not the guy who made your troubles."

"If it wasn't you or yours, who did this? Who set me up? Who cracked my head? That's the second time the last couple of weeks." I swallowed the pills and took the mug and my aching body back to the dining area and sank heavily into a chair. "No filly. No deal. You don't get it. She's my life."

"You don't know if she will even live or keep developing. None of us do. She won't be ready to run again for a few months. But we have the money to take that chance. You lose one race... and the price? You get almost nothing."

"She won't die. They just took out a piece of her intestine. untangled the mess, and she will be fine in a month."

"That's just silly. You know better than I. Horses win and lose. Even the best. How many times did *Noor* beat *Citation*, the triple crown winner? Listen, Ace, sit back, relax. Nothing is happening to you. We're here to protect you. Protect your interest in *The Silk.* I have an idea. Actually, it's my father's, really."

"He's smarter than you are."

"Yeah, yeah," he sighed. "But I'm getting better. You're one of my teachers. You know what you told me once? You said, 'Don't get wild, get even'."

"That's an old saw. So, what do you want?"

A broad grin came across that Tyrone Power face. "We should become partners. Best thing for both of us. Mondozos put up the money when necessary for the upkeep and all that, and get the filly entered into the good races. That lady trainer stays. We see to it that *The Silk* wins another handicap which should convince Miss Wiseman and the powers that be that she qualifies for a Grade One. We think she is that good. Saw her workout before she got sick and after the race. Breezing to a one ten and three six furlongs. Easy. Fabulous workout. Nothing that fast anywhere. And then we hope we've done everything right and she gets into another and then the Breeder's cup and other great situations, the Travers, the Hollywood Gold Cup, the Santa Anita. Derby. The ten million-dollar race in Dubai. Maybe this girl can do it all. Beat the boys. And then she has four, maybe six, babies at a half mil or more apiece, plus breeding fees of a couple hundred thousand a shot. And we are all a lot richer and happier. It's a fair deal."

"And you and your dad get fifty-one percent."

"No. We get fifty. No monkey business. We stay out of it. We give you a big number for our half. Listen, my dad said fifty-fifty was better than fifty-one-forty-nine. Why, you ask. I'll tell you why. He said 'cause then you absolutely *have* to work out your differences. No one person runs the show. No resentments. You have to *listen* to the other person and compromise or nothing gets done. I hate the idea. I like to run the show. Totally. Pretty smart. My father, of course."

"Aure, are you sure your father wants this?"

"Positive. He said, he didn't mean to make war with you. He wants to set things straight. You know this about him. But don't cross him, that's the thing."

"Is he just looking to park money… anyplace and everyplace he can?"

"Don't get into my back pocket or presume anything. That's a no-no. That's what the old man said to tell you. He knew you would ask. What he does you don' wanna know. *You* don' wanna know. This is a straight forward business deal. You're not interested in what my old man does."

"You're talking about cash, I suppose."

He nodded, pointed at my cup. "Some tea?"

I told him to get his own cup. Which he did. Seemed to know where everything was. "So what were these vandals who messed up this place after? And popped you that good one?"

335

"Really wasn't you?"

He looked at me. His never out of sight bodyguard shook his head and shrugged.

"I'm telling you. Wasn't me! Not interested in looking for your jewelry or such. Need you healthy. You're going to be part of the legit part of our life. You gotta stay legit and healthy. I'll even help you get this place cleaned up!"

Shook my head. Beginning to feel human. No way I could believe this fellow. Took a sip of the hot tea. Hard to believe the Mondozos. They didn't think like normal people. Six months would go by and we would be all huggie and nice and boom I would be dead. "Don't worry about cleaning up. I'll do it tomorrow. Got to get some more sleep. Head's killing me."

"Well, what do you say?"

"You're paying me in cash?"

"Right."

"I can't deposit cash. Can't go to a broker with cash. Can't think right now. Just know that *Silk* is my life. She can beat the boys. She wins I stop playing the gambling game. She wins and I give up booze. You get it? She's my life."

"You're whole life rides on a horse? Shit even *I know* that's crazy and I'm only thirty-two."

I got up and walked to the couch by the large window and dumped myself onto it.

"Tomorrow, Aure. Too damn tired now. Your father maybe explained that the rough stuff wasn't going to work with me. 'cause I rough back and he just wants to make piece. Problem is, he gets *Silk* and *then* kills me."

"That's crazy. We don't do that. He just said. Talk like a business man. Act like a business man. There is no problem."

"Wait." I closed my eyes. "Give me a half hour."

"Here's more hot water for that tea." He poured.

"Talk to me when I know the result of the next race."

"OK. Maybe I talk to him and say OK, we wait."

My eyes closed. I didn't hear anything for maybe an hour. Eyes opened. Dark inside and out. Tried to sit up and felt the head and it wanted to lie back down.

"You feeling better?" He was sitting in my Eames chair.

"Jesus, Aure, you still here?"

"Yeah. I made some soup. It's canned but I found it in the shelf. So I made it."

He put a bowl in front of me. Handed me a large spoon.

"Gotta tell you somethin', Harv. That filly. She's gonna be OK. The filly —which we own fifty/fifty – is gonna be the best. Gertrude says so."

"Go away, Aure. You talked to Gert? You're right, she will be the best. Ever see a filly do one ten and change on a six-furlong workout? Breezing? – Never saw it before or even heard of it. Except they say Seabiscuit did a fantastic workout, CS Howard saw it and that what got the Howard family interested in him. Thanks for the soup. Appreciate it. But don't count horses before you have them. Now get outta here. I'm way too tired to deal with you."

"Let us know quick. My father wants an answer. So do I." He smiled at me. Something about that grin I just did not like. "You keep making mistakes, Harv. It's a legit offer. I'm trying to be a business person like my very serious father insists."

"I'll give him that."

"This isn't going to stop, Harv. You know my father won't let it be. He drills at you. Time will come when he won't be business like anymore."

"So, meanwhile, who smacked me? If not you?"

"You gotta lot of enemies, Harvey. Maybe more n' I do."

"Need time. Too tired. Let me get this head straight."

When they were gone I threw off my clothes and fell into bed. I knew I would never let anyone own a piece of The *Silk*. She was my way out. My way to the end of what was. Perhaps to Sarah. Whatever that past was, good, bad and indifferent, that filly was my way to the future, like resurrection.

Chapter Thirty-Five

A day and half later, I was sitting in a corner booth at Glenn's California Grill on Sixth Street, low lights and suede walls. Billy, in his red Christmas stripped jacket made in a thin silk like material, sipped a vodka martini. Two young ladies with skirts more than halfway up their thighs sat across the aisle and stared at us. The legs were appealing. But, I thought, old man that I am, what's the world coming to? I avoided their eyes. Billy's jacket was an eyes full, anyway.

One of the young ladies, in a near holler, said, "Hey you, in the jacket! You wear that to bed?"

Billy swiveled toward them and stared silently. The girls turned their faces away. Grew silent. Billy said, "I'm gonna call your mothers."

Both giggled and one said, "My mother has everybody, but she wouldn't have you."

Billy rose, reached for his glass of water, took two steps to their table and poured the water on the lap of the girl who made the remark. He said, while pouring, "You shouldn't say things like that about your mother." And came back and sat down and raised his martini and took a sip.

I sipped my Orangina and Paul, quiet all along, nibbled at a crock of cooked, still in the skin, hot shrimp, with his diet creme soda. Three old guys wondering what was going on with the world and its kids. After each of us took a deep breath, Paul said, "You got a visit from Mondozo, Tell about it."

I nodded. "That why you called me?"

"One reason."

"He wants to dump money on me. Gotta be bad dollars." Paul started to say something, but I stopped him. "Relax. I told him no. Gotta be hot money. Can't prove it but gotta be. So, What about Sarah?"

"No news."

"Then why are you here bothering me?"

"Harvey, maybe you better go along with those Mondozo boys. We'll follow money and maybe come up with something. Get him off your back. Just don't sign anything."

338

"How do I do that? Paulie, you have to find her. I'm going back to Wheeler and squeeze his neck and make him talk. We can't just have a newspaper advert do our work. You don't understand all of this, do you? About Sarah and my horse and me."

"I do. We will find her. We'll get her back just for you. We will, Harvey. We're think it's one of those hifalutin Board members who is behind it."

"No reason for them unless to please Franklin Wheeler. As for the horse, no. I don't understand. It's a horse. A horse is a horse. We'll find Sarah. Hundred percent. Go ahead, you can sign anything with them, the deal won't be an enforceable one. Just call us when you did it and complain that you sign a sale of a valuable product under threat of force."

"You guarantee that? I'll have his money. I'll spend some of it on *The Silk*. But it sounds like an enforceable contract."

"With dirty money and under threat of your life? It won't hold up."

"You're wrong. I have to rely on your legaleze?"

"Bet title to the animal goes into a small Nevada corporation with names I don't recognize, a bunch of small corporations and your poor horse will disappear with a new tattoo and win everything in sight. By the way, did I tell you about Simon?"

"Simon?"

"Doctor Stanley Simon." Paul raised a finger, "When they chose Oritha Durden, they knew what they were getting. She was an inmate of Patton State Hospital about five years ago. For a full year. She gets bailed out by a doctor – guess who?" He waited. "Doctor Simon. Stanley Simon. Then her trail goes dead. Until Mara Bay and Sally Augers. And, by the way, Moss isn't the controlling owner of the institute, Harvey. And that place, what do they call it, Tucson Rest or something? He owns about forty-one percent and has a management contract over four other hospitals. Franklin Wheeler owns the balance, at least he did until he put his share into his personal FK Wheeler Trust which Harry arranged a few years ago."

"Look who's been doing his homework. The hospitals in which John was the trustee." It seems you and the kid own controlling interest. Unless Sally turns up. Control of the Wheeler Trust and/or the Foundation is what everyone is after. And in the meantime this Jeff Malin fellow is buying a ton of Wheeler's shares in the FK Wheeler Construction and Development Company And this Jeff Malin is manipulating the price. For sure Malin is not using his own money. We're following the money with him, too."

Billy said, "All we have to do is get all of John's accounts, all of Sophie's accounts and whatever else Wheeler may have in various named accounts and check everything – every nickel in and out. This is a five-hundred-piece puzzle. Takes months to get it organized, put all the pieces in place, and about the same to pull it apart."

I said, "A fellow named Christokos is actually managing the Foundation day to day. He just slid into the catbird seat. And I bet he isn't checking with Wheeler or Sophie for anything he does. And I'll bet he doesn't write anything down or tell anyone anything."

"He's next on the list," Paul said. "We've called the SEC, a couple weeks ago and they are going after those buzzards."

"If it's Sophie, she's in this with Malin, or maybe with that accountant, Cable. Or Ann. It's like they all have their claws into one another. Malin buys thousands of shares for his account which I'm sure is for the Wheelers or one of their little partnerships. Does same thing in small bundles. Round and round she goes and where she stops nobody knows."

We watched Paul's thin fingers peel a shrimp, dip it, chew once, and swallow the remains. "Everyone's gotta eat," he shrugged. "These damn things are good. Tell you something else. This Durden person? She is an employee of Harry's ownership in the hospitals and he answers to Wheeler."

"Pick him up. Charge him."

Sampson smiled. "Just sayin'. It's the SEC now and the damn FBI and God knows who else. The bean counters will tell us when and if they come up with something."

"Takes time to trace down a bank account. Never enough money, never enough time, etc...."

"Bureaucrats win. They always do."

"So, now what?" Billy leaned back as he spoke. He summed up the whole Augers affair. "Pretty easy. Number one, Franklin hired Harvey to start with. Then Sophie does the same. Best way to keep tabs on one another. Two, each of them think Sally is alive, or maybe that's what they want everyone to think just to make everyone go in different directions and lose sight of who killed John and grabbed the boy. And maybe Wheeler and his wife are both really bonkers and all we have is this Oritha and Jimmy as suspects with a dangerous unknown behind them.

Then there's Harry Moss and Jeff Malin. Sort of something like variations on Harvey's beloved Quantum Mechanics theme. Everything going every which way except where you aim."

My head ached horribly. I blinked and closed my eyes, just for a moment.

"Go home," Paul said.

"I will when you do." I grabbed another four 200 milligram Ibuprophens and swallowed them, sans liquid.

Paul smiled again and stuffed another shrimp into his mouth. "Take care of yourself. Go home."

"Maybe in a day or so Jimmy will be talking. We can find Sarah. The kid is the key. Someone has to find him. Going back to the institute."

Paul said, "If someone wanted Frankie out of the way he would be dead by now and we would probably know it. Their eight and a half million demand? That number is supposed to tell us something. Someone knew what was available. That answer doesn't take genius."

We contemplated the puzzle for a while and then Billy added, "Joe fits perfectly – somewhere. He's involved. And Sophie. She is likely to know. It could not have come all together without both Sophie and Joe. The Institute is practically next door to his station. Of course, Franklin, the old man... hard to figure. He is in everything."

"Joe is out. He doesn't have a stake in any of it. If we find Sally Wheeler Augers alive, what you've got –" Paul summarized. "What you've got is child molestation, revenge, remorse of gigantic proportions, killing by a person without mercy, kidnapping, and legal shenanigans all stemming from events in the deep dark past between Franklin and his daughter and John. Then there's merely a little matter of power and greed and hate and madness, with a little bit of real estate development on the side. An ordinary day in sunny Southern California. I think your friend John promoted bad stuff between Wheeler and his daughter and got is reward, manager of all those thrusts."

Glenn limped over, one leg straight as a board, leaning his mop of thick black hair deep into our conversation and said, "Suppose I bring you a pot of steamed clams?"

"No time," Paul smiled.

"I've got time," Billy said. "This is on the house?"

"Everything but the price," Glenn replied, smiled, pushed his hair back and waved at one of his waiters.

"I'm not buying," Billy said, and Paul joined.

The pot was delivered, wafts of steam drifting lazily up from a metal garden pail with hot clam juice at the bottom, and lots of napkins. Glenn waved, "On the house."

We jabbed at the open clams with tiny forks and dipped in the juice and ate quietly for a few minutes. Paul interrupted. "You can't figure this one with logic. Not with the history these people have – nothing is explicable except by believing that all these people are, you might say, genuinely upside down."

Billy said, "We have to quit talking and do something."

Paul smiled, "Harvey, you wanted to handle this on your own, OK, go at it." He turned his palms up like he was finished. "We don't have jurisdiction in Mara Bay or that County or in Tucson. But maybe I can get a warrant to search the children's section of Bright Paths at the request of the Santa Barbara DA. Should be enough facts to persuade a judge to sign one. We can't barge in like last time. If you try it alone, just remember, I don't know your name when things go wrong. I'm not involved."

"Finally," I replied. "You're becoming as smart as I always thought you were."

He poked out one more shrimp, peeled it, downed it, and said, "Thanks for lunch. Catch me at the office. If you don't go, I expect you to go home one more day and stay there or you're in for a long siege of headaches." His lanky form disappeared out to a red zone on Sixth Street.

Billy and I were on our own. I broke my habit of one only occasional drink and had a warm sake. It went down something like warm syrup. With a kick.

I said, "Paul wants things to play out without being involved. He's just not going to get his department any more deeply involved. It's in the lap of Santa Barbara County and Mara Bay. I'm sure Joe is figuring out how to get the Sheriff to take over. Joe is not doing anything but figuring out how to capture and keep the money flowing through his city with that shopping center deal of Wheeler's. Joe knows Pillar, he knew Simon, he knows the Wheelers. But," I mused, "if Sally Augers is alive, she has got to be in that Bright Paths place. With her son.

Doesn't seem likely but there isn't any other logical place. He's not at Wheeler's home. Bring your pistol. Let's figure Paul got his warrant and go straight there. Call Nails and tell him to bring his lock picking kit. He's going to have to open that place wide if we need him."

"If Joe is the bad guy, or go-between, he isn't going to let you get close."

"He will. He won't do anything but act the part of a good cop. I don't think he is involved at all. But, if he is part of it, he already has the money and that's that – and he'll smile that silly grin and humor us."

"Which means when and if you get close, he shoots."

"I'm telling you, he's not the problem. All he has to do is sit tight."

"You're kidding yourself."

"Not to worry.

"Like you always say, famous last words. Watch yourself."

***

I dropped off Billy at his car lot on Figueroa Street. American flags were rustling in the breeze. A Hamburger Delight store servicing students from nearby USC, neons blazing midday, was disgorging a half dozen young men as we drove up to Billy's lot. Large white numbers filled the windshields of the half dozen cars parked along the front of the facility. One potted sad azalea stood at the foot of the stairs to his clapboard office. Billy's nephew strolled up and down and immediately headed to the office. As he left my car Billy struggled with my damaged door and said, "Maybe we can get a good deal on this severely damaged vehicle."

"Over my dead body."

"I'll wait. Can't be that long."

Later, sitting in my Eames chair about 2.00 am, staring out into the dark at the somber sea, its white lips of foam against the shoreline titillated by lonely breezes, and a drizzle that had drifted down the coast. Sea winds had character, they were angry, resigned, smooth, twisted, happy, or unhappy. They fit one's mood. I was scribbling something into my journal about Joe and the missing black and white. Snippets of clouds were persistently shoved back and forth from the face of a slightly clipped moon. It was the hour of divorces and domestic violence. I can't tell you why but bad things always happen at that time of night. Paramedic sirens and emergency room visits with sick kids and emergency visits by people with ancient and feeble hearts. It was as though God, He or She or It, depending on whether you were a native American Indian, an African Tribesman, a northeastern Presbyterian, the Pope, or a militant member of NOW, reserved these hours for the worst events. It was when people like me get terrible phone calls, which I did.

Chapter Thirty-Six

"I've been hoping you'd call," Ann Whitson said, sounding as if she had muffled her cell phone. "I'm sorry about all the hassles."

"I don't like them, either. But this is business. I assume you know the difference."

"Don't be difficult, Harvey. I don't know what you mean by 'this is business.' And you have no right judging me." There was silence. A definite tremble rose in her voice. "How about let's just start from the beginning?"

"You okay?"

"Fine. Just fine. Can't you tell?"

None of us were fine. Ann was a lady alone with a big kid she was responsible for and no one anywhere to help. It was a modem story, I thought, but it probably wasn't. "No. I can't tell. But I don't know how to help."

"So answer me. It's a plain and simple question, dammit. We can begin again. You like me. I know you do. You hate all these other people. For God sakes, this isn't fun for me."

"None of it has been fun... well, maybe some of it."

I heard a small giggle. Sex thoughts almost always made girls giggle. Or retreat.

"Ann, look, starting over is a job and a half. Right now I don't much care about me or any combination involving me. There are things out there. Things that are hanging like on a gallows rope. And things I have to do. Harry's story is part of it. Your petition is part of it."

A breathy nothing came from Ann's end. I waited. It was her turn to swing. She said, "I should have told you at the start. I'm sitting here outside of intensive care room 540 at Cedars Hospital, LA. Harry will make it. But it will be a while. Don't know how he got down here. People like Harry are made of cast iron, you know. They survive. Who did this, I don't know, but they have a gang of police trying to find out. Even if he gets better, I'm not sure what will be left for either of us. He doesn't have much left. Sure as hell doesn't have Wheeler any more. Don't know where Sophie is… don't know anything right now."

"Wouldn't worry. People like Harry don't bleed, like bad generals, they just fade away."

"Harry isn't evil, Harvey. The world just began passing him by. He just got caught in a storm. Both of us, I guess. Sophie was my angel and maybe his. Try to understand. But, please don't start lecturing."

"He made choices. You made choices."

"And all of yours have been so great?"

She had me there. "But they haven't been designed to damage innocents, and I haven't spent a lot of time or effort trying to justify them." Very defensive and I was sorry the second I finished with my excuses.

"That's what you think? That I'm justifying Harry and me?"

"I give up," I said. "This is not a useful conversation. It's right out of my first marriage. What happens to your petition now?"

"You're right. Not useful. Nothing about us is useful. Have no idea about the petition. The hearing date is set. I imagine it will be continued to another date until Harry can make it or get someone else to handle it. He called someone at the Foundation, so we'll see. Forget the damn petition for one minute, Harvey. What about us? Does it just stop?"

I thought of Sarah. I said to myself, you're a callous son-of-a-bitch, Harvey, Ann is stuck in a pile of manure. Only way to move forward with your life was to clear the air – clear the past. And I went at it like a lion at dead meat. "Who hired Oritha Durden to take care of Sally? Was it Harry? You must know where Sophie is. She is supposed to be your friend. Who knew what was in the files at Herrara Pillar's place? At Stan Simon's office? Why the hell kill him? His connection was just as a doctor for Sophie. Have you or someone been blackmailing Harry or Franklin – or both? Or, all of the above?"

The phone went dead. No more Ann. She had to fix herself. I couldn't do it.

***

A morning drizzle bleached the remnants of thick night clouds. The prodigious Pacific gleamed under the rising sun. Seagulls were at it again, sounding liked pissed off ten-year-olds. I couldn't tell if they were playing or protecting territory or just plain angry birds. They could dive, float, glide in the freedom of the nearly infinite space they occupied.

If I had to I intended to break and enter every closed room at the remaining children's sections of *Bright Paths*, engage in every criminal act contrary to the Fourth Amendment of the US Constitution, and if that didn't do the trick, I would do the same to the Wheeler home. I dared anyone to arrest me. I called Sophie Wheeler at the number she had given me. No answer. "I don't know where you are," I said to the message system. "But I promised to call. It's all going to end today. You're in the middle. I know that now. Has to be you. I'll find Frankie. I'll track you down. And, if there is any substance to your fixation about Sally, that will end, too. Or I'll confirm her death. You had better call back." The silence stretched out. I added, "Did you or Franklin hire a person named Oritha Durden to watch over Sally Augers?"

There was a muffled something at the other end of the phone. Perhaps my imagination. But there it was again. "Why John? Why him? You constructed all of this, didn't you, Mrs. Wheeler? Or both you and Franklin. You needed to get rid of John in order to take over."

I was certain I heard a muffled click.

***

Chapter Thirty-Seven

I caught Wheeler at home and was let in the Fremont estate by Franklin himself with the housekeeper standing behind him, apparently making sure he knew how to open and close the door. His shoulders were bent. Seemed to mw had become a little spavined, shoulders bent a little more, cheeks hollow. He waved the servant away and motioned me in. She disappeared into the dining area as if blown away. Even bent, he was still a formidable presence, still my height and broad shoulders. However, he was subdued within his green and tan Pendleton shirt, untucked and floating on him. His glasses rested on a receding hairline as if forgotten. His eyes had not forgotten anything. What was left of his hair was tangled. There was a fleeting moment of resignation on his face as though he was expecting a priest-confessor. "What the hell do you want?"

"Answers."

"Can't help you. Sophie's at the hair dressers." Then he murmured a "thank you" for what reason I didn't know. "Alicia, ice tea!" He called out.

We sat in the living room with the blue couch. "So, whatdya want?" Sunlight poured through the French windows and bounced off the couch creating a blue tinge that spread about the room and onto his lean figure. We stared at each other for a hard moment. "I don't do anything without Sophie," he said.

"Not according to this note."

I tossed it at him.

He didn't bother to look. "So? You SOB. I knew you would come to me. I knew it. You found her. She's alive, isn't she? Let's have it!"

I had rehearsed all the way from the front door, but wasn't sure exactly how to begin. I shook my head, just tell him. "I haven't found anyone yet." The tea arrived.

He grunted, "Then, goddammit, why bother me?"

"I need facts." I pointed at the note.

He grunted and gestured and I poured myself a half glass. "What are you afraid of, Franklin. Just tell me that?"

"Fuck you. You find that boy! I paid you!"

"Sophie? got you, hasn't she?"

"Don't be ridiculous. Don't change the goddamn subject! Find him! You've been paid. I want that boy. He means everything!" He rose, ran his hand over his eyes and started to leave.

Maybe shocking him would twist him open. "Sophie knows where the boy is," I said. "She knows."

He stopped in his tracks.

"Yeah, it's true."

And then, as he stood in place, I gave him the whole spiel, the whole low down about Ann Whitson, Hannah Deets, Donna Camina and Harry Moss He took it like jabs to his belly. His eyes narrowed. Told him about Stan Simon's parcel of land that he needed in order to complete his development deal along the highway.

He came back to his blue couch and we each took another sip of the tea while he digested my remarks. He didn't look at me for at least three long minutes. Finally, he said, "You want one of these cookies?"

It was a defensive a remark that anyone could have made. Even if he was the 'bad guy,' I had a twinge of pity for him. "I told you what I want. It's not a cookie." I sat back and decided to finish it. "Frankly, Wheeler, you are in the middle of every event in this puzzle. You hold the strings. You can sit there and act surprised, but for all I know you might be a wholesale murderer. John Augers, Stan Simon, Pillar, And a nearly dead Harry Moss.

"Wherever I turn you are involved. Number one, in the assassination of John. The shooters were probably your hired hands. Harry Moss is nearly dead thanks to you and your note. It tells me you are in the middle of this mess with Sophie and now you suddenly might be antagonists. They may charge Donna Camina for the murder if he is dead. But I don't think it was that little girl who did the deed. It was someone else who perhaps came to her rescue and then used her presence to cover his tracks, or her tracks. And here I am – wondering if it was you and wondering what to do about it. But still, you act worried and even frightened about your wife and about the damn ghost of your daughter. The funny part is, I don't think you're acting."

With my last word he laughed aloud, slapped his knee, threw his head back. "You are a first-rate asshole!" he shouted. "You think I could overwhelm Harry, or shoot John Augers from a distance? Thanks a lot but if you're looking for a confession, you not getting it here, sonny boy! I have ten witnesses as to where I was every minute the last twenty-four hours…or more."

"But not Jack Gordon. Or Christokos. They'll do anything for you. Kill, maim. Anything."

"Bullshit, Ace." His eyes widened. You could tell he was, for some reason, all at once secure again. "You are full of it, Ace. We'll see. Jack Gordon doesn't take orders from me. Thinks he's somebody. He isn't. But acts like he would like to be. Christokos is a lamb. Everything exactly by the book."

"OK, Wheeler. If that's all you have to say. You know more. I told Saul Sampson that. I've told them all I know. Showed them your note. And from this point it's up to them. However, let's stay focused. Where is Sophie? Who beat Harry if not you?"

"Goddammit, get up and get out!"

"I'll find Frankie, you old fart. And soon. And Sally, too, if she exists. Then you're shit out of luck... if she is alive. The trusts are now in her control. Sophie says she saw her. I'll find all the answers. Every damn one. If you would just tell me the truth, the whole truth, about Sally and Sophie and that *Bright Paths* place. I think you know the whole damn story that relates to this mess. Don't worry, I'll find out. At your expense. It's your money."

He smiled. The sly smile was his way of saying you know nothing and I know it all and always have. "Keep the fucking money, Ace. There's not much more I can tell you. John was like a son. And my grandson is part of me. I need him. I put my life into John and Frankie's Trusts. Harry had all these ways of saving a dollar. Relied on him and on John way too much, I realize now. Why would I hurt them? That fucking Moss." He wagged his head, placed one balled up right fist into the palm of the left hand. "That's why you came?" His features turned. "To squeeze my life story out of me? To run through a thousand regrets? Don't worry, Ace. That's what you want? All my regrets? You get nothing. Find my grandson! Someone is out there, Ace!" Then suddenly, he leaned back and laughed, a huge maniacal laugh that went on too long and too loudly. "Regrets? You don't know anything about actually living. And that idiotic secretary with her stupid petition? She's dead meat! A walking carcass! And so is Harry. So is Harry! Bring me Frankie!"

He went on for another few minutes, shouting and swearing. And I said nothing and did nothing. Finally, when he seemed to run out of breath, I said, "Not interested in your threats, Wheeler. Wasting your time. Who killed John Augers? That's what I want to know... right now. You are the best suspect I've got. The LAPD must have concluded much the same. They are probably on their way. Telling me about John might save your grandson out. Save his ass. I promise you. The police get here and your lawyers get here and Frankie is probably a goner. You will lose the power to save him. Time isn't your friend. John had all the trust powers. We know he is dead. And even had power of control at your Foundation. You had the motives. All of them – and then some. You quarreled about something. Probably not even anything serious and you realized your mistakes. John had the power and you no longer do. But your daughter does, presuming she is alive as you and Sophie think. Harry had sweet talked you out of your life. John must have threatened you. He had that kind of moxie and balls. You saved a bundle of tax money but you made every mistake in the book. Smart guys make very big mistakes just by being way too smart. I guess that's the lesson. John was too smart. Creates arrogance. So you did what you could to fix the mistakes."

He had this smile that said I am smarter than you, better than you, a smug, wispy grin coming over a now gaunt face. "I don't deal with assholes, Ace. And you are one of the myriad I have trashed over the years. That can be remedied. But, you want to know my regrets, Mr. Ace? My regrets?"

Mistakes and regrets. The stuff of life.

"Regrets haunt all of us. All those regrets." Ensconced in his blue funny shaped satin couch he relaxed and spoke quietly. "John was like a son. An exciting son. A rascal. Made me laugh and made me angry all at same time. But smart. All I ever had was that daughter. Sick and hateful. A hateful child by my own doing. My own creation." He shook his head, remembering.

"John's boy is part of me. My only male heir. Yes, yes, and my only power and salvation. Maybe Sally is out there. But Frankie is all I have and his existence saves the day. Find him."

"You have a wife. You have her and Frankie."

He looked at me and began a low gurgling laugh. He put his head in his hands. Laughing a low crawling laugh. Then sobbing.

"I'm not sure you really give a rat's ass about Frankie," I said. "Or anyone, Wheeler. A social piranha. A cruel man. You're not fooling anyone. You need him now, for legal reasons. For control of the Trusts. For your own safety. That's what all of this is about. That's why Ann Whitson is such a threat. Maybe in cahoots with your charming wife. Do you really, I mean really, give a damn and want Frankie? That little boy who is undoubtedly scared shitless and suffering right now? Do you really want him back? In the clutches of Ann Whitson and Harry Moss?"

He didn't answer. He was all at once dragged out and pale and getting old by the minute. His hands twined together. Large blue veins on the back of them. The window curtains rustled and fluttered in a sudden breeze, then stopped and fell silent and limp. Then they fluttered again as if Mother nature was playing a game. He raised a hand and slowly made a fist and held it up as if to strike me. I didn't move and he didn't move. He let go. The hand came to his lap. He rose slowly as though made of crystal, gazed at me with a new steely, hateful look, tossed a paper napkin to the floor and with an angry gesture, walked out. I called after him. "The police ought to be here soon – with all their questions."

From the distance I heard, "Fuck you."

I had hoped the confrontation would yield secrets, a surrender of some kind, which would guide my next step. I watched him slowly climb the entrance lobby circular stairs. He suddenly turned back, furiously. "Talk to Sophie! Talk to Sophie!"

Chapter Thirty-Eight

I kept thinking about Frankie Augers, suddenly rescued and resurrected, becoming normal; and of Sally Augers suddenly appearing and caressing the kid's brow and becoming a real mother. It's the resurrection business brought down to neighborhood level. But I was and am too cynical to believe that that's the way it would all end. In my heart of hearts, I knew terrible things were on the way.

I drove home, washed hands for the fourth or fifth time since the Harry Moss, Donna Camina encounter, and my confrontation with Wheeler. Though I inspected, I could not actually see Harry Moss's blood anywhere on me, but I scrubbed anyway. I had an extra hour before meeting with Paul. An idea that had been simmering in my mind for a couple of days struck me again. I called a friend who sold stocks for a local brokerage house and asked him to see what was going on with the publicly traded shares of FKW Construction. In a minute Alan Stockton was able to tell me that the shares had risen from about 17 to more than 22 dollars in the past two weeks, then it had suddenly plummeted back to 16. He knew nothing about the Mara Bay development planned by the company. He was very curious and wanted to know more. I didn't know more.

Then I asked him to check on who was buying and who was selling the FKW shares if that was possible. "Maybe," he said. "We make a market in that company so maybe." I replied that it seemed a lot easier to understand a "Pick Four" at the races and certainly a lot safer than figuring and playing the stock market. The only thing I knew about the stock market was not to pay attention to the daily nonsense, but to watch the hundred and two-hundred-day trend lines. I waited on the line for about four slow minutes and he came back and told me that one Jeff Malin, as an attorney for the probate of Dr. Stanley Simon's estate had been a heavy buyer – he didn't know if he had been acting for someone else as he wasn't able to find any significant money in his probate estate, which was public record, to explain the purchases. The shares were bought primarily from one of the only sellers of the narrowly held shares –Franklin Wheeler, who was not only the largest seller, but was the largest owner of the publicly traded portions of the stock.

"Whoever is running the Wheeler interests ran it up by buying and then caused the Wheeler interests to just dump it slowly. Nearly two hundred fifty thousand shares already. The first sales made up for any losses by a large measure. Then it stopped. Nice way to make a living. I'll refer it to my managers, although I'm not sure they care as long as we got the commission."

What a fine business! If Moss was behind the accountant who was buying, and also behind Wheeler who was selling, the old man was making a profit going in and coming out. Made no sense to me. Wheeler or his family would be receiving cash from the sale of FKW stock and this Malin fellow would have acquired a ton of it. I knew he couldn't be buying for his own account. He was a not the bookkeeper type but still it was too over the top not to be a scheme, except Malin didn't seem to be the thief type. A call to the Superior Court in Santa Barbara made it clear he was also involved often on probate matters as an appointee of the Court, and made a nice quiet living running errands with Wheeler's books, but not enough to buy fifteen or twenty thousand shares of a $15 or $20 stock. He was definitely not buying for his own account.

***

A little while later, I was sitting in a comer booth at Glenn's California Grill on Sixth Street, low lights and suede walls beginning to subdue our moods. Billy sipped a vodka martini. I sipped a warm sake and Paul nibbled at a crock of cooked, still in the skin, hot shrimp. Three smart guys without answers. "How smart can we be? I'll bet that Harry Moss owns a significant portion of that highway 101 deal. The title is in a small corporation with names I don't recognize. As to your question about Durden, I figure that it's likely she is at least one of the trigger people in this mess. It's not Harry and it's not Jimmy...I don't think."

"A well-fixed Jimmy Gaines."

"Listen, someone has a copy of the tapes and is sitting out there waiting for you," Billy finished.

"And which explains," Paul raised a finger, "why they, or whoever it is who chose that big bear of a female, they knew what they were getting. A former inmate of Patton State Hospital. We tried to trace her. But the trail went cold. Until Mara Bay and Sally and Joe's records pop up. And, by the way, Harry Moss isn't the controlling owner of the institute, Harvey. He owns about forty-one percent and has a management contract for it and over four other hospitals. Franklin Wheeler owns the balance, at least he did until he put his share into the FK Wheeler Trust."

"In which John was the trustee. He controlled, didn't he?" I looked at Billy admiringly. "Look who's been doing his homework. I guess you know that Wheeler has the controlling interest in his Foundation but John had the Trusteeship and control of the Wheeler trust through Sally and Frankie. Which is what everyone is after. And in the meantime Franklin is selling a ton then manipulating the price of the stock and Jeff Malin is buying a ton of the shares at the lower price in the FK Wheeler Construction and Development Company. Malin is for sure not using his own money."

Billy said, "All we have to do is get all of John's account in line, all of Sophie's accounts and Franklin's and whatever else Wheeler may have in various named accounts and check everything in and out. This is a five-hundred-piece jig-saw puzzle. That's what they do, the wise guys at the force. They have a group of brains who do just this sort of thing."

"You think maybe someone else is calling the shots? Not Wheeler himself?"

I said, "A fellow named Christokos is actually managing the Foundation day to day. And I bet he isn't checking with Wheeler or Sophie about anything he does. And I'll bet he doesn't tell anyone anything, including his Board. Doesn't the Los Angeles Police cover such things?"

"Somebody had to start the selling spree of Wheeler's Company."

"If it's Sophie, she's in this with Malin."

We watched Paul's thin fingers peel a shrimp, dip it, chew once, and swallow the remains whole. "Everyone's gotta eat," he shrugged.

"So have you compiled all the accounts?"

Sampson smiled. "Not my department. The bean counters will tell us when and if they come up with something. DA's office has a securities fraud division. Their department."

Billy, quiet all this time, leaned back. His jacket was almost stylish, brown, orange, and white in a pattern resembling a committee decision in a local school district. "What you're saying is that you guys know nothing."

Paul smiled again and stuffed another shrimp into his mouth.

"Pretty clear to me." Billy continued. "One, Franklin hired Harvey to start with. Two, he didn't trust his lawyer or anyone else." He stuck a finger into my shoulder. "Three, Sophie hired you. They were both looking for an independent person to check things out knowing they might have to trip you up along the way. Looks good. Meanwhile, you are getting nowhere. They used you. Looks good. You being independent and all. Four, they didn't trust one another. Best way to keep tabs on one another. Hire the same guy. And five, each of them think Sally is alive. They get the LAPD, Joe Dobrowski, and you going in different directions. Could be that Wheeler and his wife are both bonkers and all we have is this Oritha person and Jimmy as suspects. Simple. Right? Not a mystery."

"Sort of like variations on Harvey's Quantum Mechanics theme. Everything going every which way except where you aimed."

"Maybe we can get Tucson PD to pick up this Durden person." Everyone nodded knowingly. And no one jumped up to make a call. Like local politics. Anyway, the kid is the key."

I agreed. "He is the center of it all. One way or another. Along with Sarah. Pulled into this mess because of me."

"We'll get her, Harvey. We will. I promise. I'll pick Wheeler up tomorrow, in the meantime Chief says let him ride, he isn't going anywhere. They are all convinced that Sarah is not really in harm's way. Of course, she doesn't know that."

"We would probably know it if Frankie was dead by now and. And, about that number – why would anyone ask for suck an odd amount? Someone knew what was available. The Foundation Board must know what's available to Wheeler. That answer doesn't take genius."

We contemplated the puzzle for a while and then Billy added, "It's behind those scary doors at Bright Paths. The juvenile section, the closed doors we didn't cover."

Glenn limped over leaning deep into our conversation and said, "Suppose I bring you a pot of steamed clams?"

"Shrimps were enough. And no time," Paul smiled.

"I've got time," Billy said. "Is this on the house?"

"Everything but the price," Glenn replied, smiled and waved at one of his waiters.

"I'm not buying," Billy said, and Paul joined. The pot was delivered, steaming hot in a metal garden pail with hot clam juice at the bottom and lots of napkins. Glenn waved, "On the house."

We jabbed at the open clams with tiny forks and dipped in the juice and ate quietly for a few minutes. Paul interrupted. "You can't figure this one with logic. Not with the history these people have – not explicable except by believing that all these people are, you might say, like you said, really upside down."

Billy said, "So where do you go from here?"

"I go my way and you go yours," Paul said, a clam on the end of a little fork, next to his lips." Just stay out of my way. If we find Sally Wheeler Augers alive, what you've got –" Paul said. "What you've got is child molestation, revenge, remorse of gigantic proportions, killing without mercy, kidnapping, and legal shenanigans all stemming from events in the deep dark past between Franklin and his daughter and John. And that Harry Moss. Then there's merely a little matter of power and greed and hate and madness, with a little bit of real estate development on the side. An ordinary day in sunny Southern California."

Hard not to laugh. But we knew there was more to come. Paul Sampson coughed. Stuck a napkin to his mouth. We waited. Finally, he said, "Harvey, you wanted to handle this on your own, but just remember, I don't have jurisdiction in Mara Bay or that County or in Tucson. Joe doesn't want us. But maybe I can get a warrant to search the children's section of Bright Paths from the Santa Barbara DA. Just remember, I don't know your name if things go wrong on your end. LAPD is not involved. Now, I'm going to get that Wheeler fellow and lock him up and squeeze for a day until that bunch of lawyers get him released."

"Finally. You're becoming as smart as I always thought you were."

Paul opened and picked out one more clam, downed it, and saluted quickly. "Thanks for lunch but I'm outta here before the check comes. Catch me at the office." Out he went.

I broke my habit of one only occasional drink and had another warm sake. It went down something like warm syrup, "Paul's not going to get a warrant," I said. "He wants things to play out without any of us involved. LAPD wraps it up. I know him. He's got a murder in Arcadia, a murder up beyond Point Dume, a confession from Jimmy in Mara Bay, and by now an assault against Wheeler. The disappearance of a kid and of Sarah Finkel. Most of it is in the lap of Santa Barbara County. I'm sure Joe is figuring how to get their Sheriff to take over. He doesn't need this. No help there. That Jeff Malin is probably doing his best to hide his ill-gotten gains. He might even get away with it. The SEC will handle that. As for Harry—who knows? Maybe just an old broken-down trial lawyer who is not so broken down, with a good-looking smart secretary who can be used. But," I mused, "if Sally Augers is alive, she has got to be in that *Bright Paths* place. With Frankie. There isn't any other logical place. If they're alive. Bring your pistols. Call Nails and tell him to bring his lock picking kit. He's going to open the tin can if we need him."

"Joe isn't going to let you get close."

"He will."

"Do you really think he has a hand in this?"

"No. He doesn't. Not eliminating anyone. He knows the whole town, Simon, Ebrons, even Wheeler. But, like you say, he's a good cop."

"That means when you get close, he shoots."

"Yeah."

Chapter Thirty-Nine

I didn't recall that the front door squeaked. But it did – like some special announcement – Harvey is here! The Bright Paths Institute had all the answers. I was certain. Maybe this is where I would end up anyway, so it might have been easier to walk in and demand an inspection tour in the name of my father, my son, and Billy's fucking ghost.

Lugubrious yellow night lights glowed every ten yards or so. No matter how bright the lights, or smiling attendants, a TV room, a game room, retirement homes are not fun places. For anyone. Billy wore rubber soles which squealed on the linoleum. I pointed at them and he slipped them off. Real burglars don't wear rubber soles, they wear thick socks over their shoes. He tied the shoe laces together and carried them over his shoulder.

A mixture of age and infirmity coiled into the scents of urine and Lysol. "I don't want to end up in one of these places, Harv. You kill me and I'll kill you when we get close."

"It'll be a pleasure – if I can remember."

We found the entrance another section with a sign attached to the main *building – **Section Two – Patients and Staff only.*** The night caretaker behind a U-shaped station was dozing when we eased in. Billy stuck a pistol on his nose. He woke with a start, slid to the floor, pale as a bathroom, and raised his hands. Unfortunately he didn't faint. He turned sheet rock gray and began to breathe in short gasps. "See? I ain't got nothing!" He emptied his pockets. "See?"

"Relax. You still have your good looks. No one's going to hurt you." I said, as we taped his arm and legs and stuffed two Kleenex in his mouth. I leaned down to his ear and whispered, "We will kill you if you even move. Where are the kids?" He nodded to our right. We pulled him into a janitor's closet. "We leave him a twenty when we leave," I whispered to Billy.

"If we remember."

The first office to our left was open and I flashed my light over the room. The shelves contained paper and the usual medical supplies, syringes, a desktop refrigerator with a three-inch padlock, that was negligently unlatched and which contained small batches of Demerol, Sodium Pentothal, Adrenaline; a couple of phones all next to a small basin. There ought to be a law about all this dope hanging out like that. Especially where kids were being held, or treated… or mistreated. There was cabinet with stuffed toys resting happily in a half dozen shelves. Smiling bears, puppy dogs, and fleecy elephants. Companions of damaged children. The next office required one of Billy's picks. He stuck something into the lock and in less than thirty seconds flipped it open and we peered into what was clearly one of the visiting doctor's offices. The name on the desk was John Holcomb, MD. We opened the file drawers and found nothing useful.

"We gotta do each room?"

I nodded.

"What if we find a living breathing Sally Augers?"

"Tie her up. But, we're looking for Frankie. This is the kid's section. Doubt if there will be any Sally here. But, we find her alive, we'll think of something."

"Keystone cops," Billy murmured, upset. "We're not even in the right place yet." His foot caught in a throw rug and he stumbled and swore. Whose idea was this?

"Keep going."

We went through supply rooms and play rooms, and a television room. We finished that portion of the wing. As we walked toward the north wing where the Juvenile living rooms began we could hear the clicking of the overhead clock. One-fifteen. The hall led to an alcove and directly to the rooms. There was one hallway bisecting the area. An open nurses business section, with desk, comfortable chair, files, typewriters, and pale-rimmed Apple computers. The end of the hallway was dark and I had the feeling that someone was hiding in the darkness. I heard a rustle in the next room as if someone was warning us. Held my breath. Heard it again. My pulse levels hit atmospheric heights, like untethered balloons. I threw the light on Billy. He was white. Not just white. He looked like the inside of an operating room.

I leaned toward the door. Slippers padded on the floor, a door opened, and in a few seconds a toilet flushed; the person sighed, slippers dropped to the floor.

Slipping quickly into the room, I switched on the overhead light and shoved my pistol into the startled person. One hand went to his mouth. "Not a word," I whispered. "Not even one."

I recognized Arthur, the bulky attendant who was supposed to guard the section. He stared cross-eyed directly into the pistol. "Not one fucking word," I repeated. He shook his head. The vote was unanimous. Guns do that. I motioned him to a corner. Billy said, "This isn't good. We can't have someone loose like this. We gotta kill him." He turned away suppressing a smile.

"You mean with a pistol shot in his ear or something messy like that? Blood all over the place?"

"Why not?"

Arthur's knees buckled slightly and he grabbed at the wall. He looked like the color of a hotel bathroom. Words that wouldn't come out of a mouth that tried. I tapped him on the nose. "Shhh. I don't want to kill you and leave a mess. We wouldn't want that." I looked at Billy. "Get the Pentothal and a syringe out of that first office. You'll see it there in the fridge."

In a minute he returned. I held up a capsule to the dim light. "I figure half of one of these capsule things ought to do it."

"Or kill him." Billy answered.

Arthur turned yellow then gray and back to white. I hoped the variations in color didn't mean he was dying or something inconvenient like that. "I'll keep quiet. I'll keep quiet," he pleaded. "You can trust me. Really."

"We trust you, Arthur. Really. Now, roll over, on the floor."

He did. "Now onto your stomach, unless you want to die quickly." Billy stifled a laugh. "We trust you," I repeated.

"No, no," he said, gutturally. "You said you trust me. Don't do that. A quarter cc. Only a quarter. Plenty. Please. Look on the syringe. Please. A quarter."

I checked it. "All right. A quarter. But if you wake up too soon, you're dead meat."

I filled the syringe to the quarter mark and added just a touch. This doctoring business was a new experience for me. I wasn't sure how far to shove the needle in or how fast to discharge the liquid.

"Do it already!" Billy whispered.

I shoved it about a quarter inch into his ass. He moaned as I squeezed the fluid out. I pulled it out and for a second was afraid I would throw up all over him. I felt my face flush. "I'm not good with needles," I muttered. "Not good at all."

The dose worked almost immediately. The fellow began breathing in great gulps of air. "C'mon, Dr. Ace, let's get with it."

I automatically put the cap back on and stuck the syringe down in my pocket. Stupid. But stupid came later like superman at the right time.

A light leaked from beneath the door of the next room. It went on and off as if warning ships at sea. On – off – on – off. We watched it for a minute. The door had no lock. I motioned at Billy to stand to one side. I swung the

360

door open and stepped quickly into the room with a two-handed pistol stance. On – off – on. It was like one of those nightmares when you're partly in it and partly out of it.

A gaunt child's face, gazed at the light switch, transfixed by his own finger which was flipping the switch controlling the yellow wall bulb – on, then off, in perfect two-four time. The boy was not more than seven or eight years old, wild tangle of sandy hair, pajamas falling off his shoulders and hips, holding them with one hand and flipping the light with the other. He was transfixed – composing his personal symphony. I hoped the movements had meaning to him. Music for his soul. We couldn't turn away for a full minute. The tragedy of this transfixed little boy hit home.

Billy gasped. "There's more than lights going on and off in those eyes. Makes you want to cry."

"That's the worst part. When there's still something going on in the brain."

There was nothing we could do. We spoke to him softly. "How about leaving the light on?" He wasn't interested. I pulled down the blankets of his bed and fluffed his pillows and invited him into it. He shook his head and flipped the lights. On-off-on.

Further down the hall some of the low wattage lights were burned out. The world of these children was dim. Dreary. Worrisome. We entered the next room and while Billy stood at the door, I motioned him to turn on the light and simultaneously pulled the cover away from the shoulders of the person occupying the bed. This time a young man, probably fifteen or sixteen years old, sat up, left arm and head shaking in palsied unison. He tried to formulate an objection. I put my finger to my lips and gently went to him, gently as I could I put him back into a reclined state and drew the blankets back over his shoulder. "It's OK, It's OK," I whispered. "Not to worry." Billy switched off the light. There were two more rooms with sleeping children. The next room beyond was empty.

The elevator at the end of the hall stood open, a foreboding black cave, dark carpeted black hole sucking light from all directions. The hallway in front of the next room was in near darkness. There appeared to be only a couple more occupied rooms on this floor, the remaining were either empty or used as sitting rooms overlooking the lawns or TV and game rooms – except for one more. The sounds of frightened children receded.

The overhead fixture was on in this last room and we used the same routine, Billy entering after me guarding the light switches and door and me rushing the bed and pulling the covering off. This time nothing.

A tiny woman, white hair flying about her head like a tangles of frozen ice, sitting in a large stuffed chair next to the bed, smiled a wizened smile and said, "Oh my, goodness sakes, what a surprise! Oh my, oh my. Good evening gentlemen. Are you here to take me home? That would be very nice. I would like to go home."

It was as though she knew us, that our entry wasn't such a great surprise. She was happy to have the company. Her eyes were Monet blue, eyelashes unevenly mascaraed, lipstick violent red and missing the mark. She beamed. "I have tea ready. Then I can go home. I always have tea ready. You never know, do you?" She pointed at my pistol. "Are we playing games, dear ones?"

Billy turned to me and said, "I thought this section was for kids. You wanted me to shoot first?" Then he smiled and said to the little lady, "We'll call it playing good guys and bad guys. And we're the good guys. We're looking for children."

"Oh, yes, the children. The doctor said the children can't resist me. They like me, you know. Oh, yes indeed. Everyone likes me. The doctor says so. He says I'm wonderful. Better than the children." Vanity spread across her thin features. She ran her fingers through her tumbling white hair and smiled her best smile. She picked up a small mirror with a tortoise shell handle, looked into it and smiled.

"He's right. You are the best. You're ready for your close up," I said. "Are there children here?"

"Indeed, silly. Indeed." She replaced the mirror. "They love me. Everyone loves me. Shall I pour?"

I looked around without finding a hot plate or a pot or anything resembling a tea service. I said, "Miss –?"

"Esmeralda Victoria Rawlingswood. I made up the Esmeralda. I like it, don't you? They said it was fine. But they all call me Miss Vickie." Her eyelashes fluttered. She was flirting. "Are we going home?"

"Of course, Miss Vickie, but we're a bit pressed for time. Suppose we come back in an hour or two and you'll pour for us then? Meantime, I need some help. I need to know if you've seen this person. She is a great friend of mine." I handed her the photo of Sally and then one of Frankie. "In the last few days? Either one?"

She turned the Sally photo around in her fingers. "Well yes, indeed. That's her, that's her."

"Have you seen her lately?"

"Oh yes. She came through the garden. She was coming to see me. I can tell you that much. They all come to see me. I am their favorite. I waved at her and she looked at me. And I kept waving. But they wouldn't let me see her. They stopped me. She's my daughter you know."

She stopped. "No. That's not it." Trouble spread over her face. A shadow tinged her eyes like a cloud over a half moon. Her lips thinned. "No, perhaps, my friend from the card game, that's it." She brightened. "She's my friend from the card game."

"This lady here in the picture?"

"Well, I think she is the one who plays cards. So many visitors come to see me. Are we going home now?"

"And the children. Do you see them at all?"

She smiled. It was pasted on her countenance. Perpetual contentment. Hard to fault. Pills and contentment. "We play cards, you know."

"Well, Miss Vickie, I hope you win. But do you see them? I mean the children?"

She was all at once set in concrete. Nothing getting through, nothing getting out. We left. In the next room there were four additional young occupants in bunk beds, each of whom turned sleepily over onto another side when I poked my nose at them. They were used to being bothered. We finished glancing into the corners of the remainder of the floor, and then climbed more stairs. We holstered our pistols. There was nothing menacing about the remaining children who already had enough problems.

We took one row of rooms at a time, leaving the alcoves and offices for last. Three more rooms with worried and disturbed faces. Fear was the common denominator. When we came out of the third room, there was a dark silent and shadowed parade behind us, Miss Vickie and several of the children in nightclothes dusting the floor. Poking our noses here and there brought out disturbed and bewildered faces in the dim light. We could do nothing to diminish the parade of confused children, apparently left to their own devices, with no one in sight, beginning to emit little cries of perplexed fear, children who were not able to make appropriate connections in their lives, many of whom could only become canny or dull and some who someday would be the strong, bright, and famous, all rising above their incapacities. I wanted to believe there was hope for them. The children followed us in their robes, their pajamas trailing along the floor, Billy leading them like a pied piper hiding under a horse blanket. He stopped and stood on one side of the corridor and I on the other side.

Mr. Rigor Mortis, also known as Jack the Mack truck, emerged from one of the rooms, fully dressed and ablaze with purpose, a baseball bat in one hand and a .32 caliber revolver in the other. He aimed it at me, drew closer, shouting commands. "Move out there, soldier! Move away!"

Billy timed it perfectly. He came up behind Jack the Mack and placed the barrel of his pistol against his left ear and said, "Start smiling for the children. This is play time. Remember, this is play time." Billy pushed the pistol harder into the fellow's neck. "Hand me the gun, and please keep smiling. We don't want the kids to panic."

One of the children began to moan loudly. He couldn't have been more than ten or twelve, hair trimmed down to a quarter inch. "They're coming," he said, holding his head rocking back and forth, seeing broken shadows and skeletons rising out of his delusions. "They're coming."

Jack the Mack handed his pistol to Billy, dropped his bat, and went to the boy. "No, no, Wally, it's all right. We're having fun. It's a game. Quiet now. No one is coming. No one will hurt you." But Wally began to cry and to shiver. Jack quickly slipped his jacket off and tossed it around the boy.

Ageless fear suddenly took complete command of these lonely, vanquished hearts, and they began to scream anguished screams, eyes stained with fear, searching for peace in the dark galaxy of time. Arms were raised seeking solace in a ceiling that was strewn with peeling paint. They were tiny beings, stars lost in their special melancholy universe.

"Where is Frankie Augers?" I asked Mack. "Frankie. Where?"

Two additional members of the staff came up the stairs. Billy Fitzer pulled out his pistol once again and they saw the lay of the land and stopped, got a nod from me and began to tend to business, attempting to diminish the fears of the haunted young crowd.

"Over there," Jack said, hoarsely, glancing quickly at me. "Down there, at the end of the hall, in the next building," he said with a jerk of his thumb. "Make it quick and make it quiet. I don't go there ever."

"What about Ebrons? And the rest of the children?"

"He should be in his room. Third floor. We'll take care of the kids."

"Thanks. You sure he's there?"

"If he's not there he's nowhere. But I think so."

"You're doing the right thing." I said.

He nodded and pointed.

"Where?"

"The other building I said. Far end of the parking lot. Go before they get hysterical here."

"The Augers woman too?"

"Not sure about anyone., but that's the only place I don't know about." Billy waved a thank you.

"Good luck," Jack the Mack said. His job was to protect the kids, his patients – which he did.

We reached a closed door at the end of the corridor. Billy began to pick it. I stood watch expecting to have hordes of madmen descend upon us. Emissaries of Master Caligula Ebrons, or a Medusan Oritha Durden. Finally, the lock slipped.

Billy looked at me. I motioned that I would enter and take the left, he would follow and take the right.

We attacked the heavy door, rushed through into the lurid shadows. We stopped. Remained still for that unknown moment in a gray silent room. Our eyes gained control of the strange light. Gold and deep red draperies hung from the walls. Elaborate picture frames, blank within the frames. The scent of jasmine hanging in the still air. There were standing candelabras at each corner of the room, much too close to the draperies. The white, thin candles were barely burned. The ceiling had been painted black, parts of walls looking like a graffiti creation without discernible form or meaning. All in black. Everything over the top.

We caught our breath and let the dimness open our irises. There she was, two stairs above us, sitting on a massive golden throne, candlelight from two additional silver candelabras on small doily covered tables at her sides, flickering a blue light over golden hair. Her hands caressing carved exotic woods and the burnished threads of the chair, one arm moving strangely like a lazy eel not yet recovered from its latest gorging. One arm, however, was chained firmly to the chair. In spite of the constraints, she commanded the space.

We were enraptured for that moment, fixed in place... a thousand judgments slot machining around and around in our minds, trying to snap a world of fantasy and madness into fact. Everything had a golden glow, yet all of it in shadowed and cinerarium red darkness. I reached over and shut the door as a smile came over her face. I approached, carefully.

The face looked familiar... but it wasn't.

Chapter Forty

Was this Sally Wheeler Augers? Hair wild and white, minus the auburn wig. Her eyes burning, sallow pockets of blue, deeply sad, but ominous. This person all at once recognized me. Eyes suddenly exulting a great triumph. My amateur diagnosis was that she was in a psychotic state of joyful insanity. Rage subdued by purpose and pleasure.

Carly Klein? Was that crazily grinning female, looking like an Oscar Wilde portrait, actually Carly Klein? Nee Sally Augers? One arm tightly chained to the chair. A carefully restrained prisoner in the midst of some mad pleasure? One arm was free like a soft white boneless appendage as it waved snake-like in the air as though in religious fervor. Whatever deceit had consumed her for the past few years, it all seemed to have been erased by a sly yet formidable plan of action affecting her as a manic narcotic addict might. But that smile – it seemed achingly human, aching to be something else. It made you want to believe it was all some silly mistake. However, it was also a wily smile that had turned truth on its head and into deceit.

Deep crevices just above her eyelids were blackened. There were black lines outlining the edges of her eyes. Rock and roll mascara at its idiotic excess. Candlelight cast small flickering waves through the cleft in her chin. Her wide forehead, her blazing golden hair and pale skin were incongruously and impossibly like a child's.

"I thought you would put two and two together – a trifle earlier, Harvey Ace," she said, in a hoarse monotone. "I'm disappointed." Then she laughed, coughed, and grew tense. "But here we are, ready to kill." It came out as a rasp deep in her throat that rose incrementally with each syllable.

I considered the answer. "Took me a while."

"If you understand everything now count yourself with the best."

"Ebrons has been hiding you."

She nodded. "In this forsaken cell. This prison. Wonderful. Isn't it? Could not reveal myself. I created my dear Carly Klein. I should say we created her. And now... this." She pointed at her chains and her limp arms. "They think I'm crazy. As you can tell, I'm not. They will find out

366

differently. Just wait… There's more you could not know. More." She looked down. Turned her face away from the flickering candlelight. "More surprises. Never dreamed of."

"This began, didn't it, when John couldn't resist getting into the middle of it. Thinking about not just millions but the entire Wheeler estate. It grew, didn't it? Like some nasty carbuncle. But," I reproached, "he lost all the way around. You weren't about to let that happen."

"Poor John. Stuck with me. Guilt did him in, didn't it? The house was mine. But that was hardly enough. Franklin didn't deserve…" She stopped and smiled. "He didn't." She reached with her free hand, grabbed and tossed what appeared to be a dark rag at me. "This is for you, Mr. Harvey Ace." It was her dark wig.

Billy said, "I don't get it."

"You actually do," she growled. "But can't believe it, can you?"

I waved at the majestic prison of that grand golden chair with the chains, holding Carly Klein. I did a majestic bow and presented her with a wave of my arm, "Here, friends and countrymen, you have Sally Wheeler Augers. In her full resurrected glory. This daughter that Franklin swore was dangerous to everything he had built. He wanted her dead, so," I paused for effect, "so, follow me, after this unhappy person got into Ebrons' hands, he conspired to make her disappear, make her over into Carly Klein. With the help of Ebrons and wigs and history she was rather easily transformed, a shot of this and a shot of that and she became the crazily sensuous Carly. A fabulous job. Franklin was mad with guilt and remorse. He knew she was dangerous. But he wasn't up to eliminating his daughter. Simply killing her. That wasn't in him. So here she is."

As I spoke the face of Sally/Carly twisted into a triumphant grin, the loose arm fanning the emptiness around her, as the panoply of the deceit was revealed, forgetting where it led. I moved closer to this flickering vision of madness. "He was losing it with the fear and worry that you were actually alive, not cremated." She waved her free hand dismissively. I went on. Sophie got Simon to swear you were dead. And Pillar. She needed the records. The good doctor used you while you thought you were using him. Franklin did his terrible deeds when you were very young. Just a child. Right? And you responded by hating. You turned your insides off. That was your best protection against him. And plotting revenge. He thought John was the answer. It was a mistake. Your father conspired to secret you away with a false cremation, Sophie and Stan Simon sealed that deceit. They kept you institutionalized and safe. It was easy to fake your death. Good old Pillar helped willingly. All it needed was the right amount of money. But John had other ideas. That bundle of busy molecules that was John at his best wanted it all. He became fearful that Franklin would cut him out of his schemes and managed to keep you nullified. Locked up. Too many moving parts. Didn't work. You got out. Didn't you? With Oritha. And Franklin feared the worst. Ebrons was beside himself. He and Pillar needed, shall we say…*fixing*. Franklin saw you around every corner. But how could you manage all that without help? Oritha's brains were not the issue. Jimmy and money were the answers. Franklin didn't know that there were other silent conspirators.

"You were double-crossed. When John was killed and Frankie was kidnapped your conspiracies bit by bit began to unravel. But who did the killing? A regular mystery movie double cross. Fortunes were at stake – all those trusts. Your trust, your son's trust. John's trust, and last but not least, Franklin's and the Foundation. So here you are. Manacled like a common thief. Didn't believe this could happen, did you? You could be Carly one minute and be Sally the next and plan for your future. Scare the piss out of everyone – until Ebrons himself got caught in his own web, in the same deceit. You are a clever one, Sally. You and Carly created a believer out of everyone. You got Oritha to deal with Ebrons and Harrara Pillar. And Jimmy loved money. He was the expert in your grand design. So, Sally Wheeler Augers, alias Carly Klein, could shift between reality and shadows. Until one of you became dangerous and madness took over. Do you even know who you really are? Ebrons not only hid you away, he made you his prisoner and his creation."

A growl came from Sally's lips. From the deepest part of her. "You don't know, do you?" She laughed a large throaty laugh that at the end was a hateful sneer.

"I know. Your silent co-conspirator is still out there," Carly. "Somewhere. As well as that monster Oritha Durden."

Billy asked, "Who was the person that attacked you at the Hancock Park house?"

"That was Arthur," I said, "he thought there was a ton of money planted there. He just wanted to cash in."

I turned directly to Sally. "Franklin will find out and then what? You're crazy and certifiable. One way or another you go back to some State Institution. An accomplice to murder. Franklin would like to see to it, but he is likely to reside in prison, too, for the terrible assault on Harry Moss. He finished the job Donna started. Donna hit him a good one fighting him off but Franklin finished the job. Franklin may finish all of you off before this is through."

"All hubris, Ace. Mere hubris. And all foolish guesses by you." Her voice was a persistent sneer. "I'm quite able to handle that old fool. I can handle anything. Trust me. Trust me. I'm not really crazy. Just smarter than most. You know that don't you? I'm not an unbalanced person at all. Not at all." Her voice grew. "Not at all. But I am clever."

"And look at you. A prisoner of a doctor who fooled all of us. Ebrons was the clever one. Look what it got him. Someone turned on him. Wonder who."

She laughed. "Greed."

Billy couldn't resist. "You are a number-one hotsie-totsie nut case lady, if you ask me. You're the one who got to Ebrons."

Sally looked at him for a long quiet moment. "So, Ebrons is gone? How? When?"

"Don't act innocent, Carly or Sally, whoever you are," Billy finished.

"We don't need you here, Mr. Fitzer. I can arrange for your absence if you wish."

"You're in chains, lady. Can't see to anything." Billy waved a hand and grinned.

"Just cut me out of these chains. And you will see. There has to be a cutter here. There has to be."

"There isn't. Ebrons and the past won't let you go. Not for anything," I said. "Who is that someone? You know. Dr. Simon, in spite of being bought off by your father to cooperate with Ebrons, agreeing to a piece of the new project on highway 101, Simon couldn't resist using all these new drugs on you. He had this stupid idea that maybe he would surprise everyone and stabilize you, make you fit into the real world again. Maybe he even felt a little sorry for you. I don't know. Anyway, Franklin wanted you institutionalized so he paid Simon to turn you over to Ebrons. He fired the good fat doctor. But the good Stanley Simon, however, made you at least modestly functional. He couldn't get rid of your bellyful of hate. But he got you back to a decent functional state of being. You used Ann... then you used Pillar."

"I didn't use Ann. I used no one!"

"And in the process you escaped from the clutches of your father and Harry Moss and everyone else and with the doctor's and Pillar's help faking your cremation – and someone else – there's always a someone else – you became Carly Klein. Pillar had to be paid, but we'll get to that. Sally was officially dead. No one had come face to face with you for years. Except John. John always loved Sally. Loved you."

"That's quite enough," she said. She struggled with her bindings for a moment. "Enough. That is quite enough from you."

"I'm not done, Sally. John loved you, that's why he willed the Hancock Park house to you – as Carly Klein. He knew who you were and are. Franklin kept him in the chips and John did his best to keep nearly everyone believing that you were dead. But then came Carole. John betrayed you and betrayed Gert Wiseman, and the betrayal grew like a cancer in both of you. He had to be in the middle of everything. He had to be careful about everything he did. But not careful enough. Hard to understand John except there was so much gold at the end of the rainbow. Jimmy was a doper since his Cuban days. Ebrons kept him in dope. It all became more bloody than you would have liked. My bet is, as Carly you were nearby, unseen, when Oritha killed Carole and nearby when Jimmy and Oritha and probably a hired hand killed John. That's the horror Frankie saw and it made him shrink into his, what is it? – his great silence. And now? Ann was easy. Money did it with her. You thought Ebrons was hiding you until he locked you in and shackled you. Somebody had to help him. It might have been Oritha, or even Jimmy. Jimmy locked you up and then got himself overdosed with Ebrons' help. Or it was with a third person, the brains? I have the sense that someone smarter than all of you was behind this madness."

At the mention of Frankie her countenance shifted to the edge. A dark antique patina edged into her eyes. Her neck betrayed milky excesses of flesh. The black around her eyes deepened them, made them evil.

"No Mr. Ace. Wrong, wrong." She murmured softly. "You still don't have it. It's all corrupt." She struggled again. "Get me out of these shackles? Out! Out!"

"Can't do it. Won't do it, Sally. You're stuck here. Stuck there. Corruption spreads like a greedy flame."

Candlelight reflected tears flowing down to the crest of her mouth. She said, "I came to a place where I could see the sickness in all those mad years. My Father couldn't control his future or mine. I wanted him out of my life. I wanted to be safe. I saw all of this with the medications Simon forced me to take. I wanted to be in control my own life. I wanted to make a new life.

"But poor Dr. Simon was in the clutches of a shopping mall and my father. Can you imagine? My father was everywhere. Then came Carole." She laughed a slow rolling laugh. "I had hate all right. But it wasn't me, Mr. Ace. It wasn't the real me. John made us all crazy." A furtive grin came over those wan features.

I drew closer to her sensing the truth might force its way out? Or was she beyond truth?

"So John was the master of it all. If so, why destroy Simon and stick with Ebrons?" Billy was itching to get into the fray.

That laugh again. "Said he would reveal everything unless I 'worked with him.' That was the way he said it." She surveyed Billy and me and waved us away with a weary twist. "You don't know what crazy is. You know nothing. Get me out of here. I'll prove it all. I can prove it. You know, none of you will likely leave here alive. That's the funny part."

Her view of the truth and of good and evil was all Sally had. I thought perhaps that's all any of us have. We get behind our embattlements. Staying with what is familiar, and we hold out as long as we can. We keep telling ourselves we're OK. Watch out for the other guy. All I wanted was to find John's killer and the young Frankie, when actually I wanted to preserve the pristine nature of my motives, my status as the white knight. I was behind my embattlements, holding on.

"Mr. Fitzer, it was all quite rational, I assure you. Quite rational. Just as I am right now. Difficult perhaps, but not crazy." Her head dropped. "Warm isn't it. Very warm." She looked up. Her free hand went through her thick hair that reflected the room's candlelight.

Billy held out an arm as I approached her. I waved him aside. I kept moving closer, wanting some absolute and final truth.

"Tell me who," I said, "if not just you – then –?"

"I want to see my son." She said, "I haven't been able to see him. They kept him from me. But I know he is here. Ebrons prevented it. He is the crazy one. You see? Here I am, tied to a post. Helpless. Help me. I want to see my son." She reached out. Majesty gone. She was a mother deprived of her child. I reached her and held her free hand. Her fingers curled themselves into my own.

"It had to be Oritha who killed Simon. Killed Harrera. But it wasn't you, was it? You were just too damn sick."

"No more, Mr. Ace. No more deductions. You are wrong. Bring Frankie to me."

Her fingers squeezed mine, cold fingers, as though not attached.

Billy moved into the circle of light with me.

"Let's get rid of these damn candles." He growled. "This is all –"

"There are no lights in here Billy," I said. "And no windows. Just air ducts and the door. Notice?"

He looked around and stepped back toward the door. "Let's get her free and get out." I nodded.

With her free hand Sally began to pull me to her, fever rising into her eyes. "It's so hot in here."

"Tell me," I said again, "If not you –?"

"You certainly know, Mr. Ace. You know –"

The door behind us banged open. Illumination from the corridor outlined the figure. A pistol was leveled at us.

"I'll tell you!" the voice screamed. "I'll tell you!"

Chapter Forty-One

A shot. A thud. I leaped and reached the extended pistol and slapped it sideways and rolled over. Another shot. Sally was screaming. Trapped in those manacles. Children cried. Candlelight flickered out from the breeze of the opened door. Except one which remained stubbornly aflame. Not enough light to pierce the darkness more than a few feet.

Before I could find the light switch I heard, "Don't move, Mr. Ace. Stay exactly where you are. I can see you. Yes, I can. Clearly. I've got Frankie. Be very careful. If you have a pistol don't think about using it. Drop it. I want to hear it drop." I pulled my own gun and held it close to my body.

I recognized the voice. "I'm not dropping anything."

"Don't be stupid. Whatever you have will do you no good here."

I heard a rustle outside the door.

Sounds only.

"Let him go, Sophie. I can see you, too." I could make out the outline of her form. "Let him say something."

"Move at your peril—and his." I heard a muffled scream.

"She has him. She does, Mr. Ace," Arthur's voice interposed. I was suddenly a permanent fan of the young man. I couldn't see him. One shot burst into the shadows in his direction.

"Not close," Arthur said. I heard him rustle about, a moving target in the blackness.

The voice said, "The next one will be into Frankie's brain. I can see both of you quite well."

"No one's moving," I answered. "You can have everything, Sophie. I'm sure. Everyone will agree. Whatever you want. The old man's entire fortune."

"She gets nothing!" Sally's voice out of the darkness.

"Quiet, silly woman! I've got what I want. Everything I want. Get away from the door, Mister Ace. We are going to leave you. We have more business, Frankie and I. Yes, we do. We have to attend to our other requirements, don't we, Frankie?"

In the dismal light I could hear movement near the light switch. "Don't do that!" A shot in that direction.

Arthur did not respond.

The last candle expired.

"Let me see Frankie," I said. "Let go and let him speak! You'll never leave here, Sophie. You are not getting out. We may both end up here, very dead. I have to see him! Just let him say something!"

There was no response. I could make out the forms without definition. Arthur was probably in a comer unless he was hit.

There was another shot in Arthur's direction.

"Missed again, you crazy bitch. Never get me."

"Just remember, Frankie is alive now but he won't be if you interfere. He doesn't like you. Any of you. He doesn't like people getting into my way. So we will simply leave you here, locked in. With bullets in your brains, of course. With the lovely Sally – right, Frankie? Stay away from the door!"

The question crested a muffled response. I moved. No one was in the same place, except Sally. Nor could any of us see one another.

"I hear you! That must be you, Arthur. Don't be stupid! Don't try anything!"

More movement in the dark. I stood still.

Sally Augers called out for Frankie. Another muffled cry. "Let the boy go to his mother." I shouted.

"He's mine!"

I pointed my pistol at where I thought the sound was. But there was no way I could risk a shot. Suddenly the lights blazed on. Arthur stiffened in his spot, hand still on the light switch, glowering at Sophie Wheeler holding the boy. She held him tightly around the neck in the crook of her arm. His small body had stopped struggling. His eyes were wide, his breath short. Arthur lowered himself to the ground and moved very quickly. Another shot at him. Not easy to hit a target coming at you from the side, someone as quick as a young man in great fear. I was afraid to shoot at Sophie.

"You're through, you're not going anywhere!" I pointed my pistol at her head. Frankie was no longer screaming but she held him high. I shot into the air next to her.

"Can you understand? Stop there! You're through!"

Sophie Wheeler's very large gun pointed at my heart. It looked like an old-fashioned gun duel was about to take place with me the loser. She kept a cool eye but her face was crooked with rage, hand shaking. Gray hair streaming in all directions, arm holding the boy in a strangling grip. "Try this. Stand right there," she said and stuck her pistol into Frankie's ear.

Arthur was nearly at her side. Frankie's wide frightened eyes moved back and forth from me to Arthur to his mother. His chest heaved, trying to grab air, trapped into the tight restraint. He was fading. Sophie was propped rigidly against the wall next to the door. First she screamed, "We have to be done with Sally. That's what we have to do."

The boy continued to struggle preventing her from any clear pistol shot. She began to move. We were stalemated for the moment. I shoot her without instantly killing her and Frankie would be dead. Not a good trade. Arthur was still looking for an opening moment.

"I did succeed, Ace. I have more power than Franklin ever had, I could vote him out and put him out on his ear. Put him on the streets. I am like a good idea that all worked out, and it was easy. I control it all – the Foundation and the Trusts. Ann is my great friend. She was useful. I control the Construction Company. Dr. Simon's land is mine. He hated Franklin. But he wouldn't deal. Just before we signed and I told Ann. Then Oritha. She does what she is told. What a lovely weapon she is. They all had a price. Everyone has a price. Even you had a price. And you found Sally. The poor demented creature sitting in this mad candlelit room. You were my instrument, Mister Ace. You gave her to me. She is now going to die the second time."

"You could have just killed your husband. Easy solution."

"Simple minds, simple solutions. He'll go to jail for his stupid attack on Harry."

"But you're not getting out of here, Sophie. You will certainly die."

"Not me, Mr. Ace. I won't have to do anything. Sally's protector, lovely Oritha will do the honors. On her way. No one could possibly believe I'm the culprit. Especially with all of you dead and Oritha with the pistol in her hands. She did it all. An escapee from mental institutions. In her paranoia she believed that you were all out to get her, to put her away again. Four walls, no windows, no ice cream, no candy. Could they convict me of anything based on her testimony?" That cackle came out again, as if her sorry unraveling scheme was still perfect. Delusion wasn't sufficient word for her insanity. It was a sick, greedy, paranoia.

Arthur began moving again, slowly. Billy slid, moved like a quick shadow.

"Stop, Ace! Don't move! You shoot, you will hit the boy!"

I heard them struggle. Perhaps Frankie could wiggle free. "Frankie dies!" She screamed again. Everyone froze. A wild moaning sound rose from Sally's mouth. "No, no." It was a low guttural emission as if from a different creature. Sophie laughed and moved with Frankie.

Sally's moaning grew. It was not a human sound. The sound of a wounded creature that had lost everything. "No one's moving, Sophie! Remember, if you hurt Frankie, everything comes crashing down, doesn't it? You need him alive. Didn't think about that, did you? You can't do anything to harm him. He's your key to everything. You've miscalculated. You need him alive. You need Ann to be his guardian. In short you've fucked up. That's what you've done." I wanted to keep her talking.

She laughed a tiny, screech of a sound. "I haven't miscalculated. I own Ann. I am simply smarter than any of you. You see that now, don't you? Ann is in control. And who controls her? I don't need Frankie."

"You're wrong!"

"I'm not! I'm leaving now. But I don't want to leave any of you behind. Oritha will handle you. My grandson and I have meetings to attend, papers to sign, pronouncements to make. We have orders to give!"

She stopped as if hearing herself for the first time. I could see her mind move with the words. I could see a cunning smile, twisted lips. She pointed her pistol in Arthur's direction. I wondered where Billy had disappeared. "I am wasting my time. I won't even wait for Oritha. Arthur, dear boy, I think I'll shoot you right here. Yes. You silly bundle of stupidity. That would fit nicely. I was attacked by a vindictive cretin named Arthur and I tried to save my grandson."

"Norma Desmond has nothing on you, sweetheart," I said. "Where's Ebrons, Sophie? Where is he? Is he dead, too?"

"Surely you can't be worried about him at this late date?" She hissed.

"When Franklin had you committed, Ebrons got you out and you hatched all your schemes. If Ebrons is not dead, you are in big, very big trouble."

I hoped Billy was getting close. It would take a hard blow to her hand to dislodge the gun. Wasn't sure Billy could manage it.

"The doctor is already being attended to, Mr. Ace. Thank you. In fact, I think we can cross his name off the list by this time. Now, I have to walk this lovely boy over to his mother. You can do so much as an innocent old lady." She smiled. "Yes you can. OK, Frankie, we will go over and talk to your mother. I promised her. Slowly. Careful now."

"And Jimmy?" I persisted, trying to insert all the delaying possibilities into the mix. "Where is he at this moment? Don't you think you should make sure he is dead? You certainly have to catch up to Jimmy."

"Why Doctor Simon, Sophie? Why him?"

She took a deep breath. I did the same. Someone would have to shoot sooner or later.

"He is dead. Simon is dead."

"Sure?"

A look of alarm flashed over her face. "There's so much to do."

"There's more to attend to, isn't there?"

It was clear to me that she would kill us all while protected by the child. She would not need Oritha.

"Not difficult, you fool! Not difficult!"

She dragged Frankie toward his mother. He wiggled and twisted.

All at once, as if figuring out a method, Frankie twisted just enough and bit her arm. He held on like a bulldog. She screamed and jumped. Through his frailty he wrestled one hand momentarily free. And in spite of her age and modest size, a burst of insane adrenaline permitted her to pull him back into orbit. However, in that instant of struggle, Arthur leaped at her and I shot at her, she whirled, her face betraying a flash of uncomprehending fear and pain. Her pistol fired. Twice. She had no sense of how a pistol reacted when fired. Her hand jumped. I felt the heat and fired again and she was thrust, arms flailing like a rag doll onto the floor... But her arm came up like a separate entity, alive to possibilities. Arthur twisted and fell into Sophie and grabbed the boy in his arms. I fired again. Billy reached for the boy and Arthur. Blood splashed out at me. I held Sophie's bloody body down and kicked the pistol away. She had a hole where a bullet hole should be when guns are in play. In the middle of her belly. Her life was descending into a puddle of blood and old flesh.

"Arthur!" I pointed at a wound in his shoulder. Billy grabbed a handkerchief from his pocket and shoved it into the wound. "9-1-1, get them," Billy called. I punched out the number. Arthur looked at me, smiled quickly, said, "Shit, I fucked this whole thing up, didn't I?" and sank to the floor next to Sophie. Frankie was screaming. Sally was screaming. Each reaching for the other. Perhaps the first sounds from his mouth since the moment Oritha Durden had shoved Carole off the parapet at the Palisades. He continued to scream bringing his hands to his hair and beginning to pull in despair and recognition. That sudden onslaught of recognition contorted his face into a tormented mass of confusion, of emotion. Sally sounded more like the ending of a distorted whine. I lead all of us back to where she was still chained. Her eyes were into black pools of anguish. With her free arm she reached out for her son.

The sounds of the boy's pain pierced the night like cries of suffering dogs. He kept looking around as if expecting to see an apparition ooze out of the walls.

We moved toward her. "I know," I said. "I know," trying to find the right words. But there were no right words as I carried him to his mother.

He screamed all the unhappy screams he had failed to scream and cried all the cries he had failed to cry for the last several weeks. He looked at me wondering why I was not screaming too. His mother was moaning deep dreadful sobs. Her eyes did not focus. I put him into her free arm and went back to where Sophie lay and with one arm I pulled her to my face. Blood streamed down her forehead from her fall. I gazed into her eye sockets. "Where is Oritha, Sophie? Where is Oritha? Tell me –"

I wanted to shake her in spite of her wounds.

Arthur went to Sally and Frankie and holding the handkerchief tightly against his shoulder tried to reach out and stroke the child. Then he suddenly realized his position and bolted out of the room. I let him run. They would grab him soon enough. His present deeds would be mitigating factors. I needed to find Oritha Durden. Perhaps she had not yet reached Dr. Ebrons.

I ran to the door at the end of the corridor. It was locked and I shot away at the handle and crashed the door open with my right foot. As I burst into the room a waiting pipe smashed my fingers. My pistol bounced away from me. I rolled over twice, eluding a series of pipe swings thudding against the wooden floor. I lurched to the side and tried to find an exit. A frustrated shot came at me and kicked into the wall. The room reflected the barest light of the dim yellow hallway. Without seeing her I could feel her malevolent presence. I rolled into something warm. It groaned. On my feet, I ran directly at the sound of a second shot and, elbows first blocked the huge body against the wall. From a foot away I saw the eyes, shot through with yellow and red, beady pin points, pure hate, pure anger, Mr. Hyde, female and enormous, swathed in that same dark scarf so that there was no neck and no shoulders, just the head gleaming out like a sick beacon above a mountain of diseased flesh. She turned trying to get the nose of the pistol at me again. I remembered the syringe which I had stuffed into my pocket, and grabbed it, pulled off the cap, and as the pistol came inexorably towards me threw the biting end of the needle which hit her as close to an eye as the best dart thrower could ever have managed.

An agonized wail erupted. She turned, one hand pulling at her face. The pistol went off in the air. Guttural mouthings came from that strange head. I was next to her and got a quick karate chop at her upper lip. She fell back down. I kicked and rolled and found my own pistol; there was an instant within which I decided that the encounter was all over. But her hands went up again. These white butterball hands went up, emerging from the mountain of flesh like a gluttonous poised albino snakes and my brain ceased all reflection and I pulled at the trigger of my square two pound, forty-five caliber pistol – I pulled twice.

Durden's body fell next to Michael Ebrons. Through the mass of beaten flesh, through the black wire of his beard, I discerned a smile. I pulled him away from the heap of Durdens' ponderous form and carried him onto one of the beds.

His eyes fluttered.

"Take it easy. The rescue guys will be here soon."

"Not dead yet," he whispered.

I left him and went back to Arthur. Billy was there with them. "Methodical, wasn't she?"

Arthur whispered. "I didn't mean to hurt anyone."

"Yeah, I know. No one ever means it. Take it easy. All the medics will be here in a second. I can hear the sirens now. Just hold on."

Chapter Forty-Two

"Will we ever see Jimmy again?"

"At the Federal pen in San Pedro."

Wally Dorrance at the hundred-dollar window at Santa Anita said, "Well, he's getting three a day and medical care. Off the drugs. So how bad can it be? Got old didn't he?"

Bought two hundred to win and place on number three and number eight in the fifth race. And the Exacta, as I couldn't separate them and both trainers were sure their horses would win. Then I walked into the Turf Club lounge, crystal chandeliers blazing, found Billy in one of the alcoves with a TV on the table and two glasses of iced cokes on the table. Grabbed one.

"Whatcha got?"

"Three and eight."

So it was. What we are, what we were, sticks around like a magnet on our hearts. Magnets don't let up.

Joe Dobrowski had been instrumental in keeping everyone not Wheeler or Sophie or their paid-for doctors away from Bright Paths so he was no longer the chief of Mara Bay police.

Hedy remained as a deputy and was up for election as the chief.

The whole Augers Affair had been exposed in the local Santa Barbara newspaper and was picked up by the large metro dailies and appeared on the inside pages of these metro papers.

Except for the involvement of Franklin Wheeler, the affair was of local interest only. The article written by two of the Santa Barbara City News Service Bureau and did a careful job of detailing only what the reporters actually knew as fact about the murders and conspiracies. Well laid plans never seem to go as planned; in war, in peace, or otherwise. So it was with Sophie and her cohort of players. Torment slowly overwhelmed Franklin Wheeler and he settled into a quiet life of bare recollections and regrets. At least he wouldn't have to face his daughter ever again. In the ironies of all ironies, he was eventually committed to Bright Paths Institute in the care of Doctor George Ackerman, whose family had bought the place for him. The planned large complex just off the 101 highway was never even started and the land sold to a Chinese group for "future development."

Pretty clear that past had risen like a Christmas ghost and had devoured the whole gang that comprised the affair.

Every now and then I visited him. Can't say what sense of duty forced me to check up on him, but I did. On the last occasion just two weeks ago he was sitting out by the entrance gate, just to the side of an old elm tree that had been carted in and planted by the Ackerman clan. He was alone and quiet. And seemed to be contemplating something in the distance. I stayed until a somber twilight descended, now and then asking him how he was, and if anyone else came to visit, and about the dead Sophie. "Finding out about her didn't make you happy, I assume." Second I said it I realized how stupid it was. Trying to make conversation does that.

He managed to mumble something about "Sally."

"I guess they try to keep you busy around here, don't they?"

He studied me. I couldn't help but imagining that he was thinking what an idiot I was and recounting the way he had once ruled his known world. I was curious if he still disliked me as intensely as he had in the recent past. However, I didn't go there. I stayed until a somber twilight descended. Misty with a cool breath of air that came up from the west and rustled the dry leaves of the great elm. They drifted down to their natural resting place on a welcoming green earth.

Finally I came up with, "Frankie is doing fine, you must be happy about that."

His eyes came alive and then turned to wet misery. "I ruined them all," he murmured, "All of them. How do you tell such things to God?"

I didn't reply. Beyond my job description, indeed, anything sensible I could think of.

Arthur came ambling slowly toward us, down the grassy hill. He was smiling. The first smile I had ever seen on his square face. "Surprised to see you."

"Oh, I come by now and then," he answered, brightly. "He seems to be doing OK," he remarked and sat on a bench next to us. "I come by and see Frankie now and then, too. He is doing really well."

"And Sally?"

"Doin' good, too. Takes a million pills. They have all this new stuff. Seems to help. She's not very nice, though. Sort of angry." He leaned over close to Wheeler. "How'ra doin' Mister Wheeler?"

Wheeler gave him a hard look like the young man was mad.

"Aha, doin' better. Right?"

He put a small box of Sees peanut brittle on the old man's lap. "I know you like these." He patted Wheeler's hand. "Well, I'll be back. I'll be back, Franklin."

Arthur hurried away. He had done what his soul told him he had to do and that was that for the moment.

Now we sat in the dark. Growing cold. I was alone and he was very alone. "Better wheel you back, Franklin."

***

I heard from Aureliano Mondozo later that night.

"OK. Three fifty. Old man says he'll go three fifty."

I spent two full minutes calling him every nasty name I could think of, then, "No!"

Five minutes later I called Gert and told her to put on a couple more grooms with *The Silk*, "And someone who knows how to use a gun."

Then I called Mexico City. After several repeat calls, all within fifteen minutes, I heard back from, old Miguel Cervantes Redon Mondozo. I told him about his son and the threats. In clear, well-mannered English he told me he had no power over the boy. I said, "We had many years together, Mr. Mondozo. I respect you greatly. Now it is all forgotten? You simply want what you want...without any care who gets hurt...or killed?"

He sighed and said, "Why not just sell, Harvey? I can't control everything. We want the horse. She fits. We can help you. We should really own her."

I hung up. The rich are different. They actually believe they're entitled.

***

I came out of the house early one morning to take a run. The front of my Condo is like the back Street of most houses. It "fronts" on an alley. As I came out I heard a shot and then a great big nothing.

When I woke I was in an all-white room with Paul Sampson leaning over me. My shoulder was thickly bandaged.

"Told you to watch it."

"Fuck you."

"Whyn't you just sell the horse? You said the price was right."

"You don't sell dreams. Get the sonofabitch. You don't get him, I will. I know where he lives."

382

"Don't be stupid, Harvey. We will get him. We'll connect the dots."

***

Four days later, after struggling to understand the crazy hospital bill, I walked slowly along the boardwalk along Santa Monica beach, near the Condo. I made myself conspicuous. Then I tore the hospital; bill in half and tossed it into the next garbage pail.

After an hour I gave up trying to understand anything. I was tired and I realized that Mondozo knew I was trying to set him up.

That next frosty morning I stood with Gert and groom Eddie Morona, they liked to call him Eddie the Moron, but he wasn't, just a bright kid too big to be a jock or an exercise boy. He was leading *The Silk* onto the dirt road in front of her stall. The chill was wearing off, and Gert and Eddie were smiling.

I noticed quickly that Eddie was carrying what appeared to be a .38 Caliber pistol.

"Is Eddie the only one watching this girl? Does he know how to use that thing?"

"Don't worry," she replied. "We're watching her."

"No police, Gert. Putting them together with armed Latinos most of whom have an axe to grind with the police is not a winning combination. Especially with the Mondozos. They can just disappear and you never know when they return. Your guys have guns. Billy and Larry have guns. So, we cross our fingers and wait."

Billy and Larry could not shoot worth a damn. But Billy was reliable and he could actually hit a barn door if he had to. "We'll stay the nights. We'll hang out here and there."

That's what we did.

We told everyone Billy was from the LA Magazine wanting to do a story with *"Atmosphere."* No one believed it, but they went along. Among them had to be an Aureliano man. Or two. We hid among the barns and the bales of hay and tubs of feed and water. We dressed like the grooms and stayed close, trying to be part of the "scene." Gert's grooms were everywhere, except by nine pm they retired to their backside apartments or nearby homes and were safe. They understood these games and refused to be pulled into them.

It was the same routine for three nights. I called his number the second night. No answer, except the machine. "You're not having her and you're not succeeding in anything. So fuck off." I slept in front of *Silk's* stall and behind a bale of hay. Billy roamed until about eleven and then retired to the same place at the barns across the street in the shadows. Larry took the end of the shed and curled up into a sleeping bag, pistol ready. Then we changed it. Billy roamed and went to the other streets, whispered with the new night watchman, Jorge Salverias. We kept switching. I kept getting calls from Paul wondering where I was. I ignored them.

After two weeks of this nonsense, Billy said, "Enough is enough" and I replied, "That's what they're waiting for."

"I got a life, Harvey."

Larry shrugged. "Go get him. Where he lives."

"Good idea."

Billy left about midnight that night. He advised Jorge Salverias to keep a special eye out.

Larry left in the morning and said he needed a night to get his stuff done. What that was I couldn't imagine. During the previous day I had bet a couple horses and won one and lost one and made a few dollars.

The next night I roamed the darkened alleys and streets of the backside always back to Gert's stalls within a couple of minutes. Finally I laid down on a blanket I had set out at the front of the stall. Moths flickered about the dim light bulbs. Flies buzzed my ears. I kept my pistol hidden as I lay on my side. Sometime before dawn I was awakened. There he was. Good old Aureliano Mondozo, pistol in hand, a great big forty-five aiming at me. I turned and did the same. Forty fives at five paces. "You want to see who dies first, Aure?"

One of his "people" hung to the right of him, grinning. "Call off the idiot or we both shoot and you die for sure as I never miss and that pistol of yours jumps in your hand and you'll miss the first one."

He hesitated. Then he smiled. "I don't miss. Neither does Freddie."

"OK," I pointed at his heart, "I'm ready to hit the heavens. What about you and your friend, 'cause he goes with you? Check out what's just down the street."

"No one. They're all gone."

"Too bad," I said. "Too bad." I smiled and then shot the sonofabitch before he could think. I hit just above his knee and hit the idiot guardian in the groin who had been dumbstruck that I actually shot his boss. He stood still for about a full two seconds. That had been enough. He might be dying. I flipped my cell and called 911. Told them to bring an ambulance. Jorge Salverias was next to me along with a gathering crowd of grooms and walkers and everyone within the sound of the gunshots. Aure was screaming and holding his leg.

"I told you I would shoot, you numbskull. Wasn't going to wait for you to shoot. I'll call your father and tell him what is what. This is after fifteen years of dealing with your family."

I thought then that there was almost no one you could trust. No one in whole world was actually trustworthy. Maybe horses. Maybe my *Silk*.

After a night with Paul and all the minions of the various police departments I took a cab home from the LA police building. My car was still at the track.

I was empty inside. There wasn't even any ear wax left in me. No thoughts, no emotions.

Empty. My tank was dry. It was like being sea-sick and dumping everything inside of you. Alone.

But there was my filly and my dreams. And no one can steal dreams.

A month later Ann Whitson surprised me with a call and we talked. Her trial was close at hand. My guess was that she wanted me to testify for her. Not sure. That was our last call.

Can't be sure of anything. The Aureliano business' ended with a whimper, a loud one, but that was that. The muscled guardian of Aure did not die and was transported to Mexico the minute he could be moved.

***

Larry and Billy and old Doc Lee are sitting with me. Doc is smoking. It's a good clear day. We do not talk about The *Augers Affair*. The San Gabriel Mountains are crisp and clear. Eastward along the mountain range Mt. San Gorgonio rose clear and cold looking with its vanilla topping. The heavy lady at the table just down the row is still screaming bloody murder at some horse that is either winning or losing. If she weren't screaming I would miss it.

And so, like others have written, we deal in the past; guided by it, perhaps controlled by it. Indeed, the past is the invisible magnet of our psyches. I have the conviction that we are all irretrievably and "ceaselessly borne" back in time to the days of childhood because it is what we know, that is what feels safe for most of us. It is the essence of who we are.

My filly will win in the future. I am sure of it. It's in the stars. I'm feeling pretty good. Safe. Well, so be it. The sun shines, the moon beams, I have a wad of bills in my pocket – tell me truly, what else is there?

I think maybe I'll call Sarah. Assuming I can find her.

Chapter Forty-Three

Frankie's screaming had ceased, replaced by the unhappiest haunted stare I had ever seen. Abject isolation and fear. But, he was alive. It was an open question, at least in my mind, whether he would actually ever be well and live a decent life without demons. No father. No mother. No grandmother. He was alone in the world. Except for Franklin. And he was not in control of his life.

We were sitting at a picnic table in the back yard of a foster home, where he had been for a week. Gert somehow pulled him out of his almost demented loneliness, and applied legally to become his adoptive parent. She filed the necessary papers and crossed her fingers that Franklin would not object. He didn't. He was a beaten old man.

Sophie Wheeler was alive but was now a patient of one Doctor Alan Camov, a young fellow with horned rimmed glasses, New York accent, looking exactly like a psychiatrist should look. He thought it might take quite a while to get her "straight and in line," whatever that meant. Her open eyes seemed strangely untroubled. Her peaceful look made me furious.

Ebrons was alive and silent. A patient at *Bright Paths*.

Moss was no more than half alive. Frankie and I smiled at one another. He told me liked Gertrude.

Aureliano Mondozo semi crippled body was still hanging nearby, waiting for the ripe time to pounce. His message was simple, *I'm never going away.* His father had gone onto other 'bigger and better' things, not thinking *The Silk* was enough of an asset to worry about.

But, I could handle him and Aure. My young friend wasn't smart enough to make more trouble.

***

Not all conspiracies unravel. This one had, though. Too many players with too many differing agendas, too many upside-down personalities, all converging at one place at one time. Had Sally Augers, nee Carly Klein, remained stuck and helpless in the insanity of her "chemical imbalances," Sophie might have succeeded. Paul Sampson and an ambulance had waited for us just outside the *Bright Path's* entrance door. Until he heard my shot into Aureliano's leg, he had, with deputies from Santa Barbara, stayed outside the gate, faithful to the limited nature of his warrant. He knew that it might ruin a couple of good arrests otherwise. When the shooting started, Paul called the paramedics and then rushed in.

***

On a Friday night soon after these events, Gert came to my condo. Dressed in an actual dress, blue with quiet patterns, hair swept back. She told me that the prior Sunday *The Silk* won the Palos Verde Handicap at $350,000 and won it going away by over six lengths. I explained briefly my preoccupations. She knew. We spent a few moments trying to understand our personal relationship and realized that it would not quite get there, we were people pretty much set in our ways. There would have been no "home life" and few home cooked meals, life interrupted by my travel schedules to Monmouth, Saratoga Springs, Florida, and Chicago, and Santa Anita during the extended winter months and thus we resolved to be content with what we had. She said, "Maybe twenty years ago" and I said, "I would like to have those years back now that I know what I missed."

I was in a different world… So was Gert. A boy of nearly teenaged years in her care and custody. A good thing for both of them. Frankie slowly began to act like a teenager and Gertrude would shake her head and wipe that red bandana over her face and wonder what it was that drove little boys to be— little boys. Nevertheless, they were both better off in the new lives.

I was not merely a gambler any longer. I was in business – in the business of Thoroughbred Racing, not in the business of gambling, although gambling was the foundation of my new *business… go* figure. I didn't bother.

***

The last few moments at the side of the ambulance, Sally Augers, nee Carly Klein, just before being slid into place, had a remarkable few moments of sanity. She raised her head and smiled, a rather touching and warm smile. Who knows how the hell she pulled it up from her depths. And then she shrugged as if saying – *it is what it is* – and damn if she didn't wink.

387

Frankie saw her. It set him off. Maybe it was that smile. He began to sob quietly perhaps knowing all of a sudden what his losses were, his hands reached out. It was a moment I won't ever forget: the understanding of two lost souls about the full measure of what had been lost. Sally's grin disappeared and she began to cry with him. She reached out also, hoping, praying, for one moment of sharing between them. You could see *reality* creeping in.

A medic reached over to administer a sedative to the young man. I waved the medics down. "Let it happen. Let him get it out."

The medic ignored me. Medical people are certain they know best. In a moment of layman's wisdom Arthur wrapped his remaining good arm about Frankie and moved him towards his mother's gurney. The boy's sobbing subsided. Mother and son gazed at one another again and then the sedative took hold and Frankie fell into Arthur's arms and into what dreams I couldn't imagine.

***

What Sally managed to say, little by little, over time, during my several visits to the hospital and then at a new outpatient division of Bright Paths, was that she felt very early in life that she was crippled while being in full possession of all her limbs and senses; that her father dealt with her in a way that made her certain she couldn't get through the day without some internal fury to keep her life fires burning. He treated her as if she was a threatening and dangerous animal. In the vortex of her growing and uncontrolled hate, and her need to retaliate against her father, she felt this continued necessity to obtain his approval, even after Sophie came on the scene. "I wanted to kill. I'll have to admit, but I wanted him to want me and love me. Not attack me. That's truly strange isn't it?"

Sophie's entry into the family created a special bond between herself and Sally. They were allies from almost the beginning. In fact, it was this bond that gave rise to the schemes against Franklin. Her purpose, in the beginning, in marrying Franklin, was merely to insure her permanent comfort, certainly not a unique purpose in the history of marital contracts. But Franklin's worsening boorishness and Sally's increasing instability and hostility to her father began to touch the nerve endings of Sophie's agile mind. Whether she knew about Franklin's abusive liaisons with his daughter, I never found out.

Then John came along, almost as much Franklin's savior as Sally's. Good old John was the opposite of the savior type.

Sophie quietly began to gather shares of FKW Construction, insinuate herself into the management of Ridge Savings and Loan, see to it that Sally's caretaker was in her employ and not Franklin's. Like plucking ripe fruit, she gathered her conspirators. And so it grew for several years. The genie simply wouldn't stay in the bottle. Billy always says, "Life isn't a movie. Can't write the script."

My knowledge of Ann Whitson's relationship with Sophie Wheeler and Harry Moss was hurtful at first. Then I realized that I had nearly forgotten about Sarah and our relationship. In my narrow focus on John and revenge, lovely Ann was a way to forget my misery. Okay, I was not a wonderful person. She, on the other hand, had excuses, had good reasons for the path she had been steered into.

Ten years ago when Sophie saw how Franklin's aging could be used in her schemes, she referred Ann to Harry Moss as needy, efficient, pretty, and possibly susceptible to his over-the hill charms. In a while it was clear who Ann was working for.

"You're working for me dear. Do you understand?" Sophie made clear as she handed her small amounts of cash every month. "Harry works for me and now you do."

***

Ann explained, "Haven't you noticed? It's not Lake Woebegone. It's wanting more than window dressings on Rodeo Drive, or a week in Cabo in the Spring, New York in the fall. It's my kid in private school and a decent college. A person forgets what one was taught as a child and soon emotions trump logic. But, I didn't do anything so terrible, did I?"

Didn't know how to answer that.

"You've never done anything terrible or less than honorable? Never?" She asked.

I thought for a minute. There were some little things like screwed up marriages and messed up fatherhood. I had killed people, but only when it was one of them or me situations.

Finally, I gave up judging even those moments.

I said, "Yeah, yeah of course I have."

"Can we just table this?" she asked.

"Sure we can. Let's table the whole thing."

We had to. She was sitting across from me in a little dinner house, The Bella Roma, in west LA, her jaw set. She knew beginnings and she knew endings. "That sounds like something very definite," she answered.

"I'm not sure."

"That's a hellava note. What do you mean, 'I'm not sure?' That's really a hellava note."

"Ann, you got a year-long probation out of this whole mess. You're going to be fine."

"Just because I worked for Harry."

"Tell the truth I don't know what to expect. Not sure exactly who you are or what I am any longer except no longer merely a gambler. You had to know that this whole Sophie scheme would end badly. No one could come out of it whole except you."

"Ah yes, here come the judgments. The Harvey Ace 'Judgments.' Strict, puritanical, damn silly gambler's world judgments and payoffs."

"Hey, gamblers pay their gambling debts; maybe not the rent. The shrinks tell us not to be judgmental. Baloney. Judgments are necessary. A person judges everything. Especially his or her lovers."

She got up.

"Where you going. I've got the car."

"I'll take a cab. I wish it was different. I really do."

"I'll call you," I grinned. It was a joyless moment, not time for grinning, but I couldn't help it.

"I would like to hold my breath until then, but I won't." There was a trace of a smile on her face. It made her very desirable. Then she got up and walked away and out to the Boulevard and raised her hand.

***

It was exactly the time I got a call from Paul Sampson.

Chapter Forty-Four

"We found her! On the 101 highway. North of Santa Barbara. Stumbling on the wrong side of the highway. They just dumped her. A truck driver stopped after she stumbled nearly in front of his truck. Called the Mara Bay police and one of them picked her up quickly and Joe got her a helicopter and she was in Cedars within a couple of hours. She's in Cedars-Sinai, north tower. Don't get too excited, she's OK. I'm telling you, she's OK. Bruises and bump and scratches. Apparently let her go deciding there was no money to be made with her anymore. She said something about a closed room, no doors. They're done checking her out. In Room 426 North. They figure a couple days."

Within thirty seconds I was in the car and on my way to Cedars, the enormous medical/hospital complex on La Cienega Boulevard in west LA. The seven-building group of Cedars buildings, for special situations and diseases, a special research complex, three main hospital buildings as well as out-patient buildings. Parking in the garage built for the shopping center a block away.

I shoved my car through the fourth-floor parking structure and ran down the walkway to the street and half a block to the north tower. The six elevators were to my right after I entered. I pushed every button I could until one came. Fourth floor followed the signs down the corridor to 426. It was closed.

I knocked but no response. A nurse came by and told me it was OK to go in. "She's awake. Someone is with her."

I opened the door and saw her half raised to a semi sitting position. Her eyes widened like I was about to strike her. She tightened. I could almost hear her mind scream oh, my God!

Next to her, standing, smiling, holding her hand, was Jack Gordon, highly respected member of the Wheeler Foundation Board of Directors; very trim, slicked back gray hair. He stepped back, crouched a little like his hand was caught in the candy jar. "We wondered when you would get here."

"Paul called me just an hour ago. You OK?"

I went to her bedside. But Jack stayed in place, half blocking the space. Sarah had a bruised cheek and one hand was wrapped as though her wrist was broken. The other held onto Gordon's hand.

"She's OK. Fractured wrist. Bruises. They're doing tests to make sure, then dismiss her possibly tomorrow, maybe the next day."

"How did you find out so quickly?"

Sarah answered for him. "I had them call Jack when they got me here. Been with me the whole time.

"We were just talking about explaining things to you," Gordon said.

"Let her do the talking, Jack."

"I was just trying to explain. Take it easy, Harvey."

I looked at Sarah.

"I wanted Jack here. He's been a big help to me…"

I interrupted, "Before all of this – your kidnapping?"

She nodded. "Before."

"How long?"

Jack Gordon leaned over her as if to protect her from me. "Move it, Jack. Don't make me move you."

He straightened up as if to challenge me. Sarah murmured, "Please, Jack, let me handle this." And patted his hand with her bandaged one.

He pulled back. I moved closer. Her voice was not much more than a whisper. "We have been… seeing each other for a while."

"A while? What's been going on?"

"We were having our difficulties, Harvey. You know that. He was just there. Not important how we met, really. But we did and then I moved out…"

"Did he know you were kidnapped, probably by Wheeler, his boss, so to speak? The old man who calls the shots? Did he chase after every lead trying to find you? Did he do anything?"

"I don't know anything, Ace. Really. I still don't."

"Just so you know, Harvey, I don't know anything yet either." He looked just like he should, a little sheepish and tentative. "I resigned the Foundation when you cast your vote like that. Just down the Wheeler line. I suspected there was some monkey business going on when you caved in like the rest of his lackeys. I voted the way I did because it was the right thing for the Foundation. Then I got out. I have several friends in the DA's office, one of them is a neighbor, and called them. Seemed like a sort of betrayal but I didn't want to get mixed up in, well, Wheeler stuff. The DA is looking into the whole Foundation business and into Sarah's kidnapping. It was a missing person and then a possible homicide and now it's an investigation into the whole group of Wheeler enterprises… they're looking, especially into the disappearance of Sarah. And, well – she and I have been dealing with the Ace connection for a few weeks…"

"When you walked out you, had someplace to go, right?"

She closed her eyes. "You're a gambler, Harvey. You know…"

"That doesn't excuse anything. Doesn't excuse your conduct. *The Silk* is winning big. I'm adding to the Stable. Going to Florida yearling sales next month. It's different now. I have a business to tend to."

She closed her eyes again as if she didn't want to hear. "That's great, Harvey. Great. Jack and I are going to set a date."

A blanket of silence descended over us. Three silent people, not sure how to deal with their emotions. Emptiness and a sort of darkness held us in place.

A nurse came in, looked around and left.

"Will you come? Please? Think maybe the spring…"

"How long this been going on?"

'It's hardly important anymore, Ace," Gordon said. He started to put a hand on my shoulder and changed his mind.

"I'll be in Florida with Mrs. Wiseman," I said. "I have to think about the future of this new business of mine."

"That's great, Harvey. Great." Sarah smiled a wan, but contented smile.

I leaned close and kissed her cheek. And nodded at Jack, grabbed his hand, shook it, and left.

Like all gamblers, you win some and lose some.

***

The Turf Club at Santa Anita is a crystal-etched, gilt-edged, mahogany and buttoned up world. The beautiful people sit in the lounge – being beautiful, the smart being smart, the rich being rich, and the pretenders, pretending. When a race starts they all take their box seats and gaze out at the beautiful, mauve, and ice-creamed winter tops of the San Gabriel Mountains.

Billy, Nails, Larry, and I were none of the above. Well, actually, Billy is smart. I was running on empty, and it wasn't downhill. I was more like a slug in a rose garden…without roses. Billy, looking over a cold cup of coffee just under his nose, said, "Harvey, we actually need to win today."

"Your words to God's ears. All I know is what I see and what I read in the form and what I can hear on the Backside. After that, horses are flesh and bone and they have their own characters and it messes statistics up. Anyway, what difference? We live a stupid existence, and in case you want to know, it's number eight in the next race."

393

His eyebrows rose as if surprised by sudden daylight. "I refuse to believe we live a stupid existence. We just don't. You can knock us if you want but it's as good as any life anywhere." He looked like a balding high school kid just then, not knowing which way to turn. He straightened all at once. His jacket in full bloom. "It's not stupid, Harvey. And it's not number eight."

Doc lee leaned in. "It is stupid. But who cares? Nothing we do here affects the world one iota."

"Suit yourself. It is stupid and your money ought to go on number eight."

"You're wrong... as usual, Harvey. We gamble on horses. Some people gamble on the market, on real estate. On oil prices. On gold they don't have and can't get and which probably doesn't exist. As I understand it that guy Buffet gambles on everything. Even on the price of cotton next winter. And wins. People gamble on the weather. Will the oranges freeze over? Shall we harvest the strawberries now or wait? Will it rain? What could be crazier? Are they all stupid? Are we all stupid? It's number three in the next race – not eight. When are you leaving for Florida?"

"Day after tomorrow."

"Listen," Doc Lee continued, "get it straight, what we do is use a little brain power to buy an emotion. Betting on an athlete that can't talk. Can't tell us anything about how he or she feels that day. Other people – who call themselves investors – look at a company and write their thoughts onto a slip of paper and some guy puts it into some computer thing and then some buyer says oh-boy this looks good and buys a piece of some asset he can't see, can't use, can't identify. Certainly can't feel. Those bets are better than ours? "Take a vacation, Harv. Go find your daughter. Go fishing. Get laid. Call that Sarah girl. I thought she was a good one. But don't *think* anymore. *Thinking is bad.* Besides, its number three. Look at the Stallion – out of a Storm Cat mare. Number three wins."

"Not calling Sarah. She seems to be otherwise engaged."

In my heart of hearts I knew that my life wasn't simple. I don't care what they say. Nothing is easy. It's fucking hard. Everything seems to be hard. And nothing gets easier with time or age. Like I said, I don't care what they say. I'm right, they're wrong."

Billy added, "Anything else you're holding onto? Get it off your chest. You've been driving everyone crazy past couple days."

"You can always sit at another table."

"I don't want to sit at another table."

"So, don't."

"It's number eight."

We were silent and sipped our coffee. I picked at a crab salad.

Doc Lee leaned in again and said, "Won't be here next week. City of Hope gets me."

"How bad?"

He waved his cigarette in the air, "Let's just say no more of these things... maybe ever."

Billy sad, "Shit! I'm sorry. We'll be there to see you."

Doc Lee smiled. He didn't care. He knew when the end was the end.

Finally, I said, "So, you want to hear the story?"

"Go."

I told them. The two-bit version.

Billy was quiet for a while after I finished telling him about Ann and Sarah and me and Jack Gordon.

Doc Lee sat next to Billy. He lit a new Merit, inhaled deeply, blew it out slowly, eyed me with one half closed eye, a deep crease in his cheeks, and said, "You look shitty, Harvey. Your story is old as the hills. I got no sympathy for you. Maybe a little. But you're a big boy. You're not in high school. Try some vitamins. And a good night's sleep. What d'ya like in this race?"

Cigarettes were killing Doc Lee, but he didn't mind. Social suicide. I told him a dozen times and he laughed. A peculiarly unhappy soul. Soon to be a dead soul.

"Told you. Number eight."

Ten minutes later number eight won. Drawing clear at the end. Six to one. Eleven hundred and thirty-one dollar payout. Three came third.

When I was deep into the Racing Form trying to figure the next race, Billy said, "Listen, Harvey, there's plenty of guilt to go around. For god's sake, don't wallow in it. It doesn't make us a buck. It just ain't worth it."

"I gotta write that one down, Billy. I don't want to forget these original thoughts you keep having."

Then I pulled out my new flip phone and dialed a number that was not stuck in there.

"Hello, Ann?"

She answered.

"Hi, it's Harvey. Harvey Ace."

"Harvey? Really you?"

"Yeah, really me and I'm calling..."

"Wow!"

"I wanted to ask you, do you like horses?"

"Wow!"

CPSIA information can be obtained
at www.ICGtesting.com
Printed in the USA
LVHW080930011120
670383LV00012B/1351